THE HERO'S WALK

THE
HERO'S WALK

Anita Rau Badami

BLOOMSBURY

First published in Canada by Alfred A Knopf

First published in Great Britain 2001
This paperback edition published 2002

Copyright © 2000 by Anita Rau Badami

Grateful acknowledgement is made to Grove Altantic, Inc., in New York for
permission to quote from "There's No Forgetting (Sonata)" by Pablo
Neruda, published in *Selected Poems of Pablo Neruda* in 1961.
Translation copyright © 1961 by Ben Belitt.

The moral right of the author has been asserted

Bloomsbury Publishing Plc, 38 Soho Square, London W1D 3HB

A CIP catalogue record is available from the British Library

ISBN 0 7475 5796 9

10 9 8 7 6 5 4 3 2

Printed in Great Britain by Clays Limited, St Ives plc

For Aditya

ACKNOWLEDGMENTS

Many thanks to Louise Dennys, my editor, for her astute comments, wisdom and guidance, and to Denise Bukowski for her unwavering faith and encouragement. Thanks also to Noelle Zitzer and Nikki Barrett for their editorial suggestions. I am particularly indebted to Ven Begamudré for his friendship and for finding time in his own busy life to provide an insightful critique of an early draft of this book. My gratitude to the Canada Council for financial support, to Shubi for sharing her journals with me, and to Madhav Badami for his constant love and support. Last but not least, I would like to thank The Centre for India and South Asia Research at the University of British Columbia for their assistance.

CONTENTS

1

BY THE EDGE
OF THE SEA

I T WAS ONLY FIVE O'CLOCK on a July morning in Toturpuram, and already every trace of night had disappeared. The sun swelled, molten, from the far edge of the sea. Waves shuddered against the sand and left curving lines of golden froth that dried almost instantly. All along the beach, fishermen towed their boats ashore and emptied their nets of the night's catch. Their mothers and wives, daughters and sisters, piled the prawn and the crab, the lobster and the fish, into large, damp baskets still redolent of the previous day's load, and then, leaving the shimmering scales and cracked shells for the crows to fight over, they caught the first bus to the market, laughing as other passengers hastily moved to the front and made way for them and their odorous wares.

In a few hours the heat would hang over the town in long, wet sheets, puddle behind people's knees, in their armpits and in the hollows of their necks, and drip down their foreheads. Sweaty thighs would stick to chairs and make rude sucking sounds when contact was broken. Only idiots ventured out to work and, once there, sat stunned and idle at their desks because the power had gone off and the ceiling fans were still. It was impossible to bat an eyelash without feeling faint. The more sensible folk stayed at home, clad only in underwear, with moist cloths draped over their heads and chests, drinking coconut water by the litre and fanning themselves with folded newspapers.

Even though it was the middle of July in this small town that crouched on the shores of the Bay of Bengal about three hours by bus from Madras, the southwest monsoons that provided a minor interlude between periods of heat had not appeared. So all of Toturpuram longed for December when the northeast monsoons would roar in. The memory of those cool, wet mornings was so appealing that everyone forgot that December was also the beginning of the cyclone season when winds blew at 150 kilometres per hour, smashing everything that stood in their way. They did not remember the torrential rains that knocked out the power lines and plunged the town into stinking, liquid darkness. And they utterly forgot how the sea became a towering green wall of water that dissolved the beach and flooded the streets, turning roadways into drains and bringing dysentery and diarrhea in its wake. There was so much rain that septic tanks exploded all over town, and people woke suddenly in the night to find their belongings floating in sewage.

Today the morning light touched the squalid little town with a tenuous beauty. Even the dozens of angular apartment blocks that marched stolidly from the beach up to Big House on Brahmin Street were softened by the early glow. Sheaves of television antennae bristled up from the roofs of those apartments and caught fire as the sun rose. Big House was the only building on the street that did not flaunt one. Sripathi Rao, the owner, had reluctantly bought a television set a few years ago, but it was an old model that only had an internal antenna. His mother, Ammayya, had been disappointed.

"Nobody will even know we have a television," she protested. "What is the use of having something if nobody *knows* about it?"

Sripathi would not be swayed. "So long as you get your programs, why does it matter who knows what we have? Besides, this is all I can afford."

"If you had listened to me and become a big doctor you wouldn't have been talking about affording and not affording at all," grumbled his mother. She never missed an opportunity to remind him how much of a disappointment he was to her.

"Even if I was one of the Birlas, I would have bought only this television," Sripathi had argued. Or the Tatas or the Ambanis or, for that matter, any of India's mighty business tycoons. He did not believe in ostentatious displays—of possessions or of emotions.

When the phone rang for the first time that day, Sripathi was on the balcony of his house. As usual, he had woken at four in the morning and was now reading the newspaper, ticking off interesting items with a red marker. He stopped when he heard the high, fractured trill, but made no move to go down to the landing halfway between the first and ground floors to the phone. He waited for someone else to get it. There were enough people around, including—he thought with some annoyance—his son, Arun, asleep in the room across the corridor from his own.

Afterwards Sripathi wondered why he had felt no twinge of pre-monition. He remembered other times when tragedy had occurred: how uneasy he had been the day before his father's lifeless body was discovered on Andaal Street, and how strange the coincidence that had taken him there the next morning where he had joined the curious crowd gathered around it. And before his beloved grand-mother, Shantamma, was finally claimed by the Lord of Death, his nights had been full of restless dreams. Weren't disasters always heralded by a moment of immense clarity or a nightmare that rocked you, weeping, out of sleep? This time, however, he experi-enced nothing.

The phone continued to ring, grating on Sripathi's nerves. "Arun!" he shouted, leaning back in his chair so that he could see the length of his bedroom through the balcony door. "Get the phone! Can't you hear it?" There was no reply. "Idiot, sleeps all his life," he muttered. He pushed the chair away from the square iron table on which he had arranged his writing material, and stood up, flexing his rounded shoulders. As a youth, Sripathi had found that he was taller than all his friends and, because he hated to be different or conspicuous in any way, had developed a stoop. His thick grey hair was cut as short as possible by Shakespeare Kuppalloor, the barber on Tagore Street. An expression of permanent disappointment had settled on a face dominated by a beaky nose and large, moist eyes. After the softness of the eyes, the thin, austere line of his mouth came as a surprise. Once during an argument, his wife, Nirmala, had remarked that it looked like a zippered purse. He remembered being taken aback by the comparison. He had always found her to be like a bar of Lifebuoy soap—functional but devoid of all imagination.

The thought crossed his mind that the call might be from Maya, his daughter in Vancouver, and he paused in his passage across the bedroom. If it was, he didn't want to answer it. His eyes fell on a photograph of Maya, with her foreign husband and their child, on the windowsill next to Nirmala's side of the bed, and immediately his mood became tinged with bitterness. Every day, whenever he found an opportunity, he turned the picture face down on the sill and piled some books on it, feeling slightly childish, only to have it reinstated right-side-up by Nirmala. But Maya phoned on Sunday mornings, he reminded himself. At six-thirty when, as she knew, her mother would be waiting, sitting on the cold, tiled floor of the landing, right beside the phone. And every Sunday, for several years now, Sripathi had avoided that moment by setting off for a walk at six-twenty.

His younger sister, Putti, who was also downstairs somewhere, was too scared to answer the phone.

"I don't know what to talk into that thing," Putti had explained to Sripathi once, embarrassment writ large on her round, babyish face. "And anyway, it is never for me." A sad thing for her to say, he had thought then, feeling guilty that he had not done his duty as her older brother and found a husband for her. After living in Toturpuram for forty-two years, Putti had nobody to call a friend. Except perhaps that horrible librarian, Miss Chintamani.

Sripathi's mother claimed that she was too old to climb the stairs, but Nirmala insisted Ammayya was a fraud and that she came upstairs regularly to snoop around when she was alone in the house.

"She steals my saris," Nirmala had grumbled. "And I found my comb under her mattress. Did it walk there by itself, or what?"

The phone stopped ringing, and silence draped itself around the house once more. Sripathi went back to the balcony and settled down in the faded cane chair that had survived at least twenty years of ferocious sun and rain. He picked up *The Hindu* again and started to read it carefully, ticking off articles that he wanted to comment on.

He could hear soft music emanating from the apartments that loomed beside the house, the thin notes drowned almost immediately by the sound of the Krishna Temple bell—a clanging that competed for attention with the nasal call of the mullah from the Thousand Lights Mosque on a parallel street. The temple was straight up the road from Big House, which had been built eighty-two years ago by Sripathi's grandfather on what came to be called Brahmin Street for the number of people of that caste. However, when the ruling party won the state elections, it decreed that no street could have a name that indicated a particular caste; so Brahmin Street was now merely Street. As was Lingayat Street, Mudaliyar Street and half a dozen others in Toturpuram. This led to a lot of grumbling from visitors, who typically spent half the day wandering the town trying to figure out which Street was which. In addition, Brahmin Street had changed so much in the past decade that people returning to it after several years could barely recognize it. Instead of the tender smell of fresh jasmine, incense sticks and virtue, instead of the chanting of sacred hymns, the street had become loud with the haggling of cloth merchants and vegetable vendors, the strident strains of the latest film music from video parlours whose windows flaunted gaudy posters of busty, thick-thighed heroines, and beefy heroes with hair rising like puffs of smoke from their heads.

Older inhabitants of Toturpuram remembered how beautiful Big House used to be—its clean, strong walls washed pink every year before the Deepavali festival, its wide verandah and several balconies in front and along the sides, all held back by painted iron railings cast to look like fish and lotus flowers floating on stylized waves. The gigantic door of carved teak had been custom-built for the house and, in the past, had been varnished annually. The windows had stained-glass panes that Sripathi's grandfather had bought from a British family that had smelled the winds of change several years before Independence and moved back to England. Since his father's death, the house itself had slid into a sort of careless disrepair and looked as if it was tired of the life within its belly and on the seething, restless street outside.

"If my husband was still alive, we wouldn't have descended to this state," Ammayya complained to her cronies, conveniently forgetting that Narasimha Rao had been solely and utterly responsible for their decline.

The paint had curled away from the decorative railings leaving them cratered by rust. The door had lost its gleam, and the beautiful carvings were now anonymous nubs of wood. Cracks ran across the tiled floors like varicose veins on an old woman's legs, and it was years since the walls had seen a fresh coat of whitewash or paint. Most of the windows could not be opened any more, so much had they swollen in the moist heat of the place, and the brilliance of the glass was dimmed by layers of grease and dirt. The jammed windows did cut out the constant din of traffic from the road outside, as well as the devotional music that was played late into the night from various local temples, so nobody attempted to pry them open. The tall iron gates, eternally blocked by heaps of granite or gravel dumped by construction truck drivers who appeared to take a malicious pleasure in making the old home inaccessible, leaned inwards as if slowly yielding to pressure from the aggressive new world outside.

The temple bell continued its clamour and Sripathi rustled his newspaper with irritation. A few months ago, the sound of the bell had not bothered him at all. Recently, however, a devotee had paid for a pair of loud speakers, and the bell had become deafening. Sripathi had complained to the temple trustees, but nobody had done anything about it.

"What Sripathi-orey," the head priest had said with his pious smile. "This is God's music. How can you object to it? Nobody else has complained. You should learn to be more tolerant. And may I remind you, your esteemed grandfather himself purchased this bell for our temple?"

"Yes, I know all that." Sripathi was uncomfortably aware that the priest was insinuating that he was not as generous to the temple as his grandfather and even his father, had been. In fact, Sripathi avoided the temple whenever possible and refused to contribute more than fifty paise to the aarathi plate when, on special occasions, Nirmala forced him to go. "All I am saying is, why do you have to make it so loud? God is not deaf, is he?"

The priest had shrugged dismissively. "What to do? The mosque has megaphones. Also the Ganesha temple. So tell me, how will our Lord Krishna hear us with all this competition?"

The bell finally ceased its tintinnabulation. A fragile peace descended. All that Sripathi could hear now was the chittering of squirrels as they raced up and down the old lime tree directly below the balcony, and the fluid trill of the lory bird from the untended garden behind the house. Sripathi remembered how neat that garden used to be before his daughter had left for America. Maya and Nirmala together had lovingly tended the mango and guava trees, the banana plants and coconut palms, and had been rewarded with a steady supply of fruit.

He shook his head to dispel the memory, turned to the last page of the newspaper and scanned it quickly. The Indian cricket team had done miserably in the test match against the West Indies. Although he was not particularly interested in any sport, the cricket fever that swept through the country during the test matches infected him as well. Unlike his colleagues at work, however, he did not spend his lunch hour with the radio glued to his ear, cursing every time Indian batsmen were bowled out or missed a catch, or going into a state of ecstasy when someone hit a sixer. Sripathi read the sports section because he believed in keeping himself informed about every single thing that happened in the world around him. Besides, there might even be a potential letter to the editor buried in the sports page.

When he was a young man, Sripathi had discovered that writing letters to the editors of newspapers and magazines was the perfect way to vent his spleen and express his deepest thoughts—those blatant, embarrassing emotions that he was so reluctant to display in speech or action. He could write about anything under the sun and occasionally his views found their way into print. In the past few years, Sripathi felt that his writing had matured considerably, and to his delight, almost every letter he dashed off to *The Indian Express*, *The Hindu* or *The Toturpuram Chronicle* was published. So it was with a delicious sense of anticipation that he opened the paper each morning. And only after he had read the first page and the second and the third, postponing the moment as long as he could bear it, did he turn to the editorial section and feel a thrill when he spotted his byline—Pro Bono Publico—at the end of a missive. He would reread his piece, surprised at how different and removed from himself it looked in print. Then he'd scan the other letters, his long upper lip curling at a particularly weak piece of prose or an ill-argued point of view.

Sripathi was particularly pleased with his pseudonym. He had found it in an old American legal journal that his father had pinched from the public library on Moppaiyya Street. Pro Bono

Publico. On behalf of the people. Like his boyhood heroes—the Scarlet Pimpernel, Zorro, Jhanda Singh the Invisible—he was a crusader, but one who tried to address the problems of the world with pen and ink instead of sword and gun and fist. He wrote every day on anything that caught his attention, from garbage strewn on the roads to corruption in the government, from lighthearted commentary on the latest blockbuster film to a tribute to some famous musician whose voice had filled his soul with pleasure.

Sripathi reached for a large wooden box on the table before him. Like almost everything else in Big House, the box had been in his family for as long as he could remember. He loved the smooth edges, the solid weight, the thick key that locked it. He opened the lid and removed the upper layer that held his collection of pens, a few unsharpened pencils, some erasers and a penknife. Below it was another compartment for paper. There was also a secret drawer that could be opened by sliding a rod out of the side of the box. There was nothing in that drawer. A long time ago, when Maya—or perhaps it was Arun—had asked him why he kept nothing in there, he had replied, "Because I am too ordinary to have secrets." The box sat under his side of the bed and emerged every morning when he settled down on his balcony.

He contemplated the pens that jostled for space inside. Thirty-two of the finest, and growing. This was his one indulgence, although he added to the collection with diminishing frequency in these days of high cost and low affordability. He touched them one by one, lifted his favourites, and wondered which one he ought to use. The marbled blue Japanese Hero? Or the gold Parker? For letters about politics or government he always picked the Mhatre Writer—the maroon colour seemed authoritative. After dithering over the pens for a few more seconds, he settled for the Mhatre Writer again, unwilling to change his routine. It was pleasantly heavy between his fingers, the angled nib giving his writing a sharpness he relished. He wrote in his usual florid style learnt at the end of Father Schmidt's bamboo cane at St. Dominic's Boys' School almost fifty years ago.

Dear Editor,
   The streets are suddenly full of verdant trees, the garbage
has been picked up (after months of being ignored by the
municipal powers that be), and our walls have been
whitewashed overnight. A new government? A government
that has suddenly realized that it is of the people, by the people
and for the people and has decided to stop taking coffee breaks
and holidays and get down to work? Ah, no! Unfortunately
not. All this amazing work is in honour of the chief minister's
son's wedding . . .

He added a few more lines and signed with a flourish. Yes, that was a good letter. Forceful, to the point, and with an edge of sarcasm to make it truly effective. He was about to go over it again when Nirmala rustled in, fresh in a crisp pink cotton sari, her black hair a sliding knot at the nape of her neck. She had a smooth, sweet-tempered face that belied her fifty-two years, and she looked much younger than Sripathi, even though there were only five years between them. On her broad forehead she had a round, red sticker-bindi. Sripathi remembered that in the past she had used powdered vermilion. She would lean over the sink in the bathroom after her ablutions, her body still warm and damp, her buttocks outlined heavily against the straight cotton of her petticoat, creating a stir of desire in Sripathi, and with the ball of her middle finger would apply a dot of Boroline cream to the centre of her forehead. Then, just as carefully, she would dip the same finger into a small silver pot of vermilion and press it against the creamy circle. But a few years ago she, too, had yielded to modernity and abandoned her ritual of cream and red powder for the packs of felt stickers that came in a huge variety of shapes, sizes and colours. Ever since, Sripathi had

had a running argument with her about the bindis that she left stuck to the bathroom mirror like chicken-pox marks on the glass.

She handed him a stainless-steel tumbler of steaming coffee. "Why didn't you answer the phone?" she wanted to know.

"Why didn't you?"

"I was busy emptying out the vessels in the kitchen. Today is water day, remember? In between I was trying to make breakfast before your mother started shouting that she was hungry. And you want me to run up to get the phone also? Enh? What were *you* doing that couldn't be stopped for one moment?"

She began to remove the towels from the balcony wall, where they had been spread out to dry the previous night. Sripathi caught a glimpse of her bare waist as she leaned forward and the sari pallu fell away. There were extra folds of soft flesh there now, although he remembered how, when Nirmala was young, that waist used to arch deeply inwards before joining her hips. He couldn't resist pinching a fold of her waist gently, and she jumped, startled, before slapping his hand away.

"Chhee! Old man, doing such nonsense first thing in the morning!" she exclaimed.

"What nonsense? I was just administering the pinch test." He had read in the Thursday health section about a test that fitness instructors used to determine the amount of fat their clients had to shed.

"I forgot to tell you," Nirmala said, ignoring his teasing, "yesterday evening at the temple I saw Prakash Bhat and his wife. So uncomfortable it felt. They pretended not to see me. Can you imagine?"

Tilting his tumbler, Sripathi poured a stream of milky coffee into a small bowl on the table, stopping just before it frothed out. Then he poured it back into the tumbler. To and fro he went, expertly, until he had created a hillock of foam over his coffee.

"Maybe they really *didn't* see you," he told Nirmala. "You imagine all sorts of things."

"I don't imagine. I know they ignored me. I'm not a fool, even though I don't have big-big degrees in this and that. That Prakash used to call me Mamma, do you remember? He was almost married to our Maya and now see how little respect he shows me. And I thought that he was a decent boy!"

"Okay, so they saw you. Now leave me alone. I have work to do." He didn't want to be reminded of old troubles. And why should she expect Prakash to show any interest in the mother of the woman who had discarded him like a used banana leaf? Why did Nirmala persist in bringing up these memories? The unpleasantness of the incident would stay with him like the bitter taste of kashaya.

Nirmala carried the towels into the bedroom but continued to talk to him. "Prakash's wife is very plain-looking," she said. "A potato nose and tiny eyes. Lots of jewellery, but. As if shining stones can blind one to her face. She was wearing the diamond necklace. Do you remember how lovely it looked on our Maya? And now that lumpy creature has it. Tchah!"

Sripathi scowled at Nirmala's back. She was bent over the bed now, straightening out the wrinkled sheets. "I told you, stop going on and on about forgotten things. I don't want to hear them."

She patted the pillows briskly and stretched, her palm pressed into the small of her back, rubbing the tension away. "Yes-yes, it is all right for me to listen to your boring office stories every day," she protested. "But the minute *I* open my mouth, you tell me to keep quiet. Anyway, what I wanted to say was that the girl is pregnant, and they were talking to Krishna Acharye about performing the bangle ceremony."

"Why do you have to listen to other people's private conversations? Eavesdroppers never hear anything good."

Nirmala came back to the balcony to take Sripathi's empty tumbler and looked indignantly at him. "I didn't listen. Krishna Acharye himself told me. How bad I felt, you can't imagine."

"Why should you feel bad about some stranger's bangle cere- mony?"

"Don't pretend you don't understand. That girl could well have been Maya, and I would have been the one talking to Krishna Acharye about buying green bangles and saris and all. What an unfortunate woman I am!" She waited for him to say something in response. But Sripathi had decided to put an end to the conversa- tion, so she peered at the letter on the table.

"Who are you writing to?" she asked.

Sripathi quickly covered the letter with a blank sheet of paper, making sure that it was thoroughly concealed from Nirmala's pry- ing eyes. "None of your business," he said. He saw the hurt look she gave him and added, "Just some office work that I have to fin- ish. Now stop disturbing me."

Nirmala hid a smile and turned away, but not before Sripathi spotted it.

"What? What? It makes you laugh to see me work? Henh? I will take retirement today itself, and let us see if you will smile then. Maybe you can support us with your dance classes."

A year after Maya had left for the United States, Nirmala had agreed to teach a friend's daughters Bharat Natyam two evenings a week after school. She herself had studied this traditional dance form until she got married. "It will be good for me to pass on what I know," she told Sripathi obstinately when he teased her about capering around the house with her bulk. Soon the number of stu- dents swelled to six, and the living room resounded with the slap of bare feet and the tap-tap of her baton as she beat out a rhythm on the floor. Two of Nirmala's students were granted entry scholar- ships to a Bharat Natyam school that a famous dancer from Madras had started, and that was attended by people from all over India and abroad. Word spread in Toturpuram that Nirmala was a good person to get basic lessons from before trying for the school. When more parents arrived at her doorstep, she decided to charge a small fee. She was glad to be making the extra money, although she never told Sripathi that his income was not enough any more. A good Hindu wife had to maintain the pretense that her husband was supporting the family.

The telephone started to ring again. This time Sripathi slapped his letter pad down and hurried across the room, his heels touching the cold floor over the worn ends of his rubber slippers.

"As if we cannot even afford a twenty rupee pair of slippers," Nirmala remarked. "You might as well not wear anything on your feet!"

"Why should I waste money? These are okay for the house for another year or two. If I am comfortable, why should you be bothered?" Sripathi argued over his shoulder.

He went down the stairs to the landing and picked up the receiver. "Yes? Sripathi Rao here," he said.

In the bedroom Nirmala shook out a sheet. Snap! Snap! So hard that the sound travelled outwards as sharp as a bullet. She spread the sheet out on the bed, collected an armful of clean shirts, trousers and saris piled on a trunk that doubled as a table, and heaped them in the centre of the sheet. Then she drew the four ends together and tied them into a loose knot. The dhobi's boy would be here any minute to collect the clothes that needed to be ironed, and she didn't want him to run away before she had given him instructions on how to press her silk saris. Not too hot, she would have to remind him. The last time the dhobi had scorched a dark patch on one of her favourite saris.

She smiled again. She knew all about Sripathi's letters-to-the-editor business, had discovered his secret quite by accident while searching the waste baskets for a receipt for a piece of material that had shrunk horribly in the wash. Jain, the owner of Beauteous Boutique, would never acknowledge that she had purchased the fabric from his shop without proof of purchase, even though she was a regular customer. She had rummaged through the shreds of paper, annoyed by Sripathi's habit of tearing everything into quarters. A sheaf of neatly penned, whole sheets stapled together caught her eye. Had Sripathi thrown away something important by mistake? To her surprise, it was a letter to the editor of *The Hindu* about the heavy-water plant that had opened on the outskirts of Toturpuram and was dumping its waste directly into the sea. Now she realized what he wrote so busily every morning on the balcony. She had placed the letter on the table and waited for him to tell her about his pen-and-ink crusades. When he said nothing, she decided not to mention it either.

Slip-slap, slip-slap. Nirmala turned at the sound of Sripathi's footsteps entering the room. "Who was it?"

"God knows. Nobody answered," replied her husband. He went back to the balcony, flapping an irate hand at a crow that had landed on the table and was inspecting his shining pens.

"You should have waited for a few minutes. Sometimes the line is bad, and it takes time for those repair fellows to let the voice come through." Nirmala harboured the vague notion that phones were regulated by the telecom maintenance men who spent all day perched atop the lines along the road.

"I did, madam, I did. Waited five minutes. I happen to know how to use a phone."

"Why do you have to talk to me that way, enh?" demanded Nirmala. "Simply-simply you lose your temper." She picked up the sheet full of clothes. "Don't forget, today is water day," she reminded him. Her voice came out slightly muffled from behind her bundle, and Sripathi couldn't see her face at all. She had turned into a large, blue cloth turnip. He laughed aloud and she peered around the bundle at him, surprised at the unexpected sound. For a moment Nirmala looked to Sripathi like the young girl he had met thirty-five years before in her father's house. He had eaten six bondas that evening, he remembered, simply because he had been too shy to refuse another helping and another and another. After their wedding, Nirmala had told him how amazed her father had been by his appetite, and for years after, every time she made bondas they had a good laugh. But somehow the laughter had run away from their lives. They were like a pair of bullock yoked together, endlessly turning the water wheel round and round and round, eyes bent to the earth. Not even a note of eccentricity to set them apart from other couples. Even that pleasure they had denied themselves.

He waited until Nirmala left the room, her toe rings ringing against the cool tiles. Then he skimmed over the letter again and folded it meticulously in thirds. In addition to dinning the rules of grammar into their heads, Father Schmidt had also taught his terrified students letter-folding etiquette. Sripathi placed the letter in an envelope and slid it into his briefcase to mail on his way to work later in the day. Twelve years ago he would have had two letters nestling against the dark, old leather of the case. The thicker one to Maya, full of snippets of information about the family and even the political situation in the country, newspaper clippings, recipes from Nirmala, gossip from Putti, adolescent secrets from Arun. Sripathi suppressed the memory angrily. Had he not banished his daughter from their lives?

———

Since everybody had forgotten to take her home, she would just have to get there by herself, decided Nandana. She had never done it before, but her father had often said it was only a hop, a skip and a jump away. She knew her address—her parents had made her repeat it nearly every day—250 Melfa Lane, Vancouver, BC, Canada, North America, The World. Her father had always added the last two, and it made her mother laugh and say, "Don't confuse the child, Alan."

"How many sleeps before my parents come home?" Nandana had asked Kiran Sunderraj a day ago. And she had replied, "Just one, sweetheart." But it was already one and a half. Her friend Anjali had gone to day camp and come back, while Nandana was still here in Uncle Sunny's house. Anjali, also going into Grade Two, was Nandana's best friend number three, after Molly McNaughton and Yee Loh. It was fun to sleep over, despite Anjali's tendency to sulk when she did not get her way.

Yesterday evening—that was Sunday—two policemen had come to the door and then Aunty Kiran had started to cry. Uncle Sunny had run out of the house and still hadn't come home when she and Anjali went to bed.

Nandana was scared. Her parents had never left her anywhere for longer than they said they would. She wanted to go home.

This morning she had asked Aunty Kiran if she could call her parents. "I want to ask my daddy if he can get me some Fuji apples." She didn't want to hurt Aunty Kiran's feelings by asking to go home, so she'd made up the story about the Fuji apples. She knew that Anjali and her family always ate red McIntoshes. "I *need* Fuji apples for my eyesight," she had explained. But Aunty Kiran had only said that she would buy her some when she went for groceries in the afternoon.

"You don't have to buy them. I can get them at my house," Nandana had reminded her, but Aunty Kiran did not seem to have heard her.

Nandana hugged her cloth cow and peered out of the window. It was drizzling slightly. She picked up the pink-and-purple backpack that her father had bought for her seventh birthday, two months ago. He had filled it with lots of small surprises, such as a matching comb set, a bottle of sparkly purple nail polish, two books by Roald Dahl. It was now her favourite bag. Right at the bottom she had packed her baby blanket, even though she was too big to want it any more. Her father had told her to take it, just in case she felt like being a baby again. She had only recently started going for sleepovers and sometimes wanted to go home right away. The blanket would help if she felt homesick, her father had said. "You don't need to take it out. Just knowing it is there will make you feel good."

Earlier today she had tried calling home when Aunty Kiran had gone for her bath. She got the answering machine. "Mummy, Daddy, please come and take me home," she said to the machine. Then she added, in case they had forgotten where she was sleeping over, "I am at Anjali's house. It's the white one with the maple tree, behind Safeway."

Nobody had called her back or come to get her. She was beginning to think that Aunty Kiran had decided to keep her here for ever and ever. Hadn't she often said as much to her mother? "Maya, your daughter is such a cutie-pie, I think I shall keep her." And her mother would laugh, "Ah, not so cute all the time, believe me. She can be a little pest." Then she would stroke Nandana's cheek and say, "But I wouldn't give her away for a zillion dollars."

She wondered if her mother had changed her mind.

2

MORNING IN
BIG HOUSE

OWNSTAIRS THE HOUSE bustled with activity. The maid,
Koti, washed the dinner dishes from the previous day in
the backyard under a sloping asbestos roof. The laundry
soaked in buckets of soapy water beside her. After the dishes were
done, the maid would turn on the brass tap that spewed forth only
saline water and wash the clothes. The tap was chained firmly to the
wall and had to be unlocked every morning; Sripathi had reluctantly installed the chain after several of their taps had been stolen.

Koti scrubbed vigorously at the pots and pans with a piece of
coconut fibre dipped in an ash and soap-powder mixture, and conducted a loud conversation with Putti over the sound of splashing
water. Like her brother, Putti was tall and heavy. There was an air
of apprehension about everything she did, as if she constantly
expected to be scolded. Even her gait was timorous. Her dark hair
hung in two long, oiled braids and made her look like an overgrown
schoolgirl. She was sixteen years younger than Sripathi. At forty-
two, she was still waiting for her mother to approve a bridegroom
for her, even though her hope dimmed a little more with every passing year.

"So many times the phone is ringing," remarked the maid.
"Who do you think it is, Akka?"

Putti twirled the end of one braid and smiled vaguely. "I don't know," she said. She had been up since three in the morning as usual, woken by Gopala Munnuswamy knocking on the front door with the day's supply of milk. He used to leave the aluminum can on the verandah, until a cat moved into the Big House compound and began to help itself to the contents.

"What is wrong with you these days?" asked Koti, giving Putti a shrewd look. "In another world you are living, or what?"

Without answering, Putti wandered away from the cemented wash area and into the messy garden. Dew still lingered on the grass in the shadow of the house and felt pleasantly cool under her feet. She glanced quickly at the large house to the left of Big House, freshly painted a bright blue absurdly out of place on this ruined street. It belonged to old Munnuswamy, the local member of the Legislative Assembly. He had started his career as a milkman with two cows to his name. People remembered him knocking on their doors early in the morning and milking his cows before their eyes, while his nine-year-old son, Gopala, ran up and down to the neighbouring homes delivering buckets of frothing, warm milk. That was thirty-four years ago. Now Munnuswamy owned Justice Raman Pillai's ancestral home, and it was whispered about town that he also owned most of the property on Brahmin Street.

Ammayya had been indignant when the rumour reached her. "This is no longer Brahmin Street. Cow-shit Street would be a better name for it," she said bitterly. "If only we had known that the rogue was saving *our* money to drive us out of here, we would have drunk water instead of milk. Much safer for all of us it would have been!"

Although he no longer needed to sell milk to make a living, Munnuswamy still maintained a dairy on the outskirts of Toturpuram. Old customers such as Sripathi continued to buy milk from Munnuswamy, even though it was cheaper to pick up a bottle from the Aavin Milk Booth a few blocks down the street. Tethered to the front verandah of his newly painted house was his favourite cow, Manjula, and her calf, Roja.

Putti thought guiltily of Gopala's dark eyes on her face. They made her breathless with excitement. And this morning when he gave her the can of milk, his hard hands had skimmed over her smooth round ones, soft from constant applications of sandal paste and cream. "Be careful you don't let it slip, Putti Akka," he had said gently.

The touch of those warm hands had made Putti grow faint with pleasure, although she was annoyed that he had called her Akka or elder sister. Just her name would have been acceptable, but she would never be forward enough to say that to him. Miss Chinta-mani, the clerk at the Raghu Lending Library and her long-time friend and confidante, had informed her (backed by the authority of *Eve* magazine) that only loose women and silly film heroines allowed their innermost feelings to show, to say aloud to a man what churned in their hearts. So she had not replied to Gopala, merely nodded politely and, heart thudding, retreated to the safe womb of her home.

"My darling, where are you?" called Ammayya from inside the house. "Come here and take a look at my eye, how red it is."

Putti sighed and went back into the dark, old house. If she did not respond to her mother right away, the old woman would start a scene, weeping and smacking her forehead with her palm and accusing her of being an unfeeling daughter.

She entered the kitchen and smiled at Nirmala who was now busy chopping vegetables for the afternoon meal. "Do you need any help, Akka?" she asked.

"No, you'd better go to Ammayya," said Nirmala, grimacing at her sister-in-law.

"Who was that on the phone earlier?"

"I don't know. You could have answered, no? You were doing nothing."

"Ayyo, I never know what to say." Putti shuddered.

Nirmala snorted. "What is this nonsense excuse? Are you a small baby, or what? Your brother sits up there like a god in heaven writing big-big things to this person and that, your nephew sleeps till ten o'clock, and you say you are afraid of a plastic dabba. I am the only one running here and there like a madwoman!"

Putti looked guiltily at her. She was fond of Nirmala. "Okay, Akka, if it rings again, I promise I will pick it up. Do you think it was Maya?"

"No, she would not call on water day."

"Putti! Are you building a house, or what? Come here quickly," called Ammayya, her voice thinly edged with petulance.

"Go, go," whispered Nirmala, her bangles clinking vigorously as she diced a large eggplant, "otherwise she will say we are talking about her. I don't want any trouble first thing in the morning."

When Putti entered the dimly lit room that she shared with her mother, she found Ammayya seated at the dressing table. As soon as her daughter's reflection joined hers in the floor-length Belgian mirror, the old woman swallowed a spoonful of some dark liquid from one of the many bottles before her. "Unh!" she said, scrunching up her mouth. "Can you see it, my darling?" She leaned forward and examined her face, wrinkled as a crushed paper bag, as if expecting to see some miraculous change wrought by the medicine she had just swallowed.

"See what?" asked Putti.

Ammayya pulled down the skin beneath her right eye with her index finger and rolled her eyeballs around. "Chintamani told me that one should always watch the eyes. If they are yellow, then it is jaundice or some other liver trouble. If the skin inside the eyelid is pale, it is leukemia. Mine is too-too red. My blood pressure is high, that's why. I can feel it going ghash-phash in my veins, my pet."

"I can't see anything," said Putti.

"So I am telling lies, or what? Look properly." Ammayya yanked her eyelid down again. "Any time now I could explode. Chintamani's father died of high blood pressure. He had red eyes like mine, do you remember? But everybody just thought it was an infection. Conjunctivitis or some such thing. Poor man." She allowed a few tears to gather in her eyes and sighed heavily. "Nobody cares for old people. Such is this modern world. My mother-in-law was blessed, truly. Because of me she stayed alive till she was ninety years old."

Putti didn't remind her mother that she, too, was eighty and in fairly good health for her age.

"You and I will go to Dr. Menon's clinic today," decided Ammayya. "Maybe the library also."

"Why do we have to go all the way to that crazy old man?" grumbled Putti, her lips pouting over her twisted front teeth. "Why not Dr. Pandit's son, where Sripathi used to take the children? At least he has all the latest devices to check heart and blood and everything."

"Pah, these modern doctors are shameless. They make you take off all your clothes, I have heard. Even your knickers. Why should I go to those perverts?" Putti refrained from reminding Ammayya that she wore no knickers at all.

A door flew open in a second-floor apartment in Jyothi Flats, Block A, one of two unimaginative structures that stood back to back, like oversized boxes, to the right of Big House. The Burmese Wife had lived in that apartment for more than five years, and yet it seemed nobody knew her name. Some said she was from Burma, and others whispered that she was actually a Chinese prisoner of war held captive by the morose Lieutenant Colonel Hansraj, her husband. Sripathi had never discovered whether this was true or simply a story inspired by the woman's slanting eyes, her slight body and the unrecognizable language in which she cursed her maidservant.

The Burmese Wife was hugely superstitious and had a running feud with the family in the flat above her own because they hung their washing over the balcony rail.

"Bad luck to have another woman's wet sari touch my face," she screamed, her shrill voice with its rounded Bengali-sounding accent startling a pair of crows away from a neighbouring balcony. "It will make me a widow!" The maidservant upstairs ignored her and continued to drape the washing over the railing. To Sripathi's relief, the Burmese Wife stopped screaming and marched inside her flat. But in a few moments she came out again, brandishing a pair of gardening shears. "To teach them to respect other people's feelings," she said, catching sight of Sripathi. "Some people have to be taught everything, even when they are grey-haired." With a grim smile, she chopped off the ends of all the saris and sheets that encroached on her space. There was a commotion in the flat upstairs as the maid realized what the bits of fabric were. She yelled for the mistress of the house, and moments later war broke out.

Then, from the first-floor apartment directly below the Burmese Wife's, there came an awful howl. It was Gopinath Nayak, the young civil servant, exercising his vocal chords. Sripathi winced as he launched discordantly into an old Tamil film song. One of these days he would tell the fellow exactly how he felt about that racket. "Gopinath Nayak," he would say firmly, "you sound like a donkey in labour. If you don't shut up, I am going to jam your throat with cement."

He gazed down, smiling at the sight of a group of college girls in pale cotton saris, their hair done up in fashionable styles, drifting towards the gates of the apartment compound. He spotted Mrs. Poorna peering eagerly out from her ground-floor patio.

"Here darling, here," she cooed in Tamil. "Your mother has made it for you, with lots of sugar, just as you like it." A kissing sound followed.

Sripathi sighed. The poor woman was talking to thin air as usual. As the day progressed she would babble on, her voice a small wave of sound unfurling gently beneath the turbulence around her. By noon she would start to wail. She would beat her breast, clutch her grey hair and beg God to return her darling child. Sometimes, if the neighbours complained, the poor relative who looked after her in exchange for board and lodging, would drag her roughly inside the apartment. Most of the time, however, Mrs. Poorna stayed on her patio until her husband came home and coaxed her inside. Years before, they had lost their only child, an eight-year-old girl who had disappeared as completely as a drop of dew from the front yard. Everybody had seen the child playing hopscotch in her over-sized dress bought to last at least a year, her pigtails flying out like dark comets, her young voice mingling with all the others. But suddenly she was gone. The Gurkha who guarded the gates all day insisted that she could not have left the compound. But despite all of the time that had passed, Mrs. Poorna still waited for her daughter's return. Every day she made sugar parathas, every day she waited on the patio and every day she continued to hope.

"Water will be coming in ten minutes," Nirmala called from the foot of the stairs. "Better come down. The rice-seller is here and I won't have time."

Sripathi put away his writing material. He hated water day, an event that occurred four times a week on Brahmin Street between six-thirty and seven in the morning. Because of the town's dire shortage of drinking water, the municipal corporation regulated the supply by releasing limited quantities on alternate days. Each area had its own scheduled water days, when every container in the house was frantically filled to the brim. Sripathi had contrived a complicated network of pipes all over the ground floor of the house, as potable water flowed from only the kitchen faucets. Long trails of green piping scrolled like garden snakes along the edges of the rooms downstairs, some leading into a large cement tank in Ammayya's bathroom, and others into an assortment of drums, buckets and pots in the dining area. Nirmala used the fresh water only for cooking, drinking and rinsing the dishes. The clothes were washed by Koti, the maidservant, in the saline water that gushed generously from the taps all day long. As a result, their clothes developed a yellowish tint and seemed always unwashed, even though Koti vigorously thrashed the dirt out of them every day on the granite wash-stone in the backyard.

Sripathi peered into his son's room, which was almost as large as his own. Arun had shared the room with Maya until she turned sixteen. Then Nirmala had decided that it wasn't right for an adolescent girl to have a male, even her younger brother, in the room, so Arun's bed had been shifted to the landing until Maya left the household. One wall had a large window that looked out onto the road in front of the house and was partially shielded from the raging afternoon light by the feathery shade of an ancient neem tree. The other wall had a door that opened onto a balcony exactly like Sripathi's. A few years ago, Koti had gone out there to dry some clothes and had nearly fallen down one storey when the railing gave way. Now nobody opened that door any more.

After Maya had gone, Arun had moved his bed back into the room and pushed it against the locked door. Frugal even as a child, he had grown into a hermit-like adult. He owned three white shirts and two pairs of trousers. He wore each shirt twice a week and the trousers three times. Every evening when he removed his shirt and trousers, he draped them carefully on a hanger and hung them from a hook on the wall. He then wrapped one of two cotton lungi cloths around his narrow waist.

The room was otherwise full of books and files and newspaper clippings. Even Maya's bed, with its bare mattress and uncovered pillows, was layered with papers and notebooks. Arun had been working on a doctorate in social work for the past five years, in between his involvement with various activist organizations.

Sripathi surveyed the chaos of paper with irritation. He had never pushed his children the way his father had pushed him. He had believed that if he left them alone, they would do well. Maya—for a short time—had proven him right. But this son of his had only ever been a disappointment.

Arun lay flat on his bed contemplating a lizard stalking a moth across the veined wall. He willed the moth to fly away. As soon as the lizard came close, it fluttered forward sluggishly and then lay flat against the peeling whitewash, the patterns on its wings like staring eyes. Was it daring the lizard to catch it? Arun stretched his arms above his head and smiled. Watch out, he said softly, that lizard is no fool. But perhaps the moth was aware of its own mortality and was playing one last game with fate. The lizard slid forward suddenly and with a flicker of its tongue seized the moth, drawing it quickly into its mouth.

He turned his head at the sound of his father's footsteps.

"What are you doing?" Sripathi demanded. "Come down and help me with the water. Mutthal, sleeping like a labourer. If you did half the work those poor fellows do, you would have a right to sleep like them."

Arun sat up and slipped his feet into a pair of Hawaiian sandals that were at least as worn as his father's. He was a short, compact man of twenty-eight with a mild air about him. The only feature he had in common with Sripathi was a nose that leapt out from the centre of his face and made it look slightly out of balance. "I am not sleeping," he said.

"Oh? Then what are you doing, pray?"

"I was thinking about—"

Sripathi did not let him finish his sentence. "Thinking? About what? How to save the world? Like Lord Vishnu? Eh? Eh?"

The phone rang again before he could continue, and he paused, walked over to the window and peered down. He couldn't see the verandah directly below, but voices floated up to him.

"Last month you sold this rice to me for five rupees a kilo, and suddenly it has gone up to seven-twenty? What nonsense! Cheating a loyal customer," he heard Nirmala say. And the rice-seller's voice, "Akka, how can you accuse me of cheating? You are like my sister. Would I cheat my own sister? Look at these grains of rice. Threads of gold they are. Aged for five years at the bottom of my granary. Better quality than last time. You cook half a cup and you will get such beautiful rice, so plump and light and fragrant, you will think that you are in the kitchen of the lord of the gods, King Indira himself."

"Last time you told me the very same story." Nirmala was not to be swayed by the rice-man's eloquence.

"Impossible, Akka! I would never say such things about any other strain of rice. How could I? This has been fed by water from the Godavari River herself."

"She won't pick up the phone till she has finished her haggling." He glared at Arun, who stood up hastily.

"I'll get it," he offered, but his father threw him another irritated look and left the room.

"It might be a wrong number, I think," suggested Arun, following his father to the head of the stairs and leaning against the banister.

"Think!" muttered Sripathi. "If you worked as hard as you thought we would be millionaires by now. *Multi*-millionaires!"

———

Past the house with the petunias that looked like a storybook picture, past the row of cherry trees without cherries and the small store that said *Vancouver Buns*, to the crossing where she would have to decide whether to turn right or left. Nandana was going home. She was nervous about being alone on the road, but she knew it was only a hop, a skip and a jump away. She also kept a watchful eye out for strangers and killer bees. The first, both her mother and father had warned her about. *Never* talk to strangers, they had said. If a stranger approaches, start screaming or run away.

Never accept anything from someone you do not know. "Even if they offer you a Mars bar, you *have* to say no," her mother had cautioned, looking very solemn. She knew it was her favourite treat.

Not that they would ever let her go out alone. No *way*.

As for killer bees, Nandana was more worried about those. She had seen a nature program about Africa on television last week. Killer bees were dangerous. They could kill with a single sting and travel long distances without getting tired. Nandana wasn't sure where Africa was in relation to Vancouver, but on the world map in her room it didn't look far at all. She and Molly McNaughton had discussed it and agreed that it was ab-SO-lute-ly possible for those bees to fly to Canada.

Why had her parents left her for almost three whole days in Anjali's house? It occurred to Nandana that maybe she had done something to annoy her parents. She tried to think what it could be. She had taken her favourite green pyjamas with the yellow frogs for this sleepover. They were too small, and her father had wanted her to take her red ones instead. Guiltily she remembered that she hadn't put her toys away before Aunty Kiran had come to pick her up. Perhaps *that* had made her father mad.

She was standing at the crossing, trying to decide which was her left hand and which her right, when she saw Aunty Kiran running down the street after her.

"Oh Nandu, you silly girl, I was so worried," she started to cry. Then she insisted on carrying Nandana back part of the way, even though she was a big girl and far too heavy. She let herself be carried, so as not to upset Aunty Kiran further, but she stuck her legs out as stiff as two sticks because she felt stupid. Finally, she was allowed to slide down to the ground, and that was better, she thought. But she still had to hold Aunty's hand until they reached the white house behind Safeway.

"Oh God, oh God, this is terrible," Aunty Kiran wailed as soon as she shut the door. "What is this poor child going to do?"

Why, thought Nandana, is she getting so agitated about me going home?

Uncle Sunny took the backpack from her and looked grim. "We should tell her," he said to his wife. "It isn't good to keep it from her. Sooner or later she will have to be told. Better soon."

"I want my mom," said Nandana firmly. She was getting a funny feeling in her stomach, as if there were beetles crawling around inside. "I told my daddy I would help him recycle the newspapers. I want to go home. Please."

Aunty Kiran blew her nose on a tissue that she pulled from the pocket of her jeans. She took Nandana into the living room with the big sofas.

"Those sofas look like fat tourists in Hawaiian shirts," her father had commented once.

Her mother had poked him in the side and giggled. "Don't say things like that in front of Miss Big Ears. She will go and blurt it out for sure."

As if. She knew all about not hurting people's feelings. It was called being diplomatic.

"Honey, I have something to tell you," Aunty Kiran began, holding Nandana very close.

3

THE STORM

S RIPATHI PICKED UP the receiver and said hello breathlessly.

There came a series of beeps followed by a clear voice. "Is that Mr. Sripathi Rao's residence?"

Sripathi didn't recognize the voice. It sounded like that of the American social worker who had arrived to work on some project with Arun and had gone back shuddering with malaria after a week.

"Yes, yes, this is Sripathi Rao," he said.

"My name is Dr. Sunderraj. I am calling from Vancouver. May I ask if you are the father of Maya Baker?"

Baker? With a small shock Sripathi realized that, for a moment, he hadn't even remembered Maya's husband's last name.

"Mr. Rao, are you still there? Can you hear me?"

Sripathi cleared his throat and said, "I can, yes. Maya is my daughter. Um, we haven't been in touch for a while now." He cleared his throat, embarrassed to be admitting this to a stranger and wishing that he had not.

"Uh-huh, yes. I see, I see." There was a small pause and then the man continued in a rush. "Sir, I am a friend of Maya and Alan's. A family friend. Your daughter asked us to contact you."

The voice floated in and out of Sripathi's head. *Accident*, it said. *Very tragic. Thought she would pull through. Really sorry.* What was this man talking about? Sripathi sank to the floor near the telephone, his legs unable to hold him up any longer.

"Pardon me," he said. He could hear his voice shake suddenly, as if from cold. "Could you please repeat that? I didn't catch . . . Are you talking about Maya Rao? Who works at Bioenergics?" He remembered the name of that company. Nirmala had made a point of telling him about it, despite his pretending not to hear.

And the man's voice, soothing, calm. "I understand. No problem, I'll go over it again. I know this is an enormous shock for you. I am terribly sorry. We thought that Maya, at least, would come through. And sorry for the delay in calling. We tried several times, but couldn't reach you. I thought, let me try one more time to talk to you personally before sending a telegram and all . . ."

A roaring wave of shock crashed over Sripathi. He hardly registered the rest of the man's words. Maya and her husband had died the day before. But why didn't anyone tell us earlier? Why, what could you have done? he argued with the voice that grew louder and louder in his head. You didn't talk to her for nine years, cut her off as if she were a diseased limb and now suddenly comes this concern? Sripathi could hear his heart pounding urgently inside his chest. His breath was indecently loud in his ears.

In between he heard bits and pieces of the family friend's voice: Maya's car had crashed off the highway. Alan had died immediately. The doctors had hoped that Maya would survive, but there was severe internal damage. Fortunately, Nandana wasn't with them. She was safe in Dr. Sunderraj's home, with his wife, Kiran, and their daughter.

"Alan has no immediate family, Mr. Rao," said the steady voice: It occurred to Sripathi that the call was probably costing the man a lot of money. He would have to offer to reimburse him somehow.

The man continued to speak. "As you are probably aware, Maya appointed you legal guardian and trustee some time ago."

Yes, Sripathi thought numbly, I remember. I signed the papers, but that is all I did. He wondered briefly how the family friend knew so much about his daughter's affairs—much more than he did.

"There might be some problem with Social Services. They may not release the child immediately to a stranger," continued the voice. "I believe you have never met your grandchild. Is it possible for you to arrange to stay here for a few weeks? Let the child get used to you, as it were? And there are other legal and financial matters . . ."

The polite, reasonable voice went on and on. Wills. Financial papers. Death certificate. Cremation. The possibility of Alan's relatives surfacing and contesting the will—a distant chance as Alan likely did not have anyone who was close enough to him to want the responsibility of a child. Police check. Adoption. Sripathi put down the receiver gently, aware that the man was still speaking. Enough, he thought. He could not bear to hear another word.

A long distance away Sripathi could hear water running, cascading down the sides of the cement tank in Ammayya's bathroom. It occurred to him that Koti must have started filling it and that if he didn't move away from the phone and help her, there would be no drinking water for the day.

He heard his mother's querulous voice calling him. "Sripathi, H_2O started coming long ago, so I turned on the pipe. Now the tank is overflowing and I can't turn the pipe off. What are you doing? Come quickly, big mess it is becoming." At any other time, Sripathi would have been mildly amused by Ammayya's habit of using chemical formulae, the occasional Latin term, or some other bit of information gathered during those days when her husband was alive, when he had forced them both to memorize the *Encyclopaedia Britannica*. But today it barely registered. Instead he imagined water flooding the floor, snaking out from under the door, spreading silver into the bedroom. *Waste don't waste don't waste don't waste.* An alarm went off in his brain, the result of years of careful budgeting, of trying to make sure that there was always enough money for decent schools and clothes and good food.

Ammayya called again, more urgently. "Ayyo! Look at this mess. I am all wet also. Sripathi!"

Sripathi sat motionless, unable to move. He stared at his hands, knotted with the weight of the years they had carried; the paper cut on his left hand, just below the thumb, which began to burn the moment he noticed it; and the three black moles on his palm, which he had believed for years would bring him untold wealth. These were the hands that had cradled a small body, stroked unruly curls off a sweaty forehead, swung a little girl—his first born—in the air above his head. The same hands that had written such hard, unforgiving words nine years ago. He glanced down at them, empty now, their palms seared by lines of time and fate.

In a daze he heard Nirmala climb the stairs.

"What is wrong? Why haven't you started filling water in the kitchen? Who was that on the phone? What happened?" she asked. Sripathi could feel her anxious gaze, even though he couldn't look her in the face.

"Ree-ree, why are you sitting like this without saying anything? Are you ill, or what? Tell me."

Sripathi felt her hand on his shoulder. Felt her shake him and, when he did not respond, yell for their son. "Arun, come quickly! Something is wrong with your father! I don't know what. Must be that oily food he keeps eating at the office. How many times I have said, after a certain age you must be careful of your diet, otherwise all sorts of heart problems you will get."

She shook him again, and this time Sripathi looked at her, afraid of what he would see in her eyes after she heard what he had to say.

"Our Maya," he said. His voice came out in a croak, and he cleared his throat before continuing. "Bad news. That was a call from Vancouver." He frowned. Had that call really come?

"What? What happened? Is she sick? Tell me no, why you are keeping things from me?" begged Nirmala.

"Maya is dead," said Sripathi. He heard his own voice again, and now it seemed to be coming from somewhere else. "So is her husband. Car crash." Again that clutch of panic in his chest—a sticky, dark tightness that caught his breath and refused to release it in the waves of grief that he craved.

Nirmala stared at him. "What are you saying? Who was on the phone? Some idiot playing the fool probably. You know how the phone idiots climb on the poles—"

"Didn't you hear me? Maya and her husband died yesterday in a car crash. Why are you babbling about phones and all? Is something wrong with your ears?" Sripathi asked savagely, willing himself to feel something other than numbness, to feel a rightful sorrow. He glared at Nirmala, hating her for making him repeat the awful news. Repeating it would make it real. Didn't the silly woman realize that?

Without any warning, Nirmala launched herself at him. She hit him on his chest and wailed in his face, "Your fault, your fault, your fault! You killed my daughter. You drove her away from me! You! You! You!"

Again and again she hammered her fists against his body, slapping and punching in a frenzy. Sripathi sat still, his head in his hands, like a penitent being flogged for his sins. For once he had no argument, no quick sarcastic remark to shut her up. He wanted to apologize, to say something, but perversely he found himself becoming angry with her. How dare she raise her hands to him, her husband?

"Stop it!" He tried to grab her flailing arms. "Stop making such a scene. Behave yourself!"

Nirmala's heavy, normally pleasant face was ugly. Her hair had worked free of its pins and fell across her face and down her back. "I am *tired* of behaving myself," she panted. Sripathi noticed with faint disgust that mucus had dripped from her nose and was smeared across her left cheek. One of her hands landed hard on his face, knocked his glasses away, caught his eye and made it water. Without thinking he slapped her back, and she stopped crying abruptly.

"You *hit* me?" she said, stunned. "You killed my child, and now you are hitting me also? Evil man." Again she launched herself at him. Now her blows caught Sripathi deliberately on his nose, his cheeks, his mouth. He was enraged by her lack of restraint. He got to his feet so that he loomed over her, and she was obliged to swing upwards at him. He grabbed her arms and she struggled to release herself. "Let me go!" she screamed. "Let me go!"

"What are you doing? Mamma. Appu. Stop it!" Arun's voice brought Sripathi back to his senses. His son was running down the stairs, and at the foot of the stairs, staring up in horror, stood the rice-seller, Koti, the maidservant, and his sister Putti. In all these years, Sripathi had never touched his wife in violence, only with desire and affection. Now he had hit her in front of his whole family *and* the maidservant *and* the man who sold them rice.

"What happened?" Arun asked again. "Mamma, stop this nonsense and tell me." He pulled Nirmala away from Sripathi, held her firmly against him and glared at his father. "Aren't you ashamed of yourself?"

Sripathi noticed that his son was wearing a faded green kurta that he himself had thrown away only days ago. The wretched boy had fished it out of the garbage bin! He looked so much like Maya, thought the father painfully, and then threw the thought away. Only the shape of his face. Only that. Nobody looked like Maya. Certainly not this shabby creature standing before him.

Nirmala raised her voice again. "I told him, begged him so many times. Let us forget the past, I told him and told him. But no, when has he ever listened to me? I am a fool, no? Can't use big-big words and say clever things."

"*Calm down* and tell me what is going on. Who was that on the phone?"

Sripathi sat down again and held his trembling hands folded tightly on his lap. He was afraid of what they would do to him if he let them loose. He didn't think he could control them. Now his legs were beginning to shiver, so he crossed them as well, tucking the loose folds of his lungi in between—once at the knee and again at the ankles, until they looked like bright, twined snakes. There was a large purple bruise stretched across his ankle. He had missed the starter pedal on his scooter and hurt himself badly. Funny he had never noticed how purple it was. Like an aubergine. A roasted one. Did Maya have purple scars on her poor body? And her husband? His skin would surely bruise in different shades. He was so much fairer.

"Appu?" he heard his son ask.

"Her head used to fit into my palm," Sripathi said, to no one in particular. "Do you remember?" Maya's baby breath had seemed like the touch of a feather on his neck as she slept on his shoulder, he thought—and he, too frightened to take a deep breath or move his head in case she woke up. Her face a bright portulaca flower, waiting for him, her Appu, to return from work. She always had her feet wrong in the tiny green Hawaiian slippers he had bought her from the Bata shop on the casino corner.

"This is your *left* foot," he would tell her. "It goes into *this* slipper. And your *right* foot goes into that one."

But of course she never listened, dancing around impatiently for him to take her for their ritual ride around the tulasi planter in the front yard, checking his pockets to see if he had hidden a treat for her. And as they rode round and round in slow, tight circles, she would bring him up to date on her day: "Appu, I saw an enormous spider. It wanted to eat me. It was green and yellow"; "Appu, I hurt my left toe on my right foot"; "Appu, I did susu in my pants by mistake because Ammayya would not come out of the toilet"; "I ate a *big* mango, and Mamma said I must drink milk to cool the mango in my stomach. But Appu, I waited for *you* to come home and give me the milk."

She had never indulged in baby talk; the unformed words that sounded unbearably cute in other children had never appeared in his daughter's vocabulary. Always such a precise little creature. She had carried that fierce precision right through to her adult years, along with an ambition that Sripathi had never entirely understood—to be the best at whatever she took on.

He turned a frozen face to Arun and said, "Your sister is dead. There was an accident. She and her husband are no more."

In a detached sort of way, he watched the shock wash over Arun's face. *Your sister,* he said again mentally. *The child who came six years before you.* He looked away before he blurted out something unforgivable. Such as, "Why your sister and not you?" Arun flirted with danger every other day in his efforts to change the world, but here he stood healthy and breathing and shabby in faded green.

"Nandana too?" asked Arun.

The child.

"No, she wasn't there."

"The child is okay? Where is she? Poor thing—what will happen to her?" Nirmala cried.

"How did it happen?" Arun asked.

Sripathi felt forced to reply. "An accident."

"Who was driving?"

It hadn't occurred to Sripathi to find out, and now that Arun had brought it up, he was filled with an urgent desire to know. Was Alan Baker to blame? Was he drunk? Was he careless? Yes, most certainly it was that man's fault. The same fellow who had taken Maya away from her family, her duties, her home—that same bastard must have taken her life, too. He scrabbled for the tattered phone directory on which he had jotted Dr. Sunderraj's number. It was important to know right away who was behind the wheel. Who was to blame.

"What are you doing?" asked Nirmala. "Who are you phoning?"

"That doctor who called just now," explained Sripathi. "To ask who was responsible."

"Does it matter?"

"Of course it does. We have to punish the person who did it. The one who murdered our child," said Sripathi calmly.

"What is this nonsense you are talking? Punish, how you can punish somebody all the way there from all the way here?" Nirmala demanded.

"Sue them, that's what I will do. Set our lawyers on them."

"What lawyers? Why are you babbling like this?"

Sripathi ignored her, and with a trembling finger he dialed Dr. Sunderraj's number. I am not the one you should be blaming, he thought; it is somebody else. As soon as he heard it ringing, though, he lost heart and dropped the receiver. Nirmala was right. They had no lawyers, and even if they did, he had no money for legal fees. Besides, how could he, Sripathi Rao, a man of no consequence in this world, sue somebody thousands of miles away in another country? And so, to hide his lack of worth from his own cruel gaze, he turned on his wife, as usual.

"Why you always have to tell me what to do, what not to do?" he snarled at her. "Is this my house or not? Did I ask you for money to pay lawyers? Did I ask you for anything at all? You came like a pauper to this house, and you talk as if you are some maharani."

Nirmala stumbled away from him, down the stairs, and he watched Putti and Koti lead her away into the familiar warmth of the kitchen. Arun pushed roughly past him and followed his mother down to the kitchen. Sripathi was left alone on the landing with the silent phone. He struggled to control his inchoate feelings—rage and despair, sorrow and guilt. He cursed himself for the way he had behaved with Nirmala. He had destroyed what should have been a moment of mourning together for their lost child. But then, he reminded himself, she was the one who had attacked him. From the bedroom downstairs, he could hear Ammayya's voice again. "H₂0 has stopped. Only my tank is full. No drinking water today. Oh-oh-oh, what to do?"

He heard her chair scrape and then the tap-tapping of her walking stick as she made her way to the living room.

"Henh? Why were you all shouting and screaming? I was trying to pray, and God himself could not hear me with all this galata." She rapped her stick impatiently and, a moment later, Putti's voice reached Sripathi.

"Ammayya, some bad news." His sister sounded very calm, thought Sripathi. Why wasn't she weeping like Nirmala? Wasn't she affected at all?

A shudder tore through him. He thought he might fall. He clung to the banister and shut his eyes. Control, he whispered to himself. If he could control himself, he could deal with anything in the world, including this. He forced himself to stand and climb down the stairs. His legs quivered with every step he took, and he felt very old and far away from everything that was happening around him. His mind seemed to have stopped working altogether. What was he supposed to do? How was he supposed to react to the death of his own child? My daughter is dead, he told himself. Devoid of life. The mechanical reduction of fact into words soothed him momentarily. He emerged into the unbearable light of the verandah and sat on the steps already baking in the sun. He barely felt the cement burning through his lungi to the skin of his thighs. The sky was a shining steel drum inside which the world was trapped. On the dusty ground before him was a rangoli pattern, made of white dots and swirls, drawn by Koti early that morning. A pattern made from rice-flour paste to keep evil away from the house. Koti had a whole array of designs in her memory—a certain order of dots laid out in strict, organized rows, all connected by sweeping lines. Without the dots the lines were meaningless, and when the dots left the design, there was only chaos. The rangoli had lost its perfection by now, smudged by a dozen feet, flung apart by the wind, carried away by ants. But tomorrow, thought Sripathi, it would be there again, a new design laid down by Koti's patient fingers. But who was there to wipe out that phone call? To reorganize his life? To erase time like the rice-flour paste and set out a new pattern of dots and lines prettier than the last?

Slowly, guilt grew in him like a balloon. I, Sripathi Rao, mediocre, trivial purveyor of words, he thought miserably, am placidly alive, while my daughter . . . He could not complete the thought. Could not bear to put the incident into words.

A truck loaded with broken concrete reversed down the road, furiously honking its horn all the way, and stopped in front of the gates of the house. Sripathi watched the lorry vomit its load with a great sliding roar of sound, cutting off all access to the house. A cloud of grey dust rose slowly above the pile and hung motionless in the air. The truck driver was oblivious to, or totally unconcerned by, the fact that he had jammed the gates shut. Sripathi felt a rage rise in him like a fire. He was glad to be able to *feel* something at last. All the helplessness about his daughter's death, all the guilt and the shame and the pain came together in his breast against the man who was blocking his gate. He charged down to the front yard, past the tulasi planter and the oleander bush, squeezed through the jammed gates and banged on the door of the truck. "Yay! You! What do you think you are doing? You think this is your father-in-law's road, or what?" he shouted.

The driver peered down at Sripathi and turned off the engine. "Who are you?"

"I am the owner of this house," screamed Sripathi.

"Achha, that is very good. And I am the owner of this lorry. Now why you are doing dhama-dham on my vehicle like a madman? Please to tell me?"

"I will report you to the police. You do this nonsense every week. Dump all your rubbish outside my gates. How do you think I will get them open?"

"Don't have a heart attack, sahib," laughed the truck driver, his enormous moustache jerking upwards with the movement of his cheeks. "You say you can't open the gate, but you are standing here in front of me, no? Are you a bhooth or what, that you went right through the bars? And anyway, my load is not inside your property, it is on the road." He laughed again and started the truck. "Better move out of the way, or you will be like the concrete—small bits!"

Sripathi watched helplessly as the truck roared off, its brightly coloured tail ribbons undulating eagerly in the underdraft. He returned to the house feeling savage. Ammayya was, as usual, stationed in her chair at the entrance to her room, from where she had a clear view of the living room, the dining area, the kitchen and, beside it, the gods' room. Putti crouched beside her, patting her knee with one hand and talking in a low voice. Sripathi stalked past them and into the kitchen. He thought vaguely that he needed to eat something, that if he filled his body with food there would be no room left for grief.

"What is there for breakfast?" he asked Nirmala, who was in the gods' room that led off the kitchen. There was no reply, and he clattered a few pot lids noisily. Still no response. He stamped into the small chamber where images of various divinities were kept and worshipped. Nirmala was crouched on the floor in a corner, tears streaming down her face. Next to her was a shallow tier of shelves holding rows of silver and bronze idols of Krishna and Shiva, Ganesha and Lakshmi. Their placid metal faces gleamed in the subtle light of cotton wicks burning in tall brass lamps. Incense sticks sent up dark spires of smoke and a dense perfume that tickled Sripathi's nostrils. Nirmala did not even look up from the sheet of paper in her hand, which, he realized, was a letter from Maya—one of the many that she had sent over the years and that he had never read. The sandalwood box containing the rest, which usually sat inside her bedroom cupboard, was open on the floor beside her. There were a few photographs scattered around as well. Sripathi saw only

Nirmala's bent head, the straight white line of her part shooting through her dark hair, the few strands of grey that branched away from that line. He was filled with a childish desire to scream.

"Did you hear me, madam? I asked for some food."

When she continued to read in stubborn silence, Sripathi rushed onto the covered verandah, to the shoe rack along one wall, and picked up as many shoes as he could hold. Then he raged back into the gods' room, startling Nirmala. He dumped the shoes on the shelves, dislodging some of the idols. He swept the remaining ones off with one violent swing of his arm.

Surveying the damage, he said breathlessly, "There! That's what I think of your wretched gods and prayer and all. They deserve only dirty shoes, not flowers. What have they ever done for us? Tell me? *What?*" He kicked at the fallen idols. "And still you spend money on flowers and incense and oil!"

Nirmala cowered in her corner, rendered speechless not by grief or anger at her husband but by his act of desecration.

"Useless nonsense rituals she does every day," Sripathi muttered. He aimed a final kick at an idol of the elephant god, Ganesha, that had landed near his foot. "This elephant-faced fellow is supposed to remove obstacles. Hah!"

"My rituals are no worse than yours," cried Nirmala, goaded out of her silence.

"I don't have any, madam."

"What do you call those idiotic letters you keep writing to this paper and that?" she asked recklessly. "That's all you are capable of—writing big-big words with different coloured pens, hiding behind some funny name that nobody can understand. And then you dare to call my son useless! At least he has the guts to go out and do something about garbage and pollution and all, while you only scribble on the balcony to strangers. Couldn't even find it in your heart to write to your own child!" She bent down and agitatedly started to gather the scattered photographs and letters, piling them into her box, showing Sripathi her back, the deep curve of her tight, pink blouse and the sweat that had stained the thin cotton dark where it touched her skin.

"How do you know about my letters?"

Nirmala threw him a spiteful look over her shoulder. "My gods told me, that's how!"

Sripathi teetered on the edge of uncontrolled rage before wheeling around and leaving the room. He collided with Arun, who caught his father's arm and asked, "Again you were hitting her? Appu?"

"No, I wasn't. And don't make it look like I do it every day. I have never laid a finger on your mother before."

"Then what was all that shouting about?"

"Why don't you go and save some more animals, instead of sitting around at home and cross-questioning me?" Sripathi demanded. He felt he had to leave the house immediately and occupy himself, otherwise he might do something he would regret. But where to go? Not to the office. He was in no mood to see all those sympathetic faces, to hear their condolences. No. He would go to Raju's house. He felt calmer at the thought of visiting his closest friend. And then he would have to visit the travel agent on Pyecroft Road to find out about flights to Canada.

"Where are you going? Do you want me to come with you?"

Sripathi hated himself for the words that forced themselves out of his mouth. They seemed to have a life of their own. "Oh? You don't have to save the world today? You can help your father with mundane things like airline tickets and all? Surely today the sun is going to set in the east!" He marched out of the house and past Putti, who had left Ammayya's side and was sitting on the steps of the verandah.

Arun shrugged and entered the gods' room, where he knelt beside his mother. She was still distractedly shuffling the photographs and papers in her hands, putting them in the box and taking them out again, sobbing softly all the while.

"He is behaving like a baby," Arun remarked. He picked up the idols and replaced them on the shelves.

"Don't say things like that about your father," Nirmala said automatically, anxious as always to maintain peace in the house. "He is very upset."

"Yes, and so are you and me. But we don't go around shouting and throwing shoes and all that!" Arun picked up the shoes and stood up. "Are you okay? Do you want me to do anything, Mamma?"

Nirmala shook her head. "What can you, or I, or anyone do now? Too late for everything. Too late." She leaned back against the wall and shut her eyes.

Arun carried the shoes out to the verandah and arranged them on the shelf before going upstairs to his room. He was still unable to believe the news about Maya—his older sister, the person who had been part of his everyday life until he was eighteen, who had protected him fiercely through elementary school, shielded him from bullies and fights, held his hand when they had to cross the road to catch the bus, carried his bag along with her own and once gave him her lunch when he'd dropped his on the ground. Maya had written to him from America, always including interesting bits of information about the world across the seas, and later, when he had decided to get involved in social activism, she had sent him clippings, books, any material that might be useful. As a child, he had followed her like an eager puppy, as she marched in and out of trouble. At school, in his crowded baby class presided over by Mrs. Mascarenha with her terrible billowing voice, ordering them to *settle down*, he had felt safe in the knowledge that Maya was in the same building, just three doors away. During the lunch break, while most of the toddlers were shepherded to the toilets by Mary Ayah and Ruthie Ayah, he had waited for his sister, and when she arrived he had clutched her sticky hand—so certain and comforting—and trotted obediently to the girls' toilets with her. She had knocked Susheel Prasad's big head through the bars of the Class Four window for teasing him to tears, and then stood stubborn and unrepentant when the principal punished her for such un-girlish violence.

"But he was bullying my younger brother," Maya had argued, when Mother Superior asked how she could have been so wicked.

And she had dared to sneak up the forbidden stairs to the terrace, where old Mother Claudette stood all afternoon taking potshots with a Daisy gun at stray dogs copulating in the football field behind the school, screaming obscenities in French every time she missed.

His sister had dared everyone that Arun could remember and had always lived to tell the tale. But she'd been no match for the God of Death. And with the memories came the shame—that he hadn't cared enough to write back to her, to keep in touch. That he had allowed himself to forget.

———

Dr. Sunderraj wasn't crying, but he kept taking off his glasses and rubbing his eyes. For the past few days—since Nandana had tried to walk home, and he had told her that her parents had been in a bad accident—he hadn't gone to his office. Lots of people had come to the house, one after another. Two women had wanted to talk to her as well. They had said that they were from Social Services. Nandana had answered their questions politely. Yes, she liked staying here. Yes, she liked Anjali a lot, even though she wouldn't let her play with her new Lego. But she wanted to go home. She liked Aunty Kiran and Uncle Sunny, yes. But she wanted to go home. The women had nodded and had written things in notebooks and then talked for a long time with Uncle. There were many phone calls that he answered and many calls that he made.

Now, in the living room, he was sitting on the ground at her feet, so close that she could see herself in his eyeballs. She and Aunty Kiran were on the fat-tourist sofa. If she concentrated really hard, she thought—if she didn't speak, if she sat absolutely still—she could see her blue house and her parents and her room with its Minnie Mouse lampshade, all reflected in those eyeballs. She could see her mother moving around in the kitchen, making supper, and her father hunched over his computer, typing away.

"Do you think she understands what has happened?" she heard Aunty Kiran say.

Of course she did, she thought indignantly, trying to concentrate on those eyeballs that kept moving and destroying the picture of her house. Her parents had gone away for some reason. They wouldn't be coming back for a while.

"Nandana, sweetie, do you understand?" Uncle Sunny asked. She saw her house. Her mother was washing something in the sink. Her father was using swear words, she could hear him. Then Uncle Sunny spoke again and the picture vanished. Why couldn't he understand that if he kept quiet, if all of them kept quiet, her parents would hear her and come to take her home?

"Your Daddy and Mummy were badly hurt in a car accident. They did not survive," Uncle Sunny leaned forward and put his arms around her and Aunty Kiran. She could smell his aftershave lotion. Like her father's. No, just a little bit like his.

Survive—that was a word she did not know.

"They died, honey," said Aunty Kiran.

She had seen a dead butterfly on their patio once. It was a beautiful yellow and black one, and it was being dragged away by a troop of ants. She had been so sad that she had not wanted to speak to anyone that day. Her mother had explained that all living things died.

"But will you die too? And me and Daddy?" she had asked, after she'd thought it over.

To which her mother had replied, "Yes, but only when we are all a hundred years old."

Her mother was only thirty-four and her father thirty-six, so they couldn't be dead. No *way*! She pursed her lips. Aunty and

Uncle were lying to her. She knew that for sure. Her parents had gone to a wedding in Squamish. Aunty Kiran was an old witch, she could see that now. She wanted to keep her here for ever, just like she had said, and so she was making up stories. She decided she had better not say another word.

"We spoke to your grandfather in India, Nandu," continued Uncle Sunny. "He'll be coming here. That will be nice, right?"

How would she know? She had never met her grandfather. She wondered if he counted as a stranger, even though Nandana had seen his photographs in her mother's album.

"You will be going to India with him. You'll meet your grandma, your uncle, lots of nice people."

To India? No *way*. How would her parents find her when they came home?

She heard Aunty Kiran's voice above her head. "Sunny, I think the child is in shock or something. She hasn't said a word."

4

HISTORIES

A LONG TIME AGO, when he was about seven or eight years old, Sripathi had believed that death was something that happened to people who reached the end of Brahmin Street, the end that curved around the two-hundred-year-old banyan tree and meandered like a dull black river for a few more yards until it reached the beach. On Saturday mornings, he used to swing on the gate of Big House and wait for the goat boys to pass with their noisy, skittish herds.

"Where are you taking them?" he had asked a goat boy once, and the boy had replied, "To the palace of the King of Death."

And in the afternoon he would see brawny men, their checked cotton lungis folded up to their knees, slowly wheeling bicycles back from the palace of the King of Death. Slung like dirty black-and-white washing over the back seats of the cycles were headless goats. Their necks still oozed blood and bubbled with shimmering, buzzing bluebottles intoxicated by the scent of raw flesh. Until finally someone started a written petition against the butchers who used the street as a short cut to the Saturday market, the place the goat boys drove their herds, and they stopped going past with their gory purchases. For several months after, Sripathi used to scream with fear every time his father offered to take him to the beach on a Saturday morning, down Brahmin Street and past the old banyan tree.

But until he was thirteen, Sripathi had never really lost anyone close to him. Death was as distant a possibility as Mars or Venus. He believed, in a vague sort of way, that the god Yama came swaying on his buffalo, dragging his lasso behind him, only to the very poor or the very old. The first time it touched him was when his grandmother Shantamma passed away. She had struggled long and hard to stay on in the world, and Sripathi couldn't believe it when she was finally vanquished by time and age and ill-health.

When Shantamma was eighty-two, she had suffered a stroke in her sleep. But she had come out of it determined to fight Lord Yama tooth and nail because there were too many things that she had not done in her life. Such as smoking a cigar. Or colouring her hair like the women in foreign magazines. Or flying in a plane. Or eating an egg fried in a vegetarian pan and using the same pan for Brahmin food. Or gossiping with Rukku, who had been exiled by the people of Toturpuram for sleeping with three men since her husband's death. Nobody had actually *seen* her with any of these men—nobody even knew who those men were—but it was obvious that she had done it, declared Ammayya, horrified by her mother-in-law's desire to associate with the woman. Years of suppressing rage at her own husband's philandering had made Sripathi's mother righteous and judgmental from a young age.

"How can you know for sure?" Sripathi had asked. His father, the lawyer, had trained him to question everything.

"Have you seen her face?" Ammayya demanded. "She looks like she fell into a tin of powder. What respectable widow uses so much kohl and colours her lips? And wears flashy earrings and saris flaming with flowers? See how she slants her eyes and snares men. Innocent married ones even!"

Despite Ammayya's poisonous rantings, Shantamma liked Rukku, although since the woman had become an outcast, a whore, a trollop, an unmentionable in decent homes, she had not had the courage to go near her or to even to smile at her. But after her stroke, she decided that she was too old to care about rules and manners and self-respect, and all her secret longings surfaced like lava erupting from a volcano. She developed a loud hectoring voice, gagged and choked over strong beedis that she forgot to extinguish and, on several occasions, nearly burnt down the house as a result. She sat with her legs spread indecently wide, she got the dhobi's son to smuggle her a bottle of illicit liquor, which he brewed in the empty plot behind the house, and she summoned Rukku for a chat, driving Ammayya into such a froth of panic that she almost had a stroke herself. Shantamma refused to lie down any more because she didn't want Death to catch her unawares while she slept. Having triumphed over him once, she wasn't about to let him lasso her until she was good and ready.

"You see," she told Sripathi, her voice like the crackle of butterpaper, "in our mythology, there is the story of Savitri. Do you remember? How she argued and bargained with Lord Yama for the life of her husband? Well, if a snivelling little thing like her could do it, why not me? Eh? Eh? Am I any less beautiful?"

She would, Shantamma said giggling, tweak the god's enormous curled moustache and flirt with him a bit, but for all that she would have to be awake. So she sat in her favourite chair, the huge carved teak armchair with its faded yellow silk cushions that looked like her own spreading, liverspotted buttocks, and never went to sleep. When she finally did die, her eyes were wide open and challenging, and her bony, ridged fingers were curled around the arms of her chair so tightly that they couldn't be pried loose. The chair had to be sawed away from her body, and—since rigor mortis had stiffened her so that she could not be straightened without cracking several bones—Shantamma was cremated sitting upright, two pieces of teak in her tightly closed fists, her face clenched in a grimace of triumph, as if she had actually confronted Lord Yama and bargained her way out of his clutches.

Sripathi was devastated by his grandmother's death. She had been his buffer against his mother's expectations for him to be the best son in the whole wide world, to be a renowned heart surgeon, the president of a company, the prime minister of India, a hero. She had protected him from his father's increasingly tyrannical rages, loved him for what he was, and that unconditional affection had been his strength. Three years later, when Sripathi's father, Narasimha Rao, B.A., M.A., LL.B., died, he was devastated again, not so much by the loss this time as from his sudden ascension from being the son of the house, with no responsibilities, to being the man of the family, with Ammayya and his unmarried sister, Putti, to look out for. He had barely figured out what he was going to do with his own life, and now he was in charge of two others as well.

Sripathi often thought that, if not for chance, fate, call it what you will, he might have been the seventh of eight children instead of the only son. Unfortunately for him, after six miscarriages, he was the first living child Ammayya produced.

The day of his birth was cautiously celebrated. He was deprived of the traditionally grand ceremonies that heralded the arrival of a first son because his parents were afraid of inviting the evil eye along with the other guests. One could not be too careful after the loss of so many infants.

Janardhana Acharye, the family priest, was summoned immediately, and he sat hunched over the infant's birth charts, alternately consulting the panchanga (which he wrote himself and sold for fifty paise a copy), and doing complicated calculations on a piece of paper. He hated being dragged out of bed so late at night, especially as he had been engaged in foreplay with his coy but excited wife, who drove him wild with her mixture of reluctance and eagerness. But one did not refuse summons from old and respected clients like Narasimha Rao of Big House. Neither did he have the guts to tell the family that Sripathi had nothing extraordinary in his future: no fame, no name, not even a modest fortune. Why spoil things for them? This was their first living child after all, and a son at that. Why tell them that by his sixteenth birthday, the child would be fatherless, and that later in life he would see the death of his own child as well? Could anyone alter the future that Lord Brahma had written on the infant's forehead the minute he emerged from his mother's womb? Then what use to worry about it? It was a long time away, and Narasimha would be dead by then. No need to worry about it now and ruin his eyes looking for planetary loopholes through which to pull out threads of hope. Besides, if he made a bad horoscope, the family would ask him to perform rituals to counteract the mischief of the gods, and that would take all of the night and the next day as well, and Janardhana Acharye really wanted to return to his bed and to his waiting wife.

So he wiped his sweating bare chest with his shalya, used the same cloth to sponge out his underarms (which smelled as if someone had boiled onions there, a stench that always heralded his arrival), and said to Narasimha Rao, who paced impatiently as if he was in a courtroom debating a case, "The boy has favourable stars shining on him. He will always be one step ahead of life and one step behind death. So not to worry-murry. Other details not so important; I will inform you later. After one month, bring him to the temple for a special puja that will clear any lingering shani kata circling his future. Until then do not dress him in red clothes— not a good colour for this boy. That's all." Then the Acharye packed away his almanac, and with it disappeared his air of authority. He shuffled his feet and became ingratiating—a signal for his clients to pay him for his services. The priest found it demeaning to ask for money himself and even more humiliating to haggle for greater than the amount he had received. After all, he was a Brahmin, not a trader-caste fellow who had no shame asking for this and that.

Narasimha and Ammayya had high hopes for their first child. They gave him the grandest name they could think of, an entire orchestra of a name: Toturpuram Narasimha Thimmappa Sripathi Rao. Deep drum beats, airy flute notes, the high twang of a sitar. It was a name that carried the full weight of Sripathi's village, his ancestors, his immediate family and all his parents' ambitions. He, as first son of a first son of a first son, had a serious obligation to grow into his marvellous name. Ammayya fed him fat balls of fresh buffalo butter, basmati rice, almonds in milk. His grandmother told him gallant tales of heroism and cunning and wit and honour; of Arjuna the great archer; of King Harishchandra, whose honesty shook even the heavens; of Bhishma of the terrible oath; and of Bhageerathi, who persuaded wild and whimsical Ganga to flow down as a river and wash over the ashes of his thousand brothers. At the end of every story, she would gather him in her jowly arms, pinch his sharp little chin (which in adulthood would give him the look of a prim bird), and say creakily, "Now, you, my darling Sri, my raja, my beautiful boy, you will grow up and become like Prince Arjuna, won't you? You will conquer every obstacle. You will come first in your class and become a great doctor, a heart doctor, and you will do big-big operations all over the world."

While the young Sripathi adored his grandmother's stories, richly trimmed with Sanskrit verses from the Mahabharata or the Ramayana, a dread grew within him that he would never be able to do the things that she seemed to expect of him. How could he learn archery, philosophy, music, art, politics, science—all the things that great heroes of yore seemed capable of excelling at simultaneously? As for utter, heaven-shaking honesty, like that of King Harishchandra, who sold his wife and child for the sake of truth— why, just the other day he had lied to Ammayya about eating everything she had packed in his lunch box. Not to mention the fib he had told Father Schmidt about his missing homework. ("I'm sorry, Father, my grandmother threw it away by mistake," he had mumbled, knowing that if the grim-faced English teacher did indeed ask Shantamma, she would support his story.) But the thing Sripathi loved most about his grandmother was that she herself never followed any of the morals expounded in the tales she narrated to him. And when one day he confided his fears to her, she clutched him against her breasts, kissed him all over his face and said, "My raja, you will be my prince, even if you end up as a street sweeper."

Narasimha Rao bought his son the complete *Encyclopaedia Britannica* on his fourth birthday and expected him to start absorbing every page immediately, even though the child could barely read. The volumes sat like plump potentates on the shelf in the drawing-room, dressed up in maroon and gold, a sign to everyone who visited that this was a house of learning.

"You read one page to him every day," Narasimha commanded Ammayya. "Make sure he by-hearts it." At dinner time he would quiz Sripathi on the page of the day, and if the boy failed to answer, he would explode.

"Idiot, idiot, you have given birth to an idiot!" he would shout at Ammayya, his heavy face flushed with emotion. Turning to his son, he would fix him with a look that paralyzed Sripathi and made him forget all that he did know. "Don't think your father will be around for the rest of your life, mutthal," he continued. "One of these days, when you are sweeping the streets, you will wish you had listened to me and studied harder."

Sometimes, when Sripathi had looked numbly at him for more than three questions, Narasimha would rise ominously from his chair. He would fasten his fingers like a vice on the lobe of his son's ear and pull him up until he, too, was standing. Wordlessly, he would drag Sripathi out through the living room, with its looming cupboards full of ancient books and its dark, brooding furniture, through the verandah and out of the gate. Down Brahmin Street they would go, Sripathi sobbing with pain and shame as pedestrians gazed curiously at them. A few of the old men who gathered daily at the gates of the Krishna Temple to gossip and bemoan the ways of the younger generation would shout encouragement;

"That's it, Narasimha-orey! Teach the young fellow right from wrong. Otherwise he will climb on your back like the vetaala and never get off!" Past Sanskrit College, the pressure of Narasimha's fingers burning on Sripathi's tender ear, and into the squatters' colony, where the road grew narrow and huts made of rags and tins and stolen bricks crowded around open drains.

"There, you see, idiot—*that*'s where you will end up if you don't learn the things I ask you to," Narasimha Rao would say. The slum-dwellers were so accustomed to seeing the big, dark-skinned man hauling his thin son by the ear and pointing to them as examples of wasted lives that they did not even look up. Idlers clad in nothing other than striped and grimy underpants continued to lounge outside their huts, smoking beedis or gazing at the ground in despair. Women continued to scrub listlessly at aluminum vessels around the tube-well that had recently been installed by the Lions Club of Toturpuram, or to spread out ragged clothes to dry on flat stones beside the festering drain. Naked children played with tops and marbles on the dusty road. Some of them squatted near the drain, next to the women drying clean clothes, grunting with concentration, their bums hanging over piles of worm-ridden feces.

His father would make a sweeping gesture with the hand that wasn't pinching Sripathi's ear and say, "Do you see that loafer there? You want to end up like that?" And just when Sripathi thought that his ear was going to tear away, his father would release it and slap the side of his head hard. Once. Twice. So that it snapped backwards and forwards. Then, casting a look of disgust at his son, he would stalk back home. Sripathi would cross his thin arms over his head and, bawling loudly, run after his father.

Sripathi had never dared to ask his father how an intimate knowledge of the mating habits of kangaroos would help in the pursuit of a career—or how familiarity with the exact dimensions of the Hope diamond, which he was never likely to possess, would assure success in life. But by the time Narasimha died, both Ammayya and

Sripathi had a stock of esoteric and wholly unnecessary information in their heads. The chemical composition of salt. The botanical name of every tree on Brahmin Street. Who invented the radio. Who invented fountain pens. Why leaves were green. When Brahms wrote his first symphony. The first person to cross the Karakoram ranges. The name of Queen Victoria's dog.

Slow, heavy steps came up the stairs, across the landing, and into the bedroom behind Sripathi. He knew it was Nirmala by the sound of her toe rings on the floor.

"What are we going to do?" she asked, her voice still thick with tears. "Why you are sitting here by yourself? You can't come down and be with the rest of us?"

"Oh, now I can't even sit quietly and think, is that it?"

"Our child is dead, and you can't share in the sorrow? What hard kind of person are you? I want to know every word you and that man spoke on the phone. You didn't tell me what is happening to the baby. Our Nandana."

"You didn't even let me open my mouth. Hitting me like a crazy lunatic." Sripathi turned around and glared at her.

Nirmala looked down and pleated her sari pallu between the fingers of her left hand. She sniffed, wiped her nose with the end of the sari and said, "Okay, but you also hit me, no?"

Sripathi did not reply and Nirmala continued. "What will you do about Nandana? What did that man say? Where is the child? Poor thing, how she must be feeling, God only knows."

"I am her legal guardian," Sripathi said. "The child will come to us. I will have to make arrangements to go to Vancouver, stay there for a few months, lots of things to do."

"She is coming *here*? I will see my grandchild? Ah, what wickedness is this, that I have to lose my own child to see my grandchild!" Nirmala started to weep again.

"It is all going to cost a lot."

Nirmala gave Sripathi an angry look. "Cost. Always you think about unimportant things. Our daughter and her husband are dead, and this is all you can say to me? It will cost a lot?"

"Don't talk to me like that. If I don't think about cost, who will? Your dead grandfather? Henh? Maybe you should ask those stupid gods of yours to give me a pair of wings to carry me to Canada. Or better still, ask one of your rich cousins to buy me a private plane. They keep showing off about this and that. Ask them and see how much real help they will give."

"Why do you always bring my family into everything? You can't take care of us, and then you curse my relatives." Nirmala replaced the sandalwood case full of Maya's letters inside her cupboard.

Burn them, they are useless now, he wanted to say to her, but stopped himself in time. Nirmala gave him another wounded glance before she left the room, and Sripathi was alone once again.

The clock on the landing chimed the hour, and he looked at it as if at an old friend. Its benign ivory face framed in polished rosewood was as familiar to him as his own. Sripathi had received it as a gift for his Brahmin initiation ceremony forty-seven years ago from one of his father's friends. Large and jolly, Varadarajan Judge-sahib, had patted the young Sripathi's newly tonsured head, pinched his cheeks and given him the clock in its fancy box.

"Here, my boy," he had said in his rotund voice that seemed to form in the depths of his stomach before emerging. "Now that you have received your sacred thread, now that you have entered the world of knowledge, you will appreciate this gift of time. A valuable gift that goes as soon as it arrives. So learn to use it wisely, and you will be content."

Narasimha found frequent occasion to repeat this wisdom to his son. Sometimes Sripathi had to be dragged back from a cricket game in the alley behind their house to study his text books. And at other times, when the boy brought home low marks from school or did not have an answer to some question from the *Encyclopaedia Britannica*, Narasimha would first thrash him with a rolled up magazine, and then remind him of the time he had frittered away. "A valuable gift, did you hear? Not to be wasted the way you are wasting it, mutthal. Time and tide, time and tide wait for no man. Today you are merrily playing with loafers like the cricket in that Aesop fellow's story, but tomorrow, while industrious ants are living like rajas, you will be sweeping the streets. And *why*? Because *they* used time properly, and *you*, mutthal, did not."

Sripathi remembered his initiation ceremony as clearly as if it had happened yesterday. He was the centre of attention, up there on the small wooden platform where he sat between Ammayya, who was dressed like a new bride in all her finery, and his father, whose silk dhoti fell in graceful folds from his waist. The priest chanted prayers that floated around them as frail as the smoke from the sandalwood fire in the middle of the platform. The ritual shaving of Sripathi's hair; the solemnity of the moment when he disappeared under a sheet of unbleached cotton with his father to receive the secret mantra that initiated him into Brahminhood; the sacred thread that was looped over his shoulder and across his chest; and later, the tenderness with which Ammayya fed him delicacies from a silver plate—he remembered them all. He had stepped out of his mother's shadow and into his father's, no longer a child but a man.

Varadarajan Judge-sahib had teased him about the thread. "See, now you have only three strands in this thread. Your responsibilities are small—only to yourself and to your parents. But when you get married, ah, then you will have six strands. A wife means twice the responsibility! Eh? What do you say, Narasimha Rao?"

The two men had laughed, and Sripathi, too, had chuckled, a little frightened at the thought of being responsible for any one at all.

He couldn't remember precisely when the woman in the green-and-gold sari had entered the large hall crowded with people, but it seemed to him now that a whisper had moved like a hot wind through the room, marking her arrival. Sripathi could still feel the burning sensation on his wrist where his mother had clutched him, her nails digging painfully into the tender skin. In her shame and rage, she did not realize the force of her grip.

"Why is *she* here?" she had whispered angrily, glaring at Narasimha, who didn't seem to have noticed the woman. He had his arm around Sripathi's shoulders, and he nodded and smiled as people streamed past, congratulating them on this auspicious occasion.

"Who?" Narasimha had asked.

"Your whore. Don't pretend you haven't seen her," said Ammayya.

The memory unwound before Sripathi, a film in slow motion. The woman dressed in green and gold, making her way through the crowd towards them, the pallu draped carefully over her shoulder, her eyes slightly anxious, the nervous movement of her left hand as it smoothed the pleats of her sari. His father's whore? At ten years of age, Sripathi wasn't sure what exactly that word meant, and why it made his mother so furious that she was tearing off his wrist with her fingernails.

The woman reached them and pressed an envelope into Sripathi's hands, not looking at his parents or at anybody else but him. "Blessings," she said in a low voice. She reached out, stroked his head and was just turning away when Ammayya grabbed the envelope, ripped it into small pieces and flung it at the woman.

A hush descended on the hall, and it seemed to Sripathi as if all five hundred guests had chosen that very moment to stop talking and stare at the scene in the centre of the room.

"Don't come near my son," hissed Ammayya. "Whore!"

Then followed the greater horror, when Sripathi's father moved away from him, towards the woman, and led her carefully out of the hall, his hand hovering just above the small of her back, as if she were one of Ammayya's precious Japanese teacups that allowed sunlight to filter through their eggshell fragility. A feeling of great abandonment swept through Sripathi as he watched his father's stiff back, the rigid body carving a path through the crowd of friends, relatives and well-wishers. He and Ammayya stood there, becalmed like two small dinghies, linked by their shared humiliation. *Never* would he allow this to happen to himself again, Sripathi had sworn bitterly. *Never* would he fail in his duty to his family or subject them to such shame. He did not want either his father's fame or stature because the higher one was, the greater the fall. No, he would be only an ordinary man, but one with good standing in the eyes of the world. He would be a simple man, respected for nothing other than his qualities as a father and a husband. He, unlike his father, would always remain dutiful to the mother who had brought him into this world, to the woman he married, to the children he had—first and above everything else. This the young boy vowed to himself, as he stood there feeling the fierce pain of Ammayya's grip on his thin wrist, as he willed the tears not to fall and shame him in front of this gathering who had come to witness him crossing the threshold of innocence.

Sripathi hated his father completely at that moment, and the feeling grew stronger with time. No longer did that tall, stately figure fill him with pride and awe, or even fear. No longer did he care about his father's opinion of him or his wrath when he brought home bad marks on his school exams. He watched scornfully when his father went to the temple for morning worship, his cotton towel draped severely over his left shoulder. And in the evening, after dinner, Sripathi watched him leave for his mistress's home, with that same shalya now slung rakishly over his other shoulder.

When he was sixteen, he was horrified and disgusted to see his mother swelling with child again. How, he wondered, enraged, could she allow that man to lay a finger on her? The hate had built up and coagulated in him so violently that when he first gazed at

Narasimha's bleeding, lifeless body abandoned on the road, he had felt nothing but a remote sense of contempt. For all his grand ways, his mighty father had died like a pariah dog, his passing noticed by none but other dogs. But with a jolt of anger, he realized that the street was the very one on which his father's mistress lived. It was on her door that people had knocked first, not on his own mother's. Sripathi had seen the woman in the crowd that gathered around his father's body, her eyes liquid with tears, her sari bunched tight in her hand and pressed to her mouth, as if to prevent her agony from spilling forth. He had wondered what his father had found in this illiterate, plain, crude-looking woman.

Narasimha's death brought with it penury and the sharp fear that always accompanies a lack of money. Sripathi discovered that his father had not saved a single paisa. There was a tiny pension, but there were also loans to be repaid—to friends, relatives, even to the bank. The sixteen-year-old had remembered the fate of a distant relative who had died a pauper. Narasimha had taken his family to visit the relative when Sripathi was eight years old. He had never really known the reason behind that visit. Perhaps his father had been a kinder man than he remembered. The relative lived in a single room at the back of somebody's house. He had two scrawny, wide-eyed daughters and a sullen wife. He had been absurdly pleased to see Narasimha, Ammayya and Sripathi, treating them as if they were royalty and ordering hard vadais from a restaurant nearby for them to eat with the sugarless tea his wife made. Sripathi remembered with shame the hunger in the eyes of the two young girls. He had not even thought to offer them some of the oversalted lentil rings that tasted as though they'd been fried in rancid oil, and which he eventually left half-eaten on his plate.

When the relative died, his wife had sent a letter around to the family, begging for money. They could not afford to buy a clean cotton shroud to wrap around the dead body; they had no money to pay for mango wood for the funeral pyre. Their abject poverty was not merely wretched, it was terrifying.

"Sell the house," suggested a trustee at the Toturpuram Bank.

Both Sripathi and Ammayya had turned down that idea. The house was all they had to mark their former status. "We will manage," Ammayya told everybody. "My son is already sixteen. He will finish school soon and become a doctor. He will take care of us." She did, however, sell the house in which Narasimha Rao's mistress lived. Sripathi was taken aback by his mother's ruthlessness and even felt sorry for the woman, who disappeared from Toturpuram. But the money from the sale allowed them to repay some of the loans and to continue to live in Big House.

On the third Sunday of every month, Ammayya took Sripathi and Putti, dressed in their best clothes, to her uncle's house in the neighbouring town of Royapura. Hari Mama was a wealthy old bachelor who, people suspected, preferred young boys to women. Ammayya had always avoided the old man, but now she had a purpose in life.

"Two purposes," she told Sripathi when he protested that, since they had never kept in touch with the old man, this sudden affection might look suspicious. "You and Putti are the two purposes in my life, and it doesn't matter what people think of me. The important thing is to take care of you two."

Hari Mama lived in an enormous house with a swing on the verandah, which was reserved for unwanted visitors and hangers-on. Inside the house, in the centre of a mirrored hall, was another swing made of sandalwood and ivory. Its decadence both repelled Sripathi and fascinated him. This was Hari Mama's favourite swing. Only specially chosen people were allowed on it. Sripathi was granted that privilege just once, and he couldn't even remember the reason. He did, however, recall the strangeness of the experience— seeing his reflection repeating endlessly in the mirrored walls of that room, swinging towards himself and farther away all at the same moment.

"Don't forget to be polite to the old man," Ammayya used to tell Sripathi, as they hurried in the raging heat of morning from the bus terminal to Hari Mama's house. "Always agree with him. He might decide to leave you something big, *Deo volente*—God willing. After all, we are his only living relatives."

As soon as they arrived at the house, the old man would give Sripathi and Ammayya two bananas each, insisting that they eat them right away. "Good for health—vitamins, phosphorus, iron. Never say no to a banana." And later, on their way home, Ammayya would grumble that if she collected the bananas in a basket and sold them, at least they would have one bus fare home. Instead she would pretend that they were going to catch a taxi, just to give Hari Mama the impression that they had come for purely altruistic reasons. Money, she took pains to remind the old man and the dozens of other people who always seemed to be in the house—money was no problem for her. Narasimha had left them well-off. She was here merely to ensure that her children were acquainted with their only great-uncle.

Sripathi always felt angry and humiliated in that opulent house. He despised himself for laughing uproariously over every one of Hari Mama's jokes, even when they were laboured and unfunny, and for leaping up to fetch a glass of water each time the old man coughed. Deep inside, he knew that the old man was not in the least deceived by this show of devotion.

"What, boy," Hari Mama had teased him on one occasion, to the great amusement of the other sycophants in the room. "What, boy, if I asked you to lick my shoes clean, would you do it? I hear that spit is good for shoe leather!"

And Sripathi, too, had been obliged to chuckle and lower his head, when all he wanted was to drag his mother away from the kitchen where, with the help of several other women, she was making an endless supply of hot coffee.

When they left for home, Ammayya would lead them a mile past the nearest bus stop, pretending to look for a taxi, and they would catch the bus to Toturpuram at the next halt.

When Hari Mama died, he left all his property to a small theatre group.

Ammayya swallowed her disappointment over Hari Mama's lost fortune and set about pushing her son towards a career in medicine; she had found out that there was a code among doctors that obliged them to treat each other's families free of charge. When she was old and needed medical care, she calculated, her son would be able to ensure that she was looked after without incurring any expense.

Having decided Sripathi's future for him, Ammayya then concentrated on becoming the perfect widow. She was determined to erase all memory of the whore from people's minds, to show the world that *she* was Narasimha Rao's bereaved wife. To Sripathi's embarrassment, she insisted on having her head shaved like the widows of the previous generation and ordered Shakespeare Kuppalloor, the barber, to come to the house every month to remove the new stubble. It didn't matter when relatives pointed out that even her own mother-in-law, Shantamma, had maintained her snowy fall of hair and that there was no need for such old-fashioned observances. She wore only maroon cotton saris, even though she continued to wear her gold chains and bangles. She was afraid that her jewellery, the only thing of value that she owned, would be stolen by thieves. "If I keep them on me, they will have to cut my throat to remove my chains," she told Sripathi. She swore off certain vegetables, like garlic and onions, that were believed to have aphrodisiac qualities and were therefore forbidden to widows. She dug up archaic fasts and rituals and became more rigidly Brahmanical than the temple's own priest. When Sripathi, in his hoarse adolescent voice, told her that she was being foolish, excessive in her zeal to be faithful to Narasimha's memory, she berated him for his lack of respect.

"You will have the right to order me around when you are earning a living. When you are a doctor, *then* you can tell your mother what to do and what not to do," she told him fiercely. "Your job now is to concentrate on doing well in school and on getting into medicine. We have to show people that Narasimha Rao's son is as brilliant as he was."

Even after all these years, Sripathi felt a sharp twinge of shame at the way he had abandoned medical school after barely a year. His admission to the school had been so hard. He remembered wistfully Ammayya's solicitous attentions as he stayed up all night mugging up volumes of information for the entrance exams. He had got in, but he hated it from the very beginning. He had struggled through the courses, the dozens of medical terms buzzing in his head, refusing to let him sink into sleep at night. The relentless pressure of learning every tiny detail of the human body—the things that make it work, the things that kill it or make it falter in its long walk through life—piled up on him and pressed him down until he felt that he would end up as one of those bodies in the morgue. The smell of corpses that reeked of formaldehyde seemed to stick to his skin for weeks. He found it impossible to look at food without imagining its journey through the glistening pink coils of his body, and he couldn't sleep for the thunder of his heart in his ears. He had never been so aware of the labouring machines of lung and kidney and brain that pulsed and pounded within his fretwork of bones, of the veins and arteries that shunted his blood up and down his body ceaselessly, of the cells that contained secret, ancient memories of growth and decay and death, and of the taut fragility of skin that contained it all. Medical school revealed the mysteries of his humming body and rendered it gross and ordinary. Finally, he had run away from the place, jumped into a third-class train compartment and arrived home at midnight. He had walked all the way from the station, carrying his bedroll and his tin trunk, their weight a penance for his failure.

He had lied when Ammayya asked what had happened. "I could not stand the smell of the dead," he had told her. "They say that even the hostel food is polluted by human blood. They cook vegetarian meals in the same pots used for meat." Any lie to hide his cowardice from the mother whose heart had burst with pride when he'd got into the school.

Ammayya had believed him for a long time, and when she did accidentally read the letter expelling him for prolonged and unexplained absence, it was too late. Sripathi was already married, in a job and about to become a father. She had never forgiven him for betraying her dreams and ambitions, for cheating her like her husband had done for so many years, for taking away the possibility of a comfortable old age. For a while after he had joined the tiny advertising agency, he wished that he had kept on somehow at medical school. Or listened to his father-in-law's advice and become a weather man with the meteorological department in Madras. "The weather is always with us," the old man had told him. "Where it will go, tell me? As long as this earth exists, we will have wind and rain and storms and all. You will never be out of a job."

When Sripathi started his career at the advertising agency, it was only a small business run by one of his father's old friends out of the ground floor of his home. In moments of self-doubt, he wondered whether Chandra Iyer had taken him on out of pity or because he was Narasimha Rao's son. The job involved nothing more demanding than dreaming up jingles for local products like tooth powder, hair oil and incense sticks. Their biggest customer was the government hand-loom factory that manufactured brightly checked bedsheets and coarse cotton saris. The agency also printed invitations for weddings, christenings and upanayana ceremonies. The local branch of the Lions Club got its newsletter printed as well, and Sripathi had to write florid tributes to every member, to accompany blurred black-and-white photographs of them planting trees or inaugurating tube-wells in various parts of Toturpuram. Once in a while, when Chandra's daughter visited, Sripathi was given the task of entertaining her three young children. He had to tell them stories, take them for ice cream to Iyengar Bakery, make origami fish out of scraps from the wastepaper baskets, and once even take them to the circus.

Soon after Sripathi's twenty-fourth birthday, a friend in Bangalore sent Ammayya a photograph of his niece, along with a copy of her horoscope. "Nirmala is a quiet, steady girl," he wrote. "Wheatish complexion, slim and pretty. She is also an accomplished dancer. She will make a good wife for your son and a loving daughter-in-law."

Sripathi liked the gentle eyes gazing at him out of the black-and-white photograph and agreed to marry Nirmala as soon as their horoscopes were matched and found to be compatible.

"What is the hurry?" Ammayya wanted to know. "Wait and see other girls. There will be a long line-up. After all, you are a big man's son."

But Sripathi was adamant and a few months later the marriage took place.

Three years after his wedding, Sripathi, bored by the routine triviality of his work, applied for a job as a newspaper reporter in Delhi. He had even gone for the interview and was delighted when he was offered the job. The salary was not very much more, but the thought of having his own byline, of being recognized for his work, was thrilling. Nirmala was excited too, mostly because it would mean a house of her own and freedom from Ammayya. She would miss Putti, and so would two-year-old Maya, but they could always visit.

Ammayya would not hear of it. "What will I do here alone?" she asked Sripathi. "With a young daughter to look after?"

"Why don't you come with us to Delhi?"

"Ayyo! You want me to die of cold there, or what? And what will we do with our house? Sripathi, you are the son, it is your duty to think about your mother and your sister." She began to cry. "You want to abandon us like your father did. I knew this would happen some day. Oh God, why am I cursed with such sorrow?"

Eventually, Ammayya's tears persuaded Sripathi to refuse the Delhi offer. He never tried to change jobs after that, even when Chandra Iyer's son, Kashyap, returned from the Wharton School of Business in Philadelphia and took over the agency. Kashyap had big ambitions. Within a month, he had changed the name from Iyer & Son Printing and Advertising to Advisions Marketing. He moved the business out of his father's house, renting instead a small office on the first floor of a modern building on Mahatma Gandhi Road. He ordered new desks and chairs, hung pictures on the walls and even got a few potted plants to fill any empty corners. He hired a secretary and travelled frequently to Madras, Madurai and Chidambaram, energetically collecting clients. In the early years, the business grew rapidly, simply because advertising and marketing were new concepts. People were impressed with Kashyap's enthusiasm. They saw how the advertisements attracted more customers. Then Kashyap's father died, and he took over the business entirely. He hired two more copywriters and another artist. There was a receptionist now as well, who sat behind a desk near the entrance. She was constantly pressing buttons on the phone console and speaking in a low, rapid voice to callers. Sripathi realized that, apart from the accountant, Ramesh Iyengar, and the artist, Victor Coelho, he was the oldest person in the office. He also noticed that Kashyap had become very critical of his work. "Too trite," he would say, flicking at the sheet of paper with a contemptuous finger. He made Sripathi stand like a peon before his desk. "You need a hook to grab your customer." Or, "Your concepts are too old-fashioned. You should learn to use more modern terminology."

The young owner gave him all the low-budget clients' advertisements. Minaret Beedis. Champak Hair Oil. Ranga's Shoe Store. And even when Sripathi wrote what he considered scintillating copy for those cheap cigarettes and oils and shoes, Kashyap made him rewrite each a dozen times and frequently decided to use no copy at all. "A picture is worth a thousand words," he would tell Sripathi, not even looking up from his glass-topped desk that was littered with paper. Then he would tell him to write something for a cement company that had just opened its business in Chintadripuram and needed some cheap publicity.

The fear of poverty haunted Sripathi. He thought of his pauper relative often. He remembered how, when he was twenty, he had tried to find out what had happened to the relative's daughters who would have been about his age. Nobody in his family knew. Nobody wanted to know about the failures, only the successes.

Sripathi plodded on doggedly through the years, wondering when Kashyap would find an excuse to sack him. Then Maya had got her letter of admission from the American university. Soon after came an offer of marriage, and Sripathi's life began to acquire a glow.

Her grandfather was coming to get her on the first of September. How many tomorrows was that? They said he wanted to take her to live with him, but she wasn't going to leave Vancouver. No *way*. She had become used to Aunty Kiran's house, and she did not really mind living in the upper bunk in Anjali's room. Her friend had told her that she would adopt Nandana, if she wanted, because now she was an orphan and orphans got adopted.

India. That's where she was supposed to go with the Old Man. Many times her mother had shown her pictures of the house in India, and she hadn't ever thought much of it. "Are there ghosts inside?" she'd wanted to know. Her mother had laughed and told her that there was a mango tree in the backyard, a snake in a hole at the foot of the tree and a big fat frog near the well, but not a single ghost. "Soon we will all go there—you and me and Daddy," she had added. And Nandana had asked, "How soon is soon?"

Once she had heard her mother crying, and her father had said to her, "Why do you torture yourself like this? If the Old Man doesn't want to see you, to hell with him. You have us, don't you?" The Old Man was the grandfather who was coming to take her away, and he had always made her mother cry. Once a week, in the evening, her mother would make a long-distance call to India and talk to her own mother, whom she called Mamma. Sometimes she spoke in English and at others in a language called Kannada that Nandana could follow in bits and pieces. Her father didn't understand it at all and said he felt left out when she and her mother spoke it. Nandana had seen a picture of her mother's Mamma in an Indian dress called a sari. One time her mother had visited school in a sari because Mrs. Lipsky was having an International Day, and everybody was supposed to bring their parents in their special dresses. She had cut up one of her old saris and made a long skirt with pleats for Nandana. She had also cut up Nandana's blue tube top, so that her belly button showed, and made her wear it with the long skirt. That was the kind of outfit, she said, that she had worn when she was a small girl in India. Nandana felt silly in the dress, especially since she'd had to braid her hair and wear some flowers in the braid, and put a small round sticker on her forehead like the one her mother wore with a sari. But afterwards, when her friends and Mrs. Lipsky told her that she looked cool, she felt better. They all wanted to wear the stickers on their foreheads, and the next time her mother went to the Indian store on Main Street, she bought a pack full of multicoloured felt dots for Nandana and her friends.

As for her grandfather, Nandana did not like him. He made her mother cry.

5

IMAGES IN
A MIRROR

PUTTI SAT ON THE VERANDAH, silently watching her brother as he wheeled his scooter to the blocked gates of Big House. She wondered whether she ought to go back inside and sit with Nirmala. She thought of Maya, and a sadness settled over her. What had got into Sripathi to make him cut the girl out of his life like that? Granted, she had disgraced the family, but people had done things far worse.

In Munnuswamy's house next door, the cow Manjula, tethered to one of the pillars in the portico, lowed and flicked its tail to keep away the flies. Its newborn calf tottered weakly around, butting its head against the mother's swollen udder. The cow stopped chewing cud and licked the calf gently. There was a law against keeping livestock in residential areas, but Munnuswamy had somehow got around it.

When Putti was a child, Munnuswamy used to come over with a scythe once a week to hack the long grass in their back garden for fodder for his cows. In return, he would tie up the jasmine, prune the roses and weed out the parthenium from the vegetable beds. He was always accompanied by his son, Gopala, a bold, noisy boy clad in ragged shorts donated by one of his father's customers. A year or two older than Putti, Gopala climbed the trees and helped himself to their fruit. When she threatened to complain to Ammayya, he made hideous faces at her through the leafy branches. He whistled tunes from films and imitated bird calls. Once, she had caught him pissing against the far wall of the compound, and she had watched wide-eyed and silent as the golden fluid arced from between his fingers and splashed into the grass stubble at the foot of the wall.

She had never imagined that one day Munnuswamy and Gopala would live in the house next door. That in addition to being a successful businessman, Munnuswamy would become a member of the Legislative Assembly. From an obsequious milkman who had carved deep, bleeding crevasses into his heels by trudging barefoot from house to house with his cows, he had turned himself into an imperious, powerful character, with two gleaming cars parked outside his house all day. He still walked barefoot, though. "The earth is my mother," he would tell his voters. "How can a humble cowherd like me insult her by wearing shoes?" Sometimes he would make a dig against a young minister who was in the opposition party and say, "Appapa, I don't have the money to wear Gucci loafers and fancy clothes like our young prince. When my fellow countrymen have nothing to eat, can I spend on useless things like shoes?"

Munnuswamy's dairy business was also known for its trouble-making services, offered to any and all political parties at rates as reasonable as the milk that he continued to sell to his old customers. Munnuswamy's "Boys"—a euphemism for his horde of hard-eyed thugs—specialized in religious unrest, fasts-unto-death (or at least until the newspapers arrived on the scene) and suicide squads. Its services were most in demand during elections, when political parties were ready to try extreme tactics to garner votes. If, for instance, a party needed Muslim votes, the Boys spread rumours among Toturpuram's Muslim population about violence being planned by an opposing Hindu party, churning up rage and rioting as easily as they did butter. And if it was the Hindus who needed a stir, the Boys ran over a cow or two and blamed a Muslim truck-owner for the outrage. Munnuswamy's suicide teams threatened to detonate themselves at busy bus stops, and his rally masters gathered groups of discontented youth to hold up traffic and generate chaos. Some of the Boys lived with the Munnuswamy family and ran errands or helped around the house. Putti was fascinated by one of them, a young, tense-looking fellow named Ishwara with a look of controlled violence about him who was famous for his dreams. One morning, after a complaint about livestock in residential areas had been registered against his employer, he had woken up and rushed out to Manjula, the cow, kissed her on the forehead, decorated her with hibiscus blossom and vermilion powder, and declared that she was Munnuswamy's saintly sister who had died twenty years before of typhoid. It was he who, on behalf of the Hindu Mahashakti Dal, a fanatically religious organization, dreamt that a stone on a local mosque's valuable property contained Lord Shiva's toenail. And to balance the scales, he discovered a hair from the head of a famous Muslim saint inside the trunk of an ancient tree that grew in a rich Hindu farmer's field.

The Boys' latest accomplishment was the International Beauty Parade incident in Madras, organized to push Munnuswamy onto the front page of every national newspaper. He had already gone on a hunger strike to protest the display of female bodies clad only in bathing suits, but the strike had attracted one sole reporter from *The Toturpuram Chronicle*. The national press was on the beaches of Goa, where the pre-parade photo shoots were taking place, holding out tape recorders to bikini-clad beauties from around the world who charmingly offered their impressions of India. Munnuswamy sent a group of earnest young women, dressed in long-waisted blouses and sober saris to lie down on the stage built for the Beauty Parade at the cost of a million rupees. They threatened to set themselves on fire after swallowing a double dose of cyanide, to detonate bombs in the audience, and to hold the contestants hostage until their demands were met. These demands were never really articulated, but nobody noticed this omission, and the press arrived like a flock of crows, eager to capture the rivetting combination of violence, beauty and politics. Munnuswamy was photographed several times standing self-righteously beside a hysterical young woman holding a grenade. She clutched a megaphone in her other hand and yelled tearfully that everybody in the country appeared to have abandoned Indian values for American ones, except the honourable MLA beside her, who clung to all things good and proper. The creative genius behind these acts of disruption and vandalism was widely believed to be Gopala, who had grown into a handsome man with passionate eyes. He had been married once. His wife had died in childbirth and he had stayed resolutely single. Since he had become a widower, his mother had paraded troops of women before him. She had begged him to provide her with grandchildren, with heirs to inherit Munnuswamy's fortune.

Now the milkman's son appeared suddenly on his verandah, clad only in the loose, striped cotton shorts commonly worn by labourers. Putti blushed at the sight of his dark, taut body, burnt and robust as strong Mysore coffee. He stood straight. His arms grew out of his wide shoulders like sinewy branches and his sturdy legs were planted firmly apart. He spoke in a soft murmur to the calf. With his right hand he absently rubbed the mat of greying curls on his broad chest. Putti gazed at him for a few minutes, and then, ashamed of herself, hurried inside before Gopala caught her watching.

When Putti entered the house, Ammayya was still in her chair at the entrance to the bedroom. "My darling, were you standing in the sun?" she asked, looking up from the newspaper she'd been scanning. She read Sripathi's copy of *The Hindu* every day, as well as the local newspapers that she borrowed weekly from a young couple who lived in the apartment building across the road. They were both busy lawyers, the new breed of well-to-do, upwardly mobile Indians who bewildered Putti (and whom she inarticulately envied) with their confidence, their careless affluence and their amazing ability to throw things out after a single use. They did not seem to care that Ammayya never returned their papers. The old lady pored over them, her nose a few inches away from the thin sheets. She stored them under her bed—the Tamil ones on Putti's side, the English ones on hers—before selling them to the rubbish man, triumphant at having made money out of somebody else's property.

"Not good for your skin, how many times have I told you?" She peered at her daughter. "What is wrong? You are looking very funny. Are you falling ill? Maybe we should go to Dr. Menon for some medicine. Let us go now itself, before it becomes too hot. On the way back, we can stop at the lending library. Miss Chintamani told me that the new book by K. Sarojamma will be in today."

"I was on the verandah," Putti replied, squeezing past her mother's chair and into the dark bedroom they shared. "Nothing is wrong with me, and I don't want to go anywhere. How can you think of going out when we have had such a tragedy in the family?"

"Tchah-tchah-tchah!" Ammayya exclaimed. "I was only thinking of you, my darling. Inside my heart is breaking, my grandchild is dead and I am alive. Why can't Yama-raja take *me* away from this world?"

Putti hoped that her mother would not launch into one of her weeping, dramatic acts. Ammayya could cry any time: at weddings, funerals and birth ceremonies; when she didn't get her way; when she was bored or in need of attention or sympathy; and when she wanted to play the bereaved, long-suffering widow. She had a whole repertoire of scenes. After living with her for so many decades, Putti thought she knew them all, but Ammayya could still surprise her at times. Her martyr act was the one that annoyed everyone the most, although the tragedy-queen role was the one she performed with the greatest aplomb. Both were lubricated with copious tears and eloquent pauses between dialogue that was guiltlessly lifted from

the torrid Kannada romances that Miss Chintamani had intro-
duced into her life. Putti dimly understood her mother's need for
attention, her growing fear and loneliness. But today, her mind in
a curious tumult, she ignored Ammayya instead of offering to
massage her sparse white hair with warm oil or to look at old
photographs with her or to take her to the library.

She sat before the Belgian mirror inherited from her great-
grandmother on her dead father's side and moodily worked the tan-
gles from her damp hair with her fingers. The mirror had a bubbled
silver surface, yellow in patches from long contact with the sea air,
and returned only a faint reflection. It should have been discarded
years ago, but Ammayya did not believe in spending a paisa more
than necessary to keep body and soul alive. Narasimha Rao, the father whom Putti knew only through other people's memories, had
stolen so much from Ammayya that she clung to everything he left
behind. So the mirror stayed in the room, concealing in its mottled
depths the tiny wrinkles matting the skin around Putti's mouth, the
vertical line beginning to carve a channel on her forehead and the
anxiety that filled her eyes a little more with every passing year. The
dim 20-watt lightbulb, coated with oily vapours from the kitchen,
did its bit to hide the truth from her and give the impression that she
was still young and attractive, and deserved, as her mother kept assuring her, a prince among suitors, a Rishi Kapoor film star for a
husband. The bulb was another of Ammayya's economy measures.
A few years ago she had acquired a vast stock of them, at a quarter of
the original price, from a small trader whose business went under.
Until she ran through the entire stock, the whole house was obliged
to use them. When Putti gazed at herself, she saw only her high,
round cheeks perched on either side of a slender, sharp nose
(which, Miss Chintamani told her, were the attributes of a perfect
beauty according to her favourite fashion magazine), and her lips
pouting over a pair of overlapping front teeth. Her hair was jet black
and shone with perfumed hair oil, and her eyes, not quite as large as

she would have liked, looked dramatic as a Kathakali dancer's thanks to a lavish lining of kohl. They were not always the same size, though, for Putti could barely see her face in the dark, corroded mirror. Of course, she could have opened the shuttered windows— there were two large ones—but Ammayya had warned her about exposure to sunlight. "Puttamma, my darling, listen to me, I have lived years longer than you, so I know. Light will make your skin darken and dry up. And it will turn your hair completely white. Then who will marry you, tell me? Besides, you don't want all the loafers we have in this neighbourhood to peep at you!" Especially not people like Gopala next door, or the bunch of ruffians who distilled illicit liquor in the empty plot behind Big House, burying the wretched stuff in the dry, hot soil to ferment, where it filled the air with the fetid stench of rotting rice. You never knew what those rogues might do, the old woman said, even with the windows shut tight. Smash them down in a liquor-coloured haze? Anything was possible. Sometimes, late at night, when she lay awake beside her snoring mother, Putti could hear the muffled sounds of laughter and voices from beyond the windows, and she shuddered voluptuously at the thought of those rough-bodied men bursting through the wood and stained-glass panes to watch her turn in her bed.

Deep in the mirror, beyond her own image, Putti could see the enormous, carved rosewood bed that she shared with Ammayya. Its canopy of mosquito netting hovered like a grey cloud above it. They needed a new mosquito net; this one had been patched so many times it looked like a beggar's shroud. But her mother was obsessed with saving, with holding on. Everything was necessary to her: pieces of thread picked up from the street that she rolled into large balls of multicoloured twine; nails, nuts and bolts collected as she swayed her bulky way to the temple, Dr. Menon's dispensary or the lending library; scraps of cloth begged from the two tailors down the road, sorted by colour and stored in gunny sacks that had once held rice; discarded bicycle tubes, if she was lucky enough to find them before Karim Mechanic's assistant-boy did. She refused to let Nirmala throw away Sripathi's or Arun's old singlets, cutting them into pieces for Koti to use as dusters or mops. If they were torn only near the bottom, Ammayya lopped off a couple of inches and wore them herself as brassieres. Frayed trousers turned into shopping bags, petticoats became tablecloths, and saris were potential curtains. Yes, Ammayya held on to everything, including— thought Putti bitterly—me.

From the outside, Putti looked as content as a well-milked cow, but within her seethed an ocean of desire that would have shocked her mother. She could feel frustration building inside her like heat in a pressure cooker. She had only recently realized—slowly, unwilling to believe it at first—that her mother meant never to let her marry. Every time Ammayya rejected another of Gowramma's suggested suitors, she insisted it was only because she wanted the best for her daughter, the very best. Five years ago, for instance, there was a college lecturer who taught political science at Madras University. Putti was thirty-seven then, and he was forty. Putti liked the thought of being a lecturer's wife, of having students worshipfully approach their door to clear doubts before exams. She was already half in love with his sad eyes trapped behind metal-rimmed glasses, with his narrow, earnest shoulders and his habit of sweeping an uncontrolled wave of hair off his forehead with the curve of his palm. But Ammayya had an awful premonition about him.

"I can see him lying there all bleeding and hurt. Because some of those students threw stones at the poor man. Tchah! Such violence in our world, Rama-Rama!"

"Ammayya, he is a nice man. So why should his students suddenly turn around and attack him?"

"Violence has taken over this country, what to do?" Ammayya had sighed. "Why, only last week I read about a boy who went to an examination class with a foot-long knife, I believe, and stabbed the invigilator who objected to his cheating."

Then there was the smart young engineer from America, whom Ammayya turned down because she had heard rumours that men from abroad already had white wives and used their Indian ones as maidservants. A doctor from Bangalore was rejected because Ammayya suspected he would die of a disease caught from a patient, leaving Putti a widow. Business men were crooks destined to end up in prison for shady practices. "And the pathologist from Bombay," Ammayya had said, squashing Putti's hopes of settling on the opposite coast of India, far from her mother, "that fellow has a harelip under his moustache. Why else would he hide the mouth that God gave him behind a hedge of hair? Do you want to be the mother of a brood of harelipped children?"

Putti's schooling had been acquired at home from an Anglo-Indian woman named Rose Hicks, the ex-principal of a school that did not exist any more. Private tuition, apart from the exclusive ring it had, was particularly attractive to Ammayya because it was much cheaper than school. No need for a uniform or a big parcel of books. Putti could acquire knowledge dressed in her underwear if she wished. School boards also had the bad habit of delving into parental pockets for replacement chairs and desks, for ceiling fans, for a new wing for the science laboratories—the list was endless. Not to mention the teachers who had to be placated with gifts during Deepavali and Christmas. When Putti did go out, to the neighbourhood Ayurvedic doctor—for the cough she developed every year after the rains, when the damp from the walls and the floors of the house settled into her lungs—or to the temple to send increasingly desperate prayers to Lord Krishna to grant her a husband soonsoonsoon, she was bewildered by the accelerated rate at which things occurred around her. Computers, cars, telephones— all to speed up life. Why did people need to hurry all the time? Where were they going so quickly except to the end of their lives, a destination that was common to all living things? And yet, and yet, there was something exciting about the this new, unstable, hi-tech world swirling like a magical pool just beyond her reach, and she thought wistfully that she might like to dip her fingers in it. Once, frustrated by the constant newness of the world outside their gates and the knowledge that she was always out of step with it, Putti had timidly broached the idea of teaching at the small playschool that had opened two streets away. She had seen an advertisement for part-time personnel in the local paper. They did not ask for any qualifications other than an ability to deal gently with small children.

"No-no, my baby," Ammayya said. "People will think you are an easy woman—only such types go out and work for a living. You are the daughter of a big man, dead though he is, and come from a respectable home. You do not leave the house to earn money. We will find a nice boy for you soon, *Deo volente*."

Putti felt despairingly, sometimes, that she was drowning in her mother's hungry love, helpless as a fly in thick sugar syrup. And on those nights, for hours after Ammayya had fallen asleep, she would lie awake beside her and stare gloomily at the lumpy rise of the old woman's left hip, outlined by stray light from a streetlamp struggling through the tightly shut windows, at the wrinkled hand, heavy with rings, resting firmly on the hip as if to stop it from growing. She would wait until her mother's breathing evolved into snores. Then she would slide a hand down the waist of her petticoat, past her heaving stomach into the waiting thatch of pubic hair, and the smell of her longing would rise gently in the shuttered room where she was born and seemed likely to die.

She stood up abruptly, unable to stand the mirror and the musty room another minute, and ran out, past Ammayya, who called after her in alarm. She barely noticed Sripathi enter the house and almost pushed him aside to reach the stairs. These she took two at a time until she arrived, panting heavily, on the large terrace on top of the house. She leaned over the low parapet wall and gulped the fresh air greedily. Below her lay the messy back garden, with its small forest of brownish-green bushes huddled together like shaggy dwarfs, trees weighed down by the burden of rotting fruit, and jasmine creepers clambering unchecked over everything, their flowers filling the day with a heady fragrance. That fragrance set loose a yearning in Putti. Her head buzzed with ideas and thoughts that she longed to shout aloud. She ached to add her voice to the noisy air.

Ammayya leaned back in the chair and fanned herself vigorously with the rolled up magazine that she had been reading. The power had failed, as it usually did by this time, and even inside the house it was clammy and unbearable. The old woman hitched up her sari as far as was decently possible and fanned between her legs. She had stopped wearing panties a long time ago, and while the newspaper created a pleasant draft in the area of her crotch, it also released a faint odour of urine. She was surprised and hurt by Putti's behaviour. What was wrong with the girl? she wondered uneasily. Was she so upset by Maya's death? True, Putti had been fond of her niece, treating her like a little sister, waiting eagerly for those letters that she wrote to Nirmala, full of details of a life so exotic in its foreignness. But no, there was something else that was affecting the girl. Ammayya was filled with a sudden fear. Putti was the one who sneaked little treats for her when she was overcome with a craving for something sweet, who sat and listened to her rambling stories of relatives dead and alive, who made Ammayya feel that she still existed.

"Oh Ammayya," the girl would say patiently. "Tell me again about Kunjoor Mohana's stolen pearls. Or, "My darling mother, do you remember that story you used to tell about the ghost in Kashinatha's house? Can you tell me again? So funny it was!"

Toothless and ancient I may be, thought Ammayya grimly, but not yet a corpse. And as long as I have my wits about me, my daughter will be mine. She rose out of her chair, her large hips squeezing up like dough from a tight tin, and roamed slowly around the bedroom, gazing up at the enormous photographs of her late husband that adorned all the walls.

"Have you noticed," she murmured to her favourite one of Narasimha as a young man, dashing in a suit, "how she refuses to look me in the eye? Something she is hiding, I know. My mother's heart tells me."

Ammayya chatted often with her husband's faded images. She talked more to him after his death than she had in the twenty-six years of their marriage. She asked him questions and answered them herself, arguing now and then to make it authentic. She complained to him about Sripathi and how disappointing he was as a son. She told him, gleefully, about Maya's betrayal. "Serves Sripathi right," she remarked. "He spoilt her. That's what comes of giving your children too much freedom. Look at our Putti, what a nice child she is. My darling will always look after me, I know that." She grumbled about Arun, who sneered at her caste rules and insisted on climbing the wrought-iron stairway that curled up the rear wall of the house to the upstairs bathroom and that was to be used only by the toilet cleaner, Rojamma. And she fretted about her own health, worrying that one day she might end up too helpless to raise herself off her bed.

"I have some bad news for you," she said now to the photograph in which Narasimha Rao was shaking hands with Jawaharlal Nehru. "Maya is dead. It was an accident, I was told. Why these girls have to drive cars, God only knows. Her child is coming here. What will we do with a small child?" The old lady sat on the edge of her bed, exhausted by the effort of hobbling around the room.

Her eyes, still sharp in age, fell on a photograph of herself as a bride, standing behind Narasimha, who sat stiff and tall in a chair. The photographer had arranged them in the traditional pose against a background picture of a waterfall. The bride wore her sari pallu, with its elaborate gold threadwork visible even in that yellowing picture, covering both shoulders. She had numerous chains around her thin neck, nose pins on both sides of a tiny nose, a wide gem-encrusted gold band around a narrow, virginal waist and jewels in her hair. Her eyes looked frightened. Ammayya remembered that she was only thirteen in that photograph. Narasimha had been twenty-three. She remembered the day he had come to her father's house in Coimbatore, and how she had thrown a tantrum at the thought of getting married instead of continuing school. Her father had laughed indulgently at her, his only child, and told her to get dressed. Her mother had wrapped her in a silk sari so heavy with gold that her sapling body had drooped under the weight. And when she saw the enormous, dark man whom she was to marry, she had refused to show herself to him. She had escaped from her exasperated mother and hidden behind one of the pillars on the verandah. Later, after their wedding, as Narasimha eagerly fumbled with her clothes, he told her that he had almost decided to refuse her, to say no to her father. Then he had noticed her foot peeping out from behind the pillar. A delicate, beautifully arched foot, pale as sandalwood, the ankle circled by a filigree of silver. Such a lovely foot, Narasimha Rao had told himself, must surely belong to an apsara—a heavenly nymph. And so, overcome with a feverish need to possess the owner of that foot, he had insisted on marrying her.

She, in her turn, was frightened of Narasimha, even though he flattered her with his frantic desire and spoiled her with saris and jewellery every day. She was filled with loathing when his furry body fell on her own delicate one and when the smell of their sex filled her fastidious nostrils. And after he had detached himself from her, leaving a sticky residue between her quivering thighs, she would curl up miserably, trying to ignore the deep pain that filled her. It took her a year to understand that this painful invasion was somehow responsible for making her body swell like a balloon; that after several months of vomiting, sleeplessness and discomfort, when all her relatives made much of her—coyly pinching her chin and congratulating her on her fecundity—she would be delivered of a child. It happened to her six times, and each time a stillborn infant slipped out, or a sickly one that seemed to wither and die as soon as the air touched its wrinkled skin. People began to whisper that Yama-raja, the death lord, had set up an altar to himself in the echoing darkness of the girl's womb.

After the birth of her sixth child, Ammayya noticed that Narasimha did not come to her bed as often. She discovered he had taken a mistress. When she ran to her mother's house, weeping and furious, she was told that she ought to be proud that her husband could afford two women. "Why should I be proud?" she had begged her mother. "How can he abandon me like this?" And her mother had told her to grow up, to stop behaving like a child. "How has he abandoned you?" she had scolded. "You are treated like a queen. So many clothes, so much jewellery, a big house."

Ammayya felt violated. Now, every Tuesday, the day he had allotted to lay his thick body on hers, she was nauseated at the thought that he had lain the same way with another woman. After he had rolled away, she would rush to the bathroom and strip away the old cotton sari and loose blouse that she wore to bed, and that her husband hadn't bothered to remove. She would pour mug after mug of cold water over her shivering self, scrub furiously between her legs with soap and a coarse dried gourd that scratched and tore her skin. But on the other six nights of the week, she thought miserably that if she was the perfect wife, Narasimha might decide never to go to his mistress. And to be the perfect wife, she would have to bear him a living child.

Ammayya began to pray unfailingly three times a day. She observed the many rituals prescribed by the Shastras for a good wife. She fasted twice a week and, after her sixth pregnancy, increased that to three times a week. No longer was she a flighty, playful

young girl but a fanatic who terrified the servants with her demands
for cleanliness, for purity in the house where everything had started
to smell of Narasimha's sex. Ammayya's virtue was tyrannical. Even
Shantamma, who had lost all fear, was wary of her daughter-in-
law's steely righteousness.

When Sripathi was born, Ammayya was only twenty-three. She
waited for love to overcome her but found that she felt nothing
in her heart for the tiny infant with the large nose and enormous
ears. Amazed that he survived his first year, and then another, and
another, she began to watch him like a hawk, followed him around
to make sure that he was safe. She didn't want him to go to school,
but Narasimha overrode her desires. A servant was appointed to
accompany Sripathi everywhere, like a second shadow. Although
she did not feel anything for him other than a fear that he would
die, she dreamed elaborate dreams for him, for he would be the one
to sustain her in her age. He would be a famous heart surgeon,
a Supreme Court Justice, or a diplomat in the foreign service.
She participated eagerly in Narasimha's efforts to make Sripathi
swallow the *Encyclopaedia Britannica* whole, although she
cringed every time he invited his father's wrath by not being able
to answer a question. She feared for him not because she loved
him but because she was afraid that Narasimha's hard slaps would
hurt the boy's brain and turn him into a vegetable. Love was an
extravagance that she could ill afford. If she spent it on the boy,
she would have none left for herself, none to use as ointment on
the wounds that Narasimha inflicted on her. Besides, the boy
would grow into a man and feed on her emotions the way he had
already sucked on her body and, when he was done would discard
her like an orange peel. Men always took too much and gave too
little in return.

After Sripathi's birth, when Ammayya watched her husband
shift his silk shalya to his right shoulder before he departed for his
mistress's home in the evening, she did not feel quite as wretched

and angry as before. She did not, however, abandon her rigorous Brahminical ways. If anything, in order to make sure that the gods watched over Sripathi and kept him alive and well, she prayed more intensely and became more rigid about the rituals of purity.

A few months before Narasimha died, Ammayya found out from a relative who was a trustee of the Toturpuram Bank that the money he spent so lavishly was all borrowed. In addition to maintaining his whore, she learned that he visited the race course in Bangalore once a month, when she thought he was away on business. At about the same time, she discovered that she was pregnant again. She locked up all her jewellery and hid it in a trunk, deep beneath the enormous four-poster bed that she shared with her husband on rare occasions. Just four months before Putti was born, Narasimha Rao was killed by a mad bull that raged down Andaal Street and made straight for him. It shredded his liver and a kidney and left him bleeding in the gutter a few yards from his mistress's house.

A few months later, when her daughter arrived in the world, Ammayya marked the twin gifts of life and death that she had received by lighting a silver lamp at the Krishna Temple every month—her one indulgence in an otherwise miserly life.

Ammayya rocked to and fro on her bed and sucked in her toothless gums. Her granddaughter had died. The old woman did not feel very much about it either way. People lived and died. It was sad that Maya had been so young, but these things were part of life. She pondered the changes that were likely to take place in the house, and she was not sure if she would like it. Ammayya cocooned herself in the past, in traditions and rituals, and the prospect of change terrified her. She knew her son. He would bring Maya's child to India. She only hoped that she would not be directly affected by the girl's arrival. *At my age,* she thought petulantly, *nobody has the right to upset my daily routine.* She reached below the bed with her walking stick and quickly touched the locked trunk underneath. Its solid presence was reassuring. That was her insurance plan—all the jewellery that she was not already wearing. More jewellery, she told Putti, than even the queen of England.

"That queen person's jewellery is stolen from other people anyway. Mine was given to me by your father," Ammayya took pains to point out. "Also, mine is better quality. I am telling you, no one has such startling Burmese rubies, redder than blood and of the best water. And my blue jaguar diamonds come from the deepest, darkest part of the earth. They have hoarded light in them for so many millions of years that to look at them is to gaze at the heart of the sun."

The trunk also contained gold coins and silver ingots, each one tied up in soft strips of cloth to prevent even the smallest smudge of gold from rubbing off. Ammayya had discovered that the borders of old silk saris were made of pure silver wire dipped in gold wash that could be melted off the saris into bars. Until that momentous discovery, she used to exchange her old saris with the raddhi-wallah for stainless steel tins and bowls that joined the hoard in the cupboard in a corner of the room. She haggled long and furiously with the man, pretending, in the end, to be defeated by his canny bargaining.

"Okay, baba, okay," she would sigh, secretly chortling at the number of tins and bowls she had wrested for her ragged saris. "You take everything. I have no strength to argue any more. And anyway, what will I do with so many dabbas and things? Nearly dead I am, can I take it all with me?" All the while, in her mind, she would grimly promise herself that yes, she would take everything with her. Whatever could be burnt on the funeral pyre would be destroyed along with her body. As for the rest, she would insist that her ashes be buried in the backyard of Big House, along with all of her valuables. She would put it in her will, and if her children did not follow it to the letter, she would return as a ghoul to haunt them.

There was no doubt in Ammayya's mind that she would be able to control her afterlife as effectively as she did her present one.

———————

In the kitchen of the white house behind Safeway, Nandana heard Aunty Kiran tell Uncle Sunny that she was going to her house. "The child needs some more clothes. And Mary Carlson said that she would come over and pick up the house plants while I was there."

I want to go home, thought Nandana eagerly, homehomehome. She scrambled out of the bed, where she was huddled with all her favourite toys, and raced down the stairs. She put on her shoes as fast as she could and waited impatiently near the front door.

Aunty Kiran came out of the kitchen and looked surprised to see her there. "Nandu, sweetie, do you want something?" she asked.

Nandana hugged Moona, the cloth cow, and waited for her to open the door.

"Do you want to go out to play with Anjali and her friends in the backyard?"

She shook her head. No.

"Oh, I see, you want to come with me?"

Yes.

Through the door and out to the driveway they went, to where Aunty Kiran's blue car was standing. Into the front seat—don't forget the seat belt—and then they were headed home. Her father would be wondering where Nandana had gone. For *sure*.

Her mother's snapdragons looked wild and horrible. The sunflower plant in the pot near the door had become a tree and was leaning over so far that it swept the ground. When Aunty Kiran opened the door, Nandana ran inside eagerly. She thought that the house had a lonesome smell. She ran around, touching the table in the corridor, where the magazines and letters were kept when they arrived, and trailing her hand against the dining-room wall, where her mother had hung family pictures. She stroked the big fat chair, in the corner of the living room, that was her father's favourite. Nandana checked to see whether her video cassettes were still on the shelf below the television, that her father's computer was still locked up to his desk by a long wire in the small adjoining room.

She raced up the stairs to her own room, where she opened all the dresser drawers to make sure nothing had gone away. Her father had found the chest at a garage sale. He had brought it home in a friend's pickup, and her mother had been so annoyed with the battered old thing—the black paint flaking off the walnut wood beneath, the missing knobs, the scratches in the existing paint. Maya hated second-hand stuff—it reeked of other people.

"In India," she said when Nandana's father teased her about her hoity-toity habits, "we never accept leftovers. Only beggars do."

"Snob!" her father had said. "This isn't leftovers. It's a perfectly good piece of furniture that needs some TLC. When I'm done with it, you won't even know it's old."

"I don't want it."

And her father had replied, "It isn't for you. It's for my cherry pie here."

For three weeks, he had abandoned his books and papers, and worked on the chest of drawers. First he sanded it down to remove the paint, and next he smoothed it with a finer sandpaper, and then he primed the wood to make it ready for paint, and he finally painted it white. Then he and Nandana stencilled onto it a pattern of daisies that she picked out. They used yellow paint for the flowers and green for the leaves. Even her mother had agreed that it looked almost new. She bought nice-smelling paper to line the drawers and gave Nandana a small picture of an Indian lady called

Lakshmi with four arms and a smiling white face, sitting on a lotus flower with two white elephants on either side of her.

"This is a goddess," her mother had told Nandana. "She will always look after you and make sure you are okay." She put the picture under the drawer paper. On a shelf in the corner of the room were Nandana's books—*The Cat in the Hat, Green Eggs & Ham* and all her Little Critters, Berenstain Bears and Sesame Street books. Her father had told her that books must be treated with respect. She would have to ask Aunty Kiran to pack them very carefully, so they would not get damaged on the way to India.

6

MAYA

O UTSIDE THE GATES of Big House, the scooter got going as soon as Sripathi kicked the pedal, and he looked at it with some astonishment. The wretched thing had actually started properly for once.

"Lucky today, or what? Mine is always giving me a headache. Every other day I have to pay fifty rupees for repair work to that thief of a mechanic," remarked a complacent voice. It was Balaji, the Canara Bank manager who lived in the apartment block across the road. He wore nothing but a dirty lungi and a shrunken vest that he had rolled into a tire under his plump breasts. Sometimes, when the vest was unrolled, it looked tiny, as though it belonged to Balaji's eight-year-old son. The boy wore big, loose clothes meant to last several years, so perhaps father and son shared their attire. Balaji's belly, large and hairy, sat over the waist of his lungi like a contented cat, and through the fuzz peered his navel. Every now and then he dug an index finger into the navel and twirled it around diligently, as if winding his stomach up for the day.

"You are late to work today?" he asked. His probing finger wandered from navel to nostril and then on to his left ear. He twisted the digit vigorously and examined his find with interest.

"No, I had to take the day off." Sripathi forced himself to reply politely. He disliked Balaji. The bank manager was a pompous fellow who derived enormous pleasure from making his customers wait outside his office, just to give them the impression that he was tremendously busy and therefore very important. But Sripathi would have to go to him for a loan soon enough, so he tried to hide his antagonism. "What about you? Why are you at home today?"

"I am suffering from heatstroke," said Balaji. "It is too hot these days. The monsoons should have come by now, but no sign yet. What a problem!"

Sripathi mounted his scooter, waved to Balaji and rode off in the direction of Raju Mudaliar's house. The motion of the vehicle ruffled the still, hot air and created a breeze that dried the sweat beading his forehead and upper lip. It was extremely muggy. He, too, wondered where the monsoons had disappeared this year. Around him on the narrow street grew the skeletons of more new apartment blocks. The builders had no sooner finished one construction than they went on to another, like a bunch of untidy crows. They left the road littered with chopped trees and building debris, so that it looked as cratered and shocked as a war zone. Overloaded trucks flanked the narrow street like pregnant camels, and their drivers raised the noise level several decibels by playing songs from the latest movies, sometimes through the night.

When he was a child, Sripathi had thought the road enormously wide and grand. His childish imagination couldn't begin to measure its length. What a wretched little alley it had become in less than ten years. Sripathi rode past piles of broken stone, their sharp edges jutting out threateningly. Small urchins and stray dogs rooted around in unused piles of sand. Here and there puddles of cement had hardened into strange shapes. Carcasses of old buildings waited for match-box towers to grow on them. And over those ruins, migrant labourers had built homes from what they salvaged out of garbage bins—cardboard boxes, plastic bags, flattened kerosene tins. The remains from other people's lives created new landscapes on the edges of middle-class life.

In spite of the chaos around him, Sripathi was glad to be out in the open, away from the oppressive closeness of his house. He felt his rage cool as he rode down the busy streets.

It was nine years since Sripathi had heard Maya's voice. She had phoned often, begging to speak to him, but he had refused. Her letters arrived regularly in the mail in thick aerogram envelopes with foreign stamps. Only Nirmala read them, though, over and over, storing them under her pillow so that she could examine the fine writing before she went to sleep. Often he was tempted to ask her what Maya had to say in those missives, but hurt, pride and anger intervened and silenced him. Later on, even that brief curiosity died, and with it he buried all memory of Maya. Sometimes, however, from force of habit, Nirmala would still read bits aloud to Sripathi. "She went skiing in the snow, she says. I hope it is not too dangerous. Why does she want to try such things?" Or, "Alan is teaching this year. They have to leave the child in day-care. Paapa. The poor little baby. I wish I was there, then no problem they would have." And he would snap at her. "I don't want to hear. If you want to keep babbling, go somewhere else and let me sleep."

He had chosen the name for her when she was born, for he could hardly believe that he had fathered this beautiful, perfectly formed creature. He had stayed awake all night in the small room where Nirmala and the baby lay, alert to the smallest whimper, certain that if he slept the child would slip away like a breath. Every time he peered into the cradle at the crumpled red face, the eyes squeezed shut, the curled hands like pale shells, he thought of yet another name for her. Latha. No, too ordinary. Sumitra? No, that was the youngest of King Dasharatha's wives. His daughter would be second to none. At two in the morning he had had a brilliant idea. He would christen her Yuri after the Russian astronaut who had gone into space that year, the first human to leave the grip of earth's gravity and wander among the stars. My daughter will be like him, she will reach for the skies, nothing less.

When Nirmala heard the name, she had burst into tears. "Yuri, Yuri? What kind of nonsense name is that?" she sobbed, jerking her nipple out of the baby's mouth and setting her bawling as well.

"What's wrong with it?" Sripathi demanded. She would probably want to give his daughter a name that every other child in India had, just to conform.

"What's wrong? It means nothing, that's what. We can't give her a meaningless name."

"How do you know it means nothing? Do you know Russian?"

"Russian?"

"It is the name of a Russian astronaut," explained Sripathi in the patient voice of one talking to a child.

"Are you crazy? We have a million Indian names, good Hindu ones with auspicious alphabets, and you go and choose a foreign one. And from a Communist country too!"

"I believe in the Communist philosophy," argued Sripathi aggrievedly. His first child, and he couldn't even give her a name without an argument.

"No, no, no! I don't care if you are a Turk who believes in Buddhist philosophy," declared Nirmala, "Yuri sounds horrible. Besides, when she goes to school other children are sure to call her urine. Poor thing. No child of mine is going to have such a ridiculous name. That is final. You call her whatever you want. I will call her something else."

Sripathi had to agree. Children could be cruel, and the last thing he wanted was to saddle his precious daughter with a name that would hurt her. And so he had eventually settled on Maya and Nirmala had agreed, insisting only on Lalitha as a second name after her own dead mother.

Maya: illusion. The name was singularly appropriate for a daughter who had disappeared from their lives like foam from the

shoulder of a wave. The last time he had seen her was at the international airport in Madras, where they had all travelled to bid her
goodbye, their entire family as well as Mr. P. K. Bhat, Maya's father-
in-law-to-be. Nirmala couldn't stop weeping, he recalled. It had
embarrassed him, that wild outpouring of sorrow. Even in private
he would never allow himself to break down like that. It showed a
lack of dignity. So he stood there stoically while Nirmala sniffed and
sobbed, until Ammayya, who hated being left out, had burst into
tears as well, setting off Putti in turn. Sripathi patted Maya awkwardly on the back and told her stiffly to be careful, to study hard
and to bring nothing but honour to their family. But underneath the
calm exterior he so deliberately presented, Sripathi was a proud
father. This was *his* daughter who had received a prestigious fellow-
ship in faraway America. And she had done it on her own merit,
without the help of influential relatives or friends. He who had
heard, with a faint envy, other parents boast about their brilliant offspring now joined their ranks. He, too, could talk knowledgably
about student visas, entrance exams and scholarship applications,
and bask in the sudden respect people showed him. That is Sripathi Rao, he imagined people whispering as he passed, the father
of Maya Rao.

Had he known that the admission and scholarship award letter
that had made him burst with pride years ago would take their
daughter so completely away from them, Sripathi would never have
consented to her departure. When he allowed himself, he could remember every detail of that day perfectly. It was a bright, hot morning in March, much like this one. He had come home from work
exhausted from trying to think of an interesting jingle for a new
brand of tooth powder. Maya was waiting for him at the gate, waving the letter and laughing with excitement. How flattered Sripathi
had been at the idea of Maya being selected for the scholarship. So
many bright students all over the world and the university wanted
their child. Not that they were getting anything less than the best,

oh no! How many children were there who started to speak as clear as a bell at age one and a half? who came first in every subject, from baby class, right through high school? who went on to be the very top student in the entire Madras University—not just in studies mind you but also in sports and dancing and music? *and* who got flawless scores on the GRE and TOEFL exams?

Nirmala hadn't been quite as enthusiastic. Later that night, when they had turned off the lights and lay beside each other on the big double bed (the only item of furniture in the house that had not belonged to one of his ancestors and that Sripathi had bought with his own money), she voiced her misgivings.

"The girl is already twenty-two, time for her to get married. As it is, we have your sister still at home. Two-two unmarried women in the house is not good. Okay, we couldn't fix anything for Putti, but for our Maya at least we had better start keeping our eyes and ears open for good boys. This scholarship and all is fine, but more important is marriage. I am telling you, these things take time, and before we know it she also will be sitting like Putti and counting holy beads."

"Oho, what is the hurry?" Sripathi said, still buoyant from the excitement of the letter. "Let her study, she has a good brain. She might even go in for medicine, who knows? Our Maya is smart, she can take care of herself."

If she went into medical research, he reflected to himself, at least she would be fulfilling a part of the destiny that Ammayya had envisioned for him. Sripathi hoped that the ancient disappointment he had inflicted on his mother would be lessened by his daughter's achievements. He had sought to wipe out his father's behaviour towards Ammayya by being as honourable and dutiful as he knew how and felt that he had failed when he abandoned medical school. Duty and honour, these were the twin hounds that dogged Sripathi's footsteps, and their hungry mouths gaped up at him always. No, his Maya would have to be allowed the chance to become someone respected, and educating her would be the way to do it. Arun, too, Sripathi had hoped in that happy time, would follow his sister and make him proud. She would be there to guide him, to help with tips on studying for the entrance exams, to assist with applications.

So he had turned to Nirmala and said firmly again, "Why should she get married so soon, like a villager? These days girls are doing well—we shouldn't hold her back."

"Did I say marry her off tomorrow? I only said we should start looking. Maya may be smart, but it is difficult for a girl to survive on her own. Even if she is a big scholar, she needs somebody by her side. We will not be around for ever you know."

Sripathi had laughed softly. "Okay, Mamma, okay. Tomorrow I will take a torch and go looking for the best boy I can find for our Maya. If you want I will get Victor Coelho at my office to make a poster—WANTED: *Boy for Beautiful, Talented Girl*—and stick it all over Toturpuram. That should get a quick response! Or should I hire Jayant Maama's band and a loud speaker?"

"Joking-joking all the time," grumbled Nirmala. "A head full of grey hair, and still he doesn't take life seriously, while my brain is going agda-bagda trying to think of what is best for this family. Wait and see, with all this joking Maya is going to end up like your sister, unmarried and frantic."

"Oho, Mamma, stop talking and go to sleep. Maya isn't going anywhere till August. Plenty of time for other matters."

Nevertheless, Sripathi took Nirmala's worrying to heart, and when Prakash Bhat's family appeared out of the blue, a miraculously good match with no strings attached, he was delighted. This was indeed a good time for Maya! First the scholarship and then a groom who had just started a job in Philadelphia. *And* he had a green card, that coveted scrap of paper that parents showed off to each other as if it were a lottery ticket with the winning numbers. Maya's stars were arranged in her favour, it seemed.

The Bhats wanted nothing other than Maya for their son, not even a pair of diamond earrings, which everybody knew was a mandatory part of a bride's trousseau to be closely examined by the groom's female relatives, who could smell a fake set of vaaley in a second. Never mind if the girl wore only cotton knickers to the ceremony, all she needed were those vajrada vaaley for the wedding to be a success.

"Sripathi-orey," P. K. Bhat had said, raising his hand as if bestowing a blessing, "we are not the dowry type. We only want a decent girl from a good family, one who knows how to fit into life in the West without losing sight of our Indian values. What you do for your daughter's marriage is, of course, your choice." He had even assured them that his son would be only too happy if Maya decided to carry on with her studies after the wedding. "We are liberal-minded people, sir," said Mr. Bhat with a genial smile.

In the end, Maya had offered a compromise. "I have been given this wonderful chance to study in one of the best universities in my field. How can you ask me to throw it away? I will get engaged if you want," she had said, "but marriage can happen only after I graduate."

"Long engagements are not good," said Mr. Bhat, slightly annoyed, although he gave in when he saw that his son did not seem to mind. "Too much time allows bad things to happen. But it is their decision, so why should I say anything? These days parents are there only to pay bills and keep quiet. What do you say, Sripathi-orey?"

Sripathi had nodded happily, still overwhelmed by the shower of luck that had rained on their family. Maya was born under a fortunate star, he had known that the minute he saw her in that bleached hospital nursery twenty-two years ago. Ah yes, he thought, the gods were fond of her, that was certain. She must have been a virtuous soul in her previous existence and was reaping the rewards now. Although Sripathi was bursting to tell the whole world about their happiness, he controlled himself, suppressed his elation. Suddenly he became mindful of Nirmala's warnings that evil spirits were always around, waiting for an opportunity to creep into lives that were too perfect. He would make a quick detour to the small Devi temple on his way to work and break a coconut at the deity's feet. Not that he believed in such superstitious nonsense, Sripathi had told himself, but for the sake of his child he was willing to do even the most ridiculous things. Then, afraid that his insincerity might somehow transmit itself to the goddess and invite her spiteful rage, he quickly mumbled an apology for his thoughts to the air. But he stopped when he realized that Mr. Bhat and his sister were looking at him oddly. They must think I am mad, talking to myself, he thought, feeling stupid. And so, to divert attention from himself, he frowned and snapped at Nirmala.

"Mamma, what are you doing sitting there? Can't you see our visitors' plates are empty? More snacks, more coffee. What will they think of us? Eh, Bhat-orey? You will think we are such a rude family!"

The engagement ceremony was shaping up to be an elaborate affair. Mr. Bhat was insistent on inviting every last relative and most of his office colleagues, too, as this was his only son's engagement, and it wasn't every day that it was performed.

"Don't worry about expenses, Sripathi-orey," he declared, patting Sripathi on the back. "We will both split it, fifty-fifty. We are not the dowry type, as I told you. All I want is a daughter for our home." He paused, moved by his own eloquence, and wiped the tears from his eyes. He summoned Maya and gave her a large jewellery case. "This is my dear departed wife's. I kept it for my daughter-in-law. My sister advised me to wait for the wedding, but now itself I wish to give it to you. So my dear child, wear it with my blessings."

Sripathi was startled by the magnificence of the gift—sparkling clusters of diamonds for the ears and a matching necklace.

"I wish he hadn't given it to her," he said to Nirmala when the visitors had left and they were in their bedroom. Nirmala was sitting cross-legged in the middle of the bed, closely examining the jewellery her daughter had just received, caressing the bright stones in their nest of purple velvet. "Now we will have to give something grand to Prakash, otherwise it will not look good. And so many people Bhat is inviting to this engagement—it is going to cost more than the god of wealth can afford; even if he shares the cost, it is too much. What will he expect for the wedding if the engagement itself is to be so big?"

"What kind of man are you? Aren't you happy for our Maya? Our first child and only daughter," Nirmala had argued. "What a nice family she is going to, and you are worrying about small details. Of course we will have to spend a little bit now—a good quality watch for Prakash, a suit, a shirt and shoes—otherwise, what will people think? We must do things in the proper way."

"Don't you understand what I am saying? We cannot—C-A-N-N-O-T—afford it," said Sripathi. "Already I have so many debts to pay off—father's bills, the house mortgage, Maya's airplane ticket. Do you know how much that costs? Foolish woman, just to please other people we must push ourselves into the poor house? Stretch your legs only as far as your cot goes! From tomorrow we will all sit with wet towels over our stomachs to shrink the hunger, and do you think anybody will help? Oh no, they will be too busy digesting the food we fed them at this stupid engagement!"

"Why don't you ask your mother? She has all that jewellery under her bed. She can give a gold chain for our future son-in-law. It's her first grandchild's marriage, after all. And take a small loan from the bank. Once Maya gets her scholarship, she will surely send some money home. She is a good child. She knows to do her duty by us," argued Nirmala.

Ammayya refused to part with any of her jewellery. She clutched at the necklaces strung around her wrinkled throat and said, "My mother gave me these, and your father—this is my sthri-dhanaa. They are for my Putti. You have the house, Sripathi, and all that your father left. I will give Maya a pair of bangles for her wedding. Not now."

Sripathi did not want to remind her that Narasimha had left him only debts. It would lead to a scene. And so he went to the Canara Bank for another loan. He had cringed at the thought of meeting Balaji, the loans manager, of listening to his supercilious voice going over the details of other unpaid loans. But it was marginally better than facing the trustees of the Toturpuram Trust Company to whom he owed far more.

"This time I can sanction only five thousand rupees, Sripathi-orey," Balaji had said, leaning back in his chair and tapping his fingers together. "And only because you are my neighbour and acquaintance. For anybody else I would have said no. You have defaulted twice already on past loan payments, so it is not in bank's interest to advance another loan, you understand?"

"I didn't default, Mr. Balaji," Sripathi objected. "The bank was closed for three days in a row. What could I do? And the second time I came in, you were on holiday."

"Look, sir, I am doing you a favour," Balaji said in an injured voice. "Some people don't appreciate the problems I will have if you do not return the loan in time. It is my good name that I am endangering for your sake, and you want to argue!"

"No, no," said Sripathi humbly. He would grovel for his children if necessary, but the man's attitude set his teeth on edge. "I didn't mean any disrespect at all. I know how much I am obliged to your good offices, so please accept my apologies if I said anything to offend you. But what to do? There are so many expenses, one after another, and I am the only earning member in my household."

"If I were you, Sripathi—and I am saying this only as a well-wisher, so take no offence please—," said the bank manager, appeased by Sripathi's abject apologies, "you should not be living in such a big house. Why don't you sell it and move into a flat? So convenient. You could wipe out your debts in one stroke."

Sripathi's blood boiled at Balaji's words. How dare he presume to advise him? Suppose I tell him to mind his own business? he thought. But once again he had to control himself. He needed the money and Balaji's goodwill. The house loan was coming up for renegotiation, and in a few years he would need money for Arun's college tuition. Soon Maya would complete her studies and be earning a salary. He knew she would send money home. He felt wretched at the thought of taking money from his daughter, but what else could he do? From a son it was acceptable; in fact, he expected Arun to share the burden of running the house and getting his sister married—these were his duties as a son and a brother. Once the boy was earning, they could return the money to Maya, thought Sripathi, happily planning the future which suddenly looked so bright.

In the months that followed Maya's departure, Mr. Bhat visited Big House frequently. He was a widower who lived with his sister in Madras and thought it important for the two families to get to know one another. Sripathi liked the man immensely. During the many long discussions they had over hot tea and Nirmala's delicious uppuma or other snacks, the two men discovered that they had much in common. Mr. Bhat, like Sripathi, did not subscribe to rituals. But in spite of his loud condemnation of those rituals, he managed to ingratiate himself with Ammayya by bringing her a box of her favourite jalebis from the famous Grand Sweets store in Madras. When Sripathi told him, with some embarrassment, that he could not afford a very lavish wedding, Mr. Bhat waved his hand and said, "Sir, wealth does not make a man rich, but good name and character do. I believe in honesty, loyalty, duty and honour. These are my gold and silver, sir, and these give one dignity. Like I said, what you do for our Maya is your business. We ask for nothing but her as a daughter."

Sripathi wrote frequently to his daughter. He was punctilious about it. The poor child must miss her home, he thought, and this is one way I can make her feel better. Every two weeks he sent her a detailed bulletin of family, relatives, friends and the country in general. He always used his marbled blue Japanese Hero for Maya's letters. This pen had a thick nib that he thought gave his writing a fatherly authority, showed the full weight of the love that he could rarely express in words.

> *My dear child,* (he wrote in one such letter)
> *Before I begin, your Mamma tells me to inform you that the Yugadi festival is on the twentieth of March this year. You are to wash your hair, say a small prayer to the assortment of gods we believe in and eat a small helping of something bitter mixed with something sweet. I am also supposed to let you know that Shanta had another baby, and Kishtamma's youngest son got married to a hideous girl who has nothing to recommend her but an enormous pair of diamond nose pins. Now for all the real news . . .*

The first year Maya replied just as frequently, sheets of paper crammed with the minutiae of student life in a foreign country, detailed descriptions of her roommates, her professors, the long hours she had to put in. She worried about her assignments, and she was amazed by the library system. She grumbled about the food she had to eat and wished that she had listened to Nirmala and taken a few extra bottles of pickle because she yearned for her mother's spicy cooking. She was lonely in the beginning and didn't like the smell of meat when her roommates cooked in the shared kitchen. Her letters were events, and the family discussed every detail for weeks, until her next letter arrived. Nirmala kept them under her pillow to reread at night, aloud so that Sripathi could share her feelings of loss or wonder or amusement. Sometimes there were photographs, too, taken with an old Agfa camera that Sripathi had purchased from a colleague at work and given to his daughter as a surprise.

Maya's letters slowed to a trickle in the second year, a fact that dismayed Sripathi but that he excused nevertheless. Let her concentrate on her studies, he told Nirmala, who worried incessantly about Maya's increasing silence. She must be very busy; she has to do everything for herself—studies, cooking, laundry. There is no Koti there for her. Where does she have the time to write? And so he continued his long, methodical letters, penned as he sat on his balcony, staring out at the changing landscape of Brahmin Street, where he had been born and his father before him. But soon even the meagre replies had stopped, and all they received was a New Year's card with a few hastily penned lines, and increasingly rare telephone calls.

Three years into her studies, shortly before she was to graduate, there came another letter from her. Sripathi did not see it when it arrived and learnt about it only after five days, even though every evening when he returned from work he asked Nirmala about the mail. He remembered the morning that he read those words in precise detail even now.

He was on the balcony as usual, reading his newspaper and making notes for his letters to the editor. The warm, rich aroma of boiling milk in the kitchen downstairs mingled with the smell of percolating coffee and teased his senses. Soon Nirmala would grumble her way up the stairs with a tumbler of the steaming beverage. At that hour, with the soft sea breeze wafting a farewell to night, the sound of Maharajapuram Santhanam's voice soaring in song from somebody's cassette recorder in the apartment block next door and the inky smell of the newspaper in his hands, Sripathi Rao was an entirely contented man. The tumbler of coffee would merely complete the sense of harmony in his being. It was the full stop at the end of a perfect sentence, the last note to a flawless melody, the dessert that crowned an exquisite meal. But that day, his sense of harmony was completely upset. Nirmala had come onto the balcony wearing a guilty expression. She had placed the coffee on the aluminum table, already crowded with his writing material, and settled down with a small sigh on a foot stool that Koti used to reach and clean cobwebs.

"Unh, this climbing up and down is too much for me. From to-morrow on, you come down and drink coffee there," she remarked and, as usual, peered at the sheets of paper in front of her husband. He covered them defensively. "Who are you writing to?" she asked. "If it is to your daughter, wait till you hear what she is doing now. Your precious Maya obviously doesn't care about your news and views and lecture-vecture. We will have to find a place to go and hide our heads at this rate."

"Why, what happened?" Sripathi smiled.

He knew his wife of old. Any little thing convinced her that the sky would drop on their heads, like the frightened chicken in the children's story he used to read to Maya and Arun. How those two used to giggle and fidget and lean against him impatiently as they waited for the line about the chicken running frantically away from a leaf that had landed on its head, screaming that the sky was falling! And when the moment came, they would jump up and down, clutch at each other, kick up their plump legs and laugh as if they had never heard anything funnier. While he, to prolong that mo-ment of sheer joy, would flap around pretending to be the chicken, clutching his head and moaning, "The sky is falling! Oh, the sky is falling!" Those days it was so easy to make them happy.

"Yes-yes, smile all you want now," warned Nirmala. "All your smiles will disappear once you read this. Here, it came five days ago." She thrust a slightly damp, much-folded wad of paper at him. The dampness was probably sweat. Nirmala had a habit of thrust-ing letters or money down the front of her bra and letting them sit there until she changed for bed. It was her secret place, one that she thought Sripathi did not know about. He didn't have the heart to disillusion her because, ultimately, she couldn't keep things to her-self. She was an open, trusting person and secrets made her uneasy.

"Five days ago? Why didn't you show it to me then itself?"

"I didn't know what to do. But finally I thought, it is his daughter also, let him manage." She glared at Sripathi as if he were responsible for the letter. "Besides," she added belligerently, "*you* spoilt her, always she wants her way thanks to you. Didn't I tell you, Maya is going out of control? But everything I say goes into one ear and comes out of the other. You think you are always right, no?"

"Oho, can you stop talking for two minutes and let me read this thing?" Sripathi asked, exasperated.

"Yes-yes, shout at *me* now, that's all you can do," grumbled Nirmala, but she subsided after Sripathi frowned at her. She knew that frown—it meant that she had aggravated him as much as he could tolerate, and any more would mean a shouting match in which he would hurl thundering insults at her, using words that she had to consult a dictionary to understand. This wasn't the time for all that confusion, so she shut up and waited while her husband scanned the wretched letter with its foreign look, the envelope thick and cream-coloured, the bright Canadian stamps that this time had, unbelievably, not been stolen by rapacious postal workers who supplemented their wages by selling stolen foreign stamps to hobby shops and collectors. Didn't Maya remember that she should get her letters franked to avoid such thefts?

My dear Mamma and Appu,

I don't know how else to say this, so let me be direct. I want to cancel my engagement to Prakash. I am in love with Alan Baker, whom I have known for two years. We want to get married and with your blessings. We hope that we will be able to celebrate the wedding in Toturpuram this summer, after my studies are over.

I know this will come as a shock to you, but I hope that you will understand. Don't be angry with me, please. I have been wanting to phone you for a while now, but thought that it might be better to write in detail. I will be writing to Prakash,

*and I know that he will understand. He is a good man, and I
am sure that he will find somebody else to marry. Could you
please return the jewellery his father gave me and explain to
him? Please, Appu? I feel very bad about hurting the old man,
but if you explain, he will be all right, I think.*

*I look forward to your reply and hope that you will not be
very angry with me. I cannot help the way I feel about Alan,
and I am certain that you will like him very much. I miss you
all and am anxious to hear from you, so that we can make
plans to come home and get married.*

There was more—about Alan Baker, their plans for the future,
the fact that they would be moving to Vancouver, where Maya had
found a job and Alan had admission in a Ph.D. program, and other
details that slid past in a blur. For a few moments after he had
finished reading, Sripathi found nothing to say. He took off his
glasses, put them on again, and reread his daughter's letter.

"Is she mad? Your daughter? Cannot help her feelings, she
says. Tell Mr. Bhat, she orders me—she doesn't want him to get
hurt! What about *me*? And *you*? We aren't going to be hurt? What
am I going to tell people?"

"I don't know," said Nirmala miserably. "You write and make
her understand that she cannot do this kind of nonsense thing."

"What should I say?" demanded Sripathi. "'My dear daughter,
your father has gone bankrupt getting you engaged to one man, and
now you are trading in his good name and family honour for some
foreigner?' Yes, of course, that is what I will write to your darling
daughter. That will definitely change her mind." He turned on her.
"*You* should have known. You are her mother, why didn't you sense
that something was wrong?"

"I am her mother, but I am not a goddess with divine eyesight!
Why didn't *you* find out? Every two weeks you write her a big fat
letter, and she never replies for two years. When she finally decides

to put pen to paper, it is to tell us that she is marrying some for-eigner. You are the one who can predict things, no? You only keep saying that! So why didn't you know about Maya? Why are you blaming me?"

Sripathi picked up his coffee cup and took a sip, grimaced at the taste of the lukewarm liquid and emptied it into the planter with its straggling money-plant creeper that had managed to survive several doses of coffee, tea and, once, some Limca.

"Will you write to her, but?" asked Nirmala again. "It might help. Maybe she needs some advice. Poor thing so far away, all by herself, no elders to tell her right from wrong. Sometimes it is good to give advice, even when it isn't asked for. I think you should tell her that we are worried and that she shouldn't do anything in a hurry. I should have guessed that something was wrong. I knew when she did not write . . . Maybe that first time she asked us to visit her, do you remember? On the phone she sounded so funny, as if she was crying, and when I asked she said that she had a cold. I am sure she was crying. We should have gone to her then. Whatever the cost. One of us at least . . ."

"Don't be silly. As if it would have stopped your daughter. She does whatever she wants." He ran a hand through his hair in agita-tion. The dense grey curls flared up around his raking fingers. "She says she loves him. How can you love somebody before you have lived with him?"

A dreadful suspicion entered his mind. What did it imply, that love business? Had Maya *slept* with the fellow? Was she pregnant? Was that why she was marrying him? How could she share her bed before marriage? When he had been married, it had taken Sripathi a whole year to get over sharing this house, this room, this bed, the bathroom and even the shelves with Nirmala. When he'd slid under the sheets and felt it stretch over the hillock of Nirmala's ris-ing buttocks, the small hump of her shoulder if she was lying on her side, he would feel a quick, guilty delight that eased into pure pleasure when he remembered that this sharing had been sanctioned by the priest before Agni, the fire god. And in the bathroom, he would open the peeling, white medicine cabinet and touch her tin of talcum powder possessively, stroke his thumb against her toothbrush, feel infinitely wealthy for having her for his own. My wife, he would whisper disbelievingly. Mrs. Nirmala Rao, *my* wife. And then immediately, even though the bathroom door was locked, he would turn on the tap full throttle, just in case she could hear him think. How shy he had felt about seeing her blouses, petticoats, brassieres and knickers nestling against his white underwear, so much so that he used to avert his eyes and search the drawers blindly for his clothes, making such a mess that Nirmala got thoroughly exasperated.

Nirmala reached around her back for the sari pallu that dangled over her left shoulder and wiped her eyes with it. She sniffed miserably, "Did we not bring her up properly? Must be that foreign place. Their ways are different, all right for them perhaps, but for a girl brought up here, it must be difficult to resist temptation."

Sripathi avoided her gaze. She might read his suspicions about Maya and that fellow in his eyes. Besides, he was probably imagining things. He had been embarrassed by his suspicions and ashamed, too. He could trust Maya. All he needed to do was to write her a letter, or perhaps phone her. Yes, it would be expensive, but a phone call would be more immediate.

"I'll go to the temple and offer a special prayer to Sathyanarayana. Give a sari for Lakshmi—the red silk I bought to wear for Maya's wedding. It is brand new, so the goddess won't mind that I didn't buy it especially for her. Maybe I will ask Krishna Acharye to perform a few ceremonies also," said Nirmala brightening up at the thought of having God on her side.

How wonderful was Nirmala's unquestioning faith in the divine, thought Sripathi enviously. He had grown up with nothing but himself to believe in, thanks to his own father who had insisted that god was only a creation of the human imagination that could not be depended on for every little nonsense matter, otherwise why should more than half the world's population be so miserable and deprived? Why did good and hardworking people have their lives destroyed by flood and famine and plague? And his mother's ostentatious ceremonies, performed to the accompaniment of bells and loud songs and elaborate rituals devoid of any real devotion, had never attracted Sripathi. His father had never told him what to do when he felt weak and helpless and his faith in his own abilities faltered. Who could he turn to then? Oh, you wretched girl, he thought. What will I say to everyone in Toturpuram, all those friends and relatives who never fail to ask how you are doing? Perhaps what Nirmala said was true—someone *had* cast an evil eye on their family.

He patted Nirmala's hand, worn with age and from the years of cutting and cooking and cleaning, and said grimly, "Don't worry, Mamma, don't worry. It's not your fault or mine. We will phone her tonight when the rates are low. In the meanwhile I will also write and try to make her see how stupid and reckless she is. She will forget this Alan fellow completely."

Nirmala blew her nose in one of the clean white towels hanging on the balcony rail, bundled it for the wash and stood up. Sripathi drew the tablet of paper towards him and picked up the glacial silver, rapier-like Parker pen. It suited his current mood. With rapid strokes he filled five or six pages with exhortations to Maya. "*Don't be silly. You are throwing away a good match. Think of Prakash's feelings. Your father-in-law will also be very hurt. He thinks of you as a daughter, you know. It is not honourable for a girl to do what you are doing. Our reputation has to be considered. Ammayya will be upset, and think of your poor Putti Atthey's matrimonial prospects.*" He poured all his distress into his letter, his frustration with her increasing with each word.

That evening they made a long-distance call. When Sripathi heard Maya's voice, he controlled his impulse to scold and started off calmly enough. He reasoned with her, told her how upset they were, and how impossible the situation would be if she did not change her mind about Alan. She explained, in an equally reasonable tone, that she could not change her mind about loving somebody and wanting to spend the rest of her life with him. But when she asked Sripathi to see things from her point of view, he lost his temper. He had forgiven his child so many transgressions, but this deliberate trampling of their dignity, of the family name that he had struggled to maintain all these years, *that* he would not forgive. "If you persist in doing this foolish thing," he had shouted at his daughter, "never show your face in this house again. *Never.*" He had hoped that his disapproval would make her change her mind, but the next envelope from Maya contained a plain wedding invitation with a brief letter to Nirmala and a few photographs—of her and Alan outside the registrar's office, Maya in a dark blue Canjeevaram sari that she had taken with her when she left home, and Alan in a suit; another at a party, surrounded by friends; and a third at the beach, Maya's legs startlingly bare in a pair of green shorts.

"Maybe we should have been more understanding," Nirmala said fearfully, when she saw how angry Sripathi was. "This girl is as stubborn as you. I want to see my Maya. Write to her and say that it is okay, no? She can come home."

No, Sripathi had replied, No, no, no. True, he had behaved like those ridiculous fathers in film melodramas, but then Maya, too, could have shown some regard for their feelings. Dishonour was what she had given them in return for the independence they had granted her.

"You write if you want to," he had said. "She is dead for me."

But Nirmala hadn't written either. She could not defy her husband; she had never been taught how to do so and she lacked the courage besides. She had scanned the last brief letter repeatedly, as if she could force her daughter to materialize out of the elegant black script, and had cried over the writing. "Tell me who sat at the dining table and made her practise her handwriting every day? Her mother. And who told her that a good hand is an indication of a good mind, that people will respect you if you write nicely? Again her wretched mother, that's who! Does she even remember that? No, of course not. Otherwise, why this little chindhi of a paper she has used? Could she not write me all the details of her wedding? *I* wasn't the one who told her never to come home. As if she does not know that I will always be waiting for her."

Then she had examined the photographs minutely, remarking over every detail, and when she had turned them over hoping to see a few more lines that Maya had scribbled there, she found only a date. "At least she could have said, 'Dear Mamma, this is your son-in-law,' no? One line is so much trouble for her?" she said bitterly. "Hard and unforgiving. Just like you, ree, just like you."

She had framed the picture taken outside the marriage registrar's building and placed it on the window ledge at the head of their bed. Sripathi avoided looking at it and frequently knocked it over so that it lay flat on its face. He had forced himself to write to Mr. Bhat, who replied with a curt note asking him to return the diamond jewellery and the saris that he had given Maya. That letter had hurt Sripathi. As if he would have kept all those things, he thought miserably, aware that he had lost a friend thanks to his daughter. He made a trip to Madras one Saturday, and, to his humiliation, Mr. Bhat had made him stand outside on the verandah like a servant. He did not even offer him a glass of cold water, despite it being a hot day and the fact that Sripathi had travelled for three hours on the bus. Then to add to it all, the man had opened the box of jewellery and checked it carefully, deliberately, before disappearing indoors without saying a word. That was it. No questions, no conversation. It was as if the years when Mr. Bhat had visited Big House, chatting for hours about politics and cricket and their children, exclaiming over Nirmala's cooking, had never happened at all. And later, cringing at the memory of that silent meeting, Sripathi had sent the man a money order for half the expenses incurred for the engagement ceremony. He had his pride, and nobody would take that away from him. He had had to borrow from Raju for that, the first time he had taken money from his old friend. Another embarrassment, all thanks to Maya.

Now Maya started to write frequently. She had got over her initial anger and addressed her envelopes to Mr. and Mrs. Sripathi Rao, as before. At first Nirmala tried to get Sripathi to read the letters, but when he tore them up without opening them, she stopped. He knew when each one arrived, though, for everyone in the house would read and discuss it, stopping as soon as he entered the room. Even Ammayya was part of the conspiracy to keep Maya alive in the house. Sometimes there would be a new set of photographs on the windowsill or on the dining table. He never looked at those either. Only once more was he obliged to read his daughter's handwriting. And that was two years after her marriage.

A large, official-looking envelope had arrived, and out of it had spilled several photographs of a newborn infant. Nirmala had been delirious with joy. "I am a grandmother," she told everyone. "My granddaughter's name is Nandana. Isn't it a pretty name?" Then tears followed the smiles. "She should have come home to me. How can a girl have her child without her mother to spoil her during her pregnancy?" She had turned to Sripathi and said, "Please stop being so stubborn, ree. How can you hold on to your kongu for so long? Be so unforgiving? I know why you are upset. It's your stupid ego. Maya did something without asking for your lordship's permission, and you can't stand that, no? Now at least you have an opportunity to forgive and forget. We are grandparents."

And he had replied in his most sarcastic voice, "Oh, now we have a great psychologist in our house! Dr. Nirmala Rao knows what everybody is thinking and feeling! My goodness, I never knew that I was married to such a perspicacious woman!"

Nirmala stopped trying to persuade him, and he gained a remote pleasure from the knowledge that he had got under her skin by using a word she did not understand.

She had framed one photograph of the baby for the windowsill, and the rest she kept under her pillow for months. Sripathi had not been able to resist a quick look at Nandana's baby face. She didn't in the least resemble her mother, he told himself, and as usual placed the picture face down. When the child was about a year old, Maya had sent a sheaf of legal documents and a letter asking Sripathi and Arun to be the trustees and executors of her will. She also asked if they would be her daughter's legal guardians, in the event that it ever became necessary.

"Why is she writing such ill-omened things?" Nirmala wanted to know. "We are so much older and *we* don't have a will-shill, nothing." But she had insisted that Sripathi read and sign the documents, even though he did not want to have anything to do with Maya. "It is your duty to that innocent baby. She is your grandchild, whatever you feel towards your daughter."

When Sripathi maintained his stubborn refusal to even touch the documents, Nirmala went to Raju's house. "Please talk to your friend. He does not listen to me at all. Raju-orey, put some sense into his head."

Sripathi was furious. He saw this trusteeship as an attempt by Maya to force herself back into his life. But he signed the documents nevertheless. As Nirmala had pointed out, it was his duty. He would never avoid doing his duty, even though Maya had no compunctions about ignoring hers.

———

On her last visit Nandana had crawled into her mother's closet. The clothes had smelled sweet: the white silky blouse that she wore when she had a meeting; the special black pants and the regular brown ones; the sleeveless yellow cotton shirt that her father said made her mother look like a sun drop. She sat silent as a mouse inside the closet, hoping that Aunty Kiran would leave without her. She spotted a spider creeping across the floor, towards the door and the light outside. Stupid spider, she thought and crushed it under her shoe. Dead, she told it. You are dead. Then she waited for Aunty Kiran to call her name.

7

JOURNEY

───────────

S RIPATHI WAS SO DEEP in thought that he almost missed Raju's house with its large, scrolled gates that hung open on rusty hinges. This road, too, had changed a lot, although it still had the rows of gnarled caesalpinia trees. Here, too, were piles of sand, concrete, stones and bricks, and new apartment buildings squeezed into spaces that had previously been occupied by single homes.

Raju Mudaliar was Sripathi's oldest friend. The two of them had attended St. Aloysius School when they were small boys, and although their fathers were on opposite sides of the legal fence and therefore fierce adversaries, their own friendship had prospered. Sripathi always believed that Raju had a lucky streak running through his horoscope. It was always Raju who found the only seat in a crowded bus to school or came upon a twenty-five paise coin on the dusty street. In school, he seemed to come first in class without any effort. The evening before an exam, while Sripathi sat at his father's desk frantically memorizing tables and formulae, Raju would play cricket with the street boys until dusk, going home only when his mother sent a servant to call him for dinner. When Father Gonsalves conducted a surprise quiz in geography, Raju managed to score better than anyone else in the class, even though he swore that he'd spent the previous evening playing.

"Tell me your secret formula," Sripathi had asked him admiringly a dozen times.

"I don't have any formula. I just don't take anything as seriously as you do. If you tell yourself it doesn't matter whether you come first or second or fortieth in class, you will end up a champ."

"It doesn't matter to *me*," said Sripathi glumly. "It's my mother who thinks I am the future prime minister of India and my father who wants me to be a Supreme Court Justice."

"What do you want to be?"

"A loafer like you," Sripathi had declared.

How ironic it was that for all the studying that his parents had made him do, he had ended up neither a prime minister nor a judge but a struggling copywriter, while Raju became the head of an important research organization. For a while it seemed to Sripathi that his friend had everything Ammayya wanted for her own son—power, prestige, wealth, a chauffeur-driven car, even a school allowance for his children in case he wanted to put them in one of the posh residential schools such as Lawrence, Mayo College or Rishi Valley.

Raju's first son was born a year before Maya, and two years later a second son arrived, at almost the same time as Arun. Nirmala and Raju's wife, Kannagi, had spent many hours comparing notes on their pregnancies and exchanging recipes for food to ensure that the child was healthy, grumbling good-naturedly about their husbands all the while. And then the Mudaliars had their third child, Ragini. How pleased Raju was when she was born—two sons and a daughter, what more could he ask? But within six months, Kannagi noticed that the child would not lift her head or turn like other babies her age. Her eyes did not focus and she did not respond to voices. Perhaps she was a bit slower than her sons had been, thought Kannagi, and kept her observations from her husband. But by the time the baby was a year old, it was obvious that something was wrong. Ragini had prolonged seizures that left her limp and exhausted.

Sripathi could still remember the day Raju had told him that the child's brain was damaged and could not be cured. Gone was his friend's smile and the cheerful assurance that nothing in the world could be so bad as to wipe that smile off his face.

"What can I say, Sri," his friend had remarked suddenly over one of their weekly chess games. They had made it a ritual to meet over the chessboard each Friday evening in Raju's spacious home. "My poor little Ragini, all her life she is going to be like this." Sripathi was aware that they had been making frequent trips to specialists in Madras, Bangalore and even Bombay, and although he was curious, he did not want to ask. If Raju needed to confide in him, he would, in his own good time. There were some things even the best of friends did not share. "Nothing is wrong with her body. It is her mind. There is nothing that can be done for her—no medicines, no operations, no magic cures. That bastard God up there must have decided: 'This bloke is laughing and smiling too much. Give him a taste of something nasty.' I must have been a murdering rogue in my last life, and now I am paying for it."

That was the first and last time that Sripathi ever heard his friend sound so dejected. Thereafter, with his usual energy, he had decided to deal with his daughter's disability as best he could. "No point grumbling," he had told Sripathi the next time they met. "It isn't going to solve anything. This is our karma and we will have to live with it." He had looked at Sripathi and smiled sadly. "Never thought you would hear me talk about karma and all, eh? Like that old crook Krishnamurthy Acharye? Remember how he used to make us put one rupee each into the plate at the temple, to avoid the weight of our wickedness landing on our shoulders? And of course the money went straight into his own greedy pockets."

"And I used to be terrified, while you never cared. That crooked old priest is still going strong, you know. He runs an empire, from what I have heard. Still in his filthy dhoti and stained shirt, and stinking like a drain, but rich as Lord Kubera." Sripathi laughed at the thought of the temple priest who had predicted such a brilliant (and unrealized) future for him, and who now presided over a company of priests and cooks like some business tycoon.

Raju's wife died when their daughter was about fifteen years old. A succession of maids came and went, for the girl needed complete attention. She had to be fed, washed and cleaned at regular intervals. One by one, Raju's sons finished their education and left the house. The older son moved to California and the younger to Switzerland. Neither came back to see their father or sister. They wrote frequently, and Raju showed Sripathi his older son's letter informing him of his marriage.

"*Dear Appu,*" wrote the boy at the end of the letter, "*please understand that my wife knows nothing of our tragedy. I have told her that you are too ill to come for the ceremony and do not like visitors either.*"

"See, he is so ashamed of his family he cannot even refer to us by name. Ragini is his sister, not 'our tragedy,'" said Raju bitterly.

When Sripathi entered his friend's house he could hear Raju's voice murmuring gently to Ragini. It was almost noon, so probably feeding time. After a succession of maids had come and gone, Raju left his job and took over his daughter's care himself.

Sripathi took off his slippers and followed the old maid-cum-cook, Poppu, who had been a part of the family for thirty years, into the cavernous dining room with its huge teak table and carved chairs, made to seat at least twenty people. It hadn't been used for years, and half of it was covered with dust. Poppu didn't see any point in cleaning the whole thing when only two chairs and a quarter of the table top were used.

"Hello, hello, Sri. What a surprise!" Raju stopped feeding his daughter for a few moments. "What are you doing roaming around in the heat, and at this time of day? Shall I ask Poppu to make you some cold lemonade?"

As always, Sripathi felt faintly embarrassed, even revolted, by the sight of Ragini, a big woman like her mother had been, but with no awareness of her ungainly body, which had galloped into maturity at the expense of her brain. He hated himself for his feelings, as if he was somehow betraying Raju, and so he forced himself to look at the girl. She lolled in one of the chairs, her head drooping to one side, her fleshy mouth opening and closing like a sea anemone as her father spooned food into it and then gently wiped away the trickle of spit and food that escaped from one corner. Her hair stuck out in spikes all over her head, and Sripathi suspected that it had been sheared at home by Raju and Poppu. She wore a voluminous frock of the kind that Raju ordered from Tailor Nataraj on Theatre Street by the dozen every two years, all stitched from the same bale of red-and-blue-checked cloth. When her mother was alive, Sripathi remembered that she used to dress Ragini well, discussing patterns of frocks with Nirmala and going on shopping sprees to Bangalore to buy fabric and lace, buttons and ribbons. The girl's deep brown eyes fixed on Sripathi, and he felt uneasily that she was trying to communicate with him.

"What ma, how are you?" he asked gently, forcing himself to pat her bristly head.

She groaned and jerked an arm, nearly knocking the bowl of food from her father's hands.

"See, she recognizes you," laughed Raju. "Don't you my child? Uncle Sri is here to play chess with Appu. So you finish your food quickly, okay?"

"How are you, Raju?" asked Sripathi. He pulled out one of the chairs and sat carefully on the once-splendid seat which, like everything else in the house, was covered with a sheet of cloth to keep it from getting dusty.

"How am I? Fine as ever, and ready to defeat you today, my dear fellow," said Raju smiling at him. "I can feel victory in my bones! But aren't you early? Took chhutti from work? Is everything all right?"

"No, not really," Sripathi said and paused. How could he put the dreadful news into words without damaging himself?

Raju looked up sharply at the hesitation. "What is wrong?"

"My daughter," Sripathi said baldly. "She is dead. And her husband too. I received the news a few hours ago."

There was a stunned silence. Then he forced himself to repeat the details of that awful phone call. And as he unburdened himself, he felt a sense of relief that he hadn't felt when he had told Nirmala and Ammayya, Putti and Arun. Perhaps he drew strength from Raju, who had managed to keep despair at bay, even though it stared him in the face every waking day.

"How is Nirmala doing?" Raju asked.

"She is very upset, she blames me for everything. Do *you* think it is my fault, Raju?"

"No, how can you be responsible for something that happened in another country?"

Sripathi gazed consideringly at his friend's thin, dark face, the sparse, grey hair neatly combed away from his forehead and the small moustache perched over a mouth now bracketed by deep lines. "But you also think, like my wife, that I should have written to her all these years, right? Come on, be honest, man!"

"You know what I think. I have repeated it often enough," said Raju, wiping Ragini's mouth one last time before nodding to Poppu to take her away. "Yes, I think you were stupid and childish to cut off your daughter. Yes, I think you should have at least allowed her to come home when she had a child. Here I am, yearning to see my sons, to meet my grandchildren, and you . . ." Raju shook his head and stood up.

"So, you are also against me?" demanded Sripathi, hurt by his friend's words.

"I am not for or against you, man. This is not a war. You asked me what I feel, and I am answering your questions."

"But she made a fool of me, don't you see that? Do you know

how humiliated I felt when I went to Mr. Bhat's house to return all those gifts? Do you realize how much she shamed me? It was okay for her to do whatever she wanted, with no thought for her family, right?"

Raju patted Sripathi's shoulder awkwardly. "What is the use thinking about all that now? It is over and done with. Too late to dissect and examine. Tell me, what is happening to the little girl? How old is she? Tchah-tchah-tchah! What a tragedy this is for her."

They moved from the shadowy dining room to the more cheerful lounge, where Raju spent most of his time now, reading an assortment of newspapers and magazines that Miss Chintamani reserved for him. He told Sripathi, with a wink, that he was sure the librarian had a soft spot for him. "She gives me these languishing looks, you know. I don't know why I can't attract any of the younger chickadees! Only these batty old ones that come running after me, tchah!"

Books rose in uneven piles from the floor next to Raju's favourite chair, and on the walls hung photographs of his family in their youth. His sons sent pictures frequently, but they stayed in their envelopes, thrust haphazardly inside drawers. A Hallicrafter's radiogram sat on a low cabinet, and Sripathi remembered how fascinated he had been as a boy with the lighted circular dial with its little markers for stations all over the world. Seychelles. London. San Salvador. French Guiana. USA. Australia. Ceylon. It was as if the entire world had somehow been stuffed into the pale brown body of the Hallicrafter and beckoned in so many languages to the listener. It seemed quite miraculous that the ancient machine still worked perfectly. On the shelf below sat Raju's pride and joy, a Bang & Olufsen record player with stacks of LPs, EPs and a few 75-rpm records. He turned on some soft music. Neither of them felt like playing chess, so they sat in silence for a while.

"What you need to do now," said Raju finally, "is concentrate on the child. It will be like bringing up your daughter all over again, think of that. This tragedy has given you the chance to redeem yourself. Take it with both hands."

"Oh, so you *do* think I need to redeem myself?" demanded Sripathi.

"Sripathi Rao, why are you bothered about what I or anybody else thinks? Ask yourself whether you did right or wrong by your daughter." Raju gave him an exasperated look that made Sripathi bristle.

He stood up in a huff and said, "I am going. I came here to get some rest from the tain-tain at home, but I only hear more of it here."

"Don't be silly, man. At least have lunch, or hunger will make you behave worse than you are now." Raju stood up as well and clapped Sripathi on the back. "I wouldn't be much of a friend to you if I told you only what you wanted to hear. Come on now, Poppu has made some bisi bele bhath. Can't you smell it?"

Sripathi allowed himself to be pacified. "Okay," he said gruffly. "But I will have to leave right after. Need to go to the travel agent and all. Lots of things to do. I am hoping that I can leave for Canada by the end of next week."

At Hansa Travels on Pyecroft Road, Sripathi realized that he didn't have a passport. He had never needed one in all his fifty-seven years of existence. Why would he when he had never left the country or even needed any identification in this town of his birth? Once, not long before Maya's departure, Sripathi and Nirmala had visited Mr. Bhat in Madras to talk about the details of the engagement ceremony. Later that evening, they had gone to the beach, and Sripathi had watched ships outlined against the seamless sky. He had wondered at the lives sailors led, unmoored, restless as the waters they sailed, always somewhere other than where they were born. What led those people to leave the familiar? What was it that had pulled his own daughter into the unknown world beyond the protective walls of home and family? Then, with some wistfulness, Sripathi had thought of his own rooted existence, and he had imagined visiting his daughter some time after Arun, too, was settled in a job, and when he had paid off his debts.

The travel agent, a thin, patronizing young man with a geyser of shiny black hair erupting over his forehead, refused to get down to business immediately. He was an inquisitive, officious man. On the narrow desk before him, a tray bristled with pens and pencils that he kept fondling continuously. Every now and then he stopped fiddling with the pens to snatch up the telephone and speak for a few minutes.

"Nateshan here!" he would bark, twirling a pencil or a pen between his fingers, his eyes fixed on something behind Sripathi's head. "Yes-yes. No problem, no problem. I am a very busy man, okay? I will phone afterwards. Okay."

All his conversations sounded the same. Sripathi suspected that he might only be pretending to speak to someone, just to give the impression of being busy. As soon as he hung up, he turned to Sripathi and gazed at him with what appeared to be astonishment, as if to say, Where did you turn up from?

Once again Sripathi explained his case, reiterating that he had no passport and that it was urgent that he leave as soon as possible.

The agent wagged his head and shook his legs. He ran a delicate hand over his quiff of hair and looked severely at Sripathi. "*Nobody* should be without a passport," he said finally.

"I didn't realize," admitted Sripathi humbly. He knew this type. You had to grovel a little to get help. "If you can help arrange a passport, I will be grateful."

The agent contemplated the mysterious spot behind Sripathi's head for a long moment. "Work-related or pleasure trip?" he asked suddenly.

"My daughter and her husband passed away." Absurdly enough, Sripathi was filled with the need to tell this stranger all about the long silence between him and Maya. "They were in a car accident."

He heard his own voice as if it were scraping its way out of a rusty tin. His legs started to shake. He crossed them quickly, alarmed by the sensation, by the fact that he couldn't seem to stop the quivering movement that had taken over his lower limbs.

The travel agent gave Sripathi his full attention now. "I am so sorry to hear. Very sorry. But I have heard about similar sudden deaths in foreign countries many times. Very sad and sudden. You know Mr. Jayaram on Car Bridge Road? His nephew was simply driving home from work on a highway in Pasadena, and suddenly a plane landed on his car. Can you imagine? Instant death, of course, what else? But the pilot of that plane survived. She was on all kinds of television shows, telling people that God had taken care of her. What about the poor fellow on whom she landed, that's what I want to know? Then there was another case . . . But why I am wasting your time? I will get you a passport, no problem. Extra charge, but."

Then the Canadian visa, which the agent said he could arrange for a further sum of money. He busied himself with the telephone again while Sripathi waited, trying to control his impatience.

"No problem. All correct and above board, okay?" he assured Sripathi, who gave him a doubtful look. Nothing these days was legal, as far as he knew.

"I don't indulge in hanky-panky, sir," said the agent, wagging his finger piously. "Honesty is the best policy." He blew out the *h* in honesty in a great gusty breath that made the papers on his desk flutter.

An hour later, after Sripathi had filled out an endless number of forms, he left the travel agency, relieved to find that his legs felt normal. He decided to stop at the Toturpuram Trust Company to see if he could borrow more money for the trip. The trust had been started by his grandfather and some of his friends to help out indigent Brahmin families and to give scholarships to their children, so that they could get that most precious of commodities—an education. Sripathi could remember the first time he had had to approach the trust with begging bowl in hand. It was soon after he had found a job. Large damp patches had developed along the edges of the ceilings in the upstairs bedrooms of Big House. The roof needed to be waterproofed immediately, and there was no money to do it. The humiliation of that visit to the trust would live with him for ever, he thought then, but that was before he became accustomed to begging.

"We hope that you will be more responsible than your father," the oldest of the trustees had said with a severe look at Sripathi from under his white eyebrows. He had never liked Narasimha Rao very much and relished this opportunity to take it out on the son. "If he had no earnings, we would have understood. Everyone in the world can't have Goddess Lakshmi sitting on their shoulders. But your father . . . tchah, tchah, tchah! He deliberately squandered all that God gave him."

The trust had given him the loan in memory of his grandfather, they had made that clear. But the interest rates were high—the burden of his father's follies were now on Sripathi's back. "You will collect punya this way," another member had told Sripathi, patting his back comfortingly. "Your children will benefit from your accumulation of good deeds." That old man was the one who had persuaded the rest of the trustees to extend more loans to Sripathi, and he was no longer alive. There was a new, youthful set of trustees now, not quite as willing to postpone his monthly payments. "This is a bank, sir," one of them had said, smoothing his trim moustache with a confident forefinger, "not your personal treasury. We cannot keep giving you extensions. This is a business, not a charity, I am sure you understand that."

Sripathi entered the old brick building that housed the trust with hesitant steps. There was a long mirror in the entrance corridor, and in it he noticed how his belly pushed like a child's bottom against the soft cotton of his ill-fitting old shirt and cratered gently around his navel. There were two dark semicircles of sweat staining the shirt under his arms, and he could feel it trickling down his back and into the waistband of his trousers. He wished that he had worn something nicer. He thought nervously about explaining the reasons for the loan to these people and wondered what he would do if they refused him. To his relief, once the trustees heard about Maya, they gave him the money without further ado. He sat there stunned for a few minutes, unable to believe that he had not had to grovel. And then he left quickly before the tears that prickled unexpectedly behind his eyes could fall on the wide, polished table that separated him from those solemn young men who led such neat lives.

When he emerged into the late afternoon heat, the rush hour had started. Shoals of school children in limp uniforms, with loaded backpacks or satchels, waited at bus stops. There were maamis with heavy silk saris in rich magentas, emeralds and purples on their way to the temple, the market or to their music groups, and young college girls in crushed cotton saris or salwar-kameez suits. Sripathi whipped past Iyengar Bakery on his scooter, its familiar blue-and-green lettering partially masked by sheets of plastic. It looked like Iyengar had finally yielded to market pressures—exerted by the sudden proliferation of bakeries in the area serving exotic things like pizza buns and doughnuts—and was doing up his tiny shop. He had even inserted advertisements in the paper, Sripathi had noticed.

A horn blasted insistently behind him. Sripathi peered into his mirror and saw a bus hot on his heels. It had a complicated licence number on its head—a series of letters followed by an illegible route number. The letters were the initials of the current chief minister of the state; an astrologer had said they were so powerfully good that they would ward off all accidents, but since the chief minister had several initials to her name, there was barely room for anything else. As a result, the number was sometimes omitted altogether or else painted on the side. The fact that nobody ever knew where they were going when they got into a bus became a regular excuse for lateness at offices around the town.

"Why are you late again today, Raman?"

"Very sorry, saar. Got into the wrong bus and it went off to the railway station, saar. Conductor himself did not know where the bus was going or what number it was."

It was true that not one bus had toppled over or crashed for some time. However, they were directly responsible for numerous other mishaps on the road, and on pavements where many a driver steered his vehicle when the road was too crowded for him to move as fast as he wanted, crushing vendors with their carts loaded with bananas, or a street astrologer who had neglected to foresee his own future, or a beggar who might have died in her sleep. But then the chief minister's initials were supposed to protect only the bus and its occupants, not every single person and dog and cow on the streets of Toturpuram.

Sripathi increased speed to get away from the bus, but the horn blasts followed close on his wheels. He glanced over his shoulder and caught sight of the driver grinning devilishly at him. Playing games, the stupid bastard. Sripathi edged into another lane and let the bus speed past. No use tangling with those bus buggers. They all thought themselves heroes, demi-gods immune to disaster. Ever since a local bus conductor had become a film star, the entire transport service had started acting smart, driving their buses like pumped-up cowboys, as if the roads were racetracks.

"Yay saar, you want to die or what?" screamed an auto-rickshaw fellow puttering close to Sripathi's scooter. In his anxiety to get away from the bus, Sripathi had veered into the path of the three-wheeler. He moved away and the auto took off, buzzing in and out of gaps in the frantic afternoon traffic like a crazy beetle. In the back of the tiny vehicle with its doorless openings on either side, the passengers, a pair of young women, held on to the canvas walls grimly, the movement of the auto turning their faces into vibrating jelly. One of them let go for a moment to grab a wing of her sari that was taking flight from the auto and, struggling to tuck it between her legs, nearly fell out.

In between lanes, at the site of some repair work temporarily abandoned by the municipality for lack of funds or inclination to work, a beggar had constructed a house with gunny sacks, sewer covers stolen from around the city, empty boxes that had once contained television sets, and even a pilfered sign board that said: *Private Property—Beware of Dog*. The last bit of the message had been scratched out and replaced with "Mr. S.S. Ishwaran, M.A. History, University of Kupparigunda."

Mr. Ishwaran himself stood outside his home, a small man with a disdainful expression on his face, as if he had nothing to do with the shack behind him. Now and again he lost his aloofness and screamed spectacular abuse at one of several naked children playing calmly in the middle of all the traffic, dashing after marbles among the churning wheels. On the ground near his feet lay a large stainless-steel bowl holding a few rupee coins. Inside the precarious shack squatted a hollow-cheeked woman, blowing softly at a coal fire, trying to coax it to life. Sripathi passed the man every day on his way to work and wondered whether he really had a Master's degree in History. If he did, look at where that degree had brought him! But such was life. Like those numberless buses, you never knew what you were getting into or where you were headed until the very end, and then it was too late to get off.

There was a momentary lull at the traffic lights when hundreds of vehicles came to a stop and waited, chugging and revving and roaring like impatient beasts. The policeman had taken advantage of the fact that the lights were working for a change and had abandoned his elevated chowki in the centre of the intersection in favour of a quick break at the nearby coffee shop. An emaciated woman had taken his place, her scrawny body draped in a ragged sari that fluttered wispily in the thin breeze, sometimes exposing a long, dry breast, an underarm or a thigh as weathered as a piece of driftwood. She swayed and jerked like an animated scarecrow, high above the traffic.

"She's mad," said a man on a scooter next to Sripathi's. "There are rumours that that policeman raped her daughter." The man had one child crouching between his feet on the front of the scooter and two more stacked like dishes on the pillion behind him.

Some urchins started to dance below the police chowki, crowing derisively up at the woman.

"Hutchee-hutchee, head full of hayseeds," they called.

The woman continued to sway, her body following the sad, disordered loops of her mind. A policeman emerged from the tea stall, his shirt gleaming white, his khaki trousers tight as drum skin against his crotch. He tapped his baton against the palm of his hand as he strolled through the pulsing traffic. He had an enormous moustache and a white Stetson hat. Until recently, traffic policemen wore turbans, but the latest chief minister had a passion for Hollywood westerns that she indulged by insisting on a change of uniform for the entire police force. She would have liked to replace the official jeeps with horses, but the municipal commissioner had objected.

"As it is we spend our time cleaning cow dung and human dung from the roads of the town, now we will have to pick up horseshit too!" he was reported to have said. "Too much, too much, this nonsense is. We will organize a sweepers' strike and then we will see about horses!"

"Look, she is directing traffic while you drink coffee, saar," shouted one of the urchins, dancing nimbly out of the way before the policeman could land a slap on his head.

The man set his hat at a more dignified angle, rapped the baton against his thigh and glared up at the woman. "You there, get down," he ordered.

The woman stopped swaying and gazed emptily down at him.

"Now itself, get down I say!" The baton pointed imperiously at the ground.

"Downdowndown!" carolled the woman, and in one fluid movement she lifted her rags and thrust a scraggy pubic patch at the policeman.

"Pappa, I saw her shame-shame-puppy-shame," giggled the child on the scooter next to Sripathi. His father thumped him on the back and shoved his head down frantically with one hand, at the same time trying to shield the two little girls behind him by leaning sideways. The scooter teetered unsteadily, and all the children screamed.

"What is this country coming to?" he remarked, smiling apologetically at Sripathi as if he were responsible for the whole absurd show.

The lights changed and the traffic streamed forward, leaving the woman leaping around in the tight circle of the police chowki, butting her skeletal bottom out at the world.

The sea breeze set in just as he entered Brahmin Street. For a happy moment he thought that the sudden drop in temperature heralded a burst of rain. He passed the egg stand—one of several set up all over town by the local government in an attempt to help the handicapped become self-supporting—and Viji, the legless woman who ran it, waved to him. She waved to everybody who passed, cheery as the bright yellow, egg-shaped stand that she ran. Recently Sripathi had discovered that the egg stand was actually leased out to Munnuswamy his neighbour, who with his usual political connections had cornered the market on egg stands. People like Viji were obliged to rent the stand from him at usurious rates.

With the cooling drift of air came the stench of sewage from open drains, and Sripathi blanched. Why not just the breeze without the odour? It seemed to him that everything good in the world came with an edging of the not-so-good. He reached the Krishna Temple, and the stink of sewage was replaced by the sweet scent of a thousand jasmines from the row of flower stalls near the gates. The deep clang of bells filled the air, and this time, instead of irritating him, soothed his tired brain. He passed Balaji, who didn't seem to have moved from his post outside the gates of his apartment building.

"Hello, you are still here?" Sripathi asked.

Balaji smiled back and pointed at the rubble in front of Sripathi's gate. "Mess! Total mess!" he remarked with the air of an Archimedes saying "Eureka."

"I know," said Sripathi gloomily. "Too much construction work. Maybe I should sell and live in an apartment like everybody."

"Oho? You are thinking of selling?"

"Maybe. Then you will be happy? No more loans to sanction for me?" asked Sripathi with a slight smile.

"Why for *I* should feel happy-sad for Sripathi-orey? I am simply an employee of the bank following bank rules and regulations. If I could, I would grant loans to everybody who came to me," said Balaji. He looked gratified by his own magnanimous instincts. "But really speaking, are you selling?"

Sripathi shrugged. "There are so many problems you know. Especially with the water. All these apartment buildings . . ."

"Naturally," nodded Balaji. "Hundreds of people flushing and bathing and brushing teeth and all. But you don't have a well?"

"Yes we do, but the water is brackish."

There was a pause while Balaji diligently scoured out his nose. He had apparently decided to clean all his orifices out in the open. A dry run before his bath thought Sripathi, disgusted.

"How much?" demanded Balaji suddenly.

"What?"

"For how much are you wanting to sell?"

"I don't know. I will have to check the market rate," said Sripathi stiffly.

"My brother is looking for property in this area," said Balaji. "He is in construction business. He will give you a good rate if you want. Straight cash, no problem."

Sripathi could feel his temper rising. Why should this obnoxious, nose-digging, supercilious bastard's relatives stay in my house? he thought. Dirty crooks in my ancestral home! He controlled his rage and forced himself to smile.

"I will inform you if I decide to sell it, Balaji," he said.

He squeezed through the blocked gate of his house, still simmering over Balaji's suggestion. Jackals, he thought. Vultures. Feasting on other people's troubles and sorrows.

Over the low compound wall, he spotted his neighbour Munnuswamy stroking his cow and singing a song from an old film. The calf was lying on the ground. It looked sickly, thought Sripathi. But what did he know about animals, perhaps all calves looked like that. Munnuswamy heard him approaching his verandah and stopped him. "Sripathi Rao, I heard about your child," he said. "So sorry. If there is anything I can do to help, don't hesitate to ask. I remember your daughter from when she was this high." He gestured towards his knees.

Sripathi nodded and sat on the rickety old cane chair on the verandah to remove his shoes. How quickly Maya had become a memory in people's minds. Such was the power of death—to strip away breath and transform a person into an airy abstraction.

From inside the house came the tap-tapping sound of Nirmala's baton and her fractured humming. He had forgotten that she had her dance class today. She must not have had time to cancel the class, and the students had arrived as usual at four o'clock.

"Not that way," he heard her say to one of the students. "You are Rama, the noble king, the hero. Walk with dignity. Walk with courage and humility. Lift your head high. And you are Ravana. He, too, is a great king, but his walk is that of a braggart. A man who is too proud and therefore not heroic."

The texture of her words surprised Sripathi. He had not known that she had such language within her homely head. He did not know either where she had summoned the strength to say anything to those children stamping the darkness of the room away with their sparkling, electric youth.

Later that night, after a silent dinner during which even Ammayya was preoccupied and quiet, Sripathi went up to his bedroom and found that Nirmala had removed her pillow from their bed. He could hear her talking in low tones in Arun's room and knew that she had made up the spare bed there for herself. Ganging up, he thought indignantly, mother and son ganging up against me—as if I care. Silly woman, she thought that he cared where she slept. Hah, it felt good to have the whole bed to himself. He flung his legs apart and stretched his arms wide. Deep within his heart a thick skein of anger unravelled against Nirmala and Arun and Putti and Ammayya, against his dead father and Maya. Especially Maya, for keeping him a stranger to his own grandchild, for disappearing from their lives as completely as she had. He had forced himself to forget his daughter's betrayal, for that was how he regarded her marriage, the life she had chosen for herself. It was true that it was he who had told her never to come home, who had refused to reply to her letters or her phone calls, but by dying she had stolen from him the opportunity to forgive and be forgiven.

Sripathi tossed and turned in his bed. His eyes felt dry and stretched, but when he tried to shut them he could not. Sleep, too, had abandoned him. There was a low murmur of voices from Arun's room, and he jealously strained to hear what they said.

But soon even those sounds died, and all he could hear was the insistent call of a nightingale from his ruined garden.

Her window was open to let in the warm summer air. It was the twentieth of August. It was fifteen days since the Old Man had arrived and two since they had moved from Aunty Kiran's house to

Nandana's. She was supposed to stay in Anjali's house while the Old Man packed everything, but once again she had stood near the car when they were leaving, refusing to move until Aunty Kiran had said, "Oh well, let her go too. Poor baby, no need to upset her about little things like this." Then she looked at Nandana and said, "All right, you can help your grandpa pack. Okay?"

No *way* would Nandana allow the Old Man to touch her things, but she nodded because she was in a hurry to go home.

Feet climbed the stairs. Nandana jumped into bed and pulled the sheets over her head. The Old Man was coming up and she did not want him to find her. He just stared with eyes big behind his glasses and did not say anything most of the time. Sometimes he opened his mouth when he looked at her, but not a word came out. He had brought her a present from India—three comic books with pictures of animals that talked to each other. They were folk tales from India, Aunty Kiran told her, and asked the Old Man if he would like to read one aloud to the kids, but Nandana had run out of the room. She did not want anyone to tell her stories but her own father.

8

SHADES
OF BLUE

F OR HIS TRIP, Sripathi had borrowed a suitcase from Raju
as well as a coat, uncertain how cold it would be in that faraway country. Nirmala dropped her stiff veil of silence and
helped him pack. She insisted he abandon his tired old sandals for
a pair of black Bata shoes that he had bought for Maya's engagement and had never worn since. She had also made him wear a pale
blue shirt she had purchased from Beauteous Boutique.

"Why are you dressing me up like a bridegroom?" He was
annoyed that she had spent even more money on this trip.

"You are going to meet our granddaughter for the first time,"
Nirmala argued, "and you want to go in that wretched checked
shirt of yours? Why you insist on keeping that shirt, I don't know.
Even our dhobi wears nicer clothes!"

"Maybe I can ask *him* to lend me a fancy shirt for my foreign
trip," Sripathi grumbled. He was secretly pleased that Nirmala was
back to normal.

"Shameless! You will do it, I know. So crazy you behave sometimes! Now stop making such a big fuss for every little thing. What will
those friends of Maya's think if you land up looking like a chaprassi?
Henh? And you have to meet all those Canadian government people

also. They will say, Who is this crazy old beggar? and refuse to let you bring our Nandana back."

In his pocket Sripathi carried a bolo tie with an elaborate silver butterfly clinging to a fat blade of grass. He had worn it when he left Toturpuram just to please Ammayya, who had given it to him. "Be careful with it," she had said. "This is pure *argentum*, not some cheap metal." She was under the impression that all Americans wore bolo ties and cowboy boots and chewed gum, and her son had to fit in, even if it was only for a month and a half. She had also heard about black people getting shot and beaten up there, and although anyone could see that her Sripathi was as fair as the queen of England, there was no point taking a chance and standing out like a sore thumb. She didn't know where to find cowboy boots, but the bolo tie had belonged to Narasimha and was genuinely American. Sripathi tried telling his mother that he was not going to the United States but to Canada, but it was quite useless. In Ammayya's somewhat limited world, there were only three countries— England, America and India. Pakistan and Bangladesh (which she still called East Bengal) did not count as countries because, as far she was concerned, India's Partition was a mistake that never happened, Jawaharlal Nehru was a womanizing fool like her own husband (God take care of his soul) and Gandhi was a traitor to decent Brahmin sentiments with his all-men-including-untouchables-are-equal nonsense. If Ammayya did not acknowledge Partition, it had not occurred.

Three weeks later, Sripathi had arrived in Vancouver dazed by the sensation of flying, of being unmoored from the earth after fifty-seven years of being tied to it. His back ached from sitting in the narrow seat for so long. His feet were blistered and exhausted from being enclosed in the new leather of his shoes. And he was afraid of what he would feel when he saw the child.

When Sripathi tried to think back on that trip, his first one abroad, he recollected very little. He had been received by Dr.

Sunderraj and stayed in his house for the first week. Then he had asked if he could move to Maya's home and to his surprise, the child had insisted on going with him. All day, though, except on weekends, she went to day camp, and he was left alone in the blue house. He was relieved when Kiran offered to stop by every evening and help with the packing and with clearing the house of clothes and furniture and utensils. She had also stocked the fridge with food for a week—orange-lidded boxes with curries and rice dishes that he merely needed to heat in the microwave. He was grateful for the food because he knew no cooking, had never even boiled a kettle of water.

During his month and a half in Vancouver, he had met no one, even though he might have at least got in touch with friends of Maya and Alan. He went nowhere, intimidated by the strangeness of the city, its silence and its towering beauty. He wanted no part of the place where his daughter had breathed her last. All that he carried back with him was a misty memory of rain and lush greenness, of things growing endlessly—enormous trees, brilliant flowers, leaves as large as dinner plates—a fecundity he found impossible to bear. He did remember, in painful detail, the blue house with polished wooden floors and large windows that Kiran Sunderraj had opened to let in the damp, clear air of the city. The air reeked of the life that coursed through the masses of plants outside, and the shrubs bowed down with the weight of their lacy, blue flowers. On his first day there, he had sat by the window and listened to a baby wail in the house next door. A young female voice had soothed it. A group of cyclists had gone by, laughing and chattering, their muscular legs encased in tight shorts, their arms bare and healthy. There were long periods when nobody passed, and all that he could hear was the sound of rain on the leaves. Sripathi had wanted to shut it all out, and as soon as Kiran left him and the child alone for the day, he had closed every single window, except for the ones in the girl's room. She had shut herself in and didn't answer when he knocked hesitantly.

The walls of the house were painted in different shades of blue. Whose favourite colour had it been, he wondered: Alan's or Maya's? As a young woman in Toturpuram, Maya had favoured bright colours—reds, pinks, yellows, greens. In most of the photographs that Maya sent home, though, she appeared to be wearing either black or white clothes, or occasionally a red T-shirt. But people were like trees, they grew and changed, put out new leaves that you forgot to count, and when you weren't watching, they even died.

There were framed prints on some of the walls, a mask of some sort, small shelves full of knick-knacks. And photographs—dozens of them—of Maya, Alan, Nandana. A record of their lives, special moments, joyous ones: at Nandana's school on her first day; on a long stretch of road graced by soaring mountains, Maya's hair whipped into chaos by the wind, her smile caught forever in happiness; Alan, tall and friendly-looking, with Nandana perched on his shoulders, her small hands clutching his fair hair. My son-in-law, thought Sripathi miserably. Curly-haired, laughing, a student of philosophy, the man who had married his daughter and made her happy.

This was the house where his daughter had once lived and that he had sold off to some stranger. The furniture was taken out by more strangers—the dining-table suite, desks, chairs, a computer, cupboards and a large chair that slid forward and backward like an opening drawer. The child had been upset when the chair left the house. She had sat on it, mute, and refused to get up. Dr. Sunderraj had lifted her off while Sripathi watched, helpless, not knowing the reason for her agitation. She had bawled, too—large tears rolling one after another down her face, her thin chest heaving violently, her fists clenched—when a buyer had carried a chest of drawers from her room. She was losing all that was familiar and beloved, thought Sripathi. He wished then that he could promise her that everything would be all right. He had even reached out to pat her shoulder, to tell her that she would be okay—he was going to take her home to India—but the child had shrunk away from him. What was going on in that small head? he wondered, observing the rejection in those dark eyes. Her mother's eyes. Large, black, depthless. Did she hate him? She must have questions about him—a grandfather who had appeared out of the blue in a brand-new crumpled shirt, bought especially for the trip from Beauteous Boutique. Had she even heard of Toturpuram, a small town halfway across the world from Vancouver—a town particularly known for its spectacular sunrise—where her mother had been born, and several generations born before her? Did Maya ever speak about him, about Nirmala and Arun and Ammayya and Putti, and the ancient house on Brahmin Street?

His daughter's daughter. An orphan. What an ugly word that was. A child bereaved of parents. "Bereft of previous protection or advantages," to quote *The Concise Oxford Dictionary*. Sripathi had looked up the word soon after Dr. Sunderraj's call in July.

"She has stopped talking," Dr. Sunderraj had told him on the evening of his arrival. His soft Canadian voice retained no trace of India. He had yielded to a new citizenship, thought Sripathi. First you change the way you dress, then your hair, your manners, your accent. Abracadabra, zippo, zippa: a new person stands before you. Had Maya's accent changed as well, from Madrasi spice to Canadian ice? Sripathi cringed at his play with words. Long years as a copywriter could reduce even sorrow to a jingle.

"We think it is the shock and only a temporary thing," continued Dr. Sunderraj.

"What?" Sripathi had been unable to remember where the conversation had begun. It seemed to be happening to him all the time, this distracted state, as if his mind had decided to stop listening altogether, to stop responding to any kind of stimulus.

"Nandana does not say a word, as you might have noticed," repeated the doctor patiently. "She is normally a very talkative child, you know, so this silence is unusual. However, these things are to be expected. Such a big shock. And one never knows how children may react."

He stayed in the blue house for a week, packing the things he thought he should take back to India—Maya's books as keepsakes for the child, photographs, letters, papers, a pair of gold bangles and two pairs of earrings. Another pair of tiny gold bangles that he recognized immediately. They had been a gift from Ammayya to his daughter when she turned one. Nirmala must have sent them somehow for Nandana's first birthday. He discarded the clothes last of all, his heart breaking at the sight of the neat shelves and drawers full of shirts, trousers and underwear, the three saris with their matching blouses and petticoats in plastic covers. He remembered the dark green, Mysore-crêpe silk sari with the edging of gold mangos—he had gone with Nirmala to the big new emporium in Toturpuram to buy that for Maya's sixteenth birthday. How astonished he was when his daughter wore it for the first time, her slender figure suddenly taller and more grown-up in the softly draped material, her face shy and expectant. He had not known what to say, his throat suddenly blocked by a surfeit of emotion—joy at her youthful beauty, and sorrow that she was almost an adult. "Appu, how do I look?" she had asked, holding out her thin arms, and the illusion of maturity had disappeared. She had gone back to being a gawky teenager dressed up in a pretty sari.

"Your mother should have listened to me and bought the pink one," he had said.

Her face had fallen, and she had dropped her arms. "I don't look nice?"

"Did I say that?"

And she had turned away and run down the stairs clumsily, lifting the sari high so that it bunched around her knees.

Later on Nirmala had scolded him. "What is wrong with you? She says that you told her she didn't look nice in that new sari. How beautiful she looked, why you told her things like that?"

"She is too young to wear saris. And that colour makes her look like Miss Chintamani," he had said, feeling guilty.

"Rubbish. *You* are the one who is like that library miss—always finding fault with everything and everyone." Nirmala had turned her back and refused to speak to him, and Maya had never worn that sari again.

Carefully, he removed the three saris from their plastic bags and placed them in the suitcase. Those were the only items of clothing that he would take back with him. He decided to wash a pile of clothes abandoned in a laundry basket, even though Kiran had told him she would do it on the weekend. He felt small enough taking so much from the Sunderraj family. Surely he could wash a pile of clothes himself before adding them to the bags meant for the Salvation Army? It took him a while to figure out the washing machine, and when he asked the child for help, she looked sullenly at him but did not reply. She also refused to let him give away two jackets belonging to her parents. She snatched them from him and raced up the stairs, dragging the heavy red and grey jackets behind her, tripping over them as she went. When Sripathi followed her, cautioning her to be careful, she turned around and glared, her eyes as wild as a cornered animal's, and he had backed down the stairs. She wouldn't let him pack her things either, stuffing them into garbage bags that she lined up against one wall of her empty room. In the end, Kiran Sunderraj had persuaded her to transfer all those toys and clothes and books into suitcases and boxes. But the child continued to regard Sripathi with suspicion, even hostility, and he gave up any attempts to make conversation with her. For the entirety of his stay, there was nothing between them but a deepening silence.

A month after his arrival, the Social Services Department gave him permission to take the child to India. Her visitors' visa had been acquired from the Indian High Commission on Homer Street in one miraculous week, thanks again to Dr. Sunderraj's innumerable contacts. He and Kiran had done more than most people would have. They had taken over all the legal formalities concerning the deaths, or as many as they were allowed to deal with. Dr. Sunderraj had also completed most of the preliminary paperwork concerning the child.

"Nandana is officially a ward of the state in the absence of any close relatives," the man had explained over the phone before Sripathi's trip. "However, I have some contacts in Immigration and Social Services. They have agreed to let us keep her, as we are long-time family friends and as Alan's parents are no longer alive. We placed an ad in the papers, but apparently he was an only child. Just an aunt in Idaho who doesn't want the responsibility. Some cousins also, but they thought that it was better for Nandu to be with us—we are familiar faces, you see. Your granddaughter is welcome to stay as long as necessary. But she needs her own people, and the sooner you arrive, the better."

At the airport, where they waited to catch their flight back to India, the child continued to be taciturn and silent. In one hand Sripathi carried a small red suitcase. He had deliberately kept the other hand free, assuming that the child would hold it the way Maya used to when she was seven years old. She did not. He offered to take her backpack that bulged oddly and seemed heavy, but she ignored him. And she looked with deep suspicion at a Mars bar that Sripathi held out to her. Sripathi decided to humour her, although he could feel his temper rising at her intractability.

He glanced down as she trotted silently beside him, her arms folded out of reach behind her back. The child had drawn an unsteady line of kohl under her eyes and looked like a raccoon. She chewed steadily on something. Munchmunchmunchmunch. A bubble grew out of her mouth like a swollen membrane. She wore ragged jeans and a sagging black T-shirt with the word *WHY?* inscribed on it in hot pink. Kiran had laid out a different set of clothes for her, he remembered, but the child had decided to be

difficult, it seemed. Sripathi noticed that her knees, which pro-
truded through holes in her ragged jeans, were scratched and dry,
bony childlike hillocks absurdly at odds with her swaggering look.
Earlier on, Sripathi had seen a drawing on one knee, a man with a
wild moustache and a large mole on his forehead. Had the child
done it herself, or was it a tattoo like the ones on the arms of those
wandering, dirty Lambani women who lived on his street in Toturpuram? Sripathi had heard that tattooing was fashionable in these
foreign countries. And her hair, what on earth had she done to it,
for God's sake? A mass of fierce black curls surged out of her scalp,
with beads strung in rows here and there. A few strands were inex-
pertly braided. She had not allowed Kiran to comb her hair either.
It must have been something that Maya used to do for the child.
Like Nirmala had done for her. Sripathi had a sudden memory of
Nirmala seated on the verandah, Maya held firmly between her
knees, grumbling and squirming as her mother braided her thick
tresses—Nirmala with her mouth full of pins and ribbons, her muffled voice telling Maya to stop fidgeting, as her hands swiftly
combed out the knots and snarls.

Sripathi found their gate and took a seat. Nandana drifted
slowly away, looking once over her shoulder at him, and stopped
near the far window of the lounge. She pressed her nose to the
glass, her rucksack pulling her shoulders backwards and stretching
out her thin neck like a chicken's. Too thin, thought Sripathi, her
collarbones barely covered with flesh, her skin a pale translucent
brown, like milk with a dash of honey. He was sure he could even
see the faint tracery of blue veins beside her eyes. She didn't eat
properly. Was she afraid of putting on weight? Did children care
about those things? He couldn't remember how it had been with
Maya. Had she been fussy about eating food because she thought
she would get fat? He realized he had not known his daughter's
inner life, the secret world of dreams and fears, the complexes and
affectations that follow children through their youth, eventually

hardening into dead weights. How had she grown up in the same house for twenty years, right under his nose? She had turned from a beloved child—who held his little finger while crossing the road, who wept with worry if he did not come home at exactly six in the evening—into a person he did not know.

The intercom in the airport lounge came alive, and everybody sat up. The elderly and people with infants were invited to start boarding. Sripathi gathered his bags and glanced at the child, hoping that she had heard the announcement as well. She was still glued to the window, her nose pressed against the glass, her breath a damp halo around it.

Another announcement that sounded as if the speaker were inside a tin. This time Nandana reluctantly began to make her way back to Sripathi. What was Nirmala going to think of her? he wondered. How would they deal with her?

The child stooped to tie a shoelace that had come undone. She looked like a turtle under the weight of her backpack. In the face of her hostility, Sripathi was afraid even to ask what she had inside it.

"Don't rush her," Kiran Sunderraj had advised. "Nandu will come to you when she is ready. Remember that she has lost all that is familiar and beloved to her. It is a shock, poor baby. You must be patient."

Sripathi kept a wary eye on her as she performed a slow, ambling circuit of the lounge before drifting towards him. She was doing it deliberately, he was sure—pushing against his authority, his patience, testing it. All the way from Madras, through Frankfurt to Vancouver, he had imagined another little Maya whom he could easily love again, who would help him wipe out his guilt and anger. This child was too self-possessed, though, too unlovely and unwilling to be loved. She was not pretty or appealing. What had he expected? A sweet storybook creature in a neat little frock like the ones Nirmala used to make for Maya when she was a girl, hair braided and doubled up in ribbons?

The child reached his side and stood there silently, one hand fiddling with a strand of beaded hair.

"Do you need to use the bathroom?" asked Sripathi, feeling awkward.

Silence.

"Something to drink before we go into the plane? Have you been inside a plane before?"

She shrugged, inserted a finger and thumb into her mouth, and drew out a long, sticky length of pink chewing gum. She shot Sripathi a quick look to see the effect it had on him. He hoped that Nirmala would know better how to deal with her. Women always seemed to have the exact words for any situation. And yet *he* was the wordsmith, the man who persuaded strangers to buy beauty cream and Ayurvedic cough paste, coir mats and tooth powder, coconut hair oil and gingelly cooking oil.

He stooped with a grunt to pick up the small red suitcase bruised by time and covered with faded, peeling stickers. It had a new-looking leather strap holding it together. He would have known that suitcase anywhere. He and Nirmala had bought it for Maya from a warehouse on Second Line Beach Road two days before she left for a trip to Ooty with her undergraduate class. The entire family had caught the No. 16 bus because it took a scenic route. This was a special occasion. Maya would be away from home for five whole days—the first time in their lives that such a thing had happened. No daughter in Sripathi's family had ever left home on her own before her marriage. The suitcase was to be an acknowledgment of Maya's new status as a person in her own right, an almost-adult. It was also Sripathi's nervous first step into a modern world where daughters went away from home to study and worked to support themselves.

Ammayya couldn't understand the fuss or the need for a suitcase. "There are so many trunks in the house," she had remarked, horrified as always at expense of any sort. "Haven't we managed all our lives with trunks? Only ten rupees my father paid for them and they have lasted all these sixty-five years."

"But Ammayya, what will all my friends think if I show up at the station with my granny's wedding petti?" teased Maya. "And who will carry them for me?"

"Pah, silly reasons you find to make your father spend. Spoiled, that's what you children are these days. Spoiled rotten!" retorted Ammayya, but did not carry the argument any further. She had subsided into a ball of discontentment instead and had filled the air with dire predictions about bankrupt parents and grasping children, ingrates and incompetents like her own son, and wound up praising her own immaculately virtuous childhood. Her disapproval hadn't stopped her from accompanying them, though, and one sunny Saturday they had all set off in a decrepit blue bus, driven by a man so short that he could barely see over the steering wheel. Every now and again he poked his arm out of the window and screamed abuse: "Mutthal, moron, donkey's arse!" People passing by jumped aside nervously and wondered whether the bus was driving itself, since they could see no driver at the wheel, only a waving arm.

They rattled past the row of flower stalls run by Mangamma and her daughters, past Judge Vishnu Iyengar's house with its tumbling waterfall of bougainvillea and the Kuchalamba Marriage Hall next to it, empty because this was a bad-luck period and no one wanted to risk blighting their wedded lives from the very beginning. They turned right at the Tagore Street intersection, where Shakespeare Kuppalloor had his barber shop, and where Jain's Beauteous Boutique stood with its incandescent display of saris, rows of brassieres padded with newspaper, and men's underwear with more newspaper stuffed strategically in the crotch. Jain's window dresser had been overenthusiastic with the newspaper; the rows of jockey shorts looked like they would fit men who had melons for balls. The bus veered past the long, battered Jesuit high school where Sripathi, and after him, Arun, had studied. At the chapel next to it, old Father Frank McMordy stood at the gate, as usual, waiting bright-eyed to catch somebody for a chat. Finally, they turned left onto the wide, paved road that traced the beach, and the crisp air reached in through the windows, jammed open by rust, and blew away the smell of armpits and old socks.

The sky was curdled milk, with lumpy clouds like paneer floating on its translucent surface. Above the asthmatic sounds of the bus, Sripathi heard seagulls. He was happy that day. Maya had insisted on buying a bright red suitcase to match her langa-dhavani, even though Sripathi preferred the handsome black one with brass buckles and a matching name tag that vaguely resembled a pirate's trunk. Ammayya forgot to sulk and treated everyone to ice cream. Infected with the pervasive happiness of the trip, she even bought flowers for Putti, Nirmala and Maya. And for Sripathi and Arun, a ballpoint pen each from the smuggled-goods market. When they got back home, they found that the pens did not write. It did not spoil the perfection of the day, though, and the suitcase accompanied Maya everywhere she went for years after that, travel-weary, flung about in planes and trains and buses.

Sripathi didn't offer Nandana his hand as they wound their way to the boarding gate, and she continued to pretend that he wasn't there.

There was nobody to receive them at Madras airport, and soon after collecting their bags, the two of them caught a taxi to the railway station. This time the child did not protest when Sripathi took her backpack from her, and she dozed off wearily in the dark taxi that smelled of old sweat and cigarette smoke. She snapped awake as soon as they reached the station, though, and gazed around wide-eyed at the crowds that were boiling on the platforms, even at that late hour. It must be strange and disorienting for her, thought Sripathi, the steady roar of sounds—vendors, children wailing for their parents, coolies shouting for customers, beggars, musicians—

the entire circus of humanity under the high arching roof of Madras Central Station. With her small fingers, the child clipped her nostrils together to block out the stench of fish, human beings, diesel oil, food frying and pools of black water on the tracks. The crowd grew tighter as they neared their train, and Sripathi gripped the child's hand, prepared to hold on even if she tried to wriggle free. Again she made no protest, and he assumed that she was too dazed by the turmoil, the relentless assault on all her senses at the same time. To his relief, there was no confusion over the berths that the travel agent had reserved for them, and soon the movement of the train had rocked the child to sleep. Sripathi sat up all night with his window open to let in cool gusts of air as the train rushed past sleeping towns and villages, and the next morning, when they reached Toturpuram, he was heavy-eyed and irritable.

Through the window he spotted his family scanning the compartments eagerly. He shook Nandana awake. Minutes later they were on the platform, surrounded by all that was familiar to him and strange to the little girl swaying beside him.

———

It was hot in India. Like the Melfa Lane bathroom after she had had a bubble bath, thought Nandana. When she arrived at the station, there were zillions of people on the platform, and all of them were talking at the same time. She clapped her hands against her ears. She wanted to get back inside the train; she liked it in there. A small group of people separated themselves from the crowd and came straight towards her.

"Ayyo!" wailed one of them, and grabbed Nandana. She was an old person with white hair and lots of bangles that tinkled loudly as she moved. She said something in Kannada, but Nandana couldn't hear it properly because her face was squished against the lady's chest. She gazed at Nandana. "Look at her," she said. "Look at her. So sad. So thin. Do you know who I am?" She clasped her again.

"How will she know, Ammayya?" said another woman. Nandana recognized her right away from her mother's photographs. It was the Mamma Lady. "She has just arrived here, poor thing. How would she know who we are?"

Nandana squirmed in the old woman's embrace. The necklaces lying on her spongy chest were biting into her cheek. She smelt like peppermint and cooking oil.

"Do you have any chewing gum?" she whispered into Nandana's ear, and then released her. "So thin she is," she continued, staring at Nandana with grey-green eyes. "I thought all American children were healthy and fair."

I am not American, thought Nandana. I am Canadian.

Mamma Lady touched her head and held her now, gently, not like the old woman. "Poor child, such a big shock she has had. Naturally she will look pulled down."

Then a young man who Nandana knew must be her mother's brother, helped a man in a red uniform pile some of their suitcases on top of his head. She was sure that if he moved, it would all topple down and kill him. But they reached the taxi stand safely, and she and the Old Man and Mamma Lady got into a black car that looked like a toffee. As they careened through the streets, Nandana was frightened by the way the driver kept looking over his shoulder and talking to the Old Man. Sometimes he stuck his hand out of the window and waved to let people know that he was turning, but sometimes he forgot and cars would suddenly stop or swerve past with squealing brakes. Nandana shut her eyes tight because she was sure that they would get smashed up at any minute. When she did open her eyes a couple of times, she thought that she was in a zoo— on either side of the car were hordes of cows and a few enormous creatures that she found out later were buffaloes. They looked ferocious with their big curving horns, and she was afraid that they would charge the taxi and push it over, stick their heads inside the window and thrust those horns into her. She was glad that she was sitting in the middle, between the Old Man and Mamma Lady.

That night, as she lay in the hard, narrow bed that Mamma Lady said was her mother's, questions buzzed in Nandana's head. How long was she going to live in this old house that was full of strange noises and dark corners? Was she supposed to go to school here? Who would help her tie her shoelaces exactly the way she liked them? She was glad that her mother's brother slept in the same room—right across from her on another narrow bed. She had warmed to him right away. But she still hoped that she would not have to live in India, in this old house, for very long.

9

A DAUGHTER
ARRIVES

Dear Editor,

Recently, there was an article in your esteemed newspaper about the new highlight at Dizzee World in Madras. Apparently, trained birds imported from Singapore astonish visitors to the park by answering the telephone, conducting polite conversations, playing basketball, riding bikes, obeying traffic rules and picking up trash. It is my humble opinion that we, the citizens of this country, might be better served if these birds were to replace our politicians, corporate thugs, the mafia who run police stations and other assorted crooks.

Sincerely,
Pro Bono Publico

SRIPATHI CAREFULLY CAPPED his pen and replaced it in the box. Since his return from Vancouver, he had felt less and less inclined to write his letters. He would spot something in the morning papers that aggravated him and then a moment later would wonder what use it was writing about it to anyone; it wasn't as if anything was likely to change as a result. Even the pleasure of looking at his box of pens had disappeared. But he would force himself to find a sheet of paper, pick a pen at random, dredge the sarcasm up out of himself and begin to write. Because he knew, deep inside, that he needed the routine of reading, of thinking about something outside of himself, and of writing to keep sane.

"Chinnamma, wake up! Time for bath and school." From his usual spot on the balcony he could hear Nirmala in Arun's room coaxing the child out of bed. She slept there now, in Maya's old cot, her eyes gazing up at the same roof that had once sheltered her mother. Nirmala had taken pains to make the room pleasant for the child, moving Arun's papers to the desk and shelves in the landing between the two bedrooms. A fairly new, yellow polyester sari had been turned into a pair of window curtains, and the cotton-beater had come in to fluff up the filling in the mattresses and pillows. Nirmala had hung a few photographs of Maya and Alan over the child's bed and lined the shelves of the large wooden cupboard with fresh newspaper. The wall cupboard had been emptied of its old boxes, bags of clothes and books. The two jackets that the child had refused to leave behind in Vancouver—Maya's red winter coat, and Alan's grey one—were hung there. Nirmala had also stored the suitcases and other unopened boxes full of memories. Someday, she told Sripathi, she would open them all out. In one corner of the room, she had placed a large wicker basket for the child's toys. They lay scattered about, bright and unexpected in this old home. Every morning Koti uncomplainingly gathered the toys from all over the house and put them back in the basket, and by evening they were all out again—little square blocks in blue and pink and purple, dolls, tiny pots and pans, coloured pencils and crayons. Once Sripathi had nearly stepped on a small pink box that opened to reveal a detailed house (complete with kitchen and bath), with three minute dolls inhabiting it. He had been fascinated by the perfection of that plastic home and wondered what his grandchild's imagination did with those little dolls. He had seen her with it often, her lips moving soundlessly, her face absorbed, as she played with the tiny family in its pink and perfect nest. Sripathi had rarely bought toys for Maya and Arun. They had invented games out of smooth stones, seed pods, sticks found in the backyard, cowrie shells. He vaguely remembered a rag doll that Nirmala had made for Maya, but he could have been imagining it. Arun had a red double-decker bus bought at the smuggled-goods market.

Nirmala's voice again, beseeching: "Come on, darling child, your bath water is nice and hot." Regardless of the girl's silence, Nirmala would often speak to her as if they were conversing. "Do you like your school? I am sure you do. Otherwise you will tell me, won't you? You know that your Ajji-ma loves you, no?" When she was with Nandana, Nirmala never revealed her private misery over Maya's death. It was only late at night, when she lay beside Sripathi, that she let her mask of practical, bustling good cheer slip. And the agony flowed out of her then, burning them both.

In the first-floor flat of the apartment block next door, Mrs. Srinivas lovingly scolded her two fat sons as she got them ready for school. Both boys stood on the balcony in tight white underpants, pouting and giggling and pushing each other as their mother massaged them with mustard oil before taking them for a bath. Every now and again she stopped cooing to shout instructions to the servant boy, whose sole responsibility was looking after her dotty father-in-law, Dr. M. K. Srinivas. The old man had to be watched every minute of the day, as he would often escape from the flat and lurk in the narrow passage between the two apartment blocks. From there he would peer out slyly until he spotted schoolgirls passing by, and then leap out holding his penis. "Do you want an ice cream, girlies? Tasty-tasty one, henh?" he would drool, waving his ancient brown organ and giggling happily as the girls ran away shrieking. Because

of his unsavoury habit, the old man was better known as Chocobar
Ajja, and he now prowled in childish nightmares along with a host
of other spooks and apparitions. "Lunatic Mansions" Ammayya
sourly called the apartment block for the number of odd people
who lived in it.

The sight of the two boys reminded Sripathi of Arun and Maya
and the same ritual that used to take place every Sunday out on
their terrace. Nirmala used to oil them down before a hot bath, "To
make your limbs smooth and supple," she used to tell them. "So
you can become strong like Shravana in the old story, who carried
his blind old parents in baskets slung across his shoulders." And
Arun would ask worriedly, "Will you and Appu become blind too,
when you are old?" While Maya, ever practical, would want to
know how they would carry Appu if he became any fatter than he
was now.

Gopinath Nayak leaned out of his balcony and hailed Sripathi
with a folded newspaper. "Good morning, sir. How are you?"

Sripathi waved a greeting.

"Trouble in Assam again," commented Gopinath cheerfully.
"Looks like there is trouble in all our border areas, what do you
think, sir?"

"Gol-maal politics as usual, that's what I think."

"Thank God these things don't happen in Toturpuram,"
Gopinath remarked smugly.

"You can't be certain of that. All sorts of ruffians are moving in.
These days it is dangerous even to walk to the temple after sunset."

"That, too, is true," agreed Gopinath. He read the paper for a
few more minutes and said. "Isn't Arun Rao your son?"

"Yes, why?"

"No-no, nothing much. Just this small article here about the
protest march he organized yesterday against mechanized fishing
trawlers. Ruffled a lot of powerful people's feathers, it seems. He
should be careful, these trawler owners are rich and don't like

problems. You know he could get into trouble, sir, interfering in other people's business."

"Yes, we should all learn to mind our own business, but how many of us do?"

There was an awkward silence. Then Gopinath said stiffly, "I just thought that you ought to know what your son was doing. No offence meant." He folded his newspaper carefully and disappeared inside his apartment.

From the bathroom in Arun's room came the sound of water being poured from one bucket into another—Nirmala mixing cold water with hot in preparation for the child's bath. It was water day, but Sripathi had not been disturbed all morning. During his absence, Arun had taken over the task of filling all the pots, pans, drums and tanks in the house and now continued to do it. He woke up unusually early, too, and frequently Sripathi, lying dry-eyed and sleepless in bed, heard him moving softly around in the kitchen.

Now Nirmala hummed snatches of a tune that she used to sing for their own children. "Hurry up, hurry up!" she urged, as Nandana dawdled over her teeth-brushing. She insisted on bathing the child just as she had Maya and Arun. Sripathi had thought that Nandana would object, but to his surprise, she stood acquiescently while her grandmother soaped her and scrubbed her and sang to her. Not a word escaped her small, tight lips, though. It was now a month since their return from Vancouver, but the child showed no desire to speak. She obediently allowed Nirmala to comb her hair, feed her and pat her to sleep, but she avoided Sripathi, ducking into her room when she saw him. He was hurt by her rejection but made no attempt to approach her either.

"Okay, now dress yourself," said Nirmala. "Then come down for breakfast, yes?" She came out of the room wiping the perspiration from her forehead and peeped in at Sripathi. "Will you make sure that she hurries up? Every day she dawdles, and the rickshaw fellow says he won't wait if she isn't at the gate by eight o'clock."

Sripathi nodded and continued to gaze out of the balcony. "You are all right, no?" Nirmala asked. "These days you just sit there doing nothing."

With an effort Sripathi used his old acerbic tone. "What do you want me to do? Work twenty-four hours? Not enough that Kashyap is breathing down my neck at the office, even in my own home I can't take some rest?"

"I am just asking, that's all," said Nirmala. She sounded relieved by his tone, and he was pleased that he had managed to fool her. He waited for her to leave and then looked anxiously at his wristwatch. Only six-thirty. The evil time started at eleven on Wednesdays, so there would be no problem leaving at seven-thirty as usual. It was Monday that was a problem, because rahu-kala, the evil time, started at six-thirty and went on until eight.

Since his return from Vancouver, Sripathi had gone from being an intensely rational man to a deeply superstitious one. He checked the almanac that Nirmala kept in the gods' room for the hours during which Saturn presided, and he refused to go out then or even to begin any work. He had memorized the little rhyme—Mother Saw Father Wearing a Silk Turban on Thursday—to help him remember the order of the evil hours: on Monday from six-thirty to eight; Saturday from eight to nine-thirty; Friday from nine-thirty to eleven; and so on. Now he went late to work on Mondays and got home late every Thursday because he left the office only after five, by which time Saturn had stopped casting its malevolent shadow on the earth. On other days, he sat in his tiny cubicle at work without writing a single word for two hours, until the evil time had passed over his helpless head. He knew that he was inviting a reprimand from Kashyap Iyer, who had suspended all criticism for the past three months as a sign of respect for Sripathi's grief. But he had a business to run, not a thriving one either, and sooner or later he would lose patience and summon Sripathi to his office. But even that did not seem to matter any more.

There were other superstitions too—three crows were a portent of death, a coconut with four eyes meant a fatal illness, black cats and lumps of vermilion-stained mud were all ill omens. He snapped at Putti for asking him where he was going one morning. "Bad luck to ask such questions," he said, coming back into the house in order to leave again. And Putti had said, "What is wrong with you, Sri? You sound just like Nirmala. Bad luck this, ill omen that." When he clipped his nails, he flushed the parings carefully down the toilet instead of leaving them in the dustbin, and at the barber's he insisted that Shakespeare Kuppalloor sweep up all the hair and give it to him in a packet, so that he could burn it in his backyard. Any of these things, he had heard, could be used to cast spells on him and his family.

What terrified Sripathi even more, however, was the mysterious way his body had begun to behave. It had started a week ago. He had been sitting on the old cane chair on the verandah when he bent down to pull on his socks and couldn't see his feet. Simple as that. They had vanished. His legs continued to his ankles, and then, nothing! He shook his head and reached forward again. One foot slowly appeared out of a red mist, and finally, the other. Was he having a stroke? Was he going mad? Sripathi pulled on his socks and waited to see if the bloody mist that soaked his feet would stain the socks, and when nothing happened, he straightened up carefully. For the next few days he walked around the office and at home as if there were snakes underfoot that he could not see. He glanced down at his feet often and was relieved to find that they were still there within his aged, much-repaired shoes, taking him from one place to another.

One day, in the middle of lunch with his colleagues at work, it occurred to him that he couldn't really see *through* his shoes. A dreadful fear filled him. He pulled them off frantically and saw only his socks, hanging limp and empty from his ankles. With a moan of terror he gazed at them. He clutched his head and rocked to and fro, whimpering softly, hardly aware of anything but those dreadful empty socks until Victor, the visualizer who had been with the company almost as long as Sripathi, touched his shoulder and said, "Hey, Sripathi, man, what is the matter with you? Not feeling well, or what?"

And somebody else suggested, "Get some water. Sri, do you need to lie down? Is it paining very much somewhere?"

Perhaps it was their voices, God only knew what, but suddenly his feet were back. Sripathi wriggled them cautiously. He laughed like a madman who had found his senses.

"What are you looking at me like that for?" he asked. "I am all right. Just my feet . . ." He stopped. They would not understand. Nobody would. Better to keep it to himself.

Sripathi became more and more preoccupied with his body. On the surface, he seemed quite normal. He went about his daily life, but out of the corner of his eye, he kept a sharp watch on his every movement. When he lifted his hand to place food in his mouth, for example, he fixed his eyes on that part of his anatomy, just in case it, too, vanished. He knew that he could never be sure of anything in the world again, not even his own body.

The clock on the landing struck the hour, reminding him that the child had to be sent downstairs for breakfast. He shuffled to her room, wishing that Nirmala hadn't asked him to do this simple deed. The room was empty. Had she gone down already? He peered into the bathroom. No one there.

"Ree, where is Nandana? Ask her to hurry up," Nirmala called from the foot of the stairs. "I tell him to do one small thing and he can't even do that."

Sripathi went down the stairs, deeply puzzled. Where on earth had the child gone? Out in the backyard, perhaps, to look at Munnuswamy's calf? She seemed fascinated by the creature. As soon as she came back from school each day, she raced over to the wall and stood on some bricks that Koti had piled for her to gaze at the creature as it butted against its mother's belly.

From the gods' room came the sound of Ammayya's voice, chanting her prayers loudly. "Oh, Rama, Krishna, Jagannatha! Oh, Shiva, Parvati, Ganesha!" she sang in her parched old voice. She recited the names of as many divinities as she could remember, thus covering every aspect of life—health, wealth, beauty, luck, good weather, food, everything. She wound up by ringing a small brass bell loudly. In addition to signalling the end of her conversation with the deities, it was also her way of alerting Nirmala that she was ready for breakfast.

"Where is the child?" asked Nirmala, bustling out of the kitchen carrying a platter of steaming idlis.

Sripathi shrugged. "I don't know. She isn't in her room."

"Well, *find* her then," said Nirmala giving him an impatient look. "She takes so long to eat. You go look in the front, and I will ask Koti to see if she is playing in the backyard."

He stepped out of the house, and the heat hit him like a blow. Sweat beaded his forehead almost immediately. He heard Mrs. Poorna in the apartment building next door, calling forlornly for her lost child: "Kanna, my darling, see what I have made for you today." Sripathi remembered how her daughter had disappeared not so long ago and was suddenly seized by panic. He hailed the Gurkha who guarded the gates of the apartment blocks, and the man came running to the wall.

"Have you seen a small girl anywhere? In a white chemise? My granddaughter?" he asked.

"No, sahib, only uniformed children I have seen," the Gurkha said. "But I will keep my eyes open."

By eight o'clock there was still no sign of the child. "She isn't even dressed properly. It is so hot, her skin will get burned," worried Nirmala. She sent Sripathi out again. He circled the house, wandering out into the backyard where he had often spotted the child playing on the cemented area near the wash-stone. She never ventured out into the overgrown garden, but he looked there as well, feeling a prickle of nostalgia as he ducked beneath the heavy canopy of the mango tree that he used to climb as a child. A pair of grey partridges stopped pecking at the ground beneath the tree and creaked in unison like unoiled hinges before fluttering into the bushes. In the last few years, the water shortage in the town made it impossible to maintain the garden that Nirmala and Maya had once lovingly tended. The dry, unkempt tangle of vegetation had become a paradise for all kinds of birds.

"What are you doing there?" called Putti from the terrace, where she was drying her hair.

"Looking for the child. Have you seen her?"

"No. Maybe she has gone out with Arun."

Sripathi didn't bother to contradict her. Arun had more sense than to take Nandana to school without breakfast. Putti was the one who was behaving witlessly these days, wandering around the house with a silly smile on her face, dreamy and vague. The garden yielded nothing, and Sripathi went back into the house faintly worried. He followed Nirmala up the stairs again and into his son's room.

"Where could that naughty child have gone?" muttered Nirmala. "I hope she hasn't foolishly decided to walk away again."

Two weeks ago, on a Saturday morning, she had vanished in much the same way. Karim Mechanic, who sat in his makeshift autoparts workshop at the end of the street, had brought her back to Big House. He hadn't come inside. Like everybody in the area, he knew of Ammayya's rigid ways. He had refused Sripathi's invitation, saying with a chuckle, "Baap-re-baap, Ayya-orey, I don't want your Ammayya to throw a bucket of Ganga water on me to purify the house! Don't worry, I am fine here on the verandah. And anyway, my job was to bring this child home to you. God knows where she was going. And only God gave me the eyes to see her wandering around. There are so many funny-funny people on the road, not safe for a young one on her own."

Sripathi's heart had jumped with relief at the sight of his grand-daughter, the shuttered little face, the hair that was now neatly oiled and braided by Nirmala, Koti or Putti every morning, the crumpled school uniform with its streak of yellow where she had probably dropped some food. He thanked God for Karim Mechanic and his sharp, kindly eyes.

But that time, Nandana had taken her backpack with her, a bright pink and purple thing that she refused to go without. She never left it behind. She even carried it to bed. He saw that the backpack was propped up on her bed, so perhaps she hadn't gone out of the gates after all.

"Look, her school uniform is still here on the bed," exclaimed Nirmala, pointing at the neatly starched and ironed grey pinafore and white shirt, and the socks and handkerchief that she had put out for the child to wear after her bath. "She is still in her petticoat. That means she is in the house only. Tchah! Naughty child. That Sister Angie will get angry if she is late for assembly."

Outside the front gate, the rickshaw driver pressed his rubber horn impatiently. He waited a while and then left with a clamour of wheels and bells and childish voices, the bright ribbons on his handlebars flapping in the hot wind.

———

Earlier that morning, after Mamma Lady had left her to get dressed, Nandana had stayed in her slip and panties, even knowing that breakfast was ready and that the rickshaw would soon follow. She hated the plump brothers from next door whose squishy thighs pressed against hers in the rickshaw. And the three girls also from the apartments—Meena and Nithya and Ayesha—she was sure that they hated her. Nandana missed Molly and Yee and Anjali; and Mrs. Lipsky and the school janitor, Bobby Merrit, who made funny faces to entertain them and sometimes helped them with math sums during the lunch break; and even the principal Mrs. Denton, who stood at the corner of the library and made sure nobody ran too fast in the corridors.

She had glared at the starchy school uniform that Nirmala had laid on her bed. Why couldn't she wear whatever she felt like? Her favourite pair of shorts and her *WHY?* T-shirt?

"Tell that child to hurry up," Mamma Lady had called from downstairs. The Old Man's steps had come across the floor towards her room—flip-flap, flip-flap—and she had jumped off her bed and crawled into the cupboard where her parents' jackets hung. It was her favourite spot. She had snuggled into the hot darkness of the cupboard, loving the faint smell of her mother still embedded in the soft, red coat.

She was not going to school today. She did not want to eat those fat white idlis the Mamma Lady made almost every day for breakfast and that tasted like barf. Why couldn't they have multicoloured cereal or waffles instead? The milk tasted funny, too, and came from the cow next door. She remembered how her father always put an *n*-shaped piece of cereal in her first spoonful of milk and guided it into her mouth. And her mother's smell of after-bath lotion as she ran past, half-dressed, frantically packing lunch boxes and calling instructions: "Don't forget your keys, I will be late home today, there's a meeting, pick up Nandu at two-forty-five, make sure she does her homework." Everything in this Indian house was so slow and old.

Nandana had tried to find her way back to Vancouver two weeks ago, and a man who sat under a tent on the road with broken things all around him had brought her home, even though she had struggled to get away. She was angry with him. If she had walked another few minutes, she was sure she would have reached the railway station where they had arrived long, long ago. And then she could catch a plane from the airport.

She did not want to live in this horrid house. She hated the cockroaches that came creeping out of the kitchen sink at midnight. Some nights when Nandana couldn't sleep, she thought that she could hear them rustle-rustle-rustle under her bed. She was glad that Arun Maama slept in the same room. He knew all about animals and bugs and birds, and sometimes he would tell her stories just like her parents used to. She liked Aunty Putti, too—even though she smiled too much, she always bought something neat for Nandana when she went to the market: a green ribbon, a comic book about a witty man called Birbal and sweet-smelling flowers for her hair. The only person she did not like was the Witch, who she had learnt was her great-grandmother, and who lived downstairs in a room that smelled and was crowded full of things.

Once, when Nandana came down to play in the kitchen, so as to be close to Mamma Lady—she was afraid of being alone in the room upstairs—the Witch had told her not to leave her toys all over the floor. She had tapped her stick hard against the floor when she said it. But Mamma Lady had hugged her hard against her chest, which was soft and damp, and rocked her as if she were a little baby. "Don't listen to Ammayya," she told her. "She is old, that's all. Sometimes old people don't know this from that. This is *your* house, and you can do whatever you want."

No *way*, Nandana had thought. This was *not* her house.

Nandana shifted in the cupboard, making herself more comfortable, her hand seeking out the soft, familiar shape of her stuffed tiger, Bosco, who waited for her in the dark.

"Mummy," she whispered to the coat, "I am never going to school again. Okay? There are *strangers* there."

The Old Man entered her room. Went out into the landing and back again. She heard him opening and closing the drawers in the desk on the landing. As if he thought she was hiding in one of the drawers! The thought of herself squished into a desk drawer made her giggle.

"Shh!" she heard her father's coat say. She rubbed her face against the soft, grey jacket.

"I won't make a sound," she whispered in the darkness, her thin feet shoved into a large pair of shoes. The Old Man left the room and Nandana dozed off, although she was beginning to feel too warm in the cupboard. She snapped awake suddenly when she heard both the Old Man and Mamma Lady come into her room. The rickshaw's horn blared outside, and the fat boys were laughing loudly.

Dust tickled her nose delicately and she sneezed. Again. A bigger one this time.

10

SHIFTING
PATTERNS

NIRMALA OPENED the cupboard door and looked at Nandana with astonishment. "Why you are sitting there in that dust?" she asked. She turned to Sripathi who shrugged helplessly. The child crawled out silently and stared at her feet, chewing on a thread of hair.

Nirmala sighed and sat down on the bed. "Do you know how worried we were? You mustn't do that again, understand?" The child continued to gaze stubbornly at the floor. Her grandmother removed the strand of hair from her mouth and said, "At this rate you will lose all your beautiful hair. Then we will have to ask Shakespeare Kuppalloor to make a wig for you, no?" The child did not even smile. Come to think of it, thought Sripathi, he had never seen her smile. Behind him, he heard Nirmala urging the child into her school uniform. "Come on, now, quick-quick. I will help you put on your clothes, and your Ajja can drop you off at school."

Sripathi was startled to hear her refer to him as Ajja. *Grandfather*, he thought. The child has never called me that. What does she think of me? Of us? This house? This place? Why doesn't she say anything? He glanced at his watch and winced. He was going to be late again today. "Why doesn't Arun walk her to school or take an auto-rickshaw?" he asked.

Nirmala gave him one of her looks, the one that silently accused him of being callous and unfeeling, and Sripathi gave in. "Oh, all right. But tell her to hurry."

Another impasse. The child wouldn't sit on the scooter. Sripathi waited impatiently for her to get on. The vehicle was puttering away, and his leg ached from having to balance the scooter while the child stood at the edge of the verandah, her small face pinched with fear.

Arun had returned from wherever he had gone early in the morning, and now he cajoled her. "Don't worry, nothing will happen. See, I'll show you how easy it is." He settled on the pillion behind his father and Sripathi rode the bike in a tight circle around the tulasi planter in the centre of the front yard. "What did I say? So safe and simple!" yelled Arun waving his arms and sticking out his long legs while Sripathi thought anxiously about the amount of time this whole drama was taking.

She shook her head. No.

"Oho! Your Ajja is very careful. He will drive slowly—very, very slowly. He used to take your mother and Arun Maama to school every day, both together on this very scooter. You just have to hold him around his waist and you will be fine," said Nirmala.

Nandana looked down and scuffed at the ground with a foot encased in a polished black shoe. The shine dimmed immediately under a patina of fine dust. Her face looked small and unhappy. She dropped her bag, clapped her hand to her mouth and gagged violently. Sripathi stopped the scooter, feeling like a clown in a circus ring.

"I shouldn't have forced her to drink milk in such a hurry," moaned Nirmala, looking conscience-stricken. "You are feeling like vomiting? Sit, sit, it will be all right. No need to go with Ajja on the scooter." She turned towards the interior of the house and yelled, "Koti, bring some cold water, quickly. From the boiled-water drum." She rubbed the girl's back.

"Oh God, enough of this nonsense, Mamma," said Arun, also

fed up. He jumped off the scooter. "I will take her to school in an auto. Is that okay, baby?"

Nandana looked at her uncle with relief and nodded.

"Your stomach is feeling all right now?"

She nodded again.

"Okay, let's go then." Arun picked up his niece, school bag and all, and marched briskly out of the compound to the beat of "We Shall Overcome," which he sang completely out of tune.

Nirmala shook her head and leaned against the verandah entrance. "Too old I am for all this daily hadh-badh," she murmured sadly. "What is going to happen, I don't know."

I don't know either, Sripathi thought. Maya's death had aged them both ten years. Where were they going to find the strength and energy to bring up a seven-year-old? He wheeled his scooter out of the gate, which was still jammed up by construction debris, and squeezed his way out. A warm breeze drifted down the road, and copper-bellied, yellow caesalpinia flowers chased after it, tumbling and skipping like merry children. Here and there lay crimson gulmohur petals, splashes of blood on the dull, black road. His spirits lifted momentarily at the prettiness of the blossoms. The flowers were falling; soon clouds full of moisture would blow across the sea, and the rains would come.

As he rode the scooter, Sripathi kept a wary eye out for lemons strung with leaves, which he avoided because they had been left on the street to draw evil away from somebody else. If he stepped on the pile of yellow and green, he would surely transfer the wickedness to his own fragile home.

When he returned that evening, he took another bath, not caring that the water supply was low in the drums and bins and buckets. He dressed in a clean shirt and a lungi that smelled of the sun and went down the stairs to the gods' room, where he fussed over the selection of fruit that Nirmala had arranged on a silver platter.

"What are you doing?" she asked from the doorway.

"We can't take any nonsense. Why didn't you buy grapes also?"

"As if God cares whether you give banana or apple. Are you trying to bribe, or what?"

"I like taking decent fruit to the temple, that's all," said Sripathi.

"You are also coming to the temple with me?" Nirmala was surprised.

"Why, you have a problem with that?"

"On festival days I have to go down on my hands and knees and beg you to come with me. Why you have become so holy all of a sudden?" she teased.

"I have to ask Your Highness for permission before I pray even? Not enough that I have to ask about everything else that goes on in this house? Henh? Are you my wife or my jailor?"

"Okay, baba, okay," she said. "I was only joking a little bit, and you go and get angry."

That night, there was a huge orange balloon of a moon floating in the sky. From where he lay, he could see the sky, dark and busy with stars, even though the moon occupied centre stage. Nirmala had left the balcony door open to let in some cool air. They used to sleep with that door open all the time, but Sripathi had woken up a few nights ago, seen the white towels floating dimly like ghosts—outlined by their own light against the inky sky—and nearly had a heart attack. Ghosts frightened him now. He had become more aware than ever that the world was full of unseen things, old memories and thoughts, longings and nightmares, anger, regret, madness. They floated turbulently around, an accumulation of whispery yesterdays that grew and grew and grew. These days Sripathi could not bear the insubstantial—sorrow, pain and other abstractions that couldn't be surgically removed like an extra thumb.

On the bed beside him, Nirmala stirred and sat up suddenly. "Listen," she whispered, her eyes wild. "Listen, did they do it all properly?"

"Do what?" he asked, annoyed with her for disturbing the silence of his night.

"The rites. For our daughter. Did they close her eyes with coins? And put one in her mouth as well?"

"I already told you all the details, Nirmala, as soon as I came back. Now go to sleep. I have work tomorrow."

"No, tell me again. Did they? And who washed her body? Did they wash her hair as well? It is not auspicious otherwise."

Sripathi shook Nirmala by the shoulders. "Stop this nonsense," he said. "What does it matter now? Everything is finished. Did you hear? Finished. She is dead, and after death, nothing matters. Maya is beyond all these rituals."

Nirmala turned on him fiercely, her eyes on fire. "Nothing ever matters to you, henh? Like a stone you are. My poor child has gone like a beggar, without any proper rituals, and you say it doesn't matter? Her soul will float like Trishanku between worlds. It will hang in purgatory for ever. Did they at least dress her in unbleached cotton?"

Nirmala rocked herself on the bed, looking dry-eyed into the darkness as if she could see Maya there. Sripathi sat silently beside her. I have not turned to stone, he wanted to say. I am full of tears, but if I let go I will not be able to carry on walking this hard path to the end of my life. Control is everything now.

"Now, if she had died *before* her husband," continued Nirmala relentlessly, "it would have been better for her. She would have gone to Yama-raja as a sumangali in her bridal finery with her wedding beads around her neck and kum-kum on her forehead."

Sripathi couldn't stand it any longer. "Stop this foolish post-mortem analysis you are doing," he said sternly. "We have a child to bring up now, and you are behaving like one yourself. We have lost our daughter, that is true, but think of that little one in the next room. She has lost her parents. Do you think I don't feel as wretched as you?" he asked in a gentler tone. "Henh?"

His words fell softly in the silvery grey silence of the room, and he was surprised and suddenly embarrassed that he had laid himself bare like this.

"Did you at least see her before . . . ?" asked Nirmala, soothed by the hand stroking her head. He used to do that to the children as well, she remembered. Such a fond father he was. What evil spirit had suddenly entered his mind and turned him against his child?

"Yes, I told you already, I saw her. She looked peaceful, as if she was simply asleep," replied Sripathi. He didn't tell her that Maya's scalp had been shaved for surgery and that Alan had no face left. He couldn't tell her about the greyness of their frozen skins, the dark blue lips, the dreadful immobility as they lay in the morgue. Dr. Sunderraj had warned him that the cost of keeping them in the morgue would be very high, but Sripathi had insisted. He had not wanted to see their lifeless bodies, but he had needed to be absolutely sure that there had been no mistake. It was his daughter's voice that he needed to hear, and her laughter. But it was better than not seeing anything but a box of ashes and a gravestone.

In the end, all he said was, "Yes, I saw them both. He was a handsome boy, our son-in-law. And Maya died knowing that we would take care of Nandana. Yes, she knew that."

Nirmala lay down again and put her forearm over her eyes to curb the tears that continued to well out of her like a spring from a dark, echoing cave. Sripathi slid down until he was flat on the bed, his body separated from Nirmala's. Ever since that telephone call months ago, she had kept this thin space between them, an invisible line of anger, one that he dared not cross. For thirty-four years he had curved his body against her back. In the beginning, and for years after, just the touch of her buttocks against his crotch had given him an erection. Slowly that desire had faded into a simple need for warmth and companionship. He knew how that stiff back tensed like the branch of a bamboo tree when she was annoyed, its relaxed doughy softness when happiness filled her, the small red mole like a monsoon beetle edging towards the valley of her spine, the curve of dark, sunburnt skin just above the line of the old cotton blouse she wore to bed, the generous dimples that marked the beginning of her buttocks. Sripathi couldn't bear the distance any more. Timidly he touched Nirmala's shoulder, ran a finger down the hollow of her back, the rich, smooth skin like old silk. She shrugged her shoulder as if to flick off a fly, but he recognized that motion. It meant, I am still angry but . . . So he kept his hand there, fingered the red mole, and when she didn't jerk away, he folded himself against her.

"I am sorry," he whispered, his hand gently stroked her hair, loving the soft surge of it against his palm. "I wish I could undo the past."

Nirmala breathed in deep and the breath travelled through her and into him.

"We performed all the rites. Dr. Sunderraj got the Hindu Temple priest to do it for Maya. Alan's ceremonies were done in the church," he whispered.

"I have asked Krishna Acharye to arrange a puja for their souls," said Nirmala after a long, quavering silence. "On Thursday. And then we will take the ashes to the sea."

And then, a few moments later, she was asleep. Calm and empty of all emotion. What a simple woman she was, thought Sripathi enviously. There were no shades of grey in her mind, no annoying little doubts that lingered and grew like scum on a pond, choking all other thought and feeling.

The coconut trees at the edge of the compound rustled and creaked. In the distance a dog barked frantically for a few moments and then subsided. Restless now, Sripathi got out of bed, careful not to disturb Nirmala, and padded out to the moonlit balcony. His eyes were caught by a vertical line of moving silver trapped between the apartment blocks next door. Why, he thought, surprised, it was the sea. He had never noticed it before and realized that someone must have chopped down one of the Ashoka trees on the other side of the apartment building. The water pulsed and shivered, contained by the two immobile blocks of cement and brick within which two hundred bodies slept and dreamed, and Sripathi was almost certain that he could hear it sighing against the sands. A bat fluttered past, and small creatures stirred and shuffled in the wild back garden. The sharp smell of ripening limes from the tree below the balcony mixed with the cloying scent of oleander blossoms. He hoped that Nirmala had warned Nandana about those pretty pink flowers, of the poison that they carried in their hearts.

The last few lights in the apartment block went off. Sripathi slipped into bed again and drifted into an uneasy sleep churning with dreams. In one of them he chased after a bus, and the faster he ran, the farther he was from the bus, until at last he realized, with a weeping sense of emptiness, that all along he had been running backwards.

At around four o'clock the next morning, a loud rumble travelled like a tsunami through the moist, heavy air and sent him scrambling out of bed, heart thudding wildly. Thunder, he thought, reaching for his glasses on the windowsill. Thunder at last! But when he looked out at the grey, pre-dawn sky, in which a pale moon still lingered, there was not a cloud to be seen. He waited for another rumble, wondering whether his yearning for rain had translated itself into imaginary sound. If only his longing could touch the still sky and turn it into a churning sea of charcoal cloud. Could one's will, strong and unwavering, touch the hearts of the gods, of nature herself?

Years ago, Sripathi had gone with Shantamma to a music concert. He had been reluctant to accompany her, bored by the thought of sitting through three hours of singing in the dark theatre with its thatched roof and humming mosquitoes. But his grandmother had told him that it was important for his soul. Music, she had said, had the power to rouse Varuna and Vayu, the gods of the ocean and of the wind, and compel them to fill the clouds with rain. "And some ragaas," the old lady had assured him—nodding her head and ecstatically keeping time with the flat of her hand on her thigh—"have such heat and passion that when they are sung, a thousand oil lamps will ignite spontaneously. But only when an ustaad, a master of music, produces them." That certainly eliminated that donkey Gopinath Nayak.

He stretched his arms wide and knocked over a pile of books and papers that had been balanced on the windowsill beside the bed. He tutted impatiently and scrabbled in the narrow gap between cot and wall, pulling out old newspaper clippings, sheets of paper (on which Nirmala had briefly tried to account for all the money they spent each month), a magazine with a sexy film star on the cover and a slim book of poetry by Pablo Neruda—a gift from Maya for his forty-sixth birthday, just a year before her departure for the States. Once in a while Koti went on a cleaning spree and piled everything neatly, according to size. But the order she imposed was only temporary. Like a number of things on the windowsill, the volume of poems, too, had gathered dust all these years, waiting to be put away, read or organized. But Sripathi had not picked it up, even to glance at it. Last week, on an impulse, he had started it, his curiosity aroused after a documentary on the poet had aired unexpectedly on television, in between the Kannada song-and-dance sequences and soap operas that Ammayya and Putti watched avidly. Sripathi liked to think that he was the only person in his family who had any taste at all, but he was also shy about this opinion and felt a delicate, hidden pleasure in keeping it to himself. He had found himself fascinated by the poems, even though he couldn't fathom the poet's meaning at times. He glanced down at the volume in his hand, noticing the slim size. How marvellous that the poet could fill such a universe of feeling and ideas into such a slender book. "*Ask me where have I been | and I'll tell you: 'Things keep on happening,*'" said Neruda, on the page that opened to a bus ticket that Sripathi had used as a bookmark.

And there is nothing you can do to stop them, he might have added.

He tossed off the thin, well-washed cotton sheet preparatory to getting up. It was too hot for clothes, let alone sheets, but he could not sleep unless his toes were covered. A rat had bitten his big toe once, and when he'd woken up the sheets were damp with blood, and he'd had the terrifying thought that he might be dead or dying. It took him a while to get over the panic and discover a nipped toe at the end of a body otherwise whole and healthy.

Nirmala was still asleep, her mouth open, a small snore emerging now and again. He went over to the balcony to see what had caused the thunderous sound that had awoken him, and then decided to go down to the verandah. To his surprise, he found the front door ajar and his sister sitting on the steps, chin cupped in the palm of her right hand, three packets of milk on the floor beside her. Putti's hair was loose on her shoulders, and she had on an old cotton sari. In the dim light of pre-dawn she looked much younger than forty-two.

"What are you doing up so early?" asked Sripathi.

"I came to get the milk," replied Putti, looking embarrassed. "I do it every morning."

"Oh, I thought Nirmala did," said Sripathi.

"No, I told her to sleep for a little longer. I am up early anyway, and since I sleep downstairs, it is easier for me. I don't mind."

"Does that Gopala still bring the milk?"

Putti looked acutely uncomfortable now. "Yes, sometimes," she mumbled.

If Sripathi had been less preoccupied with his own misery, he might have noticed and wondered at his sister's embarrassment. But he saw nothing, and after a few moments Putti patted the verandah steps beside her. "Sit down. It is so peaceful at this time, no? You can even hear the koyal bird singing."

"Yes, at least till that moron Gopinath starts his morning raaga," agreed Sripathi.

"Shh! Don't talk. Listen to the bird sing," whispered Putti, leaning forward to rest her elbows on her knees.

Sripathi stared out at the deserted street and allowed the sweet, high notes of the bird to fill his troubled mind. So must the Emperor of China have felt when he heard the nightingale's melody, he thought, remembering a story from his youth. He glanced at his sister's rapt profile and with a sudden shock realized that he had never spent time like this with her. Never. The sixteen year gap between them had prevented any closeness. When she was a child, he was frantically finishing his degree, battling with guilt for having abandoned medical school, for having knocked his mother's hopes to the ground. And then, after he had found a job, he was too tired to notice her. By the time she was ten, he was already a father preoccupied with his own children. They all lived in the same house, but Sripathi hardly knew his sister.

"Maya and I used to sit here every morning and wait for the koyal to start singing," said Putti suddenly. "We would creep out when everybody was asleep, and she would tell me about her school. I loved listening. It was like having a little sister. She made me laugh, especially when she imitated her teachers. I wish Ammayya had let me go to school as well." She paused for a bit. "Maya told me before she left for America, that she would send me a ticket to visit. But I knew it would never happen."

"She would have sent you a ticket, I know," said Sripathi, moved by his sister's wistful voice.

"Maybe. But my fate lies within the walls of this house," said Putti. "See, today I am forty-two years old and still I am stuck here. Even if Maya had sent me a ticket, Ammayya wouldn't have allowed me to go."

Sripathi clapped his hands to his head. "Ayyo!" he exclaimed. "Today is your birthday, I completely forgot."

"Too many things are happening, so of course you forgot. It doesn't matter. I don't want to remember that I am growing older and older every day, and still I have done nothing to remember the years that have passed," said Putti.

"Tchah-tchah, what sad things you say." How stupid he felt for forgetting. Every year he did something special for her—got her a new sari or took her and the others out to eat at the Mayura Palace on Bridge Road. It was a pure vegetarian restaurant, the owner had fervently assured Ammayya the first time they went there. "Everybody who is working here is Brahmin, Amma. Even our doorman is my own nephew's son—totally Brahmin. No garlic or onions we are putting in the food. Our ice cream, too, is purest vegetarian, no egg and all to increase bulk."

"So shall we eat out today to celebrate your birthday, Putti?" asked Sripathi.

"Don't be idiotic," she replied. "I am too old for such nonsense. Spend the money on that poor Nandana. Or when I get married we can celebrate!" She gave him a sidelong glance, her eyes bereft of their usual ring of kohl. "What do you say?"

"Are you planning to get married?" asked Sripathi cautiously. "To whom?"

Putti shrugged. "Maybe, if Ammayya allows me to." She twisted the end of her sari into a tight cord of blue and white cotton.

"Why worry about Ammayya? We are here to take care of her."

"That's what you say every time, but it is all big talk, nothing else," said Putti. "So many times grooms have come to see me. Why you never said anything when Ammayya refused them all? Henh? Tell me? Because you are also afraid that she will start wheezing and coughing and threatening to die!"

She gathered up the milk bags and got to her feet, leaving Sripathi to stare after her retreating back. In trying to keep his mother happy, he thought, he was neglecting his duty to his sister. He sat for a while longer on the verandah, brooding over the dilemma he was in. Absently he noticed that the pile of debris blocking his gate had grown higher; the noise of thunder that morning had been a truck dumping more broken concrete. He tried to summon up the anger that had fuelled his quarrel with one of those truckers months ago, but found that he could not do so. There was no feeling left for anything. It was as if he was standing outside of his body, dispassionately watching himself bumble through his daily routines.

As the sun came up, Koti entered the gates, green plastic basket in hand, her hair neatly oiled and gathered in a bunch at the back of her head. A cluster of white flowers sat on top of the bunch like a fragrant crown. She gave Sripathi a gap-toothed smile, her skin stretched in a million wrinkles around her eyes and mouth. From a corner of the verandah, she took up the ancient, threadbare broom with which she swept out the yard. The dust rose in plumes all around her and settled back slowly. When she was satisfied with the reorganization of the dust, she picked up a decrepit aluminum bucket half-full of water, dipped a hand in it and moistened the ground with a sharp sprinkling motion. Her fingers jerked out a little dance, throwing silver arcs that shimmered briefly in the sunlight. Putting the dust to sleep, she called it. Then she bent over abruptly, straight from the waist, her substantial buttocks in a shiny green nylon sari sticking up into the air, and rapidly peppered the calmed earth with rice-flour paste from an old Bournvita tin until there was a vast expanse of dots like stars on a dusty sky. She sat back on her haunches and allowed her imagination to swim in. The random dots became a pattern and Koti leaned forward again, her face intent as she drew fine lines. Swirling, curling, frothing, furling. The lines swept from dot to dot, a fluid creation. Thought transformed to art, reflected Sripathi, oddly moved by this ritual that Koti had performed for so many years. The lines on the ground came alive—became swans, mangoes, wispy jasmine creepers, peacocks dancing, elephants thundering, signs and symbols for happiness and prosperity.

A memory came to him of Maya skipping down the steps to the yard. Asking Koti if she could please-please try a pattern. Of Koti guiding Maya's impatient little hands through the intricacies of the pattern. "What is this for, Koti?" the child had asked, after she had managed to dribble out a shaky line between two dots. "To keep the evil eye away," Koti had replied, standing up and stretching her aching muscles. "When I put rangoli in front of a house, no evil spirits dare enter."

And yet nothing could keep bad luck away from Koti's own life. She married a drunk when she was eighteen, and every morning she arrived with her face swollen and discoloured, burns on her arms sometimes as large as the lid of a Bournvita tin, missing teeth and blackened eyes. Sripathi remembered seeing a child as well, a boy who often accompanied Koti on her daily rounds, a silent child who sat on a corner of the verandah scribbling endlessly on a slate. When his mother was inside the house, he followed her around, searching for the gap-toothed smiles she sent him as she worked, peering timidly inside rooms if she disappeared even for a moment, and then, satisfied that she had not, running back to the verandah, to his slate and chalk. Once she had come in with her lip split open, crying openly, furiously.

"The son of a whore took my money," she wailed, beating her head against the wall while Ammayya and Nirmala and Putti crowded around, patted her shoulder and soothed her. They ignored Sripathi, glared at him when he asked what had happened as if he was responsible for Koti's sorrow. "*My* money the son of a diseased cunt drank up. I had saved it up to buy a white shirt for my Kannan, for his school. Next week he goes to school for the first time, Amma, and the bastard of a father of his stole my money."

Another time she came in with her left eye swollen half-shut. Sripathi was horrified. "We should tell the police," he said to Nirmala. "One of these days her husband will kill her."

"Police, hunh!" remarked Nirmala, giving Koti ice wrapped in a towel for her eye. "They will only take down a complaint and send her home. Tell her that she must be provoking her husband. You know how people's minds work."

When Koti arrived for the umpteenth time with her hair uncombed and smelling of old sweat and oil—dragging her child behind her and weeping silently because she did not have the energy to feed him or bathe him for school once again—Nirmala gave her a towel and oil and some soap and told her that she could use the toilet on the terrace to clean herself. "Give the boy some hot breakfast also," Sripathi had urged.

This licence had outraged Ammayya. How could a servant bathe in the same place as the mistress of the house? Unthinkable! And eat the same food! Obviously Nirmala was losing her mind. What would the neighbours think when they heard about this? But Nirmala was adamant.

The years had passed, Koti's husband had left her and never returned, and her son was now almost thirty. He had a job as a doorman in a five-star hotel in Madras and lived there with his family.

"What Ayya-orey? No work today, or what?" asked Koti, her sharp voice cutting into his memories.

He smiled back and said, "If I don't go to work, my boss will tell me to stay at home for ever, then how will we pay you, tell me?"

The maid giggled like a young girl and slid past him into the house, leaving a trail of smells—jasmine, coconut oil, betel nut.

———

School again. Mamma Lady had finished giving Nandana a bath and left her to get into her uniform. "No fuss-muss this time," she had warned. "No getting into cupboards and nonsense like that, okay?"

Nandana stuck her tongue against her front tooth and wiggled it. The feeling was pleasant. Soon the tooth would fall out, and then the tooth fairy would leave a quarter under her pillow. She shook the tooth again, with her fingers this time, but stopped when she heard a rustling sound from the tree outside her window. She clambered onto her bed to see what it was, leaning her face against the grill. The smell of the warm dust that layered the grill's metal flowers filled her nostrils. This used to be her mother's room, Mamma Lady had told her, and Nandana had seen the tears in her eyes. She wondered whether the tree had been there when her mother lived in this room. She loved that tree—something interesting always seemed to be happening in it. There were ants—small red ones and large black ones—that marched ceaselessly along the branches all day long, dodging each other, sometimes coming to a dead halt for a few seconds as if exchanging gossip. Did ants sleep? she wondered. To and fro they went, like lines of the red powder that Mamma Lady kept in a box in the gods' room downstairs, twined with black on the gnarled branches of the tree.

Koti, the person who swept the floors every day, and who had shown her how to make pictures with a white powder in the front yard, had wagged a finger at her and pointed to the red ants. "Bite," she said, pinching Nandana's arm gently. "Paining bite." Then she added something in another language and moved the pillow, which was on the side of the bed nearest the window, to the other side. "Wheeen," she added nasally. She drilled a finger into her ear, screwed up her face as if in pain, and then pointed at the red ants again. Nandana finally figured out that Koti was warning her that the red ants could get into her ears and bite her inside her brain. She had smiled shyly and nodded her head, and Koti had stroked her cheek and cried a little.

The branches of the tree shuddered as two squirrels raced up and down, chittering angrily at each other. Unlike the squirrels in Vancouver, the big black ones that dug up all of her mother's precious bulbs and nasturtium seeds, these were small with grey fur and two stripes down their backs. Arun Maama, who talked to her a lot, even though she did not reply, had told her a story about those squirrels. He said that Lord Rama, a god who was born as a human being, had blessed the squirrel. Nandana had nodded. She knew about Lord Rama. Her mother had bought some books from the Indian store on Main Street and told her stories about him and his wife, Seetha, and his brother Lakshmana, and a monkey god called Hanuman who could lift mountains. She wanted to cry when she thought of her parents and their voices coming out of the darkness, warm and comfortable, reading one story after another until she was fast asleep.

"When Rama was building a bridge across the mighty ocean, to reach a kingdom called Lanka where another mighty king called Ravana lived," Arun Maama had said in a sing-song story voice that sounded like her mother's and still rang in her ears clear as a bell, "he needed all the help he could get. The bridge was built of stones, millions and millions of them. First came the bears of the forest to lend a hand, and then the monkeys and the elephants and all the other big-big animals. The king of the squirrels also came and offered a paw. In gratitude, Rama stroked two of his fingers down its back and left those stripes there. So every new generation of squirrel carries that blessing marked on its back."

Another time her uncle had told her the entire story of Rama and his war with the ten-headed Ravana, and she had sat and listened, even though she already knew it. And at the end of the story, he had said, "Some people believe that Rama was the hero and Ravana, the villain."

11

A MATCH
FOR PUTTI

A T ABOUT EIGHT O'CLOCK, soon after Nandana had left for
school, Nirmala came puffing up the stairs. "Gowramma
is here with another prospective groom for Putti," she told
Sripathi, out of breath. "Ammayya wants you to come down."

"Why does that woman always come on a weekday?" grumbled
Sripathi, combing his hair briskly. "I will be late for work again."

"Just for a few minutes you show your face and she will be
happy."

Halfway down the stairs Sripathi realized that he only had his
vest on and returned to his room to find a clean shirt. He stood in
front of the long narrow mirror in the passage and pulled at his
jaanwaara—the sacred thread that was looped over his left shoulder, across his belly and up his back, girdling his body in a diago-
nal. It made a fine back scratcher and he tugged it to and fro, so that
it rubbed satisfyingly against his skin.

"Sripathi, what are you doing? Hurry up, Gowramma is waiting," shouted Ammayya from the living room. He hurriedly but-
toned his shirt and smoothed the thick, curly hair that had a
tendency to spring up above his head like a grey fog, before running
down the stairs. He wondered who the matchmaker had dragged
out of hiding for his sister this time. Poor Putti.

"Namaskara, namaskara!" Sripathi folded his hands together and touched them to his forehead.

Gowramma nodded at him. The matchmaker was seated on a coir mat that Nirmala had spread out for her on the ground. There was a sofa against one wall, beside a looming teak cupboard full of ancient case files, newspaper clippings and books with mouldy leather covers. It was soft and smelled like decomposing mushrooms, its ivory silk tinged green with the long exposure to the humid air. In a desperate effort to preserve it, Nirmala had covered the fabric with sheets of plastic stapled together around the edges like an envelope. Too late, though, for the mould had already taken root and now thrived inside the warm plastic. Nobody sat on the sofa except on state occasions when Putti's suitors showed up. The plastic was then covered with gay Rajasthani bedspreads that highlighted the shabbiness of the rest of the room. At all other times—like the two other heavily carved mahogany chairs and the coffee table inlaid with ivory—it was pushed against the wall to make space for Nirmala's dance students. Close friends or visitors like Gowramma either sat on the wooden chairs or on the coir charpai that Nirmala unrolled on the floor.

As usual, the matchmaker had with her a woven plastic basket containing sheaves of horoscopes, letters and photographs of prospective grooms and brides. She also had her notebook and a thin handloom cotton towel that she used to wipe away the perspiration from the back of her neck and the crooks of her arms. When Sripathi entered the room, she was jotting down details of a prospective bride, suggested by Ammayya, in her book.

"Is she fair?" she asked briskly.

Ammayya wrinkled her nose and thought for a bit. "So-so," she said finally. "A little darker than our Putti. Very good features but."

"Education?"

"B.Sc. Computer Science."

"Very good, that is *very* good indeed. Nowadays these boys

only want bank or computer girls." Gowramma nodded. "Height and general behaviour? Good family?"

Only when she had finished with the business at hand did she give Sripathi her full attention. She beamed at him now, making up for her cursory acknowledgment of his greeting. Sripathi could never get used to her sudden appearances, as if she were a part of some magic show. She lived with her youngest son. Her husband had walked out of her life one morning leaving only a brief note as explanation. "I am renouncing the world," he wrote. "I will pray for all of you."

Gowramma was left with three teenaged children. In her fury, she told everyone that she was a widow, thus wiping her husband off the slate of her memory. She forbade her children to ever mention him again. There were rumours that a year later, when he returned to his home, disillusioned by the ascetic existence, Gowramma had chased him away with a knife in her hand, threatening to cut off his balls. Nobody had seen him since, although Miss Chintamani, who ran the lending library at the corner of Pilkington Road and Andaal Street, insisted that the beggar outside her library was the runaway husband. The suspicion was confirmed in her mind by the man's habit of cuddling his privates—a protective gesture inspired by Gowramma's threat.

Oddly enough, or perhaps because her own marriage had ended so disastrously, Gowramma had turned her energies to match-making, casting horoscopes, numerology, and Vastu-Shastra, an ancient science that dealt with the auspicious positioning of objects in a given space. Her business had expanded so much that she now used the first floor of her home as an office. She had hired two assistants and acquired a temperamental computer from a relative in Bangalore to handle correspondence from all over India and abroad. She also published a weekly paper, *Jataka*, in Kannada, Tamil and Telugu, and an English version called *In Your Stars* for her American and British audience. Sripathi called it "In Your

Arse" and said that the contents were as useless as the bodily wastes ejected from that orifice, a comment that found its way back to the matchmaker and gave her one more reason to dislike him.

Gowramma visited Big House at least once a month, not just to catch up on the gossip with Ammayya, whose nose for a nasty rumour was as well developed as her elephantine hips, but because she regarded Putti as her special project. Her most challenging project. She had suggested at least a hundred boys, but not one had met with Ammayya's approval, although the old woman always put the blame on Sripathi.

"Tchah!" Ammayya would exclaim each time she turned down a horoscope. "What and all I should do, you only tell me, Gowramma. My son, he is too-too fussy about the person who marries his sister. Not this one, he says, not that one. Oh, my hair has all gone grey and still the fellow is saying no, no, no."

Now the matchmaker turned again to Sripathi. As usual, he was struck by her bindi glowing like a red third eye in the middle of her forehead—she, like Nirmala, had shifted to the sticker bindis. There was talk in town about that pugnacious red dot: surely a woman whose husband had left her had no right to wear such a sacred sign of marriage. It wasn't decent, was it?

"Ammayya told me about the terrible, terrible news, Sripathi-orey," she said. "What a tragedy! And you haven't seen Maya since she left this country, no? Or her husband?" She looked inquiringly at Sripathi and when he did not reply continued, "Tchah! Tchah! Tchah! My heart is breaking for you all. Nirmala come here, my dear, sit beside me. I cannot bear to see your tears."

Sripathi pursed his lips so that they became even thinner. "I believe you have come here with a proposal for my sister," he said curtly.

Gowramma gave Nirmala a sympathetic look. But she did not ask him about Maya again. "Thanks to the computer, I found a wonderful, perfect boy for our Putti," she said instead. "Everybody who knows him, and even those who have only heard about him, say that he is a veritable prince, a paragon of all virtue. Very shy and well behaved, and of course in a permanent job, so also secure." She wagged her head several times as if confirming and reconfirming her own statements. "Not very good-looking, but a healthy and decent man he is. I always say that a girl must be better looking than her husband, otherwise he will spend his time admiring himself in the mirror instead of her!"

Which meant that the prospective husband looked like the backside of a camel, thought Sripathi.

"But a little too old. Fifty, didn't you say? With a cataract in one eye?" said Ammayya doubtfully, her hands drumming a soft tattoo on the arms of her chair.

"What can you expect for a girl who is no longer in the spring of her life?" demanded Gowramma, allowing herself to display some irritation. "You don't like *this* one because he is too old, and *that* one because he is too young. I don't understand any more what kind of jewel you are looking for, so next time find some other matchmaker. I have no more suggestions for you."

"*I* don't think he is too old," said Putti petulantly. "I want to meet him."

Ammayya smiled soothingly at her daughter and turned to Gowramma. "The poor child is tense, and who can blame her? Choosing a husband is not easy," she remarked. Then she patted Putti on her bottom, as if she was indeed a small child about to throw a tantrum and not a woman in her forties, and continued, "Yes, my pearl, don't you worry about anything. Your mother will decide what is best for you. And of *course* you shall meet this man. Although, I must say that his career choice is very strange. What kind of man likes to work with mentals and maniacs, henh?"

"A goodhearted, gentle man," said Gowramma, eager to be done with this family that kept surfacing in her search list every few months. "What this house needs is a wedding. That will drive away the sorrow that is filling it." She glanced at Sripathi to see if he was going to react, but he did not say anything. "He will be perfect for you all, very nice person, knows how to deal with all sorts of difficult characters. You should hear some of his stories, especially the one about the lady who murdered her own children. Ate them up like a cat, I hear! Our therapist taught the poor thing to weave cane baskets to soothe her troubled mind." She noticed Ammayya's expression of deep horror and stopped abruptly before trying to salvage matters. "But he is a good, very talented man. Everybody likes him very, very much. Long lineup of girls waiting to see him, but I decided, no, our Putti should have the first chance, what with such a beautiful horoscope match and all."

"A man who has been exposed to so many peculiar people is bound to be peculiar himself," commented Ammayya.

Putti stared at her mother, seeing in that loving face yet another refusal. "I want to meet him but," she said, mutiny in her tone.

Her mother pressed the end of her sari pallu to her lips and looked mournfully at a large photograph of her late husband that hung prominently on the faded wall of the living room and had a garland of dusty sandalwood shavings around it. "We'll let your brother decide," she said. "He is the man of the house after all, and like your own father."

Sripathi avoided Putti's beseeching gaze. He cleared his throat. "Nothing wrong with just meeting this man, is there?" he asked weakly. "Final decision is yours, of course."

"Yes-yes, that's what I also feel," agreed Gowramma, her eyes darting from one person to the other.

Without any warning, Ammayya burst into noisy tears. "My poor child did not even know her own father. What karma!" she sobbed.

Gowramma gave her an ironic look. "Come on, Ammayya, think of Maya's child. That girl has neither father nor mother now."

Ammayya ignored the comment, clutched Gowramma's hand in her own sharp-edged one and squeezed it like a lemon. "*You* know how difficult it is to bring up children without a father. But unlike me, you are an independent person, no need to live on the charity of your children."

Gowramma twisted in Ammayya's tight grip and nodded briskly. She wasn't in a mood for theatrics, especially not one in which she was merely the audience.

"You don't know what problems *I* have every day, Ammayya. I don't like to tell, that's why nobody is aware. Smile, smile and smile, that is my policy. But inside my heart is a big cloud." She waved her free hand wide to indicate the celestial proportions. "To think that I would one day have to earn my living. Tchah! If I didn't have to pay for food and all, I would never even ask for payment for these horoscopes. But what to do, I am obliged . . . deeply ashamed but obliged." She tried to yank her still-captive hand away, but Ammayya was not about to relinquish it without completing her scene.

"Obligations, obligations," she sighed, a large tear clinging to her craggy cheek like a rock climber on a cliff face. "Gowramma, my old friend, nobody knows the weight of obligation better than me. All my life I have carried it on my shoulders. My back has become bent under it and still I stumble on."

Ammayya released Gowramma's hand to wipe away the tear which had stalled on its journey and was beginning to tickle her cheek. The matchmaker swiftly moved away. She gathered up her plastic string bag, and her file folder full of horoscopes and photographs, and backed out of the room. Normally she would have hinted at a cup of tea and a hot snack, but she sensed a storm gathering in the house and preferred not to be present. Besides, the therapist-Putti match seemed quite unlikely, and so it might be a good idea to hurry over to the Shastris and give them the horoscope for their niece. At least I can make some little money over that match before the prospective groom dies of old age, thought the matchmaker sourly. Even though Ammayya was one of Gowramma's oldest clients, her refusal to like any of the matches she suggested reflected badly on her abilities as a finder of grooms.

"Now I have to go," she said. "Many other houses to visit. Nirmala, give me leave, henh?"

Nirmala, who had stood silently by, nodded and held out an open tin of vermilion powder in the traditional farewell ritual of women. Gowramma took a pinch of the powder and pressed it into the parting of her hair. She nodded vigorously, "I'll go and come, then," she said. Again she paused and added, "Oh, and I also wanted to inquire after your granddaughter. So sad, poor thing, must be missing her father and mother. Tchah! Tchah! Such a big tragedy. How you are all coping, I don't know only!" Gowramma's eyes shifted sharply from one person to another.

"Oh, Gowramma! What can I say?" began Ammayya, ready to fill the matchmaker in on all the details of their lives since Nandana's arrival. But Sripathi quelled his mother with a look so ferocious she subsided from sheer surprise.

"We are fine, and we will manage by ourselves. This is a family matter," he said.

"Oho, and *I* am not part of this family? Why, I have seen you, Sripathi, since you were in half-pants," Gowramma protested, increasing her age considerably in order to accommodate that falsehood. "So, if you need any help with that poor child, let me know. Surely you need some happy marriage music in this house!" She nipped Putti's cheek, taking her by surprise, and chuckled.

"Didn't you say that you had other business to finish today?" Sripathi asked.

Gowramma gave him a sharp look and stepped out of the house. She fanned her face with her hand. "Pah-pah-pah! It is burning hot outside. Why it cannot rain, I don't know," she complained, stopping on the verandah to slip into the worn black sandals that her nephew had brought back from Dubai five years ago and that she couldn't bear to throw out because of their foreignness. And then, with another reminder that the match she had suggested was one of the best in her files, she was gone.

"Hunh!" remarked Ammayya. "What cheek she has bringing such a proposal for my daughter."

Putti's face fell. "You always find something wrong," she cried. "I know you don't want me to get married."

"Enh?" said Ammayya, taken aback by the outburst. "Why am I buying saris and jewellery for you whenever I have a little money then, tell me? Why am I living if not to see you happily married?"

Her daughter stormed into their bedroom and emerged carrying her handbag and a pile of magazines. "You are going to the library, my darling?" asked Ammayya, following Putti onto the verandah. "I will also come with you. Wait for me, okay?" The old lady tap-tapped her way inside, almost tripping over her stick in her haste. But when she emerged five minutes later, Putti had gone.

The lending library was round the corner from Dr. Menon, the Ayurvedic practitioner who took care of Ammayya's ills with an assortment of herbal powders, pills and ointments. It was owned by a man named Shekhar, but his sister, Miss Chintamani, presided over it. When Putti entered the tiny box-like place, wedged in between a bakery and a jewellery store, Miss Chintamani was busy with a line of customers. As always, Putti was startled by the woman's greenish complexion. For years the librarian had scrubbed her dark skin with turmeric paste that was supposed to make her more fair. The yellow of the turmeric had leached into her skin and given it a mossy tint, as if she had stayed submerged in water for too long. Her compelling eyebrows were drawn with a very dark pencil—her original eyebrows, she confided to Putti during one of their long, whispered conversations, had been plucked to extinction by the beautician-in-training down the road.

"Little more, little more she kept pulling out, and then there was nothing left. She said not to worry, it will all grow back, and still I am waiting for my eyebrows to return," she complained, as if her eyebrows had merely left her face for a short holiday in some unknown place. "I am thinking I will never get my eyebrows back. They were beautiful and thick like yours." And she would give Putti a cloying look.

Her eyes darted about in her verdant face, constantly on the lookout for book thieves and filthy-minded teenagers, all of whom—she was convinced—lurked near the corner of the library that harboured pornographic books. Despite her vociferous objections, her brother insisted on carrying them. He had sound business instincts, even if his moral fibre was horribly frayed. But Miss Chintamani made sure that decency was observed. Teenagers and children who ventured near The Corner got a good tongue-lashing followed by threats to ban them from the library.

Putti headed for the desk where Miss Chintamani was loudly humiliating a young man in a white polyester shirt.

"Mr. Rajan," she said. "You are *sure* that you wish to borrow this . . . this Nurse Cherry book? No mistake you are making, sir?" She waved a slim volume called *Nurse Cherry Goes to School* that had a voluptuous blonde woman in a transparent nurse's uniform on the cover, her balloon-like breasts pressed into a patient's face. Miss Chintamani examined the cover with disgust, sucked in her teeth and continued, "Sometimes people get mixed up about the contents of books in this shop. If you wish doctor-nurse books you will find good ones on *that* shelf there." She pointed to the section dealing with health and natural cures, religion and philosophy, the section that carried the latest books by Deepak Chopra, Swami Chinmayananda or trusty Dr. Spock.

"Not a good book, eh?" mumbled Mr. Rajan looking thoroughly miserable. "I thought this was about hospitals and all. I *like* educational books about the human body. You see, once upon a time, I wanted to be a doctor, but what to do? Admission is impossible—such high donations and all one has to pay to get into medical school."

"Yes-yes, Mr. Rajan, but *this* is not a medical book," Miss Chintamani pointed out, her lips pursing after each sentence. She challenged the other customers, "Does this look like a *medical* book to anyone here?"

Some of them tittered nervously. One or two slid out of line and furtively replaced their own copies of Nurse Cherry and Bunny the Virgin books.

"Of course, it tells lots about the human body, *very* educational that way," continued the librarian." She paused for effect. "But sir, what will your mother think when she opens this and sees God knows what, henh?"

A few of the men in line looked around, prim and straight-backed with mutual virtue. One of them exclaimed loud enough for Miss Chintamani to hear, "What rubbish these young fellows read, God only knows!"

And another nodded and said, "*I* say it is too much foreign tele-vision with shameless women doing this and that. Spoiling our children, that's what!"

Miss Chintamani looked around triumphantly, noticed Putti hovering, and beamed at her. "Oh, Puttamma, so nice to see you. You wait a few minutes, I have special magazines reserved for you."

Lately Miss Chintamani had begun to greet her with a con-spiratorial waggle of her pencilled eyebrows. It made Putti wonder uneasily whether the librarian knew about the way Gopala Mun-nuswamy made her feel.

"You look very beautiful today," remarked Miss Chintamani. She leaned on the desk and smiled admiringly at Putti. "Somebody special is making you look like that, or what?"

Putti jumped. This woman knew everything. "Who is there to make me look special?" she protested.

"Aha! I met Gowramma yesterday. She told me about this won-derful match she found for you. So excited she was, you don't know only."

"Oh yes, him," said Putti relieved. "Well, we will have to see."

"When is he coming to see you, but? *That* is the question." Miss Chintamani liked talking about the grooms who had come and gone from Putti's life, eagerly mining all the information about those men whose horoscopes had matched hers but had been unaccountably rejected by Ammayya.

"Maybe next week, I don't know."

"What will you wear? Very important to make the right impression, I am telling you," she said. "See, it says so here in this article." She licked her thumb and churned through the pages of a glossy women's magazine until she arrived at her destination. "'First impressions are important.'"

"I haven't decided yet," said Putti.

"Tell me what colour saris you have," suggested the librarian. She didn't seem to care that another queue had formed behind Putti. "And I know all about *him*. Nice mature fellow, I was told. Working in the mental hospital. Very sober and clean living."

Dark green made her look serious and pink was too frivolous, said Miss Chintamani. What would a man who worked as an occupational therapist at the local mental asylum appreciate? Brains or froth? Young and serious, or mature and balanced? "This time you can't make a mistake," she said finally. "Otherwise you will end up like me, obliged to my brother, no future of my own." She leaned across her desk and Putti could smell her hair oil, the sweat that made damp circles under the arms of her tight blue blouse, and deep beneath it all, the noxious odour of regret. "Marrying *anybody* is better than living as a dependent sister, I am telling you."

It was still and airless outside. Putti winced as the heat hit her like a slap. Earlier that week when Shakespeare Kuppalloor had come to Big House to shave Ammayya's head, he had sworn that it was the hottest summer in eighty years.

"How you know that?" Ammayya had demanded, glad that she didn't have any hair to add to the misery of the heat.

"I remember everything that happened."

"Enh, how can you remember things from eighty years ago, you liar?" laughed Ammayya. She liked the gossipy barber.

"You know my sister Regina Victoria? She dropped me on my head when I was a baby, and ever since I get flashes from the past," declared Shakespeare, whose father had worked for a British theatre group and had named his oldest child after the Bard.

The smell of bread and cakes baking wafted out from the shop next door, hanging motionless until being dispersed by a passing vehicle. The beggar who always sat in the corner, and had been identified as Gowramma's husband by Miss Chintamani, lolled against the wall, his legs wide apart, his testicles spilling out of the loose shorts he wore. He noticed Putti and gave her a gap-toothed grin. She looked away quickly and hailed a passing rickshaw, abandoning all thought of catching the bus.

Big House loomed like a misshapen creature against the stark afternoon sky, and Putti was filled with a reluctance to enter it. She paid off the rickshaw and stood silently before the inward-leaning gates, contemplating the house as if she were seeing it for the first time. She wished that she was like Maya, who had lived, studied, worked, been happy and sad, travelled, loved somebody, created a life out of her own body and died—all in the span of thirty-four years. It had been a brief but full life. And Putti, born eight years before her niece, had nothing to show for her own existence. A car drew up in front of Munnuswamy's gate and Gopala stepped out from its air-conditioned interior. He noticed Putti standing at the gates of Big House and smiled at her. "You are going out, Putti Akka?" he asked. "My driver will take you, if you want."

For a wild moment, Putti was tempted to take him up on his offer. To drive away somewhere she had never been. But there was no place in Toturpuram that was new and marvellous for her. So she smiled shyly and said, "Oh no, I just came back. Very nice of you but."

"For you, Putti Akka, anything I will do," said Gopala softly.

She blushed and, without looking at him again, squeezed through the gates and walked hastily up to the door of Big House. Behind her, she could feel his eyes on her back. She did not know that Gopala was in love with her uneven eyes, her bucktoothed smile and the promise of her cushiony body still taut as a girl's. That he jealously observed Gowramma hurrying into Big House with new marriage proposals and wondered why she remained unmarried. And that, with every passing year, his love for her swelled like the scent of raat-ki-rani flowers unfurling in the moist heat of the night. Putti had not considered Gopala for a husband. While he made her pulse race with his flagrantly erotic glances, and she was shocked and titillated by his flirting, the idea had never entered her head.

Ammayya was waiting for her in the shadowy coolness of the living room. "I saw you," she said. "I saw you talking to that no-good milkman. What was he saying? Enh?"

"Nothing much, Ammayya," said Putti. "Only wanted to know if we needed extra milk for the festival season."

"So long you were standing there, that is all he said?"

"What else would he say?"

"And you? Did you speak to him?"

"I just told him that we are not celebrating Deepavali this year because of our tragedy. That's all." Putti turned away from her mother and went into the kitchen. Her heart was too full of unsettled feelings.

———————

Here they said *class* instead of *grade*. She was in Class Two, Section B, and she sat next to Radha Iyengar. Nandana thought it very odd that there were no boys in this school. The teachers mostly wore saris, and you had to call them Miss, even if they were married. Some of the teachers were nuns who wore black gowns and veils and were called Sister or Mother. Radha told Nandana that the nuns had no hair, which was why they wore veils, and that they had no hair because they were all married to a person called Jesus. There was a wooden figure of Jesus hanging from a cross on the wall above the blackboard. He looked sad, Nandana felt, and she wanted to know why he had to hang like that, all scrunched up on two sticks.

Radha was best friends with somebody else. She allowed Nandana to eat lunch with her and her best friend, but they talked about secret things that she did not know at all, such as how to blow bubbles with congress grass juice and a safety pin; where to find the biggest gulmohur seed pods with which to make boats in the rainy season and swords for mock battles; the secret twist of the fingers that guaranteed a win when you played pistol fights with gulmohur flowers; and about sea shells and magic stones and seeds and fruit and movie stars and cigarette sweets and ghosts under the mango tree near the chapel at school. Nandana wanted to see her favourite *Barney* show on television and eat a double-chocolate doughnut. She had seen doughnuts in a bakery nearby, but Mamma Lady would not allow her to eat anything outside the house, not even an ice cream, because she said it would make her sick. Nandana really wanted to try some of the treats sold by the two men near the school gates, especially the bright green juice that Radha bought every day without ever falling ill. But she had no money, not even a dime. She wiggled her loose tooth with her tongue again. Perhaps if she gave the tooth to Mamma Lady when it fell out, she would find a coin under her pillow the next morning. Then she could buy green juice.

The school bell rang every hour. There were two teachers and fifty-two students in the class, and sometimes it became so hot that

Nandana wanted to pull her uniform off and sit in her underwear. Asha Miss was old and kind, and never tried to make Nandana say anything. But the other one, Neena Miss, would keep asking her questions and sighing loudly when she did not answer.

"But this is ridiculous," she would exclaim, every single day. "This can't go on for ever. I am finding it impossible to teach you anything, child!" Then she would ask Nandana to draw pictures and write whatever came into her mind.

And most of the time nothing came into her mind, or at least nothing that she wanted to draw. But this morning she remembered an exciting day long ago in Vancouver. Mrs. Lipsky had got some butterflies for the class. Their very own butterflies, she told them. There was a white one with dark brown circles on its wings and a pale green one that was Nandana's favourite. She had wanted to take it home, but Mrs. Lipsky had said that the butterflies belonged to the class and would have to be let loose at the end of the day. The green butterfly sat on Nandana's hand. It felt like a snowflake. And then it started to rain and, one by one, the butterflies flew away. How sad she had felt watching them go, but Mrs. Lipsky had said that it was not fair to keep them because they were free spirits. Nandana remembered those words. Free. Spirits. She tried to draw herself standing in front of her old school with the butterflies on her hand, but it didn't come out the way she remembered, so she tore up the paper and put her head down on the desk, refusing to look up when Neena Miss asked if she was done.

12

AN ORDINARY
MAN

BY THE TIME Sripathi reached his office that morning, it was already half past nine. He found a parking spot almost immediately, narrowly beating a red Maruti to the space. He hurried towards the building entrance that had recently been painted a bilious green. Assorted odours of frying—vadais, dosas, spices, and boiling milk—emerged from the small restaurant to the right of the stairwell. In the window was a sign saying, *Café Exquisitt. Continental, Chinees, Indian availebbel—Burger, chow-meen, masala-dosa, vadai.* And below the menu, in crisp black letters, *Outside Eatables not Eatable inside plees.*

He spotted his reflection in the mirrored wall of the café, a feature installed by the owner to make the place look bigger than it was. He patted his hair, which had frothed up with the static energy generated by his helmet, the wiry curls standing straight like the cartoonish pictures drawn by small children. Was he really that fat? When did he develop such a paunch? No wonder Nirmala kept on about heart attacks. I am a man with no air of dignity, he told himself, watching his face as if it belonged to somebody else. His father's face swam into his mind. So lean and handsome he was, his thick hair always neatly parted on the left, his moustache clipped over his firm mouth. Narasimha Rao, the famous criminal lawyer.

Nobody knows who I am, thought Sripathi. A deep gloom settled on him as he stared at himself, the crushed shirt, the pants that bagged at the knees, the moustache that he had grown in an attempt to look more like his father.

There came a shuffling sound, and Sripathi found another reflection beside his in the mirror. A man, middle-aged, with an expression of deep curiosity on his face. They were joined by two young women, giggling and chattering, flicking their sari pallus flirtatiously, their hair redolent with the aroma of oil and flowers. About to rush up the stairs to work, they paused to peer through the glass, their slim figures joining the growing crowd of reflections in the distant café mirror. I don't look all that bad, thought Sripathi, comparing himself covertly to the fellow next to him. The crowd began to grow as people stopped to see what was happening in the restaurant—obviously something was going on to attract such a crowd.

"What happened?" demanded a smart young fellow in a suit. "Somebody is not well, or what?"

"I don't know," replied another fellow, jumping up and down to see over the heads of the two young women who were beginning to look perplexed.

"Someone is not well? Food poisoning? Heart attack? Did anyone call an ambulance?" demanded an officious man without any hair, whose dome head bobbed behind the others in the mirror. What on earth was he talking about? Sripathi thought as he swivelled away from the glass and edged to the rear of the crowd. He didn't want to get mixed up in anything involving ambulances and policemen; it would take too much time, and he would have Kashyap after him with a hatchet.

"Someone had a heart attack? I have some tablets in my bag. Doctor gave me three-two years ago for chest pain," offered a plump woman whom Sripathi recognized from the lawyer's office on the second floor. She always smiled at him in the lift, even though they had never spoken to each other in all these years.

"Enh? Why you all are standing here and staring?" demanded a rough voice. It was the café owner. He flapped the checked Erode towel that was always draped over his left shoulder at the crowd. "Is there a circus inside here, or what? Like monkeys everybody is staring. What is wrong, enh?"

"Ask him," giggled the two perfumed women, pointing at the fellow who had joined Sripathi first. "We stopped because he was standing. So we thought, what is happening here? Why he is looking-looking?"

"How *I* should know?" demanded the man. "I stopped because that other fellow was staring like an owl at something. Maybe something happened here, maybe somebody needs help, I thought."

"Which man?" asked the proprietor, whisking his towel over their heads, wiping his forehead and then the glass wall in one fluid motion. The man turned this way and that trying to locate Sripathi, feeling more and more absurd as the giggling and the shuffling and the grumbling grew louder. And then, mortified, he backed away from the café, tugging at his stiff, grey safari shirt. "He was standing here only," he muttered. "I saw him."

Sripathi hurried up the steps. He didn't want to explain that he was simply checking to see who he was in relation to the world around him. He entered his office on the third floor and smiled at the receptionist Jalaja, neat in a green cotton sari, her pleasant face gleaming from the coat of Vaseline that she used instead of make-up.

"Oh, Mr. Rao," she called softly, beckoning him over to her desk. "Iyer Sir is in a bad mood. Very angry. I think with you. So watch out, okay?"

Sripathi nodded gratefully at her for the warning. It helped to know what the weather was like in his boss's office. Well, he would preempt any explosion by marching right in and giving Kashyap a copy of his latest effort. Sripathi always had at least two different campaigns waiting in the wings. He had learnt long ago not to submit everything at one shot and then sit around waiting for a response.

The trick was to look busy all the time; appearances counted for everything in this office. Wasn't that what advertising was all about?

There was a note on his desk that said, *Re Govardhan account, Frigidaire and Tottle Bottles: Urgently required by the end of the day.* Sripathi checked his watch. He had another hour before Kashyap—pale, petulant Kashyap, who truly believed that bitchiness was one of the attributes required by a creative director—followed the message delivered by his peon with a summons to his office.

He morosely scratched out the jingle he had waiting. *Your day will be bright if you have a good night. Govardhan Mattresses: the height of comfort.*

"Very busy, saar? Here, something to oil your thoughts." Kumar, the office peon, slammed a cup of tea on Sripathi's desk and wiped the splash quickly with a stained, odorous rag. He stuffed it into a fold of his dhoti and settled on the floor with a small sigh. This was the last cubicle in the row that stretched down the length of the narrow office, a series of beige and yellow boxes with little privacy. If you wanted to speak to someone without the entire staff eavesdropping, you would have to go down the stairs to Café Exquisitt and beg the proprietor for the phone that he kept hidden in a drawer of his desk. Everything in the café that could be stolen or misused was guarded zealously, chained to the wall or locked in the cupboard in a corner of the tiny room.

In his cubicle, Sripathi felt furtive even about doodling in case Renuka Naidu, in the cubicle next door, decided to stand up and stretch at that moment. He could imagine her wrinkling her button nose at the sight of her fellow copywriter wasting time. People like her—with her convent-school accent, the ease with which she dealt with her superiors, her expensive clothes that looked uncrushed even at the end of a sweaty, miserable day— such people made Sripathi feel horribly aware of his own age and lack of social skills. He was a misfit in this world of make-believe that he had entered quite by accident when advertising was just a poorly paid job requiring no major qualifications. Somewhere along the way, in the past ten years, it had changed. Now only the *crème de la crème* of English departments and management schools could get a foot in the business.

Sripathi sipped the scalding tea, allowed it to cool in his mouth before letting it slide in a soothing stream down his throat.

"Sugar and milk okay, saar?" asked Kumar, his eyes fixed anxiously on Sripathi's face. He had made the same tea as far back as Sripathi could remember, but he needed to be assured that his efforts were worthwhile. He was an artist, a tea-making artist, and like all artists had a fragile ego.

"Perfect," replied Sripathi. He leaned back in his chair and felt his muscles unknot one by one. "And what is happening in your life these days, Kumar?"

"My wife has gone to her mother's house," said the peon coyly.

"Pregnant again! You goat. How many children do you already have?"

"Eight, saar, and two grandchildren." Kumar grinned at Sripathi, his long, sharp face cracking open to show large teeth, orange with paan stains and tobacco juice. "My oldest son is a school teacher, very smart. He is angry that I have filled his mother's belly. He says it is not good at her age. I think he is embarrassed, that is all."

Renuka Naidu poked her elegant head, with its smartly bobbed hair gleaming with health and henna, around the cubicle wall and said, "Your son is right, Kumar. It *is* dangerous for your wife to have a baby at her age. How old is she anyway?"

Kumar shifted on the floor with embarrassment and slapped his knee with his cloth. "I don't know how old my one-at-home is, madam," he mumbled, smiling at his knee and slapping it again a couple of times. "Forty-five, fifty, maybe."

"Oh my goodness!" exclaimed Renuka. "You should have had more sense, Kumar. Tchah, tchah! You people are so brainless. What do you think, Sripathi?"

Sripathi shrugged his shoulders. He hated getting involved in discussions like this. Kumar's life was his own, to be led the way he wanted; why spoil his mood by giving him a lecture? Besides, his own mother had allowed his father to impregnate her late in life. And he remembered how, in his anger and shame, he had started a small campaign against his father's mistress—leaving cow-dung patties on her doorstep, cutting school to spy on her and follow her around, stealing things that she had left outside on her verandah or in her backyard.

"It's not really my business," he said finally. Nothing was his business any more, he decided. Nothing.

"What do you mean? Not your business? Don't you care about the poor woman's life?" She had the same crusading zeal as Arun, the same desire to set the world right, to go out and raise awareness among the masses of their rights and obligations and duties.

Sripathi said, "Oh, I suppose you could call me a non-aligned person, like our country itself. Don't like to take sides or get into arguments."

"You are a coward, Sripathi Rao," laughed Renuka. "You don't like getting involved because you are afraid of what you might find out about yourself and the world around you." She wandered off down the office, stopping at various cubicles to say hello. Sripathi and Kumar watched her undulating behind for a few moments, and then glanced guiltily at each other.

"Pah-pah-pah, what a woman!" said Kumar. "These days girls are ruling the world, eh, saar?"

"You know she is right," said Sripathi sternly, not sure that it was the peon's place to comment about a senior copywriter in the agency. "Brainless fellow!"

"What to do, saar," laughed Kumar, unrepentant. "My Shanti is so beautiful, and that day she was wearing a pink sari. She looked like a bride and I was lost."

A pang of envy twined with regret travelled through Sripathi like an arrow. How is it that I don't see any beauty in Nirmala any more? he thought. When was the last time I noticed what she was wearing? She is the one person in the world I know more intimately than anybody else, and I sometimes forget what she looks like. When was the last time I bought her a string of flowers or her favourite magazine? Flowers had been a part of his daily ritual of loving her when they were newly married. Sripathi remembered how carefully he used to pick the plumpest buds from the flower-seller's basket, a sprig of fresh chamrani to intrigue the senses and underline the tender scent of the jasmine. The flower-seller used to tease him for the time he took over the simple task.

"Oho, someone sooper-special," she would chuckle, leaning forward to chuck him under the chin, even though she couldn't have been much older than he was. She still sold flowers in the same street, except that now it was a major arterial road, and her business had expanded into a string of small shops, wooden boxes perched on stilts where she sold enormous garlands of roses and marigolds, tuberoses and lilies—fat, multicoloured snakes shot through with silver threads—for funerals and weddings, and for political rallies, where they were piled around the spongy neck of some overfed minister. The shops were manned by her six daughters, each a carbon copy of the mother—buxom young women with gleaming oiled hair neatly wound into buns that snuggled against the napes of their necks like dark birds, their foreheads hued as richly as cinnamon, decorated with enormous red bindis, their hands knotting the flowers into strings while they laughed and chattered with customers.

"Saar, Mr. Iyer is asking you to go to his office with your work, saar," said Kumar. He had come back without his tea paraphernalia. "Immediately, he is saying."

Sripathi nodded and gathered up the sheets of paper with the scribbled jingles.

"Saar, he is not in a good mood," said Kumar.

Sripathi nodded and hurried to Kashyap's office, glad that he had something ready to show him. The secretary, Jayaram, who guarded the office like a dragon, smiled grimly at Sripathi. He was a faded man with delicate features, thinning hair, a high voice and a haughty air. There was some debate about whether he was a man or a woman, because of his arching eyebrows that appeared to have been plucked, heavily scented powder that lay in patches on his face and his predilection for strawberry-pink polyester shirts. He was also ferociously efficient and deeply loyal to Kashyap.

He gave Sripathi an ominous look and raised one eyebrow. "He is waiting for you. Please to go in."

Kashyap was seated at his enormous glass-topped desk.

"Good morning, sir," said Sripathi, stooping a little more than usual, as he always did when he was uncomfortable. "I have finished the work you asked for."

"Fine, fine," said Kashyap. "Sit down, please, Sripathi. I want to talk to you."

A feeling of dread gathered in Sripathi's mind as he took a seat. He is going to kick me out, he thought. I am going to be bankrupt. How will we manage?

"Something wrong, sir?" he asked, forcing himself to remain calm. He was amazed at how even his voice sounded.

"I am thinking of moving this business to Madras next year," said Kashyap without any preliminaries. "More work is available there. And my children are growing up. They need better schools. I might have to let some of you go."

Sripathi swallowed with difficulty. He couldn't say anything. Thirty-four years I have worked here, he thought. More than half my life.

"Of course, I am still thinking about it," continued Kashyap, twirling a pen on his desk, round and round, faster each time until it was a blue and red blur. "So no need to worry yet. But I am just letting you know, since you have been here the longest."

How very kind of you. Sripathi couldn't bring himself to look at Kashyap. He nodded, placed the sheets of paper that he still clutched on the gleaming table that separated the two of them, and left the room. He walked straight to his desk, not responding to friendly greetings from colleagues in cubicles much like his own, and sat there for what seemed like hours, unable to write anything. He picked up his keys from the small bowl that held erasers, clips, staples and other odds and ends. It had the logo of some long-forgotten company on the side. And then, as if in a dream, he left the office, even though it was only three-thirty. He was vaguely conscious of people staring curiously at him, of Jalaja, the receptionist, asking if he was ill, and then he was out of the stale green building.

He stood outside for a few moments, gulping down the warm air that tasted like flat cola. He wanted to cry. He wanted to laugh. This must be how a long-time prisoner feels on being released, he thought: relieved to see the open gates, yet terrified of what lies on the other side. Sripathi had been waiting so long for Kashyap to throw him out, that this was almost anticlimactic. And even then, it wasn't certain that he had lost his job. For a panicked second, he wondered whether he ought to return to his desk, pretend he had only gone to the toilet. Why should he? he thought defiantly. He was always doing his duty, and where had it taken him? He saw two college students waiting at the bus stop in front of the building— young women clad in summery saris with flowers in their hair. They looked to him like Maya—their laughing faces, their smooth skin, their alive-ness. As if in a dream, he approached the students and gazed at them like a thirsty man. One of the girls noticed him and nudged the other. They stopped laughing and moved away. Sripathi followed and the girls started to look annoyed.

"Loafer," said one of them, giving him a disgusted look. "Even at this age they act funny."

Sripathi turned away, feeling ill. His legs began to shake, and it was with great effort that he crossed the parking lot to where his scooter still stood. I need a doctor, he thought, panic-stricken. He wished that old Dr. Pandit was alive. When Arun and Maya were young, they always seemed to develop soaring fevers in the middle of the night. He didn't have a phone in those days, or the scooter, and he'd had to cycle frantically to Dr. Pandit's house for help. The doctor lived forty-five minutes away, and Sripathi was certain that his child had died while he cycled through the still night—past shuttered stores and empty tourist buses with tarpaulin-shrouded luggage piled on their roofs, parked along the road like slumbering elephants, and the pavements full of sleeping street people who looked like bundles of grey rags. The doctor had been a genial old man. "Ah! Don't worry about it!" he would say, waving away Sripathi's profuse apologies for disturbing him so late. "Everybody falls ill and has babies in the middle of the night. I sleep all morning in my clinic because no patients come then."

Five years ago, Dr. Pandit had died. His heart had given one final lurch and he had collapsed on top of a patient who had almost expired with shock too, so the rumours went. The doctor's son had taken over the clinic, but he finished all his business in the morning and firmly told the patients whom he had inherited that, unlike his father, he did not like to be woken in the middle of the night, and neither would he make house calls.

"Don't you finish at your office and go home at five o'clock?" he had asked Sripathi once. "Would you go back to work if somebody phoned and asked you at one in the morning? Just because my father was crazy enough to do it, does it mean that I should follow in his footsteps? No-no-no. These days even doctory is a business, sir, like everything else."

He had handed Sripathi a list of all the hospitals and nursing homes in the area, along with phone numbers, and told him firmly that, in case of a medical emergency at an ungodly hour, he should contact them.

Sripathi missed old Dr. Pandit, his willingness to listen, his involvement in a patient's family, his entire life—for as he was fond of saying, a human being is not merely a ticking body, but a sum of all that happens in the world around him.

"If you have a headache, do I immediately jump to the conclusion that you have a tumour in your brain? No, no. There are many other possibilities—a fight with your wife, too much work to finish in too little time, not enough sleep—so many things can cause pain, eh?" And all the while his wrinkled fingers that had probed and gauged and soothed so many bodies would find their experienced way around, almost as if he could hear and see with them as he did with his stethoscope and his glasses.

What a good man he had been. He most certainly would have known what was wrong with Sripathi Rao, aged fifty-seven, father of two children (one dead), burnt-out copywriter and a man whose body was out of control. Yes, he would have known.

———————

It was October the fifteenth. Only two weeks to Halloween, Nandana remembered, although she didn't see pumpkins anywhere. Nobody talked about their costumes. Her mother used to buy bags of candy several weeks before Halloween, but Nandana hadn't seen any in Big House. Of course, they could be in the kitchen cupboards, which were too high for her to reach, but she doubted it.

The kids at school talked about a festival called Deepavali that Nandana had never heard of. It sounded like fun though—they were allowed to play with firecrackers. The two fat boys said that their father burst lots of bombs. No *way*, thought Nandana. She remembered the television news that her father had watched every evening at eight—weren't bombs used only in wars? Radha told her she was getting three new sets of clothes—one from each of her grandmas *and* one from her mother. Nandana wondered if Mamma Lady would get her new clothes, whether she would get to burst bombs and eat tons of sweets, although what she really, really wanted was a Mars bar. Mamma Lady went to the market every day, but she never ever bought any chocolates or cakes or doughnuts. Only yukky vegetables and bananas and sometimes two apples, which she'd cut into slices and give to Nandana. If she didn't eat them, because she didn't really like these India apples, Mamma Lady looked sad and said, "No-no, chinna, you mustn't waste good food. There are too many hungry people just outside our gates." And slowly, she would put a piece at a time into Nandana's mouth, kissing her every time she ate one. Which she had to admit she liked, even though she wasn't a baby and could eat it by herself.

The school bell rang and Nandana ran to the door. If she could get to the gate before the rickshaw man arrived, she could slip out and walk back to Vancouver. But she wanted to stay and see what this Deepavali was all about. Perhaps, she thought, she would go home *after* she had burst a few crackers.

13

BANDIT
QUEEN

AT THREE-THIRTY in the afternoon on Brahmin Street, Big House lay like a shaggy animal, drowsing in the heat. Ammayya had just woken from her nap, irritable and hungry.

"Akka, can I leave Ammayya's room? I cleaned it properly this morning, and my daughter-in-law is taking me to the cinema," she heard Koti ask Nirmala. The lazy shani didn't want to work at all, never had in all the years Ammayya had known her. Ammayya didn't like Koti, and never lost an opportunity to yell, or throw her pillow, at her.

"One sweep will do. No need to wipe the floors. I'll come with you," said Nirmala.

"What are you both doing phusur-phusur outside my room?" demanded Ammayya. "Plotting something no doubt. I am not safe, even in my own house."

"Do you want your tea here in the room, or are you coming to the table?" asked Nirmala, drawing the curtains to let in some afternoon light. She had drawn them in the morning as well, and Ammayya had shut them immediately.

Ammayya shaded her eyes and snarled at her daughter-in-law, "Stop that! My eyes hurt. I don't want all kinds of dirty people peering inside. Thieves and lechers, all of them. And am I sick that

I should have food in my bed? Perhaps you hope that I am sick, dying even. Then you can lay your greedy hands on my jewellery. Aha, I know you only too well! I have left everything to my daughter, so don't expect a single paisa."

"Shall I make you your tea? Or will you make it for yourself?"

"Why, where are you going?" demanded Ammayya, rocking vigorously in her chair. She liked an argument if she could stir one up. It cleared the boredom that fogged her daily life.

Koti knelt down and swept under the bed. She hit Ammayya's trunk with the flat of her hand and giggled, "What is in this petti Ammayya? Anything for me?"

Ammayya picked up a rubber slipper and flung it at her. Koti laughed and ducked. She hummed a tune from a Tamil movie and started to whisk her broom around.

"Cow! Fat, cross-eyed cow." Ammayya picked up her other slipper. "Cheeky, black buffalo. Crawled out from a gutter and says dirty things about me to my face. And you, who are you?" She threw the slipper at Nirmala as she bent over the bed, straightening the sheets to check whether Ammayya had hidden any food under the pillow. Except for sweets, there was no restriction on what she ate, but Ammayya liked to pretend that she was being starved by her family. She stole food from the fridge and the kitchen cupboards, hid it all over the room and then promptly forgot about it. Once, a long time ago, when her fears of starvation first began, she had stuffed tomatoes under her mattress, and for weeks they had festered there.

Today Nirmala discovered a dry chapatti beneath the old woman's pillow. "You do this again, and I will not make any food for you or do *anything* for you," she said firmly.

Ammayya became senile. "I said, Who are you? What are you doing in my house?"

"I am Sripathi's wife, Ammayya," Nirmala said patiently.

"Sripathi, my son—ah, he is a handsome boy. I am looking everywhere for a good bride for him. It is time he got married; it isn't good for a young man to stay a bachelor for too long. So if you come across a nice girl, pretty, well educated, decent family. . ." Her voice dripped into a mumble, and she rocked too and fro in her chair. She looked slyly at Nirmala to see whether she had provoked a reaction. "He isn't a doctor like I wanted him to be. It is always good to have a doctor in the family, but the idiot went and studied poetry. Will pretty words fill your stomach, that's what I want to know? So we need a rich bride for Sripathi. Better that way. At least we won't starve." She shot another malicious look at Nirmala who had brought only two sets of jewellery with her.

Nirmala calmly continued to tuck the sheets, check under the mattress and plump the pillows.

Ammayya stopped rocking and glared at her, "What are you doing to my bed?"

Nirmala gave the sheets a final pat and straightened up, wincing as she did so.

Koti gave her a concerned look. "Akka, what happened?"

"My back," said Nirmala. "Yesterday I brought down that pile of books for the raddhi-wallah. They were heavy."

"Books, what books? You are throwing away my husband's books?" demanded Ammayya.

"Maybe it was the dance step I demonstrated to my class on Saturday."

"Nobody in this house listens to me," Ammayya shouted. "Why are you checking my bed? Are you looking for my money? You won't get any of it, I am telling you."

"Ammayya, I am going out. If you want tea, come to the dining room right away."

Ammayya rose slowly from her chair, and her knuckles whitened on the arms with the effort. Nirmala handed her the walking stick and moved quickly out of the way, in case she decided to take a swipe at her. You never knew what demon was going to spark her mind from one minute to the next.

"Do you need any help?" she asked tentatively.

"I don't need anybody's help," snapped the old woman as she shuffled out of the room. She concentrated on not losing her balance or crumpling to a heap on the floor. How humiliating that would be, especially in front of the servant maid, the squinting monkey. Neither age nor illness would rob her of dignity; she would walk by herself, no matter how long it took her.

"Don't go too fast," said Nirmala. "You'll slip and break your hip."

"Shut-up, stop treating me like I am a two-year-old, Nirmala," snapped Ammayya.

"Oh, so you *do* remember who I am, eh, Ammayya?"

"Do you think I am senile, or what?"

"Where is Putti?" asked Nirmala, holding her mother-in-law firmly under the elbow. For all her protestations to the contrary, the older woman had been losing her balance lately, and Nirmala was afraid she might break her hip bone and need surgery. The last thing they could afford right now was hospital bills, which, if her friend who had just returned from a hysterectomy was to be believed, were horrendous nowadays.

"How do I know where she is? Am I her shadow to follow her around everywhere she goes?"

"So we will be entertaining another groom for our Putti. I hope this one clicks."

"What is the hurry?" demanded Ammayya. "Is she on *your* head or what?"

"No-no, nothing of the sort," said Nirmala. But she had noticed Putti's secret interest in Gopala, the way she rushed to get the milk in the morning when he rang the doorbell and the flirtation that had developed between them.

Ammayya looked suspiciously at Nirmala. She knew her daughter-in-law only too well, especially that feeble, wishy-washy expression on her face. The silly creature was hiding something from her.

"What is it?" she demanded, tapping her stick impatiently on the floor. The sound set Nirmala's teeth on edge. "What is going on in this house? Nobody tells me anything. Nowadays I am like a guest here." She was pleased with her martyr act. It had no effect on her son, but her daughter-in-law was more susceptible, and it delighted the old woman to hone her tongue on her.

Nirmala hesitated and Ammayya pounced. "Tell me, I want to know. Is it Putti?"

"Oh no! I was just thinking whether it would be all right to buy new clothes for Deepavali this year. For the child at least, poor thing. We can't give her very much, but a new langa-choli would look so pretty on her."

"Don't ask me for money. I have nothing," Ammayya said quickly. "And I want to know where Putti is. That girl is becoming very strange these days. I will have to ask Menon doctor for some medicine for her. Have you noticed anything strange also?"

"Like what?" asked Nirmala warily.

"She stares at things all the time. At the mirror, at the walls, everything. And she is always drying her hair on the terrace in the morning, and looking at the sky from the verandah in the afternoon. God knows what is wrong."

"Maybe she is feeling the heat," suggested Nirmala.

"Unh-hunh. Who wouldn't feel it?" said Koti, giving the floor one final swipe with her broom and backing out of the room. "You should hear the stories that are going around about this heat. Why, the other day, that income-tax inspector, you know the one on Second Main, near the cinema? Well, he was quietly eating a mango on his verandah when his wife came out of the house and demanded the seed to suck."

"Enh, why couldn't she get her own seed?" Ammayya wanted to know.

Koti shrugged. "Do you want to hear what happened next or not?"

"Okay, okay, go on with your silly stories."

"Well, our big inspector-orey refused to give it to her. She tried to grab it and he ran out of the house holding the stupid thing. Can you imagine what a sight that must have been? All the people on Second Main saw it with their very own eyes. His wife raced after him screaming dirty-dirty words and waving a knife in one hand."

"Ayyo! Why didn't anybody stop her?" Nirmala asked.

"Too hot it was," said Koti. "Besides, that Gajapati-amma is like Kali Devi herself when she gets angry, and nobody wanted to get near her, especially since she had a knife. But it was the heat that saved her husband, finally. She fainted from all that running around. What a drama!"

Nirmala laughed at the thought of the income-tax inspector sprinting down the street with a mango seed in his hand and, settling Ammayya in a chair, gave her a cup of tea.

Putti entered the room just then. "Where were you, child?" demanded Ammayya. "I wanted to tell you about my blood pressure. See how red my eyes are? Jayanthi Ammal told me that that is a sign of high pressure."

"Are you going out, Nirmala?" Putti asked, not looking at her mother.

"Yes, to the vegetable shop. I need chilies and tomatoes. The child eats nothing at all. I don't know what to give her, only. And since she won't talk, she can't tell me."

"Putti, did you hear me?" whined Ammayya. "Nowadays you don't speak to me at all. I am sitting and sitting and waiting for you every single day, and God knows where you disappear."

"I am always at home," said Putti. "Where will I go, other than to the library or the temple? And if you are ill, why don't you visit Dr. Menon?"

"Tomorrow you can take me to him. Now you stay here with me, and tell me what and all Miss Chintamani said."

"Not now, Ammayya. I want to go with Nirmala. Help her carry the vegetables."

"Pah, no sense you have. That child won't eat vegetables and all. She had a foreign father. They eat meat. I am telling you. Shanti Kumar told me. She had a really bad time when her grandchildren came from foreign. They wanted cow and goat and pig and all. Every day she used to send the servant to the Military Hotel to get tiffin carriers of food for them. She said that she felt like vomiting from the smell and had to get the Acharye to do a special cleansing ceremony in the house after they had all gone back."

"Meat?" said Nirmala uncertainly. "The child eats meat?"

"Enh, what did you think? Your daughter brought her up like a Brahmana? Once she went there she forgot everything—flushed all our rules down with the shit water." Ammayya frowned at Nirmala. "But don't think I will allow you to bring meat into this house. I am not a fool like Shanti Kumar, giving in to the demands of children."

Nirmala gathered up her shopping bags and purse and left with Putti.

"Putti, you will become black as a crow with all this running around in the sun," shouted Ammayya. "And next week that fellow who is coming to see you will run away. Listen to me."

There was not a sound other than the cawing of a crow from the lime tree in the backyard. Ammayya wriggled with excitement in her chair, waving her feet that, in their thick socks, looked like a pair of white mice. Despite the heat, Ammayya never felt warm enough. In addition to the socks on her feet, she wore a woollen blouse and a shawl.

She tried to plan out her time. Sripathi was still at work, the child was at school and would be back only at a quarter past four. Plenty of time to make her way up the stairs to her son's section of the house and check the cupboards, his desk, the drawers, under the pillows, for letters, cheques, wads of money. She would go through Nirmala's cupboards to see if she had bought any new saris without telling her. She would check the child's suitcases. Opportunities like these were rare, and she cherished them. Ammayya sucked in her dentures and released them with a moist click. Nobody told her anything these days. They kept secrets from her, she knew that for sure. She could smell it in their voices, see it in the sly looks they traded with each other—Sripathi and Nirmala, and Putti and Arun. Even the servant knew more than she did about the goings-on in this house. Ammayya tapped her stick furiously on the floor. She should never have given Nirmala charge of the keys to the house. Daughters-in-law were crooks. They stole power from you before you knew what was happening.

She waddled back from the dining room to her bedroom where she settled down before the dressing table with its rows of medicine bottles, all containing Ayurvedic remedies obtained from Dr. Menon. She refused to visit a regular hospital or even young Dr. Pandit, whose father had taken care of Sripathi's children. She had a horror of being examined by a doctor, of having her dry private parts poked and prodded, of lying helpless on an examination table. Sripathi and Putti had been delivered here in her own home by a midwife. And she had read about the body-parts business that was rampant in hospitals.

"You know Sub-Inspector Krishnappa's son?" Miss Chintamani had asked. "Well, he went to that big new hospital on Nehru Road with a simple sore throat. Only that, see? And before he could say *aan* or *oon* those smart-suit doctors had him on an operating table. Took out his appendix, they said. But who knows what else they pulled out? The boy has been married six years and still his wife's belly is flat."

"They can do things like that?" Ammayya had asked, wishing all the more that her own son was a doctor. Surely they wouldn't do bad things to a doctor's mother?

"Of course they can. Do they allow anyone inside the operating theatre? No. Worse than anything, I have heard, is the stuff they put *inside* you. I have heard that these America-trained doctors do all sorts of inauspicious things, put monkey hearts in humans and what not!"

Ammayya came away from the library determined never to end up in a hospital. Besides, the sight of people in white coats with stethoscopes around their necks was a constant reminder of what her own son had tossed away. Her anger was evenly divided between all those arrogant, god-like creatures with the power to heal at their fingertips, and her son who could have had that same power. Dr. Menon, the Ayurved, was too old and poor to inspire anger or envy in Ammayya's heart, and more importantly, his advice was dispensed free of charge. He practiced ayurveda as a hobby, and anybody who went to him did so with the understanding that they were his guinea pigs and had forfeited the right to complain if his medicines did not work. His patients might not always get well after taking his powders and pellets, but at least they did not get any worse.

Ammayya swatted her stick against the edge of her bed and it hit her trunk. Her mood swung from cantankerous to contented at the heavy sound. Nice and full, she thought happily. The trunk itself was a camouflage for a smaller box, also locked with a Navtal lock, inside which there were other tins and boxes, each with its own lock. You could never be suspicious enough about people's motives, Ammayya knew that for a fact. Why, just the other day she had read in the papers about a woman (like her), old (again the similarity), helpless (there you go again), who had been beaten to death by her own son, all for a few gold chains around her neck. Not to mention the story that Miss Chintamani had told her and Putti about the decent, god-loving, charitable (she made fresh tea, even for the servants, if you please!), old Kaveriamma on Ganges Road, next to the Mother Mary Church.

"You know the servant boy, Vasu?" she had asked.

"The good-looking fellow?"

"Uh-huh! Handsome is as handsome does, that's what I say." Miss Chintamani had pursed her lips censoriously.

"Why, what happened?" Ammayya wanted to know.

"Poor old Kaveriamma, she brought up the ingrate as if he was her own son. For twenty-five years. And he tried to kill her with a rolling pin!" Miss Chintamani had been indignant.

"Ayyo! Why did he do such a thing?"

"Who knows why villains do the things they do? He said it was because she wouldn't give him the money she owed him. Worked him like a slave, he said, for all those years. Where would he have been without Kaveriamma, tell me? In the gutter, that's where."

"And what did the old lady say to that?" asked Ammayya. Why, she might have been Kaveriamma. Koti could easily attack her the same way.

"Poor thing, she could barely talk. But she told the judge that she had deposited all his money in a savings account and was planning to give it to him on his wedding day."

"But didn't Vasu get married two years ago?" Putti had asked.

"Oho, one must learn to be patient. Kaveriamma would have given it to him if he had asked properly. But the idiot goes and hits her on the head. That's gratitude for you!" Miss Chintamani had ended her story.

Well, thought Ammayya, unlike Kaveriamma, she was certainly not foolish enough to trust a soul. She patted the keys that she had pinned to the inside of her blouse, then with one mighty heave she detached herself from the chair. Tap-tap-tap, she swayed slowly across the cold red-oxide floor of the living room. Past the rotting sofa, the ancient rosewood chairs and the brooding teak cupboards that still contained the yellowing stacks of legal books, journals, case notes and files once used by Narasimha Rao. Ammayya had no particular use for all that paper, but insisted on keeping it out of a sense of perversity. She was aware how it bothered Nirmala, who grumbled about the waste of good space. With a click of her teeth, the old woman pulled a small coffee table out into the centre of the room. Like all the other furniture, it had been pushed against the wall to make space for Nirmala's students. Capering fools, sniffed Ammayya, her heart thundering as she made her way up the stairs. Dancing! She had seen better dancing from the monkeys at the temple. But she enjoyed the entertainment on Wednesdays and Saturdays, liked to sit in her chair and comment on the dancers. "Is she doing the elephant walk, that fat girl there?" she would demand. Or, "Nirmala, is this the dance of the demons you are teaching these children?" Then she would slap her thigh and cackle at her own wit.

She paused for breath on the landing, looking at the cracked floor with distaste. It was a while since she had had the opportunity to come up here, and she hadn't noticed how wretched the house had become. Perhaps Sripathi was right. It was time to sell it to the highest bidder and get some of those matchboxes in exchange. She would then rent out her flat and continue to stay with her son. Putti was entitled to an apartment as well, which could also be rented out.

In Sripathi's room, she made sure that all the windows and the balcony door were shut, so that none of their snooping neighbours would report her to Nirmala, and then she started to open the cupboards. To her disappointment, Nirmala had locked the steel almirah where she undoubtedly stored all her recent acquisitions. The wooden cupboard with everyday clothes was open, though, and Ammayya eagerly pawed through the neatly folded saris and petticoats, mumbling to herself about suspicious daughters-in-law. There was nothing there, not even money that she could pinch. Nor any secret letters for her to read. Only the sandalwood box full of Maya's letters. Ammayya was already familiar with the contents of those. The old woman cupped her palm and shook out some powder from a tall tin kept in the cupboard and that she had on her own dressing table as well. With one hand she held the front of her blouse out like a pouch and smeared the powder over her breasts with the other hand. Smelled good, smelled good. Why should only Nirmala use it? She decided to take the powder down to her room for when she had exhausted her own supply. Let her daughter-in-law wonder where it had gone. Satisfied that there was nothing else in Sripathi's bedroom that was of interest, she shuffled over to the other room. Where the foreign brat slept. With a growing sense of excitement, Ammayya dragged out the suitcases from under the bed. Ever since Nandana's arrival, Ammayya had been longing to see what her great-granddaughter had brought from abroad. She imagined thick packs of chewing gum, for which she had developed an enormous craving. Boxes of soaps that smelled so different from the Lifebuoy bars that Nirmala bought in bulk for the entire household. Dozens of pens in assorted colours. The old lady wondered whether the child had brought back any of her parents' clothes. Those would fetch a good sum of money in China Bazaar; the shops did a roaring business in smuggled goods, second-hand foreign clothes and make-up, shoes and bags. She would have to think of some way to sneak the clothes out of the house and all the way to the bazaar, but—she sucked at her teeth delightedly—she would manage. To her intense disappointment, the suitcases held nothing other than photographs and assorted books that for some foolish reason Sripathi had lugged all the way back from that America-Canada place. As if there weren't any books in this country! Trust her son to pick all the wrong things to hang on to. He never did have any sense; from the moment he was born, he was an idiot. That was obvious to Ammayya as soon as she laid eyes on his sticking-out ears, his pasty face and his bulging navel fifty-seven years ago. Although at that time, her young eyes dimmed by love for her first-born, she had thought that the elephantine ears were a sign of future greatness, in spite of the fact that they were folded down at the top like photo-corners and had to be tied back for a few months until they straightened out somewhat. She rifled through the photographs impatiently, pausing when she came across one of Maya, Alan and Nandana in front of a small blue house with a flowering bush beside it. All of a sudden, the old woman was filled with an unaccustomed regret. She looked at the smiling young face in the picture and remembered that Maya had always indulged her. Like that time she had taken Ammayya to an ancient film starring Shivaji Ganeshan playing Robin Hood. The girl had saved her bus fare for weeks, leaving the house early to get to college on foot. And then she had surprised her grandmother with a trip to the theatre, even treated her to a bag of popcorn that the vendor assured them had been popped in vegetable oil. After she went away to the foreign country, she never failed to enclose a pack of chewing gum for Ammayya along with every letter, starting an addiction for the rubbery strips in the old lady. Yes, Maya had been a good grandchild. But then again, perhaps she had hoped that Ammayya would leave her some of her jewellery. Nobody did anything without an ulterior motive. The old woman stuffed all the photographs back in the envelope and shut the suitcase, and with it her momentary lapse into sentimentality. Ammayya had lost so much in life—children, illusions, dreams, trust—that one more loss no longer really mattered to her. Things came and things went. That was life. What she could hang on to, she did with the ferocity of an animal with its kill.

Arun's belongings in the same room did not rate so much as a cursory glance. He was an ascetic, nothing there worth taking. In fact, thought Ammayya, if she had had her purse with her she might even have been moved to leave a few coins for her unimpressive grandson. He, too, had proved to be a disappointment like his father. But that was how it was with men in this family. Arrived in the world with a lot of noise and did nothing to deserve all that initial attention. Fah!

But she knew she would find something interesting as soon as she opened the cupboard. There, in the dark hollow, Maya's red coat shone like a flame, begging to be stolen. Ammayya stroked the delicious, heavy, silky surface of the coat. She loved it immediately, passionately. Ammayya snatched it up, and like a bride with her wedding clothes, she shyly inserted one arm and then another into its warm, glowing embrace. Her pouchy skin shrank with delicate pleasure at the touch of such luxury. It smelled wonderful too. Subtle and teasing, the aromas trapped in that red blaze of wool. She would never be able to wear it at home, but she could sell it for a good sum of money at the China Bazaar. Ammayya abandoned the powder tin on Arun's paper-ridden desk. Let Nirmala keep it, she thought magnanimously. This jacket more than made up for the sacrifice. The old woman cuddled it against her ancient body, remembered to open out the windows she had shut, pull the curtains she had drawn, and creaked down the stairs like a bandit queen, satisfied with her efforts. She shuffled across the gloomy living room and into her own chamber where she secreted the jacket in one of her cupboards, locking it carefully with a key from the bunch around her neck. Ah, what a good evening it had been! Thoroughly pleased with herself, she went onto the verandah and sat on the steps. Innocent as a leaf on a tree. An old woman waiting for her family to come home.

———

"Scissor sharpening! Knife polishing!" called a sing-song voice from the road outside, followed by the clash and scrape of knives against the sides of a bicycle. The knife man passed this way every single day, but no one called for his services. Last week, the fat brothers in her rickshaw had warned her that, if she was naughty, the knife man would cut her into small pieces with his sharpest pair of scissors, and feed the pieces to the sea monster that guarded Toturpuram from foreign pirates. So it was with a sense of relief that Nandana watched the man go by without stopping. As his voice faded down the road, another set of sounds started up across the compound wall, shrill voices screaming and fighting over the garbage bin. The gypsies who lived on the pavement had started scavenging for the day and were quarrelling over the discarded cloth, old tins and bottles. Nandana recognized these two gypsies, with their dirty, deeply pleated skirts slung low over their hips so that their bellies spilled over. They fascinated her. The men had curly hair that they wore in knots and decorated with peacock feathers. They sang or simply lay on the ground, staring up at the sky split into blue bits by tree leaves. The children ran around naked and played all the time instead of going to school. And the women sat on the pavement and made bead jewellery or stitched the rags that they had collected into patchwork skirts. On her first day at school, Nirmala and Sripathi had taken Nandana by bus and that was when she had first seen the gypsies.

"Thieves," Nirmala had muttered, pulling her closer. "Don't go near them. They will put a curse on you." The gypsies stole anything they could find. They were like crows. They even stole children if they found them wandering around alone. "Don't ever go out by yourself, okay mari?" warned Nirmala, squeezing her hand tight.

But Nandana wasn't scared. All she wanted to do was get to the railway station and the airport and home.

14

UNKNOWN
ROADS

B Y THE TIME Sripathi reached the street on which Dr. Menon had his clinic, his legs had stopped quivering. But to his dismay, he found the entrance to the street blocked by an enormous plywood cut-out of the chief minister of the state. It leaned against the wall of a building and was so large that it stretched right across to the other side of the street. A man was perched on scaffolding high above the ground, touching up the face of the cut-out with a large flat brush. Along the scaffolding, he had hung a tray with cans of paint that he dipped into every few minutes.

Sripathi clucked his tongue in irritation and came to a stop. "What is going on here?" he asked. "How do you expect people to go through?"

"Other way," shouted the sign painter, pausing to look down at Sripathi.

"What do you mean 'other way'? I don't have time to circle the entire town to get to the other end of this street," protested Sripathi.

"This is Madam Chief Minister's portrait. Urgently required. Cannot be moved without permission," said the man, busily darkening the eyebrows on the enormous chief ministerial visage. He added a touch of neon pink to the lips and leaned back on the scaffold to survey the effect. "Madam likes my style. She personally requested me, Chamraj Painter, to do this special portrait. I am too-too honoured."

"How much is she paying you?" asked Sripathi, shielding his eyes from the sun as he stared up at the enormous cut-out that soared over the building against which it was propped.

"I don't know. The honour is what matters," replied the painter.

"Who gave you money for the paints? At least that you could have got from the minister's office," remarked Sripathi.

"Oh, Madam will make sure that I am paid," said the painter, dabbing diamond earrings on the chief minister's ears. He used the same brush to add a kindly sparkle to her outsized eyes. "She knows that I am a poor man with a family to feed. Why she should cheat me of a few rupees?"

Why not? Sripathi wanted to ask—that's how these politician crooks become rich, by stealing from the poor and the helpless. But the poor fellow probably knew that he would not see any money, yet could do nothing. The chief minister's goons would have made chutney of him if he had refused the commission.

"Can I park my scooter here and walk across to Dr. Menon's clinic?" he asked instead. "I'll give you two rupees if you keep an eye on it for me."

"No problem, saar," said the painter cheerfully. "And you don't have to pay me. Anyway, I am here, so whyfor you need to give me money also?"

Sripathi stepped carefully across the bottom planks of the scaffolding and beneath the cut-out. The pungent smell of turpentine overrode the more subtle scent of wood and the inevitable stink of the open drain at the edge of the street. After he had walked a few furlongs, Sripathi turned around to make sure that his scooter was still where he had left it. It was there, minute beside the soaring cut-out of the chief minister, her enormous cheeks a radiant pink, her eyes like planets bulging out of their broom-long fringe of eyelashes. She smiled coyly at the sky, her lips thick slabs of red meat still ashimmer with fresh paint. Directly beneath her head were her breasts, painted twin mountains draped in a shawl strewn with what appeared to be sparkling gems. The shawl was the minister's trademark and was believed to hide a bullet-proof vest. Her hands were folded demurely in a namaskaram. During the night, probably, some loafer had clambered all the way up to those jutting breasts and painted a pair of black nipples surrounded by red aureoles. This, in combination with the pouting lips, the tragic eyes and the halo, made the minister look like a martyred slut. Sripathi hoped that the painter noticed the addition to his art before he presented it to the respected minister.

Dr. Menon ran his clinic from a hole in the wall of a dilapidated building on the street. The wall was plastered with film posters and political graffiti, so that the clinic seemed to be a part of the collage too. Women with beckoning eyes mooned at thick, muscled heroes on posters that announced in black letters: *Super-action-packed chiller-thriller! Romance! Comedy! Tragedy! Spectacular Spectacles!* And beside these flamboyant outbursts were the more sombre political messages: *Vote for VKR. He Cares for Your Cares. He Will Wipe the Sweat from Your Brow.*

People who weren't aware of the existence of the clinic were startled by what appeared to be characters stepping off the pictures. Dr. Menon, almost a segment of this whole unrealistic scene, was so ancient that he had to be hauled out of his chair by his patients and supported to a shadowed corner of the clinic where he shakily mixed pellets and powders, screwed them into tight little slips of paper and handed them to his patients with garbled instructions on dosage. It was difficult to make out if the old man actually listened to his patients, made diagnoses and then decided on the medicine, for he always coughed through the entire recitation of ills and staggered out of his chair before the patient was done. When Sripathi entered the dark hole, he found the doctor lying motionless with his head on his desk, eyes shut, surrounded by a welter of papers and books. In one corner sat a small child, probably his grandson, reciting his times tables.

"One twoza two, two twoza four, three twoza six," he droned, swinging forward and backward rhythmically to his own voice.

"Is he okay?" asked Sripathi anxiously, jerking his head in the doctor's direction.

"Hoonh," said the boy. "Just shake him a little and he will get up."

A tentative tap on the shoulder of the good doctor evoked no response. Sripathi glanced at the boy questioningly. The boy jumped to his feet and grabbed his grandfather's shoulder, pinching it a couple of times before putting his mouth against a ragged ear soft and crumpled as old velvet.

"Thatha!" roared the boy, still pinching the old man's shoulder energetically. "A patient has come. Get up. Thatha!"

The old man sprang to his feet and looked around wildly. "What? What?"

"A patient is waiting for you. Thatha!"

The doctor swivelled his milky eyes towards Sripathi. "Good morning sir, good morning. And what is your problem?"

"My legs are feeling funny," bawled Sripathi who knew that Dr. Menon was hard of hearing. And I might not have a job at the end of this month, he felt like adding.

"Funny legs. Hmm. Could be a stroke or maybe filaria. Or malaria. In this pigsty of a town there are so many types of mosquitoes." Dr. Menon leaned back in his rickety chair and shut his eyes. He was silent for so long that Sripathi thought he had fallen asleep. He was thinking of shaking him awake when the old man jerked up and feverishly scrabbled through the desk drawers. He opened and shut several drawers before excavating a little jar of translucent paste.

"My son brought this for me from Singapore. It says on the leaflet here that it is a malam good for everything. Many ancient herbs and berries have gone into it. Rub some on your legs and if that doesn't work, swallow a teaspoon with a glass of warm milk. If it works it works, if not nothing bad will happen."

Dr. Menon leaned back again, exhausted by the whole interlude, and fell asleep. Sripathi dropped a five-rupee note on the desk and slipped out quietly.

On the way back to his scooter, he spotted a tired-looking woman crouched beside the road, selling a few flowers. He was reminded of his long-forgotten ritual of buying flowers for Nirmala. And of the fact that it was Putti's birthday today. The flower-seller had just one withered string of jasmines in her basket and a few pink roses that had lost most of their petals.

"Seventy-five paise for all of them," said the woman. Sripathi paid her without trying to bargain and she wrapped it in a piece of banana leaf for him.

The sign painter had stopped for a tea break when Sripathi returned to pick up his scooter. Once again he refused the money that Sripathi held out to him.

"Come on, take it, for your children. Buy them some toffees," urged Sripathi.

"Okay, if you put it that way," smiled the man, dropping the change into his shirt pocket.

"Have you finished the picture?" asked Sripathi. He shielded his eyes against the last rays of the sun and stared up at the huge cutout. The black nipples had been painted over, he noticed, and the chief minister merely looked coquettish now.

"*I* have finished. But tonight again those opposition party loafers will come and paint something which I will have to erase tomorrow. Big nuisance and waste of paint. I have told Madam's office to please come urgently and pick up this thing, but nobody bothers," said the painter sadly. "How long I can block up this street? People shout at me, as if it is my fault. I am just a poor man making my living."

"Do you do many of these?" asked Sripathi.

"Three or four a month. It takes time to cut out and draw the portrait. I have to sketch the face in when the wood is flat on the ground. Then attach it to the rest of the body. The clothes and all are easy. The face can be a problem. Looks different when it is standing up, then you have to do it all over again."

"Lots of work involved," agreed Sripathi.

"You have seen the one over the Chettiar crossbridge? That also is mine. And most cinema posters near January Talkies. I am good at personalities. That is why I get enough work—every other person in this place thinks he is a personality, enh?" The sign painter winked and grinned at Sripathi.

He took the long, roundabout route to get home, mainly to avoid the street in which his father had died. In the dying light of the evening, everything seemed to him to be old and remote. Nothing was the way he remembered it. He lost his way a few times, even though he had lived in Toturpuram all his life. By the time he reached Brahmin Street, the sun had almost disappeared from the sky. In the gloom Big House loomed like an ugly monster. The front door was open and the back door would be as well, to release the malicious spirits trapped inside and welcome the good ones in. Nirmala would have lighted the lamps and finished her brief incantation to her gods. The gate was moving slightly, hitting against the latest pile of debris, and a small figure swung on it, propelling it back and forth with a foot. For an instance, Sripathi thought that it was Maya waiting for him to return from work. As he approached the figure detached itself from the gate and raced inside the house. It was the child, he realized.

"How are you, Sripathi-orey?" greeted Munnuswamy from next door. He was sitting next to the calf, stroking its heaving flank.

"Okay," said Sripathi briefly. He had no desire to talk to the man, his heart still thundering with the sudden hope that had arisen at the sight of that little figure swinging on the gate. "And how about you?" he felt obliged to add.

"My calf is very sick," said Munnuswamy. "She won't live till tomorrow."

There was nothing that Sripathi could think of to say to that, not even a few words of comfort. He locked his scooter against the railing around the verandah, took off his slippers and entered the house. The child was nowhere to be seen. Ammayya was sitting in front of the television, watching one of the three channels they received. It was a program with noisy song-and-dance sequences from old films. The heroine danced and wiggled around trees, mountains, fountains and gardens, while the hero chased after her, entranced. The blue glare from the television fell on his mother's rapt face, making her look haunted. Nirmala emerged from the kitchen, wiping her hands on her sari pallu.

"Why you are so late?" she wanted to know.

Sripathi held out the crushed packet of flowers that he had purchased.

"For me?" Nirmala asked.

He nodded. "And half for Putti—it is her birthday, remember? They are a little dry. The woman did not have any more."

She broke off a bit from the string of jasmines and tucked it in her hair, her eyes on him all the while, shy and a little puzzled.

"What are you doing phusur-phusur there?" asked Ammayya. She peered across the gloomy room at the two of them.

"Nothing," said Nirmala. "He just bought some flowers for me."

"Flowers? At this age?" Ammayya went back to her television program and Sripathi went upstairs. I will have to tell them about my job, he thought. The lights were on in Arun's room and suddenly he was filled with a rage against his son. If the fool had a job, at least the burden of looking after the family would be shared. There was some money for the child, her parent's insurance money.

Sripathi had insisted that it be placed in a trust fund. For her future. He would take care of her present, he had told Dr. Sunderraj. He had refused to agree to a monthly allowance for the child's education, clothing and other necessities. "I can manage," he had told the doctor, resenting the man's interference. "We people in India are not all paupers, you know."

Now, on an impulse, he entered his son's room. He looked around for the child, but she wasn't to be seen. Arun was sitting on his bed, studying some sheets of paper in the dim light of the 20-watt bulb that Ammayya had forced them all to use. Sripathi looked at the short body, the ragged hair, the unshaven visage, and allowed it all to fuel his building anger.

"Where is the child?" he asked stiffly.

"Under the bed," said Arun looking up at his father, his eyes hidden behind his glasses.

"Under the bed?"

"She goes there when she is scared."

The child was scared of him? What had he ever done to her? Did she, too, blame him for her mother's death?

He stepped backwards until he was in the doorway. From there, he could see the child's thin elbow where it stuck out from under the cot. He also noticed that Arun's face was swollen and bruised.

"What happened to you?" Sripathi asked. "You look as if you fell down or something."

Arun touched his face tenderly. "I got beaten up by Munnuswamy's thugs."

"What?"

"Oh, he doesn't know, probably. He just issues the orders."

"What are you involved in now? Henh? Some other saving-the-world project? Why are you wasting your time trying to be a big hero instead of getting a job? Here I am, head full of grey hair, going to work everyday like an ox, and my son sits at home dreaming useless dreams."

"Appu," said Arun, "I am not trying to be a hero or anything so grand. I just don't have the patience to wait for the government to take care of my future for me. They are all crooks and thieves, lining their own nests."

"I know, you don't have to tell me that," said Sripathi. "But what kind of future will you make for yourself by wasting time waving flags and banners and shouting slogans? At your age I was earning a living and looking after a family of four."

"You won't understand, Appu, so why don't you leave it alone?"

"But I am trying to. Your mother also keeps telling me that I don't. But why doesn't anybody tell me *what* it is I don't understand?" demanded Sripathi, slapping his hand on the door to emphasize each word.

The child under the bed whimpered. "Don't shout, you are frightening her," said Arun. "And I will try to explain. See, you had your independence of India and all to fight for, real ideals. For me and my friends, the fight is against daily injustice, our own people stealing our rights. This is the only world I have, and I feel responsible for it. I have to make sure that it doesn't get blown up, or washed away in the next flood, or poisoned by chemicals." He looked awkwardly at his father and shuffled the papers on the bed. "I mean, look how it is already, no water to drink, electricity keeps getting cut off, you can't even play on the beach without getting all kinds of rashes on your legs. It wasn't like this when I was small, was it? Appu? Was it?"

Sripathi didn't reply. He knew deep down that his son had a point, but still, all that talk about duty, what about his duty towards his family? And tomorrow he might get married and have children, and how would he support them?

"I knew you wouldn't see things my way. You never have," said Arun bitterly.

Sripathi glowered at his son. He wanted a quarrel, he realized with a shock. He wanted to shout and scream and rage at someone, and Arun was handy right now. Why are you fighting all these use-less fights? he wanted to yell. You idiot, I, too, dreamed of being a hero and look at me now. You will lose all that crusading innocence as your hair turns grey, and you find yourself responsible for lives other than your own. It will all slip away, one by one, your dreams vaporized by the fierce sun of reality. A house, a scooter, your child's education, the doctor's bills, food and clothes and shoes . . . All these will drown you, and before you know it you will, like me, sit at the edge of your youth and ask yourself, Why did I let it all go?

A shuffling movement beneath the bed reminded him of the child's presence, and with an effort he stopped himself from ex-ploding. "You are a fool, that is all," he said finally, in a quiet voice, before heading off for a bath.

At dinnertime that night, Ammayya glared at the child. "It's evil to play with your food," she said finally. She had slurped her way through large quantities of each dish on the table as if they were in the middle of a famine, managing to tuck a chapatti in the folds of her sari for later consumption.

Nandana continued to toy with the rice and sambhar that Nir-mala had mixed for her. Around the edge of her large, steel dinner plate she had arranged neat piles of mustard seeds, chilies, curry leaves, beans and other things that she had fished out from the pud-dle of food.

"You, girl, did you hear me?" continued Ammayya, knocking on the table with a spoon. "God put food on our plates to *eat*, not to push around here and there. What would your mother think of this kind of wasteful behaviour?"

The child's head shot up. Nirmala frowned at her mother-in-law and then at Sripathi for his silence. "There is no need to scare the little one," she protested. "She is not used to our food."

"Pah! Her mother was such a gem-child. No fuss about eating food or anything."

"Ammayya, that's enough," said Nirmala.

The old lady surged on, inventing as she went. "With my own hands I used to mix her food for her. I only used to feed her. Ammayya, she used to say to me, I feel so bad for the poor hungry orphans in the slums. Can we take some food to them? And my eyes would fill at her generosity. Although—and I don't like boasting—I am the one who taught her to think about the less fortunate in this world."

The child chased a pea around the swimming brown mess of food on her plate. "Look at her, so stubborn," continued Ammayya. "These days children are spoilt, that's all."

Nirmala stroked the child's head and cheek tenderly. "You don't like our food? This was your mother's favourite dish. Shall I feed you?" Without waiting for a reply, she took up the spoon and ladled small amounts into the little girl's mouth.

"Do you know what is the capital of Argentina?" Ammayya quizzed Nandana. "Who is the president of America? Look at her, she knows nothing, this girl."

"Leave her alone, she is too young for all this," Nirmala said.

"At her age I knew everything. Even her mother was so bright, thanks to me," argued Ammayya. "What was Oscar Wilde's full name? Who can tell me?"

"Oscar Fingal O'Flahertie Wills Wilde," Sripathi replied. This used to be one of the answers that he could never recall when his father quizzed him years ago, and now it was burned into his memory. "Now that is enough, Ammayya." He pushed his food around his plate, unable to taste anything. He had no desire to eat. His legs were feeling odd again. He had ducked his head under the table a few times to check if they were still there. It seemed to him that his left foot had dissolved into a translucent, amorphous shape.

"What's the matter with you?" Ammayya asked him suddenly. "Something is down there? That wretched cat? It should be killed, inauspicious thing. Tomorrow I will ask Koti to catch it and throw it in the drain."

Nandana pushed her plate away and ran up the stairs.

Nirmala banged the spoon down and glared at Ammayya. "Why you have to say such things in front of the child? You know she likes playing with the cat. Why you are always doing these things?"

Before Ammayya could respond, there was a scream from upstairs. "What happened? Did you hear that?"

Another scream, followed by loud, hysterical weeping. "Nandana, something happened. Maybe she is hurt," Nirmala struggled to her feet and went up the stairs as fast as she could, followed by Arun.

They found the child in front of the open cupboard, screaming and crying alternately. "What is it? You are hurting somewhere? Tell me? Something bit you?" Nirmala tried to hold the little girl in her arms, but Nandana pushed her away hard and cried even louder.

The cupboard door gaped open and Nirmala peered in uncertainly. What had frightened the poor thing, she wondered. If she wouldn't speak, how could they know what to do? She shuffled the clothes hanging in the cupboard and realized that the red coat was no longer there. So *that* was what had upset the child. By now, Nirmala was familiar with Nandana's habit of hiding in the cupboard when she was angry or sad.

"Oh, my little one," she sighed. "Your coat is not there, is that the problem?"

Nandana nodded, her sobs subsiding into hiccups. "Don't worry, where can it go, tell me? Must have fallen down."

Nirmala knelt before the cupboard and rummaged about in the darkness. Her fingers encountered nothing other than the suitcases that she had stored there. "Must be here only," she murmured. "Where else it will go?" She sat back with a sigh and looked at Nandana's tearful face. "Don't worry, chinnu-ma. Tomorrow we will ask Koti to search the whole house. Maybe she kept it somewhere by mistake."

She stayed in the room, patting Nandana's back until she was asleep and then went heavily down the stairs. She caught sight of Ammayya rocking in her chair outside her room, and a sudden suspicion filled her mind. Could it be? she wondered. Could the old woman be that mean?

All night Sripathi lay awake staring out the open balcony door at the night sky still hot with stars. Squares and rectangles of light from windows and balconies turned the apartment block into a patchwork quilt of bright and dark. Some of the balconies had small clay oil lamps with lighted cotton wicks floating in them, others were trimmed with garlands of electric bulbs that winked and glittered. It reminded Sripathi that this was the end of October, and Deepavali was just a few days away. In the past, when the children were younger and the brightness of the future was a thing to celebrate, Big House, too, would have been lighted up and redolent with the smell of festival cooking. Putti and Koti and Nirmala would have brought out the clay lamps, checked them for cracks, replaced the broken ones and spent an afternoon or two twisting wads of cotton into wicks. The silver would be polished to a high shine. All the drums and pots and pans would be scrubbed thoroughly and marked with vermilion and turmeric. New clothes and fire crackers would be bought for the children. "Can we explode one right away?" they would beg, their eyes alight with excitement. "Just one sparkler, pleasepleaseplease." And Nirmala would refuse firmly. Only at dawn on Deepavali day would they get to light one sparkler each. The whole house would be cleaned from top to bottom, for this was a festival to welcome the heroic King Rama home from battle. To celebrate the triumph of light over darkness. Sripathi had often argued with Nirmala about the festival.

"Who says Rama is the hero?" he had asked once. "Why not Ravana? After all, he, too, was a great and beloved king. He was a musician, a learned man. Just because he had ten wives and lusted after another man's wife, he is a villain? Look at your Rama. Did he not abandon his wife after all the fireworks were over? If he is a hero, I am a superhero. See how long I have stuck with you?"

And Nirmala had replied, in too good a mood with the excitement of the approaching festival to be truly angry, "Ravana had a big ego. Like you. A hero is humble."

There would be no lamps or crackers this year in Big House. All of a sudden he longed for them. The flickering lights, the thin rain that always fell on the night of the festival, the aroma of chakkuli and khara sev frying in the kitchen, the flash of silk as the women and girls dashed in and out of the house. He wanted yesterday to come back to him whole and unspoiled.

He watched the lights go off, one by one, until there was only the dark rectangle of the apartment building. He heard Arun enter the house. And several hours later, Putti opening the front door to get the milk. He dozed off briefly and was woken again by a whimpering cry from Arun's room across the landing. For a few minutes, Sripathi lay there wondering whether he was imagining it. There was a louder cry and he hurried across to see what was wrong. Nothing. The child was sound asleep, her right arm tight around a faded cloth cow. Arun's bed was empty. Must be in the dining room reading or planning another protest march, thought Sripathi wryly. He straightened the sheet on the little girl's body and sat at the edge of her cot, contemplating her thin face, the tangle of long hair curling over the pillow, the curve of her eyelids fluttering in sleep. The whites of her eyes shone from the gap between her lids like sickle moons. Maya, too, had slept with her eyes slightly open. What kind of dreams or nightmares wandered behind those tender lids? wondered Sripathi. If he and Nirmala could barely contain the grief they carried within them, how could this frail creature who had lost the two people she had known best in all the world? He had thought that, as was natural in this world governed by time, his life would stop and his children's would surge past like runners bearing the chalice of his memory. They would tell their grandchildren about him. Happen upon his photographs, his pens, after his death and say, "Ah look, these were Appu's most beloved possessions. He never let us touch them, you know." Never, not even in his nightmares, had he chanced upon the possibility of being alive after his child was dead.

Sripathi touched Nandana's head again, wishing that he could allow himself to let go, to give the child all the love that he had dammed up. He was ashamed of the distance he maintained, aware that the child could sense his unease and was puzzled by it. She never indicated that she wanted anything of him, although she seemed comfortable with Nirmala and Arun. Especially Arun, who spent patient hours with her explaining life in this bewildering place of noise and people, not in the least bothered by the child's silence.

How can I face my grandchild when I am responsible for her mother's death? Sripathi asked himself. The more he thought about his actions eight years ago, the more convinced he was that his anger had somehow brought about Maya's demise. He had cursed her for her refusal to marry Prakash, for humiliating him by breaking the engagement, for obliging him to face Prakash's father when he went to return the jewellery they had given Maya as gifts, for blackening the family name in the entire town. And the curse had killed her.

Nandana stirred in her sleep again, and Sripathi automatically patted her on the back the way he used to do when Maya and Arun were children and then placed a hand on her forehead to make sure that she did not have a fever. Her forehead was cool and moist. Sripathi rose from the edge of the bed, straightened out a few sheets of paper lying on Arun's desk and decided to go down for a cup of tea.

His son was in the dining room, books spread out on the table before him. He was busy scribbling on sheets of paper. "Working on something?" asked Sripathi, rubbing the back of his neck. He was determined to be pleasant no matter what the provocation. Even though the sight of Arun's shaggy, uncut hair and the torn green shirt made him itch with irritation. "A new project?"

"Yes," said Arun briefly.

"What is it about?"

"Do you really want to know?"

"Why should I ask otherwise?" said Sripathi. I have lost one child because of my temper, he reminded himself. Not another one as well.

"Have you heard of the Olive Ridley turtles?"

"Yes, I saw something in the papers."

"And you really want to hear more?" Arun asked cautiously.

"I am most interested in knowing what turtles have to do with the fate of this world, or for that matter, with your future." Sripathi couldn't keep the sarcasm from his voice.

"We are all part of nature, Appu. If the natural world goes, so do we. All the industrial effluents being dumped into the sea are destroying the turtles, and soon they will destroy us too. Before long the water table will be affected, and instead of drinking water we will be drinking chlorine or whatever poison is being unloaded."

"Too much talking as usual," grumbled Sripathi. "Turtles! Couldn't you find anything more useful to work on?"

Arun pushed his chair back angrily and left the room. "No point talking to you," he said. Then he came back again and glared at his father. "You lecture me all the time. You want me to get a job, no? Tomorrow itself I will find one."

"Oh, of course, the world is waiting for Mr. Arun Rao to come along and ask for a job! Yes indeed, there are jobs lying like pearls on the road for you to pick up as you walk past. Let us see what kind you will come back with."

Arun left without another word, out the back door, closing it softly behind him. Sripathi was alone with the spasmodic snorts and starts of the ancient Zenith refrigerator. He had purchased it at a ridiculous price twenty years ago when he was doing the advertisement for it.

"Japanese at heart—strong and steady" he had written flatteringly about the motor.

Almost believed it too. Until the company collapsed. The engine wasn't all that strong, it turned out, and almost every customer had returned the product for a full refund. Sripathi's was the only one in the entire country that had survived without a problem all these years. The owner had told him that on one of his bi-annual visits to look at the fridge with awed wonder. He was bankrupt, living on the goodwill and charity of his brothers, and Sripathi didn't have the heart to refuse him this small pleasure. How was it that he could find kindness in his heart for everyone but his son? he asked himself, wishing that he had not been so harsh tonight. It had not been his intention, but somehow the words had just flown out of his mouth. He remembered his father's uncle, Rama Rao, a kind old man who had lived alone on Veerappa Street in a small, bare house, perfectly content with whatever he had, with no desire for anything that he did not. Sripathi's father used to visit him once a fortnight, always taking Sripathi along with him. As soon as they entered the little house that crouched like a gnome in the squalor of the street, Rama Rao would shuffle forward, chuck Sripathi under the chin with a trembling hand and exclaim, "My goodness, how this boy has grown!" Rama Rao spoke excruciatingly slowly. It took him half an hour (or so it seemed to the young Sripathi) to pull a single sentence out of his mouth.

One day, in the middle of a long story that the old man was narrating, Sripathi, conscious that his father would be furious, had burst out impatiently, "Rama Uncle, why do you take so long to say anything?"

And the old man had gazed at him with merry eyes and replied, still very slowly, "Ah, my boy, once the words are out of my mouth, I cannot push them back in. So it is better that I think carefully before I allow them to escape."

Sripathi wished that he had assimilated this advice more thoroughly. He went out onto the verandah and picked up the newspaper, took it back upstairs to the balcony and opened it to the editorial page. One of his letters was there:

> *Dear Sir,*
>   *This is with reference to the comment by one of our esteemed ministers that the banyan tree on the corner of Beach Road and (formerly) Brahmin Street be cut down because of the number of traffic accidents in that area. May I point out that the tree is only an innocent bystander. The real culprits are drunk drivers, poor street lights, the absence of speed breakers, and other human factors.*
>
>   *Sincerely,*
>   *Pro Bono Publico*

He waited for the usual frisson of pleasure that seeing his byline produced, but nothing happened. He felt as dead as a broken branch.

———

No fair, thought Nandana. She was always It when they played hide and seek in the apartment block. She and Nithya and Meena and Ayesha. It was a trick, she knew, but she couldn't figure out how they did it.

"Close your eyes and count to twenty," commanded Nithya.

Reluctantly, Nandana leaned against the wall of the building and shut her eyes. One-two-three, she counted.

"Sweet baby," crooned a voice close to her ear, startling her. She opened her eyes. "Lovely baby, my little one, come here." It was the sad lady on the ground floor who always sat on her patio and stared at nothing. Koti had said that she was mad. Nandana backed away nervously. What did mad people do?

"Cheating! Cheating!" screamed Meena, peering around the building to check whether Nandana was done counting. "Game up! She was cheating. Her eyes are open already."

Nandana shook her head. She never cheated. Never ever. The other two girls emerged from their hiding places. "You have to be punished for cheating," said Nithya.

"Yes, yes, yes!" sang Meena and Ayesha. "She has to cross her eyes for ever. She has to be den three times."

No tears, no tears, Nandana told herself. Tears were a sign that the battle was lost. Her father had told her that when Janet Lundy was mean to her at Molly's birthday party. She had cried then, great gulping sobs that had soaked the front of her new dress and made the cake taste funny in her mouth afterwards. But she wasn't going to lose now. She twisted the end of her frock in her right fist and held on tight. She wished that she had her Moona cow with her.

"No, those are stupid punishments," said Nithya. "I've got a better idea. She has to pass a test."

What test?

"She has to run through the tunnel between A and B blocks." Nithya pointed to the dark alley that separated the two apartment buildings. Meena and Ayesha giggled nervously. "But that is a no-no place," whispered Ayesha.

"The tunnel test," said Nithya firmly.

Nandana gazed fearfully at the dark, forbidding passage. There were wicked spirits in there. All the children had told her that. And the crazy old man from the second floor hid there sometimes—the Chocobar Ajja. Mamma Lady had warned her to run away when she saw him. But Mamma Lady was bugging Nandana these days. She had not found the red coat. She had lied to her.

"If you don't do the test, we will never play with you again," said Meena.

Nandana hesitated and walked timidly over to the high, narrow gap between the two buildings. Behind her the girls giggled, a little frightened. "She is a cowardy-custard," said Nithya.

"My mother said that it was a un-sani-tary place," said Ayesha. "She'd beat me if she knew."

"Tattle-tale!" said Nithya. "How will she know if you don't tell her?" She turned to Nandana, her arms on her hips. "Are you going or are you frightened?"

No *way*, thought Nandana. She entered the tunnel, and behind her she could hear the girls gasp and squeal. "We'll wait for you at the other end," shouted one of them before they ran off.

It was twilight in the tunnel. Light from adjoining apartment windows shimmered weirdly off the slimy walls, and the ground was groggy with overflow. It smelled of rotting fruit in there and made Nandana want to vomit. Sewage pipes ran down the walls like snakes, and the sound of toilets flushing, taps running, showers jetting, teeth brushing, songs singing and families talking were all translated into eerie moans and whistles, sighs and gurgles. Something soft slithered against her sandalled ankle and with a scream of terror, she hurled herself out of the other end, sobbing with relief.

The three girls were waiting for her, but as soon as Nandana emerged, they ran around the corner of the building. All the tears that she had collected inside herself burst through, and she cried harder and harder. They were mean, like her parents. They had gone away. She had prayed every night to Hanuman to send her parents back to her, the brave monkey god Aunty Kiran had told her about, who always helped people in trouble, who made everybody happy. But it hadn't worked. The monkey god hadn't done anything at all.

"Oho, my darling, there you are," exclaimed a gentle voice, startling her.

It was the mad lady again. "Where did you go, child? I was so worried."

Nandana backed away, although the woman looked kind rather than frightening. She did not have any sticks or knives that Nithya said she carried around. She was a stranger, though.

"Come here, look what I have made for you," the lady held out something and smiled.

Nandana inched forward curious to see what it was that the woman was offering her. It was a much-folded paratha. "See, your favourite treat," said the woman, reaching out to grasp Nandana's arm. "I know how much you like it with sugar."

She looked frightening now, her eyes black and staring. So Nandana turned and ran out of the compound, past the Gurkha who dozed on his stool near the gate and leapt up when she hurtled past. "Ohey, missy-amma, ohey!" he shouted running after her. "Where you are going like the wind?"

He stopped following when Nandana entered the gates of Big House. As she ran in, she heard Mamma Lady's voice raised in song, and the tap-tap of her baton.

"Where are you going?" Aunty Putti called from the verandah where she was sitting, reading a magazine. But Nandana continued to run until she reached the back garden and the mango tree that her mother had told her about long, long ago, and she sat beneath it completely out of breath. For a change, she did not even bother to check for fire ants, killer bees or cobras.

15

CHANT FOR
THE LOST

P UTTI FINISHED THE MAGAZINE she was reading and looked discreetly across the wall at Munnuswamy's blue house. There was nobody. Only the cow, and beside her, the dead calf. The hide of the calf had been draped over a stack of hay, tied together roughly to resemble an animal, and placed beside the cow. Mrs. Munnuswamy had said that this was what was always done. "The mother has to be fooled into believing that the young one is still alive," she had said. "Otherwise the poor thing will be too full of sorrow to give milk, and her udders will be infected and she, too, will die." Putti had thought how wonderful it would be if humans were as easily deluded. Or did the cow know that her calf was dead and willingly submit to the comfort of the illusion that Munnuswamy had created with hide and hay?

She decided to go up to the terrace and sit there for a while. Past the dancing girls she went, ignoring Ammayya who sat at the door commenting on the girls, on Nirmala's singing and teaching methods.

Her mother, too, did not look at her. She was angry with Putti. Earlier that day, they had searched the house down for Maya's red coat. Except for Ammayya's room. She had refused to let them in, or to open any of her cupboards and trunks.

"Insulting me in my own house!" she had screamed, hitting out at her daughter-in-law and the maid with her stick. "Accusing me of theft! Kali-yuga has indeed, arrived and I, unlucky one, am still alive to witness it! Oh-oh-oh!"

"Nobody is accusing you of anything, Ammayya," said Nirmala, dodging the stick. "The child is really upset, so we are only looking just in case that coat got into your room by mistake."

"Mistake? Mistake? Can a coat open doors and climb in by itself? You don't fool me one bit. Or that cross-eyed bitch of a Koti! You are all after my jewellery, I know."

"If Maya's ghost can wander around the house, why can't a coat?" demanded Nirmala with some asperity. She wasn't going to let Ammayya off that easily.

"Ghosts? There are ghosts in this house?" asked Ammayya artlessly, opening her eyes wide.

"*You* are the one who told my granddaughter that there were," said Nirmala.

"Me? I never talk to that brat. What use talking to a dumb thing?" She held her heart and allowed the tears to drown her eyes. "All my life I have done things for people, total strangers too, and now look how I am treated in my own house."

After lunch, while Ammayya napped, Putti had stolen her mother's keys and found the coat wrapped in an old sari stored in a corner of the cupboard. She had quietly handed it to Nirmala. Now, up on the terrace Putti leaned against the wall and swept all her hair to one side. It was a Sunday and she had indulged in an oil bath. The combination of the thick mustard oil melting into her body and the hot water that she had used to wash it off made her feel soft and drowsy. A pleasant breeze cooled the back of her neck. Far below, in the garden, she noticed Nandana near the mango tree. The child had captured the cat and was playing with it.

"Like dark clouds her ringlets tumble," called a voice from the neighbouring terrace.

Putti looked up startled to see Gopala standing there, in a sin-glet and striped cotton shorts. She knew it was indecent of him to expose his body like this to an unmarried woman, but she felt her belly flutter with excitement.

"Her face is a moonbeam shining through," continued Gopala, leaning against the parapet and giving Putti a deep, meaningful glance. "Her eyes like twin stars beckon." Now his own eyes touched her breasts decorously covered by the pallu of her sari, and to her horror she could feel her nipples harden inside the stern cotton Maidenform brassiere, which, like the rest of the lingerie in Beau-teous Boutique, was built to last several decades. Putti blushed, embarrassed by her wayward body.

"Shall I come and carry you away my moonbeam?" called Gopala, and made as if to leap across the gap separating the two buildings, and Putti turned and fled into the safety of the house. She was so agitated she did not know what to do with herself. The last thing she wanted was to face her mother just now. She sat down at the top of the stairs, her heart thudding with fear and excite-ment—Gopala was like a film star, Putti thought. But, she reminded herself, he was also an unscrupulous, ruthless man. He was danger-ous. Nevertheless, the thought of him tainting her safe, clean world was wildly exciting.

And to complicate matters, next week the mental asylum thera-pist was arriving to see her—the fellow who had been touted as such a marvellous catch by Gowramma. Putti did not know what she would do if he agreed to marry her. Could *she* refuse? Or would Ammayya find something wrong with the fellow as she always did with every prospective groom? Restlessly she went into her brother's bathroom one floor down, and splashed some cold water on her face. Then, having composed herself, she went to her own room hoping her mother would not be there.

But Nirmala's students had left, and Ammayya was regretting her quarrel with Putti. She looked up eagerly at her daughter.

"My darling, isn't it exciting, next week my new son-in-law will be arriving?"

"I am not married to him yet. We are only meeting for the first time," snapped Putti sweeping past her into the bedroom.

"I have a good feeling about this one," sang Ammayya, rocking happily on her chair. "A really good feeling. And I saw four crows in the backyard this morning. You know what that means?"

"No."

"Of course you do, my darling. I only taught you the rhyme. *One for sorrow, two for joy, three for letter, four for boy!* Now do you remember?"

Putti settled in front of the Belgian mirror and brushed out her long hair tangled by the breeze.

"Why you are not speaking to your old mother, my pet?" begged Ammayya.

"I have nothing to say."

Ammayya looked fondly at Putti who was staring at the mirror as if she had never seen it before. A small spiral of doubt unwound in her mind. Once again, she noticed, Putti was standing transfixed before the glass. The old woman moved closer and tried to see what her daughter was looking at, but there was nothing except the two of them in the corroded silver.

At six that evening, after the dance students had dispersed, the family went to the temple. Nandana looked unfamiliar in a long, green cotton skirt and matching blouse instead of her usual jeans. Nirmala carried the fruit offerings in a silver platter—fresh bananas, a single apple (as apples were far too expensive now), a small bunch of grapes coated white with some pesticide that wouldn't wash off, a coconut with its fibre still intact (it was inauspicious to get rid of that tuft before the coconut was offered to God). A couple of a garbatti sticks and a string of flowers completed the picture. When Sripathi's father was alive, the offering was much grander and included out-of-season mangos, pomegranates, even a silver coin or two.

Now that the festival season had started, the temple was crowded with evening worshippers. Women swept by richly dressed in heavy silk saris, smelling of sandalwood, jasmine and incense. They, like Nirmala, carried platters of fruit and flowers. The men looked plain in comparison, as most of them wore white lungis wrapped around their waists and starched white cotton kurtas. There were rows of vendors outside the temple gates, shouting out their wares. More flowers, coconuts, fruit, betel leaves, piles of kum-kum powder in shades of crimson and pink, like mountains in a child's dream— every possible thing that one might need to placate, honour or flatter the gods inside that great stone building with its soaring pillars and dark womb where the chief deity resided in tranquil silence.

They left their shoes with a young boy who gave them a token in exchange. For a small charge, he would guard their footwear from the thieves and beggars who always hung around the gates, waiting for alms or an unguarded pocket. The temple was already full of evening worshippers—people singing, bending before the various idols scattered around the echoing stone enclosure, or simply praying silently with their eyes squeezed shut. One man lay flat on the ground and repeatedly banged his forehead on the floor, his murmured prayers rising and falling with each movement of his head. In a far corner, leaning against a pillar, sat an old man with neat clothes and sparse hair. He clapped his hands and shouted in a rich voice that seemed to emanate straight from his belly, "All gone! All gone! O Lord of the Cowherds, only you are left for me!"

Krishnamurthy Acharye, the old priest who had presided over the ceremonies when Maya was born, during the annaprashna when she had her first mouthful of solid food, on her first birthday, and who had blessed her before she left Toturpuram, was waiting for them. He recited prayers for her soul and Alan's, the latter in spite of Ammayya's objections.

"You and I are old enough to know better than to make a fuss over all this nonsense, Janaki Amma," he had wheezed. The priest was one of the few people who had known Ammayya long enough to address her by her first name. "Our gods won't mind if we say a prayer for someone of another faith. I know, I have been talking to them for eighty five years."

"But he doesn't have a gothra-nakshatra, nothing," quibbled Ammayya. "What was his family name? What stars was he born under?"

"We shall do it in God's name, that will be enough," said the priest. Ammayya had to content herself with eyeing the silver utensils that Nirmala had polished and brought along with the coconut, the flowers, the coins and the pieces of cloth that would be distributed to the poor after the rituals were observed.

"So cunning, did you see all the new-new things she has purchased? And she says that she has no money!" whispered Ammayya to Putti, who frowned at her.

"Those are her wedding things, Ammayya," she said, disgusted with her mother for behaving so uncharitably on even this sad occasion.

It was a simple ceremony. Nirmala had insisted on that, and the family sat in deep silence for a few minutes after the priest had finished his incantations. The ancient rhythm of the words was profoundly moving, and Sripathi could feel the tears prickle behind his eyelids. He wouldn't let them fall, though. To do so would be to acknowledge the finality of Maya's death. To do so would be to absolve himself of all blame, and he couldn't do that. Like a penitent he needed the harsh bite of guilt to keep memory alive.

Later that evening, Arun and Sripathi rode down to the beach with Maya's ashes. It was full of people out for an evening walk, children racing through the waves screaming half-fearfully as the surf snarled at their bare legs, women with their saris tucked high between their knees, keeping a watchful eye on the children and shouting, "Be careful, be careful!" every now and again. Here and there in the twilight, Petromax lanterns gleamed where vendors sold peanuts and green mango cut into lacy spirals, spicy bhel-puri and sugar-cane juice, their voices hoarse from competition with the endless crashing of the sea.

"Let's go farther up, over there," said Arun, pointing to a narrow, deserted strip of sand hedged in by large, mossy rocks.

They emptied the urn, watching the flecks of grey float away on the foam and the breeze, or settle on the rocks from where they would be washed away as the tide surged higher. Sripathi could feel some of the dust settle into his hair, stick to the skin on his face. He brushed a hand across his hair, but could still feel the weight of those particles. His face, too, felt coarse, as if the ash had scabbed over it permanently.

"We should have taken this to a river," he murmured. "That is the proper thing to do."

"I don't think it matters. Maya would not have minded," said Arun. "She never cared about silly details."

Sripathi nodded, too full of feeling to say a word. Yes, she never cared about details such as her father's reputation, Mr. Bhat's anger, nothing. And he cared about nothing but. That was the problem. He had a sudden desire to see Raju, to borrow some of his calm strength, his good humour. "You go home," he told Arun abruptly. "Tell your mother I will be back later."

He stood by the water for a while, and then walked across the damp sand to the road where he had parked his scooter. He rode past Karim Mechanic's shop, the Ace Tutorial building full of young men and women anxiously cramming for the SAT and GRE and GMAT exams, and the video store reverberating with the sound of the latest film music. Raju's house, when Sripathi reached it, was a haven of calm, but his friend was strangely silent during their visit, distracted almost. He listened quietly to Sripathi's complaints about the possibility of losing his job. And he nodded when he heard about the ceremony of the temple. "Yes, you need to close down some parts of your life without too much fuss," he said. "Otherwise you will go crazy."

But when Sripathi started grumbling about Arun, Raju gave him an irritated look. "Why are you always after that boy? At least he is with you when you need him. Look at me, my sons are strangers to me." He stopped and gazed broodingly at his book before plunging into complete silence. Sripathi sipped uncomfortably at his tea, aware that something deeper than his sons' attitudes was bothering his friend.

"Is something wrong?" he asked finally.

Raju hesitated. "No," he said. "I am okay, just a little tired."

"There is something," insisted Sripathi. "You can't hide from me, man. Come on, tell. I thought we were friends."

Raju gave a faint smile. "Too much imagination you have, Sri. Nothing to tell."

Poppu shuffled in with the tea and Raju shifted the conversation. "Why haven't you brought Nandana to see me?" he asked. "Am I not her grandfather too?"

"Yes, I will," said Sripathi. He wondered whether to tell his friend that the child would not speak at all. That she didn't seem to like him.

"When? Tomorrow? I am fed up of my own company. Why don't all of you come and have tea here? I will ask Poppu to make her famous maddur vadais. What do you say?"

"I say that you are trying to change the topic. I know there is something worrying you, and I am not going home till you tell me what it is," Sripathi said firmly.

Raju fiddled with the pages of his book. "I am selling this place," he said. "I can't manage any more on my pension. I can't handle Ragini by myself, and Poppu is getting old. We need to keep a nurse and I can't afford it, unless I sell my house."

Sripathi was too stunned to say anything for a few moments. "Why didn't you tell me?"

"What would you have done? You have troubles yourself."

Sripathi felt too ashamed to speak. Here he was going on and on, full of self-pity, always borrowing strength from Raju, never stopping to ask him how he was managing.

"You know, sometimes I dream of killing her," continued Raju. "I imagine how it would be to put a pillow over her face when she is asleep, how easy it would be to get away with it. Who will ask questions? Nobody. Why should people care about a retarded girl who has been abandoned by her own brothers?"

"Don't say things like that," Sripathi remarked, unable to hide his shock.

"Why not?"

"You don't really feel that way, I know."

"Don't be too sure of that," Raju said, giving Sripathi a tired look. "Sometimes I sit here in the dark and think, Suppose something happens to me, who will look after my daughter?"

Sripathi wished that he could say without any hesitation that he would. He wished that he had the courage and the niceness to do so. But he was silent and after a while, when Poppu came in to remove the tea cups, he rose to leave. "If you sell this house, where will you go?" he asked.

"Oh, I will still be here in this same place. The builders are giving me one flat as part of the payment for my property," replied his friend. "Are you leaving already? Don't forget, I want to see your Nandana. Bring her over the next time you come here. Yes?"

"I will," replied Sripathi, "but on condition that you don't think such nonsense thoughts about Ragini." Once again he trembled on the brink of telling Raju that he would take care of the girl should anything happen to her father, that he would always be there to help, but the words wouldn't come out. It was only after he was halfway home that he realized Raju had not said anything in response to his last sentence. This Friday, he told himself. This Friday he would talk to Raju again, assure him that he was there to help in any way he could. Perhaps he could sit with Ragini for a few hours while Raju took a walk to the beach. Or maybe they could go for a picnic with the girl.

Just as he entered Big House, Sripathi spotted Mrs. Poorna sitting hopefully in her balcony on the look-out for her lost daughter.

"She will never return, you poor woman," murmured Sripathi sadly. "The lost ones never do."

He envied her her madness. In the secret corridors of her mind, Mrs. Poorna wandered around eternally hopeful. She had found relief in the delusion that her child had only gone out to play and would return any moment. He wondered whether it was comforting to be lost in madness. He longed for such oblivion from pain. Or for the strength to be completely detached from all creation, to achieve the state that the sages of the epics had attained through years of penance, fasting and meditation. As a young boy, Sripathi was warned never to stand too long in one spot on the wet sands by the sea. The sea would suck him in, he was told. But he would wait until that cunning mesmeric movement of sand began under his feet, a sense that he was sinking inch by inch, and then, with an enormous exercise of will, he would remove himself from the insidious pull of the sea and run across the sand kicking at the waves in an ecstasy of freedom. This grief that wrapped itself around him was like the sea. The longer he stood beside it, staring at the limitless horizon of it, the deeper he sank. It refused to let him feel anything for the child that Maya had left behind, refused to let him love anyone again. Perhaps he did not want to move away from that welcoming edge of darkness that yawned open every time he heard a shard of music beloved of his daughter, every time he heard a voice with the same timbre, saw a neat head (just like hers) turning in the marketplace, or a gesture reminiscent of her.

———

Her tooth came out on Wednesday morning, just before she got out of bed, in a great gush of blood that wet her pillow and frightened Mamma Lady. Nandana was pleased, though. There would be some money under her pillow for sure. Now she could buy herself one of those bottles of green juice that all the other children purchased outside the school gates. Or the pink and black marble-shaped candy, so huge that it made your cheek bulge out and spit drip down your chin.

"So much of blood for such a little thing," marvelled Mamma Lady, washing Nandana's face and pushing her lip upwards to peer at the pink gap between two other wobbly teeth. "Ayyo! My baby, so small and sweet you are." She leaned forward, her warm smell of pickles and sweat and talcum enveloping Nandana, and kissed her on the forehead. "Now a fine new tooth will grow and you can eat your food double-quick, no?"

She switched off the electric immersion heater that she had put into a bucket of water for Nandana's bath, pulled it off and hung it from a hook high on the wall. It sizzled dry, the coil turning from a warm pink to white. Nandana had never seen anything like it. She was told not to ever-ever touch it while it was in the water or out of it. Now Mamma Lady mixed some cold water from another bucket and tested it with her fingers until she had it just right.

"Okay, today you can have a bath by yourself," she said. "Don't take too long." She picked up the tiny, sharp piece of bone that Nandana had handed to her and waddled out of the bathroom. Nandana looked at the bath water. She watched from the bathroom door as Mamma Lady stripped away the blood-stained pillowcase and re-made the bed before leaving the room. She didn't slide anything under the pillow, and so Nandana ignored her instructions to have a bath and followed her out, skipping excitedly. Maybe in this India place they *gave* you your money. Maybe there were no tooth fairies here to leave it under your pillow. Mamma Lady trundled slowly up the stairs to the terrace, out into the bright sunlight, and with one quick movement of her arm, flung the tooth on to the roof of the house. "There," she said, "now the crows can take it away, and the evil spirits won't know whose it is."

She had *thrown* away the tooth? She hadn't kept it in a special box like Daddy did? Nandana couldn't believe her eyes. But still she stood there, expectantly, close to her grandmother who was now touching the clothes on the line, left out overnight, pulling off the ones that were dry. In a minute or two she would take out a rupee note from that wet place between her breasts and give it to Nandana. For *sure*. She trailed around after Mamma Lady, the sun warm on her bare arms sticking out from the thin cotton slip, sucking a strand of her hair.

"Enh? What are you doing here still, child?" demanded Mamma Lady, noticing her all of a sudden. "Again you will be late for school and all that rickshaw confusion will happen. Didn't I tell you to have your bath? Go inside now, quickly."

My tooth money? Nandana stared hopefully at her grandmother. She opened her mouth wide and pointed at the vacant spot in her upper gum. "What is it, child?" asked Mamma Lady wearily. "I told you no, a new tooth will come soon. A stronger one, don't worry. And why don't you say something? I am getting very tired trying to understand you." With a sigh, she shifted the clothes onto one arm and propelled Nandana out of the terrace and down the stairs to the bathroom. She sat on the bed and folded the clothes stiff with salt and soap solution and old starch, while Nandana sulkily poured mug after mug of the tepid water over her head. This was cheating, she thought. Her tooth had come out for nothing at all. She wanted to go back home.

16

TICKET
TO ESCAPE

SRIPATHI DOODLED ON HIS PAD and wondered whether he could get away early. Before rahu-kala, the evil time, started. Otherwise he would have to stay until six o'clock. He had nothing to do except the aluminum tubing advertisement. It was the smallest account Advisions had ever got, and the client wanted nothing more than a picture of a girl in a low-cut blouse, posing against a pile of tubes. He had said as much at their first meeting. Nevertheless, Kashyap had asked Sripathi to write something—they both knew that it was a formality, an unnecessary exercise that would later be dropped. While he made up his mind about moving to Madras, tried to negotiate new loans with banks for the move, rounded up new clients in that city, Kashyap allowed Sripathi to remain at his desk, throwing him a few unimportant campaigns to work on. He did not summon him to the office again, and neither did he send his little notes through Kumar, the peon. Sripathi wondered whether the others in the office had also been told that they would be redundant soon. Neither Victor nor Ramesh mentioned the move to Madras during their lunch breaks, both continuing to joke and gossip and banter as they'd done for so many years. Perhaps he was the only one who was being kicked out? He was fifty-seven. Next year he would have had to retire anyway, so it wasn't too bad. The company had a provident fund plan to which he had been contributing all these years, and he would have that at least, calculated Sripathi. The notepad with its ruled yellow paper was full of such anxious notations—numbers, calculations, accounts. In his head there was no room for aluminum piping or Mangalore Jewellery or Ace Tutorials, who guaranteed admissions into foreign universities with their SAT, GRE and TOEFL coaching.

On the other side of the cubicle wall, he heard Renuka Naidu discussing the latest movie running at the Galaxy Theatre. "Superb acting," she said in her confident voice. "The female role is quite strong. But I adore Shahrukh Khan. He is such a dreamboat, and he acts so well in this flick."

She would definitely be moving to Madras. A dull envy filled Sripathi, flooding into his mouth so that he could taste its bitterness.

"You females just go for that body of his," laughed Mohan, another of Kashyap's young recruits. He was good at hustling business, Sripathi had noticed. He had an easy charm, a way of making you feel as if you were the most important person in the world. "I prefer the dame, Madhuri Dixit."

"Oh, of course, and I am sure you like her only for her acting." There was the sound of a chair being scraped back. "I have to go meet the big boss now. See you later, okay?"

Their voices faded away, and Sripathi went back to scribbling numbers anxiously on his yellow pad—loan payments, money to be returned to Raju, house tax, repairs to the roof before the monsoons, food, water, electricity—the list was endless. Finally he slapped his pen down in exasperation. With a sort of irrational perversity, he decided to leave the office early and go to Galaxy Theatre to book tickets for the movie. So what if there were bills to be paid? It was years since he had seen a film, since he had allowed dreams to drown him in their luminous sweetness. Perhaps he could pick up some tickets and surprise Putti? Poor thing, he had not even taken her out to a restaurant to celebrate her birthday this year. And Nirmala. It would do her good to get out of the house with him, and a movie with all those thick-thighed women dancing around trees would make her laugh. The child could come along as well, her first experience of an Indian movie. Sripathi was so pleased with his idea that he forgot about the mental hospital therapist who was supposed to meet his sister that evening.

He hurriedly scribbled a few more lines of copy, dropped off the sheafs of paper at the typist's desk and strolled into Kashyap's office. By a stroke of luck he had just left for a client meeting and wasn't expected back until late afternoon.

"Could you please tell him that I had to go home? Not feeling well," Sripathi said to the secretary.

Jayaram gave Sripathi a critical look from under his sweeping eyebrows. "You look all right to me."

"I am feeling dizzy," lied Sripathi, trying to look like a man whose head was spinning. "My doctor told me to go straight to his clinic if I felt like this again. Blood pressure might be very high, that's what he said. Too much tension recently."

Jayaram's eyes softened and he nodded. "How is the baby doing? Must be finding it so funny in this country, enh? So dirty and noisy after those clean-clean places she has lived in? My nephew who is in Australia holds his nose from morning to night when he visits me. Poor boy."

He handed Sripathi a few forms to fill, glanced over them and allowed him to leave the office. Sripathi felt guilty and relieved, all in the same breath.

From the ticket counter, down the theatre steps, looping around the bicycle stands and puddling outside the gates of the theatre, was a river of people patiently waiting for the clerk to arrive. Sripathi parked his scooter on the pavement that had been turned into a make-shift parking lot already crammed with vehicles. A gigantic billboard loomed up from the wall of the theatre. There was a violently coloured scene of a man in tight leather pants standing over a bleeding body. His arm stuck right out of the billboard, his fist clenched triumphantly. From the lower right-hand corner emerged the cut-out of a naked leg that was attached to a flamboyantly curved woman, bright pink and nude, save for a bikini made of sequins that shimmered in the breeze. She appeared to be dancing, her hips swinging in a wide fleshy arc, her breasts aggressive in their shining sheath of sequins.

"Deadly, eh?" chuckled a voice right behind Sripathi. It was Shyamsundar, a clerk from Advisions. *Damn the man, now he will go and tell everybody that he met me here, and then I am in trouble.*

"Hello, Shyamsundar, you also took time off today or what?" Sripathi asked.

"Yes-yes," said the man bashfully. "Today my daughter is having her maturity ceremony. She became a woman last week, so big celebration we are having in the house for that reason only."

"So why are you here?"

"It is a ladies' function, no? What I will do in the house with my better half, her mother, my mother, and sisters and all?"

"Then why did you take a day off?"

The man looked offended. "Suppose my family needs help with preparation? I am helping them all morning, getting flowers, organizing food, the priest and such things. Now I am having some time to myself, so my better half said, go and see a movie, so here I am." He gave Sripathi a curious look. "How come *you* are not at work today?"

"Oh, I took half-day off. I have to go to the doctor for a check-up. On the way I decided to buy tickets for the evening show."

"Why doctor? You are not well or what?"

"Oh, nothing much. Just high blood pressure."

"Blood pressure, eh?" smirked Shyamsundar. "And after watching this sex bomb going tingi-tingi, finished, your blood-pressure machine will burst itself!" He jabbed an elbow into Sripathi and continued. "And thunder-thighs Madhuri, giving all those kissies to hero with her wet sari sticking everywhere . . . Ayyo! Where will your blood pressure be, saar?" He winked and dug Sripathi in the ribs again.

Idiot, thought Sripathi, but smiled instead. There was a small pause and then Shyamsundar leaned close to Sripathi and whispered, "Ever seen one of *those*?" He jabbed a finger at a less conspicuous sign on one wall of the cinema. It was a shadowy poster in grey tones. In one corner a woman looked coyly over her shoulder and unhooked her brassiere, while a bare-chested man lay spread-eagle on the bed. He looked like he was dead.

Many Nights. Extremely for Adults. Uncensored XXX Scenes, proclaimed the poster.

"Once, when I was in college," admitted Sripathi, remembering how guilty he had felt, certain that he would be recognized by someone in the crowd, certain that his mother would find out and die of shame.

"How was it?" asked Shyamsundar.

Sripathi shrugged. "I don't remember, it was such a long time ago. And those days, the film quality was not very good either, very dark, couldn't see anything." Ahead of him the crowd inched forward minutely and he wondered whether he ought to abandon the attempt to buy tickets and go home. A man wearing a loud yellow shirt nipped in at the waist and bell-bottom trousers slid along the edges of the queue muttering in a low monotone, "Two for fifty, two for fifty, two for fifty." He reminded Sripathi of a rat—his beady eyes lined with kohl, his razor-thin nose that quivered every time he spotted a gullible face tempted to pay black-market rates for tickets.

He sidled up to Sripathi and grinned ingratiatingly, exposing rows of teeth corroded by paan juice and tobacco. "Two for fifty?" he asked, expelling a gust of garlicky breath. Sripathi stepped back quickly.

"Why you should waste your time standing here in this heat? That's what I feel bad about," continued the tout sympathetically. "First you have to work all day, and then you have to stand in a long line just to buy tickets for a movie. You are here for more work or for relaxation? I feel so sad about it. That is why I thought I will help my fellow brothers and sisters a little bit, is all."

"Rogue, cheating honest people and telling big stories," grumbled Shyamsundar, turning to Sripathi who nodded agreement.

The tout shrugged and moved on, leaving in his wake a cocktail of odours—garlic, hair oil, stale sweat—laced with some sugary perfume. It was now three o'clock and the theatre compound was swarming with people. After a minor commotion in the front of the queue, people started to drift away.

"Oho, ticket counter is closed," said Shyamsundar, mopping his forehead and the back of his neck. He checked the money in his wallet and pushed through the milling crowd to get to the black marketeer, who was now doing brisk business. Sripathi hesitated and then followed him. Since he had waited for so long, he might as well buy the wretched tickets, even if they were three times as expensive. It wasn't as if he did this every day.

"What, gentlemen," smiled the tout, slicking his greasy hair back with a palm. "Tired of standing in the sun?"

"Two tickets, please." Sripathi held out a fifty-rupee note. Given the sudden enhancement in price, he decided to purchase the tickets only for Nirmala and Putti.

"Seventy-five rupees," said the man.

"What? Rascal, you said fifty rupees!"

"What I can do? Prices are going up every minute in this country. Yesterday a loaf of bread cost two rupees, today it is five. Tomato was three per kilo, this morning my wife bought for seven! And please, saar, I beg you, stop this name-calling. I am educated, respectable person, doing a service for my fellow ladies and gentlemen. You want ticket, you pay the going rate. Many people are willing to give me a hundred rupees even. But for you I am making a special concession."

All of a sudden he leaned forward and pointed at a five-rupee note that was sticking out of Sripathi's shirt pocket. "You should be careful with your money, saar," he said solicitously. "Lots of thieves and pickpockets and all here."

"As if I don't know," said Sripathi.

"Just doing my *duty*, I am a God-fearing man just doing my *duty*," huffed the tout.

"All right, all right, here's seventy-five." God only knew what Nirmala would say when she found out how much he had paid, but it was far too late for regrets. Transaction concluded, the tout disappeared into the milling crowd, which seemed to be concentrated near the theatre gates. Sripathi found himself being propelled slowly by the surging crush of bodies towards the gates as well. He tried to get a glimpse of the road outside, his eyes scanning the sea of vehicles on the pavement for his battered scooter. On the road, all traffic had come to a halt to make way for a winding procession of people waving banners and flags, flanked on either side by policemen.

"What's going on?" he asked, tapping a man in front of him on the shoulder.

"Some kind of protest march, I think," said the man, shrugging.

"Big trouble, I heard," offered a roadside vendor, emptying his basket of peanuts into a large plastic bag and folding up the cane table on which he had set up shop. "Better not to get involved. They burnt a bus on Margosa Road for no reason, I heard." He slung everything over one shoulder, balanced his basket on his head, shifted to get everything settled into place, and started walking away.

Sripathi wondered whether he ought to risk leaving the relative safety of the theatre compound and make a dash towards his scooter parked outside. It would take him a while to extricate it from the mess of vehicles there, and by that time anything could happen. These people were always on the edge, a word could set them off and chaos would spread like a kerosene fire.

"Leave our fish alone!" the crowd shouted in unison. "Stop starving the poor!" Some of them carried placards and posters with more slogans: *Foreign Ships Go Home! Thieves and Robbers Go Home!* and, *You Have Taken Our Fish and Left Behind Only Blood!*

By now the crowd around him had squeezed Sripathi forward so that he found himself pressed against the gates of the cinema that had been locked by a pair of burly guards. He gazed at the procession and his eyes fell on the familiar figure of Arun, bedraggled as always, furiously shouting something that Sripathi could not catch. He stretched a frantic arm out of the gates, simultaneously filled with anger at his son's recklessness and a sneaking pride at his defiant courage. "Arun!" he shouted, but his words were swept away by the rising wave of voices on the road. Another glimpse of his son, his cotton shirt ripped clear off his shoulder. His head bobbed up and down a few times before being obscured by the crowd. Sripathi shook the gates, hoping that he could get out and perhaps drag the idiot boy away from all those policemen, take him back home where it was safe. One of the security guards prodded at his arm with a baton and said politely, "That's enough. Inside, please. No trouble or I will break your head."

"But that is my son there," protested Sripathi. The guard ignored him and whacked harder at his arm, forcing him to withdraw it. "I *said*, I will break your head." Some more burly men from the cinema pushed through and lined up with their backs to the gate so that Sripathi's view of the procession was almost completely blocked.

"I want to go out," he shouted, struggling forward against the tide of the crowd that was now being prodded back towards the theatre by the baton-waving guards.

Somebody tapped him on the shoulder, and he turned around to find Shyamsundar at his heels. "What is happening now? Do you know?" gasped Sripathi, relieved to see the dark, familiar face.

"No idea." Shyamsundar shook his head. "Come on, let's go inside the theatre and buy something to drink. Who knows how long we'll have to stay here, might as well be comfortable."

"I saw my son outside in that procession," said Sripathi. "I hope he doesn't get hurt."

"Your *son*? What was he doing with those khachda people? Is he in the police service?"

"No, he was one of the protesters."

"Why you allow your son to protest and get involved in all these dangerous things? I would never let my children do this."

Sripathi shrugged uneasily. Now the tiny bit of pride that he had felt earlier on was replaced by anger.

They pushed their way into the cool, dark lobby of the cinema, with its faded green Rexine sofas, ash-bins full of sand and cigarette butts that hadn't been cleared for days, large posters of Hollywood stars from the fifties with corrugated hairdos—all enveloped in the thick, sour odour of old coffee and popcorn. Sripathi hurried to the telephone booth in one corner of the lobby and dialed home. The phone remained mute in his hand. He pushed a rupee coin into the slot and dialed again. Nothing. Just the distant hum of static echoing in his ear. He slammed the phone down, jiggled it a few times in the receiver and tried again. This time, it swallowed his coin but gave him another stretch of silence in return. Damn thing. *Now* what to do? By six they would be wondering where he was, and starting to get worried if he didn't show up by seven. Sripathi thumped the phone a couple more times and wandered back to join Shyamsundar in the queue for coffee.

"Did you hear the announcement?" asked Shyamsundar.

"No, what did it say?"

"They are throwing stones outside, I believe. The police might put curfew on the area. So the theatre manager said that everybody who has tickets, never mind which show, can see the movie now itself. What do you think?"

Sripathi's throat tightened with panic. Stones were being thrown! A few days ago Arun had come home bruised after an encounter with Munnuswamy's Boys. Today it was the police. Why did he get mixed up in such things?

"Come on, man. Might as well see the film. God knows how long we will be stuck here."

For a moment Sripathi stood undecided. The tickets were for the Saturday show, so he could simply sit in the lobby and wait out the curfew. A refund was useless since he had bought the tickets on the black market and would get back only a third of the cost.

As if to solve his dilemma, a fat seth with hair sprouting profusely out of his nose raised his voice and shouted. "Anybody has an extra ticket? I will pay thirty rupees."

Shyamsundar nudged Sripathi and said, "Why don't you get rid of your other ticket? At least some money you will get back."

Sripathi nodded and waved to the seth. "Here, I have one."

The crowd streamed into the dimly lit theatre, and Sripathi settled down with a sense of resignation next to the seth, whose smallest movement set the whole row of seats shuddering wildly. No point worrying about his son, his scooter outside or the panic in the house when there was no sign of him that night. Perhaps by the time this movie was over, the curfew would be lifted. Perhaps the curfew itself was only a rumour—in Toturpuram, rumour ruled supreme.

The lights dimmed, a sigh ran like a low wave through the hall, the final rattle of a bag of chips, and then the sound track bounced its bright melody off the walls. The heroine appeared in a pale pink sari and turned her liquid eyes on Sripathi. He slipped deeper into his seat and waited for the hero to stride in, waited to join him in his battle against villainy and injustice, avarice and evil. While confusion filled the streets outside, Sripathi nestled in the comforting arms of fantasy and followed Mr. Hero as he chased the goondas who had killed his poor mother, raped his sister and were now after his girlfriend. He would vanquish them all with a song and a dance and a thundering monologue. He would always know the best thing to do in any circumstance, always take the right turning at the crossroad, and, if he got into trouble, would come out of it with a song trembling on his lips. In the end, the hero would win every battle that destiny flung at him.

The seth shifted in his chair and sent a mighty vibration through the row, but Sripathi barely noticed. He was the hero. The future of his job hung on Kashyap's decision, his son—instead of working for a living—wandered around the streets of Toturpuram waving flags, he had an unhappy grandchild dropped out of the blue and a dead daughter. His home was crumbling about his ears, his sister was going crazy and his mother wouldn't shut up. Did it matter? No, not at all. What else were heroes for but to swat troubles away like so many flies?

"Pop-caran?" whispered the seth, holding out a small paper packet.

Sripathi smiled at him in the dark and dipped into the greasy bag. One more vigorous heaving of the chairs as the seth resettled his bulk and then silence. A twinge of guilt as Sripathi looked at the glowing dial of his watch, until his attention was captured by the blazing funeral pyre of the hero's mother. The dull numbness that had sprouted inside him months ago and had grown like a waterweed, choking off all sensation since, began to tear apart. He had accepted it with gratitude because it had allowed him to look at his grandchild without immediately seeing her mother's dead face. Allowed him to look at Ammayya without resenting the fact that she was alive and healthy. Now, as the orange flames on the screen crackled and leaped, Sripathi felt the hero's rage boil in his own veins. Temporarily, at least, it cleansed him.

Towards the end of the film, he began to feel horribly cold. He knew that it was the latest of his body's shenanigans. He shuddered, wrapped his arms around himself and wished that he was wearing something warmer than the thin, half-sleeved nylon shirt. Now it wasn't only the fat seth who was setting the chairs aquiver, but Sripathi too. Unable to control the tremors, he rose jerkily and made his way out of the dark theatre, tired of not knowing what would happen next. He wanted someone to tell him that the world was the same, that his daughter was coming home. He wanted to push time backwards, to be a young man cradling his first child and then his second, full of hope for those two infants he had helped create. He wanted, more than anything else, to have the power to reshape the past.

The theatre door was open and he stepped out into the evening, his teeth chattering. The road was deserted and there was glass all over from shattered shop windows. A solitary policeman strolled up and down, his shoes strangely loud on the pavement. Seeing Sripathi near the scooter stand, he tapped his baton against his thigh and shouted, "What are you up to? Seeing if there are scooters to steal? Don't try any funny business, or I will bash your head in. Understand?"

"I'm not doing anything. That scooter there is mine. I just want to go home."

"How do I know it is yours, eh?" The policeman was shorter than Sripathi but looked far more fit. He whacked the baton against his palm and stared challengingly.

"I have the keys here, in my pocket," said Sripathi. "And my licence."

"I still say you have no proof. You give me some proof and you can go, otherwise I will have to deal with you." The policeman poked him in the chest with the baton. "Understand? You give me some proof, and everything will be fine." He rubbed his index finger and thumb together and grinned, his teeth gleaming dimly in the darkness of the street. It took Sripathi a few moments to realize what the man was trying to tell him. He drew out his wallet and removed a ten-rupee note. The policeman continued to prod him with the baton. "These days everything is so expensive, no?" he asked, still smiling. "The other day my son came home and said that his teacher was failing him because he did not give her good-quality sweets for Deepavali. The whole world is going down the drain."

Sripathi pulled out the thirty rupees that he had got from the seth for his ticket and handed it silently to the man. "That's all I have," he mumbled.

With a quick movement of his hand, the policeman plucked the money and slid it into his hip pocket. His smile became cordial now, and he accompanied Sripathi through the tangle of vehicles leaning against each other and helped him extricate his scooter. He even removed a green handkerchief from another pocket in his tight khaki trousers and carefully wiped the seat and handles clean of dust. He watched as Sripathi scrabbled to find the small tarpaulin sheet that he used to cover the vehicle when it was new. It was stuffed in behind the spare tire and smelled of old diesel oil and mould. Nevertheless, he draped it over his shoulders like a cape, tying the ends under his neck.

"What for you are doing that?"

"I am feeling cold," replied Sripathi, fumbling now for his keys.

"You should buy sweater. Why this dirty cloth you are using?"

Sripathi shrugged and the policeman patted him sympathetically on the back. "Sweater is so expensive. Did you like the movie?"

"It was not bad," said Sripathi, starting his scooter.

The policeman waved goodbye. "Tomorrow maybe I will bring my one-at-home. She is always grumbling that I work too much. You be careful on the roads now. Too many goondas around doing protest marching and breaking laws."

With the blue tarpaulin flapping from his shoulders like wings, Sripathi rode home. The sky was dark with towering cumulus clouds that had grouped like sombre giants. Thin sheets of lightning flared and died intermittently, and thunder rumbled in the distance.

"I am getting a new silk pavadai for Deepavali," boasted Radha. "And my father bought two big boxes full of firecrackers—one for me and one for my sister. He said that I could burn one packet of sparklers today. Maybe one fountain also. You like fountains or ground chakras better?"

Nandana shrugged and peered into her lunch box to see what Mamma Lady had packed for her. She had realized that in India they didn't have Halloween. Instead there was something called Deepavali, when people got presents and burst fireworks. She wondered why Mamma Lady hadn't bought *her* any new clothes. Yesterday, when Nandana went to the market with her to buy some bread, she had stood for a long time in front of a shop window and stared at an orange skirt with golden spangles all over that she loved. It looked just like the dress that one of those dancing women wore in the television programs Aunty Putti watched all the time.

"Why don't you talk?" Radha wanted to know. "Are you dumb? Did someone cut off your tongue? I saw a movie once where they did mean things to orphans. You are an orphan, no? Did anyone do mean things to you?"

Nandana shook her head and sucked nervously on a strand of her hair. The other children seated in a circle on the grass waited for her to say something. When she remained silent, they lost interest and resumed chattering amongst themselves about their new clothes and the firecrackers they would be playing with later in the week. Nandana sulked quietly and added up all the things that were gnawing at her: Mamma Lady had thrown her tooth away without even looking to see which one it was; there was no money under her pillow either—she had checked twice before leaving for school; she was the only child at school who wasn't getting new clothes or firecrackers for this exciting festival; this morning she got a scolding from the rickshaw man for making him wait when it wasn't her fault—she'd had to sit on the toilet for ever because the paper had run out. Mamma Lady had been irritated afterwards. "Pah! This is not clean. Why you can't learn to wash with water?" And to Nandana's embarrassment, she had leaned over so that Nandana's face was stuck in her soft, sari-covered breasts, and rinsed her bottom with cold water as if she was a baby.

She sulked all the way home in the rickshaw, kicking one of the fat brothers in the ankle for no reason and wiggling so hard that the other almost fell out. To her surprise, Mamma Lady was not at the gate when she got home. Instead she was bustling around inside the house, ordering Koti to pull the stinky sofa forward and cover it with a coloured bedspread, and frying round golden things in the kitchen.

"Hurry up, wash your hands and face and come down, chinnamma," she said as she rushed in and out of the kitchen. "I'll give you some milk and biscuits, and then you go and play next door till I come and get you. Somebody important is coming to see Putti today."

Nandana wanted to stay at home. She didn't want to stand and watch Nithya and Ayesha and Meena play and whisper secrets. She trailed behind her grandmother to the kitchen for a glass of milk. The Witch was sitting at her bedroom door reading something. She looked up as Nandana went past her and grabbed her arm. "You watch out for the Chocobar Ajja. He is very bad. He catches small girls," she said. "If your poor mother was alive she would make sure that you didn't go to such dangerous places to play."

My mother is in Vancouver, Nandana wanted to shout. I am only here for a short while.

17

INTO
THE TUNNEL

THE DANCE STUDENTS started arriving soon after Nandana had left with Koti. Nirmala spread out her reed mat and placed her book of songs beside it before lowering herself to the floor. The Kala Kendra organizers had asked her if she could participate in their year-end cultural festival—choreograph a dance-drama perhaps, a small episode from one of the epics. Over the last two weeks, she had selected the girls who would take part in the festival and had now begun rehearsals. She watched the five young girls who waited before her, legs bent to form a diamond shape, fists against their hips, straight-backed and tense in the traditional stance of Bharat Natyam dancers. So, too, had Maya stood before her years ago, her young body poised to spring to the music, her feet slapping hard on the bare floor, her eyes darting like birds after her graceful, flying arms. Nirmala blinked rapidly to stop the tears that threatened to spill over and started rapping out a rhythm on the floor, humming as she went along. What use is crying? she thought. Would it bring her child back? Just before Maya was born the nurse at the hospital had told her that labour pains were terrible, that she would feel as if she had reached the brink of existence and returned when the baby finally emerged from her womb. But it had been a quick delivery, following only an hour of pain. Perhaps it was in exchange for the agony that would follow thirty-four years later that the gods had given her Maya so easily.

"Are they rehearsing the march of the demons?" called Ammayya, dragging her chair closer to the living-room door.

Nirmala realized that her rhythm was off slightly and the students were uncertainly going through the steps. She wiped her eyes and nodded approvingly at the girl who was to play King Rama. She performed the hero's walk to perfection—graceful, dignified, measured. But the one who played Ravana, the demon king, was awkward and restrained. "Stamp harder," she urged. "Remember you are also a great king, full of valour. But you are vain, and that is what sets you apart from the hero. Thrust out your chest, child. Twirl your moustache. Flex your muscles." Nirmala put down her baton and demonstrated. "Like this, and this. Exaggerate your walk, frown and stamp. You are showing off your strength."

"Vanara sena!" called Ammayya. "This is the monkey brigade; look how they prance." She giggled and rocked.

The dance class continued, ignoring the old lady, who soon grew bored of passing comments that stimulated no response.

"Where is Putti?" she demanded. "I have a headache. I want her to rub some oil in my hair. Is she on the terrace again? What does she do there all day? Has she forgotten that Gowramma's proposal is arriving this evening? Isn't she going to dress up?"

Nirmala was relieved when the class was finally over. Ammayya's fretting all the way through had grated on her nerves. When Putti drifted dreamily down the stairs, Nirmala turned on her. "Your mother has been eating my head for two hours. Why aren't you getting ready? Nobody in this house cares about anyone but themselves. Selfish, every single one of you."

Putti gave her a startled look. "Are you angry with me, Akka?"

"Angry? Oh no," said Nirmala borrowing some of Sripathi's sarcasm. "Why should I be angry about running around doing everything while all of you are relaxing? Your brother hasn't come home yet, your nephew has also disappeared. And you sit on the terrace all evening listening to that fellow sing songs. Why should I get angry, tell me?"

"Who is singing songs?" Ammayya pounced on Nirmala's words. She looked sharply at her daughter and back at Nirmala. "Puttamma, what is going on? Nirmala?"

"Ask your daughter," said Nirmala, stamping into the kitchen to set the coffee percolating for the prospective groom.

Ammayya raised her voice. "Puttamma, I am asking you once and for all, who is singing to you?"

"Nobody, Ammayya. Who will sing to *me*?" asked Putti. "Now stop talking, and watch your favourite program." She clicked the television on and immediately the room was washed with a blue light. "I'll get dressed."

Ammayya gave her a sharp look. She smelled something in the air—ripe and bubbling like jackfruit left out in the summer sun. "My darling baby," she murmured, shuffling over to sit before the television. "Is there something that you want to tell me? I know there is. I might be old, but I am not an idiot."

"There is nothing—I am telling you, no? It is cool on the terrace, and I can't smell Munnuswamy's cows up there. That is why I go, no other reason. Nirmala is angry with me and simply saying all these things."

Ammayya examined her face closely for a few moments, and then settled down to watch her soap opera.

Soon she was absorbed in the antics of three beautiful sisters who were all in love with the same man. The hero was a plump fellow whose corrugated wig sat on his head like the roof of a poorly constructed house.

"Ayyo! Ma, what rubbish they show these days!" she exclaimed, as the hero kissed one of the sisters almost on the mouth, missing it by only millimetres. She was certain, too, that he had touched, yes, touched her bottom. And was now rubbing up against her in a way that would make a Kopraj Street whore blush. The daring new series had somehow escaped the scissors of the censors.

The mental-hospital therapist, when he arrived, had long strands of thin hair that he had wound into a spiral around his bald pate and pasted down with some heavy oil. A few rebellious strands had come unglued and stuck out behind his left ear like feathers. He had a faintly reptilian habit of rapidly licking his plump lips before he spoke. In the middle of a prolonged discourse on the benefits of basket weaving for severely disturbed hospital patients, Putti noticed that the backs of his hands were heavily marked with stiff black hair. She thought about Gopala's smooth, exciting fingers, about spending the rest of her life being touched by this other man, and made up her mind.

"No," she said to Ammayya soon after the therapist had left. "I cannot marry him."

She had expected her mother to agree with her. Ammayya had never found any of the grooms suitable. But to her surprise, her mother defended him. "Good family. Good job. High caste. Why you are being so fussy?"

Putti gave her an astonished look, but a moment later understood the reason for her mother's perversity.

"I suggested he stay in this house with us. Like a son, only he will pay a small rent. He was so happy, poor fellow. He doesn't have any family members of his own, you know."

"I am not marrying him," insisted Putti angrily. She gave Nirmala a pleading look, but her sister-in-law merely shrugged and said, "I have to go and bring Nandana from next door. It is getting late."

There was no sign of the child when Nirmala entered the apartment complex gates. She hurried around the two buildings with fear slowly invading her mind. Please deva, dear god Krishna, let her be safe, she thought, hurriedly mumbling a prayer. So many funny people and strangers in this town, nobody was safe any more. She remembered rumours of children being stolen and sold to brothels or beggar gangs in the big cities. Why, just the other day there was that big newspaper article about a Nepali girl who had been rescued by the police from a whorehouse in Bombay. Kidnapped from her village when she was seven or eight, and now—ten years later—she had gone home to a family who did not want her back.

She approached the Gurkha at the gate. He saluted her smartly. "Have you seen my grandchild?" asked Nirmala. "She was wearing a red shirt and blue pants."

"No, memsahib. I saw her playing just five or ten minutes ago, but I don't know where she went. Right there she was." He pointed to a spot in front of the building with his stick.

"Are you sure she didn't go away while you were not here?"

"Memsahib, the baby didn't leave this place," the Gurkha insisted. "I have been here all evening, no child left the compound. I didn't even go for a drink of water. I keep all that I need right here." He tapped a basket on the ground beside his chair. "When I have to answer Mother Nature's call, I lock this gate. Nobody can come or go without my permission, memsahib. I am telling you."

Nirmala nodded, relieved by the man's assurances, and diffidently approached a group of teenaged boys loitering near the entrance of Block A. They intimidated her, these boisterous young men. Although, she reflected ruefully, strangers probably felt the same way about Arun with his shaggy beard, the shapeless cotton kurta he wore, the worn sandals, the long hair.

"Did you need help, Aunty?" one of the boys asked her.

"I am looking for my granddaughter, Nandana. Small girl wearing a red shirt . . ."

"The foreign girl," said another boy. "I saw her with Nithya and Ayesha a little while ago. They were running around the building."

The boys directed her to the apartments in which the girls lived. Nirmala climbed the narrow stairs slowly, wishing there was a lift to take her to the fourth floor apartment in which Dr. Quadir's daughter, Ayesha, lived. Very few of the buildings in the town had elevators. What was the point? Electricity came and went as erratically as the wind. The stairs were surprisingly clean and smelled pleasantly of agarbatti burning in various flats, onions frying and rice cooking. Muffled sounds filtered through the doors and mingled to become a soft murmur that rose and fell like the call of the sea. Nirmala wondered about the busy lives that went on behind the closed doors. In each of those little compartments was joy and sorrow, anger and pain, memory and forgetfulness—the salt and sugar of daily existence. Did these people share their feelings and experiences with their neighbours on the same floor? As long as she could remember, Nirmala had lived in large, independent houses full of her own people. First with her parents, her grandparents and her siblings. Then, after marriage, with Ammayya and Putti, Sripathi and her own children. The only time she felt truly alone was when she was surrounded by strangers on the bus, or on the brief walk down to the temple. Once she was inside the temple, it was almost like being in her own home, the number of people she knew there. Why, even the priest was the same one who had performed all the family ceremonies. She wondered how she would feel if Sripathi did indeed sell the house and they moved into apartments. Ah, the freedom of not living in the same house as Ammayya! The thought of Ammayya made Nirmala wonder whether she had remembered to lock her cupboard before leaving the house. She knew that the old woman snooped and for years had not even dreamed of stopping the invasion. The habit of obedience, of respect for one's elders, of subservience, ran strong in her blood. Maya's death had knocked most of those habits out of her. In losing her child, first because of Sripathi's ego, and then to Lord Yama himself, Nirmala had taken more than she could bear. For all the years of being a good wife, daughter-in-law and mother, *this* was how she was rewarded? They had repaid her honest devotion with a kick in the face. Now she no longer cared about obeying Sripathi

without question or hurting Ammayya. Now she dared to lock her
steel cupboard that stored her saris, the few pieces of jewellery that
she had collected for Maya, photographs, school reports, curls of
hair, baby booties and tiny dresses—all memories of her children,
of those more innocent times when happiness lay in the sound of
their young voices and in the smile of appreciation that Sripathi
sent her way when her cooking was exceptionally good. Even a day
without a complaint from Ammayya had pleased Nirmala then, because it meant that she had not done anything to offend or irritate
her. How could she have been so like a faithful animal? She climbed
another floor and her thoughts turned to how she, too, had failed
Maya. She remembered how many times during their phone conversations, her daughter had asked, "Mamma, is it okay if I come
home?" And she, too afraid of going against Sripathi so completely,
had said, "No, not now. Wait, I will speak to your father." But
Nirmala had never spoken to him, intimidated by his solid, impen-
etrable anger, unwilling to force a confrontation of any kind. She
was too much of a coward to face unpleasantness head-on. Always,
always, she had taken the easy, conciliatory route.

The next time Maya had begged to come home, she had pushed
her away again. Of course, there was nothing she could have done
to prevent her death, but at least she could have made a stronger
effort to be a part of Maya's life all these years. She could so easily
have said, "Come home, child. Bring your family with you. I want
to see my grandchild."

Footsteps clattered down towards her and Nirmala leaned breathlessly against the wall. The Chocobar Ajja descended, accompanied
by his servant. He glowered at Nirmala, making her shrink farther
into the wall. Dirty old fellow, showing his privates to children!
What madness existed in the world these days. She didn't remember
being afraid of anything as a child. Was it just a symptom of a world
that had lost all morality, or was it a greater awareness of the wickedness that had always lurked beneath the surface of human life?

Maybe in the past nobody spoke of these things, families kept their sins hidden behind curtains of respectability. Nirmala contented herself with giving the old man a dark look as he went by.

By the time she reached the fourth floor, she was panting. She sought to subdue the trembling anxiety that Chocobar Ajja had aroused by reassuring herself that Nandana was most likely lost in play in a friend's home, that she had forgotten the time. She grew furious with the little girl. She would have to scold her. The child seemed to take her for granted, just like everybody else in the house.

Mrs. Quadir, Ayesha's mother, opened the door. A look of surprise crossed her thin, attractive face.

"Mrs. Rao? Come in, come in. You decided to visit us finally?" she asked.

Nirmala had met her often at the vegetable store or the lending library, but although they often exchanged promises to visit, they had never really done so.

"I am sorry to disturb you," said Nirmala, wiping the perspiration that beaded her forehead and formed a necklace above her lip.

"No-no, what you are saying? No disturbance. Full pleasure only to see you in our house, Mrs. Rao. Come, sit down. What you will have—tea, coffee, juice?"

"Actually, I just came to see if my grandchild was here. She hasn't come home yet, and I was a little worried."

"No, she didn't come up. Ayesha came home early to finish her homework. These teachers dump everything on them to do at home. I don't know why we have to pay such high school fees and do everything ourselves only. But I will ask her. Don't worry, this is a safe area. Nothing will happen."

She went into one of the rooms hidden from view by bright cotton curtains and reappeared with Ayesha in tow. "Say good evening to Aunty," she commanded, pushing the child forward. "She wants to know whether you saw Nandana today."

"Yes," muttered the girl nervously, staring at her feet.

"Why you are so shy all of a sudden?" demanded her mother. Then to Nirmala, "This girl is usually going bak-bak like a frog in the monsoon and now look at her! Children are so funny, no?" Again she touched her daughter's shoulder and said, "Do you know where she went? Aunty is worried."

To their surprise, Ayesha burst into tears. "What is it?" asked her mother sharply. "Are you hiding something? Look at me and tell me honestly what is wrong."

Slowly the story emerged. She and the other girls were playing Through the Tunnel. When it was Nandana's turn to go into the tunnel, they had promised to wait for her at the other end, but had run away to Nithya's house instead. And when they came down ten minutes later, there was no sign of her.

"The ghosts took her away," sobbed Ayesha, cringing at her mother's angry face. "I told Meena not to force her, but she said it was a test of friendship. Last time she went in and came out, and nothing happened."

Mrs. Quadir glared at her daughter. "Is that how you treat children who are new here? I am ashamed of you. How would you like it if someone did the same to you?"

"Don't scold her too much," said Nirmala, trying not to show her fear. "She is only a child."

"I am so sorry that my daughter did such a bad thing, Mrs. Rao. Wait a moment and I will phone Nithya and Meena and ask them if they know where she went."

Several phone calls to families in both blocks turned up no information, and Nirmala got up to leave. Mrs. Quadir accompanied her down the stairs, apologizing again for her daughter's role in the whole drama. The group of teenagers was still there, leaning against the wall of the building or standing with their hands in their pockets, laughing and chatting.

"Did you find her, Aunty?" asked the boy who had approached Nirmala earlier.

"No, I don't know where she could be," said Nirmala.

"If you want, we can go from flat to flat and check for you," one of the boys suggested. "She couldn't have gone far with our lion of a Gurkha guarding the gates."

Nirmala nodded and smiled. "No, you are right. She must be sitting and playing somewhere, naughty creature." She left the compound with a heavy heart. Should they call the police for help? Suppose the child wasn't anywhere in the block, where would they start to search for her? This was a crowded town, and not many people knew Nandana the way they did the children who were born here. Why, even then children could disappear. For a brief moment, Nirmala's thoughts turned to Mrs. Poorna's daughter, and she shivered.

Somewhere between Chamber's Road and Brahmin Street, Sripathi's scooter coughed a couple of times and expired. He waited for a break in the churning, relentless traffic and then, dragging his scooter, plunged after a cow that had languidly drifted through, forcing the entire road to slow down. As long as he stuck close to the cow, thought Sripathi, nobody would dare hit him. He pressed against it, allowing it to lead him, hoping that it would not decide to void its bowels on his feet. When he reached the pavement, he felt as if he had achieved something miraculous in surviving the wild rush of traffic. He patted the cow's flank affectionately and made his way to Karim Mechanic's shack, dim under the single street light that was still working on the road. A couple of Petromax lanterns flared on either side of the shack and lit up the piles of tires, spare parts, a dismembered car chassis. The first drops of rain thudded down, bursting against the dry road like transparent glass beads just as Sripathi reached the shack. The earth, like an eager lover, sent up a wet scent that at any other time would have exhilarated him.

The mechanic shouted at his assistants, two small boys not much older than Nandana, to cover the assorted debris of other vehicles with tarpaulin.

"What, sahib?" he greeted Sripathi, struggling to tie down one end of a canvas sheet that had torn loose and flapped in the wind. "This old lady is sick again?"

"Broke down in the middle of the road," said Sripathi.

"I will have to check it thoroughly. If the rain stops I can do it to-morrow, otherwise I will send one of my boys as soon as it is ready. You might need to buy a new scooter, sahib. This one is old and tired, like me and you, eh?"

With the tarpaulin still draped around his shoulders, Sripathi walked carefully down the road. He didn't want to disturb his crazy body any more than necessary. It scared him now, terrified him. A fresh wave of shivers washed over him, leaving even the tough bristles on his chin standing in raised cushions of skin.

Nirmala was waiting for him on the verandah. Behind her the house was dark and gloomy, which took Sripathi aback. Nirmala never forgot the ritual of turning on the lights at dusk. She had always believed that a dark house was an invitation to evil spirits. Sripathi also noticed that the smell of incense and burning wicks dipped in mustard oil was missing, which meant that Nirmala had not even performed her evening prayers.

"Where were you?" she demanded as soon as she saw him. "I have been going crazy. Nandana hasn't come home. I told her that I would pick her up at six-thirty. I told her to wait for me. I sent her next door to play and now I can't find her."

Sripathi sat down wearily in the cane chair on the verandah. As usual he perched at the edge, avoiding the frayed strands of bamboo in the centre of the chair that clung together out of sheer will power. He had acquired the chair more than twenty-five years ago and refused to get rid of it despite Nirmala's periodic threats to give it away to the raddhi-wallah when he next came to buy Ammayya's stolen newspapers.

"Stop screaming. Maybe she has run away again. You know she keeps trying to go somewhere on her own. Someone will bring her back, don't worry," he said, easing his aching feet out of the shoes. He shrugged the tarp off his back and shuddered as the cold air touched his exposed arms.

"It is one hour *more* than that now," wailed Nirmala, holding her sari to her mouth to stifle the sobs. "And dark too. She hasn't taken her backpack, I checked in her room. When she runs away, she always takes that bag with her. I don't know what to do."

"Don't be silly. How can she disappear from next door? Did you check with the other children?"

"Of course I did. And some nice boys checked in each and every apartment. And no, the Gurkha fellow didn't see our Nandana leave the compound. He says that he was sitting there all the time and would not have let her go alone. But he could be making that up just to impress."

"Why do you send her here and there alone?" asked Sripathi putting on his shoes again. "Can't you let her play here in our house?"

"You are very good at giving advice. How can I lock up a child at home, with only old people for company? Always you find somebody else to blame. Why you don't take the poor thing to the beach to play, if you know so much about children? And your son is another nuisance. He also hasn't come home yet either. Two-two men in this house, but not one is around when there is trouble!"

"I saw him from the movie theatre. He was marching in a procession," said Sripathi. He lowered his voice, "There were police involved, too."

"Movie theatre? You went for a movie while I was sitting here worrying?"

"Which movie?" Ammayya wanted to know.

"I didn't want to see it. I just wanted to purchase the tickets for Saturday, but your wonderful, planet-saving son started his protesting. There was a temporary curfew. Didn't you hear it on the news? We were locked inside the theatre."

He went inside the house to fetch a sweater with Nirmala following.

"Where is your scooter?" she asked as they climbed the steps.

"Broke down. Had to walk all the way home. It is sitting with the mechanic," said Sripathi. "Where have you kept my sweater?"

Nirmala was completely puzzled. "Why you suddenly require a sweater? This morning only you were grumbling hot hot hot, and now you behave as if you are going on a yatra to Gangotri, to Mount Everest! The sweaters are inside a box on top of that shelf in the kitchen. Too heavy to remove now. Wear something else."

"What?"

Nirmala thought for a moment and went into Arun's room. From the cupboard she drew out Nandana's father's jacket and handed it to Sripathi.

He looked at it without touching it, shocked by Nirmala's seeming lack of sentimentality. "You want me to wear *this*?" he asked. The shivering overtook him again and his voice shook. "Are you mad?"

"What is so mad about a coat that nobody uses? You are feeling cold, so wear it," replied Nirmala giving him a frosty look. He had never seen her like this before and it frightened him. Nirmala was the one person in the house that he could always take for granted, always depend on for her simple wisdom and goodness, but now she seemed to be changing before his very eyes. He had always been grateful for her stolid practicality, her ability to carry on with the business of daily living without breaking down. What a horrible parody of that practical nature this was.

"But this is *his* coat," said Sripathi.

"So what? You never bothered about him when he was alive, so why do you care now?"

He turned away from her hard-eyed, tearless gaze and went back to his room. He took out a thick flannel shirt from the cupboard where it had languished unworn for years. "What do you want me to do?" he asked without turning around.

"Ask Munnuswamy to help. He has influence. His Boys know everybody in this town. Surely they will be able to find her."

"I am not going to that crook for anything," said Sripathi. "I will walk down the road and check her school. Maybe somebody saw her. If she isn't back in half an hour, contact the police station."

"But you aren't going to Munnuswamy," Nirmala said. She was still holding the jacket, her fingers tight against the thick grey material.

"No. He is a rogue."

"Then I will go. I am fed up with always listening to your nonsense. This is not right, that is not okay, what will people say? You have ruined my life because of all this nonsense. You go to Nandu's school, and I will ask our neighbour for help." Nirmala went swiftly down the stairs.

"Where are you going? Shall I come with you?" asked Putti, trailing after her.

"Next door," said Nirmala briefly before leaving the house, her bare feet flashing defiance from under the flapping edges of her sari.

"You are going to that milkman's house?" screeched Ammayya. "Low-caste people!"

"Shut up, Ammayya!" said Putti, surprising even herself. There was a moment of silence while her mother digested this unexpected response, and then the floodgates opened. Ammayya wailed and beat her chest, she hiccupped and wheezed, turned blue in the face and declared that she was about to faint. Finally, she smacked her cane petulantly on the floor and whined, "Sripathi, did you hear the way your sister spoke to me? And you just stood there and listened like a wet mop? While I was insulted left and right?"

Sripathi followed Nirmala out of Big House, not bothering to reply. It was raining even harder now. He hailed an auto-rickshaw but it whizzed past. Another one stopped but refused to go in the direction of the school. Sripathi found that he could not even summon up any anger against the auto-wallah. He hurried down the road, past the gypsies huddled under television cartons on the pavement, past the vegetable vendors with their produce covered in plastic, and the brightly lit video parlour with its flashing neon sign. The rain, which had thinned to a drizzle, began to drum down again heavily as he reached the huddled shape of Karim Mechanic's shop, now shrouded completely in tarpaulin. He spotted his scooter lying on its side like a wounded animal amid the mechanic's debris. It was sheeted in plastic and tied with heavy ropes to a tree. Thunder rolled across the sky. Sripathi shook open his umbrella and increased his pace. A wind started up, shaking the branches of the ancient caesalpinia trees lining the road like old warriors, and the umbrella strained and bucked in his grasp. He pressed his body against the wind and continued to walk down the road that stretched out before him, long and dark and strangely unfamiliar, even though he had spent his entire life travelling it.

18

THE
WAY HOME

T HE DOOR CLICKED OPEN and Mrs. Poorna entered the room with a plate piled with parathas. "Here my darling, I have made these for you, exactly as you like them. With lots and lots of sugar," she said, sitting on the bed beside Nandana. "Shall I feed you?"

Nandana shook her head violently. She wanted to go back to the old house next door. She hated this crazy woman, this smelly apartment and the room full of blue dresses. Everywhere there were pictures of a little girl, big and small, framed or simply tacked to the wall. A naked newborn, a wide-eyed infant, a six-year-old in a starched uniform, her pinched face solemn and unsmiling. Memories of a little girl who had disappeared from everywhere but her mother's heart and confused mind. She shifted uneasily on the bed, moving away from Mrs. Poorna who was gazing at her with shining eyes.

The woman giggled and pinched Nandana's chin. "Sweet paapu, teasing me, making jokes. Of course you will eat my parathas. And while you are eating, you will say your favourite poem. Do you remember it? You won a prize in poetry elocution for it, remember? '*The boy stood on the burning deck . . .*' And see that picture there, that is you on your first birthday. You took your firststep that day. I thought my heart would burst with pride."

She frowned when there was no response from Nandana. "So quiet you have grown, child. Why don't you talk to me?" She tore off a piece of the paratha and tried to squeeze it between Nandana's tightly pursed lips. The girl burst into tears, and Mrs. Poorna hastily deposited the plate on the floor. "Don't cry, my pet. Don't be angry with your poor mother. I didn't mean to lose you. Please don't be so sad." She collected Nandana in her arms, pressed her close, kissed her forehead and cheeks repeatedly, and rocked her back and forth, humming under her breath. "Think how surprised your Appa will be when he comes home! Think how surprised that wretched Shyamala will be. She tells me I am mad. Can you imagine? Is a mother mad to wait for her child?"

After a while, she released Nandana and leapt to her feet. With a happy smile, she picked up a comic book from the small white desk beside the bed and pushed it towards her. "See, here is your new comic. You never finished it. Sit quietly and read now. Amma will go and cook all your favourite things, okay?" She left the room, still humming gaily, and Nandana heard her lock the door from the outside. The plate remained on the floor beside the bed.

Earlier that evening, Meena had challenged Nandana to run through the tunnel between Blocks A and B again. "If you do it, I will let you come to my house and use my Sony PlayStation," she promised.

Nandana had agreed. She was still afraid of the tunnel, but now the desire to play a video game in Meena's house had her firmly in its grip. It would feel just like being in Yee's house in Vancouver. So she had run through the dark passage full of slime and strange sounds and emerged on the other side, only to find that the three girls had disappeared.

She had stood there chewing her hair, mad at them. She did not notice Mrs. Poorna gliding out from her patio until the woman had caught her tenderly by the arm.

"Darling child, again you are playing outside," she crooned. "I was wondering where you were. Come, let us go home. I will show you something nice I bought for you." She pulled Nandana towards the terrace of her apartment, urging her to enter the small metal gate. The little girl had not resisted. Why should she obey her mother's warnings about strangers? she thought rebelliously. Especially when she had gone away and left her by herself. Mrs. Poorna had drawn her into the apartment, murmuring love to her as if she were a nervous foal. Once they were inside, she shut the patio door and double-bolted it.

"They said you wouldn't come back, but what do they know? My heart called and called, and you heard me," she had said, stroking Nandana's face and hair.

Nandana glanced uneasily around the small room in which Mrs. Poorna had locked her. Now she regretted allowing herself to be led here. The room was crowded with toys, books and clothes neatly folded on shelves. A blue dress hung on a wooden hanger in a corner of the room. There was a window on one wall. Nandana climbed on the bed and struggled with the bolts, which were slightly rusty. When the window swung open she peered out through the bars. There was nothing there but another wall criss-crossed with drain pipes thick and thin. It looked familiar. With some surprise, Nandana realized that it was one of the walls of the tunnel. A little above her and slightly to the left was another lighted window, and if she stuck her head close against the bars, she could see more squares of light. Sounds of laughter and talk emerged from the window but were partially drowned out by the rain that pinged off the pipes and roared steadily in the two gutters that lined the tunnel. Other human sounds floated down from various flats, bumped against the walls and turned into ghostly noises.

Somewhere on the other side was the old house in which she lived. Through the locked door, she could hear the crazy woman singing loudly, clattering pots and pans. There was the sound of a doorbell and Nandana heard Mrs. Poorna opening it. She waited, hopeful that it was somebody come to look for her. She pressed her face against the window bars and said quietly, "Mamma, I am here." Then she raised her voice and shouted a little louder. Her voice ricocheted around the tunnel—"hereherehere"—and was washed away by the splash and gurgle of water. She remembered how many times her grandmother had asked her to call her Ajji. Perhaps that was why there was no response. So she shouted again. "Ajji!" It occurred to her that Sripathi often sat on his balcony right across the wall. Now she called for him too, the word strange in her mouth, "Ajja!"

When they took her back to Big House, she promised herself, she would never be naughty again. No *way*. And she would talk to everybody in the house, even to her Ajja. The door opened and Mrs. Poorna came in with a tray of food.

"What is this?" she asked in a peeved voice. "You haven't eaten your parathas. And now it is dinnertime. Come, I will feed you." She shut the window. Again she began humming a song, and, pulling Nandana tight against her, inserted small quantities of food into her mouth. "I'll never lose you again, my chicken," she murmured. "Never." She kissed her over and over. "Can you imagine, another little girl is lost? They came just now to look for her. She was wearing a red shirt, they said."

"They were looking for me," said Nandana, struggling to get off the woman's lap.

"Why should they look for you in your own home, my chicken? Again you are teasing me, naughty thing. Now come here and finish this before I get angry."

Nandana struggled against her. Home. This was not her home. She remembered the police at Uncle Sunny's door, and Aunty Kiran telling her that her parents were dead, and understood at last that they would not ever come to find her. That was why the Old

Man had brought her to Big House. So he and Mamma Lady could take care of her for ever and ever.

"No, I don't want to finish that," she said. "I want to go to my home." She screamed as loud as she could, refusing to be silenced by Mrs. Poorna until she clapped her hand over Nandana's mouth.

———

The school was silent and deserted when Sripathi reached it. The gate swung open easily, and he made his way first to the office, hoping that somebody would still be there. To his dismay, the doors were locked shut. He banged a fist against the thick wood and made his way slowly along the long corridor that wound its way around the main building, peering through shut windows into empty classrooms. He couldn't remember where Nandana's classroom was. That first day, when he had brought her here, one of the nuns had been waiting for them at the front office. She had taken Nandana's hand in hers and led her away down the thin, dark corridors to some unknown place. Sripathi remembered the sense of loss he had felt as he watched the tall figure in her floating black robes and the small girl trotting beside her. It was the same feeling he had had when he was a child, on the first day of every year when his father left him at the doors of his school; on the first day he had left Maya, and then Arun; and years later as he had watched his daughter's plane rise into the sky.

Nowhere. She was not on any of the verandahs or in the open corridors. Not on the playground or in the little asbestos-roofed square with its rows of tables and benches for those who didn't want to eat their lunch inside the school or under the trees. As he approached the convent, a little behind the main building, a young nun in a white sari appeared and stared questioningly at him.

"Yes? Do you need any help?" she asked.

"My granddaughter, Nandana Baker, didn't come back from playing today," said Sripathi. "She is only seven years old. In Class Two. I thought that she might have wandered back to school for some reason."

"I haven't seen any children in the school after last bell. But please come into the reception area and sit down. I will tell Mother Superior and we can get one of the peons to check all the rooms."

The nun led Sripathi into a small bare office with two brown sofas pressed against opposite walls. On the table in the middle was a vase full of tuberoses that were going brown around the tips and letting off a funereal odour, and a pile of religious pamphlets with brilliantly coloured and intensely pious faces looking out solemnly from the covers. High up on one bare wall was a small wooden cross with the Christ figure draped wearily across it—a familiar icon, a part of his own boyhood at school where cassocked priests swished through the imposing corridors instead of nuns in their whispering robes. Was it a good idea putting Nandana in this school? he wondered belatedly. Would she have been more comfortable in a non-denominational place such as Vidya Bhavan? Father Joseph, the old priest who had taught Arun, was the one who had raised the question of schooling once the girl arrived in India. He had suggested St. Mary's and used his contacts to get the child a seat here. Like everything else, school seats came at a premium these days, and thanks to the priest's intervention, Sripathi had not been asked for the capitation fee or donation that was expected by most schools in the country. The better the institution, the higher the fee.

A tall, slender nun who looked barely forty, rustled in and smiled at Sripathi.

"Good evening, Mr. Rao," she said. "You might not remember me, but I used to be your daughter Maya's history teacher many years ago. I was sorry to hear about her passing."

She looked at Sripathi sympathetically and again he had to control a desire to weep. What was the matter with him, crying in front of every person who gave him a kind look? Half an hour later, the peon returned and told them that all the rooms were empty. After another sympathetic look from the nun, Sripathi made his way back past the silent school with its glassy, shuttered eyes, its barren playground where childish feet had churned up dust all day and the whitewashed wall surrounding it all.

Two hours after Sripathi left to look for Nandana, Arun came home. His shirt was torn, he had several bruises on his face and arms, he was soaking wet and exhausted. The protest march against the large fishing trawlers that were depriving the fishermen of their daily catch had not had quite the effect he had hoped for. Instead, two of the women in the procession had been badly wounded and hospitalized. Thugs hired by the trawler owners had used crowbars and bricks to disperse the unarmed group. One of them had pulled Arun aside and threatened him. "You think you are Gandhi, do you?" the man had asked. His face was familiar, and later Arun realized that he was one of the Boys employed by Munnuswamy. "If you don't keep your long Brahmin nose out of things, you will find it broken into small pieces. And we won't stop there either."

Arun had stared defiantly at him and said, "Do what you want, it doesn't matter to me. Break all my bones, we will see."

The man had grinned in reply, his large teeth stained with betel juice gleaming orange. "There are other things that we can do, mister. We have heard that you have a small girl in your house. It is so easy for a child to get lost these days, eh? She is going to school and *phuss*, gone. Or playing outside one moment and nowhere the next. You will have to be very careful." He slapped Arun hard. "Of course, if you behave yourself, we can make sure that nothing happens to the little chicken. What do you say, mister?"

As soon as he entered the gates of Big House, he was surprised to find Nirmala standing right there, water dripping down her face.

"Oh, it's you," she said flatly. "At last you decided to come home?"

"What are you doing in the rain?" Arun wanted to know.

"The child is gone. We still haven't found her. Where were you?"

"There was a protest march . . ."

"I am sick of your protesting. Your father was right to be angry with you. Here we have so much trouble, and you are outside saving the world. I am sick of all of you. All these years I listened to your father and your grandmother and this person and that. I should have done what *I* thought was right. Then none of this would have happened. I was stupid. Stupid." Nirmala was shouting now, her voice high and furious. "I waited and waited for my Maya to come home, and now I have lost her daughter too. I should have told her ten years ago to come home. Why did I wait? Why was I afraid?"

"Mamma, don't cry, please," begged Arun. He tried to wipe the water running down his face on his wet sleeve. "It isn't your fault. And we'll find her, I am telling you. Have you called the police?"

"It is my fault. I shouldn't have sent her out to play. She didn't want to go," wailed Nirmala.

Arun led his mother into the house, which was blazing with lights. He was surprised to see Gopala sitting on one of the straight-backed rosewood chairs, and Munnuswamy on another. "What are you doing here?" he demanded, the beating he had received at the hands of Munnuswamy's thugs still fresh in his memory and on his body.

"They are helping us to find Nandu," said Nirmala. "So kind."

"What do you mean kind? These two are crooks. Their goondas threatened to take Nandu away only hours ago. What help are they going to give us?" Arun advanced threateningly towards the two men. "Leave our house, please. You are not welcome here."

"That's it, give it to them, the usurpers," Ammayya shouted, delighted to find somebody of the same opinion at last.

Nirmala caught at Arun's arm and dragged him back. "No, don't do anything. They are not involved, I am telling you," she said. She smiled pleadingly at Munnuswamy who had risen to his feet. "Please, don't go. My son is worried, that's all. He doesn't know what he is saying."

"Why couldn't you call the police?" Arun asked.

"Police? I phoned and phoned so many times, and nobody has come to help."

"But these two are crooks, Mamma," said Arun, lowering his voice a bit.

"Everybody in the world is a crook," Nirmala replied. "I don't care if these two are shaitaans from hell. All I know is that they are helping me find Nandana."

A stench of gutters rose and filled the room, mingling with the smells of stale cooking and the mouldy sofa. Although Munnuswamy had gone home shortly after Arun's arrival, Gopala had stayed. Putti fluttered around anxiously, plying everybody with coffee and insisting that they eat something. "We'll find her, don't worry," Gopala assured Nirmala, pressing her hand. "Those Boys know this town like their own palms. They know everybody also. Because of this rain, it is taking a little time, that's all."

Then, around eleven o'clock, just when Nirmala decided to go out to the gate again, there was a shuffling sound from the verandah. The dim light there shone on a man whom she didn't recognize right away. Beside him stood a small figure with long hair.

"Ayyo, ayyo, ammamma!" shouted Nirmala, running to the verandah and lifting Nandana off the ground. "She is back. Oh, thank you deva!" She plastered the child's face with kisses. "Where did you go, you bad child? Are you all right? Tell me, are you all right?"

Nandana dodged the kisses and nodded. "Yes, but I am sleepy," she said shyly.

Nirmala stopped from sheer astonishment. "Did you hear? She spoke to me! Arun, Putti, did you hear her?" She gazed at Nandana. "Say something again, my chinna. Tell me where you went."

"The mad lady took me away and made me eat food," Nandana declared, now struggling to get down from her grandmother's arms.

Nirmala allowed her to slide down, but kept a tight hold on her hand. She looked around at the crowd on the verandah and noticed the man who had brought her grandchild home. Finally, she recognized him. Mr. Poorna, that poor, crazy creature's husband. "You found her? Thank you, thank you," she cried.

The man looked embarrassed. "No, she was in our house all evening," he said. "My wife had taken her inside. I am sorry, I didn't know. I was on tour. Just got back and found her. Please forgive. My wife isn't well. She didn't harm the little one. Please forgive." The relative who looked after his wife had gone to attend a wedding, he explained. Had she come back as originally planned by seven o'clock, the child would have been found earlier. But the storm had disrupted bus services, and the relative had decided to stay over at her cousin's place.

"I am sorry for all the worry we have caused," he said, backing off the verandah. "The child is unharmed." He refused Nirmala's offer of coffee. "No, I had to lock my wife in the room. She is very upset. I have to go and explain."

Long, swaying walls of rain slapped against Sripathi's body and soaked him despite the umbrella. The road had turned into a shallow river with debris hurtling in the flow. Sripathi had longed for this deluge, but it couldn't have arrived at a worse moment. All the people on the road, the pavement dwellers and roadside vendors who might have noticed a small girl with long hair, wide eyes and two missing front teeth, were gone, disappeared into abandoned buildings or under plastic sheeting held down by bricks on piles of old kerosene drums. Strings of electric lights flickered brightly from the balconies of a few of the apartments lining the road. Far away, somebody had decided to celebrate Deepavali early, and Sripathi could hear the hiss and rattle of firecrackers. The smell of onions frying came to him from the cooking fires of the construction workers who lived in every building they made. How many different homes had they inhabited? Not one of them would have his own house to die in. At the thought of homes, Sripathi was reminded of the fact that very soon he, too, would have to find a way to pay his loans or sell Big House. A car rushed past and waves of dirty water washed over his legs. He grimaced and moved to the edge of the road hoping that he wouldn't fall into the gutter. No longer was it possible to know where the gutter ended and the road began. A memory came to him suddenly. He had taken Maya and Arun for a magic show at Technology Hall. Maya was eight and Arun barely two. He did not own a vehicle then, and so they had taken a bus, although it was a fair distance from the bus stop to the house. Arun was too young to appreciate the talents of the great P. C. Sorcar, World-Famous Wizard, but Maya was enthralled, screaming with wonder each time the magician pulled off another trick. When they emerged from the show it was dark and pouring rain just like this. All along the beach they had travelled on the empty bus, watching as lightning slashed the brooding, Cimmerian sky. The sea was a pulsing roll of green fire, hurling itself at the shore, reaching its eager fingers towards the road. A high wind tossed sand against the windows, and the bus seemed to rock with the force of it. By the time they got off and started their long hike home, the road was flooded. Although cyclone warnings were in effect, and Sripathi had been reluctant to leave the safety of his house, especially with the children, he had already purchased the tickets and wasn't going to let them go waste. Nirmala and Putti and Ammayya had gone to Tirupathi for the weekend.

Maya had trotted beside him, chattering excitedly about the magician, her hand clutched tightly in his. In his other arm he carried

Arun. A truck had roared by and almost drowned Maya under the wash of dirty water swooshing up under its wheels. She had coughed and spluttered, scared by the unexpectedness of the drenching, and refusing to walk another step, had begged to be carried instead.

Even today he shuddered at the memory of that night. How he had staggered slowly down the road that usually seemed so brief and now stretched on endlessly. The children grew heavier and heavier, Maya riding piggyback, her arms choking tight around his neck, her plump legs sliding and holding, next slipping and grasping at his waist.

"Hold on," he had shouted every time she seemed about to fall off. "Hold on! We are almost home."

His arms ached with the weight of Arun's body. Sripathi had waded through knee-deep water on the edge of the road, hoping that he wouldn't slide into the invisible drain that waited, malevolent and stinking, beneath the surface.

"Appu, are we going to drown?" Maya had wailed and he had soothed her. "No, my sweet. No raja, Appu will take care of you."

"For ever and ever?" she had demanded, as always making use of the moment to get as much as she could out of him, trying to seal the small uncertainties in her mind with assurances from him, her father.

"For ever and ever," he had promised rashly. How could he have dared the future, challenged the mischievous gods with a statement as arrogant as that?

He passed a pair of caesalpinia trees guarding a familiar scrolled ironwork gate. Raju's house. A light flickered in one of the front rooms. Those trees had provided many of the long, curving brown seed pods that Sripathi and Raju had used as swords in their boyhood games, to re-enact ancient battles: Arjuna and the Kauravas, Lakshmana against a demon or two, Karna, Shivaji, Tipu Sultan. Kings and warriors and heroes, their boyish shouts rising into the dusty air and mingling with the memory of other voices, other children before them who had imagined themselves in the same games. It had all seemed so simple then, all problems solved with the swipe of a long brown seed pod. Sripathi staggered as another truck surged past, creating a strong wave of dirty water around his legs. Suddenly, he felt disoriented and weightless, as if he were floating down the dark road. He couldn't remember where he was or what he was doing in the rain. He tried to compose a letter in his head to hold on to a fragment of consciousness. "Dear Editor," he shouted, "dear, dear Editor." He laughed wildly, unable to think of a single complaint to make against the small world that he inhabited. Two women passed him, and he caught at a soft, wet arm.

"Drunk fool," she screamed, shaking off his hand and hitting him with her open umbrella. Her companion pulled her away and they hurried on, looking over their shoulders now and again.

"I am a fool," agreed Sripathi, giggling helplessly. "But not drunk. No madam, I am a sober fool, and I am terribly, terribly sorry to have discombobulated you."

He staggered and almost fell against a figure coming towards him.

"Appu?" said the figure, startling him. It was a short, thin man with glasses, carrying a torch and a bright yellow umbrella that leapt at the wind. He seemed familiar to Sripathi. "Appu, Nandana is home. She was in Mrs. Poorna's house. She is okay."

"Okay?" Sripathi echoed foolishly. Somehow standing here in the rain, in the dark with this man in front of him whose face he could barely see, the whole day seemed to dissolve into a swirl. A child had got lost. He had not found her. In fact, he thought completely exhausted, he, Sripathi Rao had been responsible for losing her.

"Okay?" he repeated to the man who now took his arm gently and led him down the lightless road.

"Yes, Appu, everything is okay," said the man, sounding more and more like somebody Sripathi thought he might know.

"Maya is back? I told Nirmala she would come back," said Sripathi confidentially. "She never believed me."

He retained no memory of that walk down the road, no memory of Arun, only recollections of endless rain, trees full of swinging swords waiting to fall on his head and a nun who had looked kindly at him through the stained-glass windows of a building he had never seen.

"She is talking," said Nirmala, as soon as Sripathi and Arun reached home. She had put Nandana to bed and was now excitedly pacing the living room. Gopala had also left, insisting that they wake him if they needed anything, regardless of the hour. Sripathi sank down on the floor of the verandah and tried to remove his shoes. He caught his foot and tugged ineffectually. Finally he gave up and just sat there, his head bent, his legs stuck out straight before him. "She is all right," said Nirmala, assuming that he was merely exhausted. "Did you hear me, ree?"

"Who?" Sripathi raised his head and whispered.

"The child, who else?"

Sripathi looked eagerly at her. "Our child is back?" he asked. "Is her husband with her? I hope you have made her favourite things for her. This is a happy event." He beamed at Nirmala who gave him a baffled look.

"Why is he talking nonsense like this?" she asked Arun, who shrugged his shoulders. "I don't know," he said, leading his father gently inside. "He was saying all sorts of things on the way back."

In the living room, where the lights were considerably brighter than the one on the verandah, Nirmala saw how ghastly pale Sripathi was and how wild his eyes were. She touched his face and gasped. "He is burning with fever!" she exclaimed. "Oh God, what a day this has been." She called Arun, who had just taken off his wet clothes, ordered him to go to the doctor's house and beg him on bended knee to make a house call, pay him whatever he asked for. Then she led her husband upstairs to their room, stripped his wet clothes from his body as tenderly as she would a baby's, feeling pity at the sight of his trembling form, the grey whorls of hair that worked their way down from his chest to his crotch, the shrunken scrotum. Was this the same man who had once carried her to bed in jest, his teeth gleaming strong and white in laughter as she shrieked in protest?

"Let's pretend we are in a movie," he had said, swinging her around, almost losing his balance in the process. "You are Vyjayanthimala and I am Sunil Dutt!"

So long ago that had been. Everything had turned topsy-turvy since then. Nirmala wiped him down with a dry towel, pushed him gently down on the bed and dressed him in pyjamas and kurta while he sat docile as a child.

She descended the stairs, slowly, slowly, to accommodate her reluctant knees that snapped and creaked as she moved, and waited for Arun to return with the doctor. *If* he agreed to make a house call in this weather. Nothing was certain these days, not even basic human goodness, she thought bitterly. The living room was dark. Putti was a huddled shadow on the same chair that had been occupied by Gopala an hour before, refusing to join her mother in bed until sleep had quietened her. She stared out of the open front door at the raindrops that briefly turned to gold when caught in the glow of the streetlights. Ammayya's door was shut tight. She had retreated there when Munnuswamy and Gopala arrived, and now she fulminated behind the thick wood, her stick rat-tatting meanly on the sticky, damp floor.

19

WHAT - WHAT
WILL HAPPEN

———————

A CHILD'S LAUGH. The steady patter of rain. Gutters grumbling with the overflow. The whoosh of traffic. Gopinath Nayak singing. The Burmese Wife and her upstairs neighbour screaming at each other over another set of chopped saris. All through the week, Sripathi lay in bed and swam in the warm, familiar tide of sounds. He was not aware that the doctor had agreed to come that night and had left a prescription for his fever and restlessness. Several nights Sripathi had woken in a panic, still feeling the rain slapping against his face, dirty water swilling about his calves, wondering whether he, too, was dying alone on the street like his father. Then he had heard Nirmala's soft, snuffling snores beside him, touched the curve of her back and slid back into sleep. At home, I am at home, he thought drowsily. He had no memory of the preceding few days. The last thing he remembered was his visit to Nandana's school. Did they find the child? He lacked the energy to ask. Now he was awake at last, and free of the dark, churning tumult that had filled his mind since the death of his beloved daughter. In the dull afternoon light that struggled into the room through the ajar balcony door, he stared at the mouldy ceiling until his eyes drooped with the effort of staying open. Soft footsteps approached, but he didn't open his eyes. Nirmala he recognized by the sound of her toe rings striking the floor, but he couldn't decide who had come with her.

"Ajji, is he dead?" asked a hoarse young voice in a whisper. He felt Nandana's breath splay over his face. So they *had* found her.

"Tchah, don't say such things," whispered Nirmala, touching Sripathi's forehead. He liked the comfort of that touch. "Your grandfather is just asleep. See, no fever also."

Her hand was replaced by a much smaller one. There was a brief silence as the two surveyed Sripathi.

"Why is he wearing that string?" asked Nandana. Sripathi jumped as a small, cold finger traced the path of his sacred thread across his chest. He was ticklish. He opened his eyes, unable to keep up the pretense of sleep any longer. Simultaneously, he realized that the child was speaking.

"Look-look, he is awake! Ajji," said Nandana, stepping back from her close examination of Sripathi's bare chest and the thread that cut across it, looping over his left shoulder and disappearing down his back. "Can I ask him about that thread?"

"Why not?" said Nirmala, relieved to see her husband awake.

"She can speak?" he asked, his own voice sounding strange to him.

"Yes, and whole day she has been going bada-bada-bada. Haven't you, my mari?"

"I want to know why he is wearing a thread," said Nandana, retreating behind Nirmala and peering at Sripathi.

"It's to keep me tied together." He tried out a small joke, slightly upset by the child's wary gaze. She was afraid of him. He got a severe look from Nirmala.

"Okay," he amended. For the first time since they had returned from Vancouver, he realized that he was talking to his grandchild without the pain of seeing her mother in her face, her eyes, her voice. "It is to scratch my back. And to remind me of my responsibilities. See, six threads." He separated each of the threads in his jaanwaara with the tip of his index finger. "One each for you and your Ajji. For Ammayya and Putti and Arun and Maya."

"What about my daddy?" demanded Nandana. "Why did you forget my daddy?"

"Okay then. Let's leave Ajji out and make this one your daddy's thread."

"Tchah! Always joking and being foolish. Don't listen to him, my darling. Come, let him sleep. I will tell you what that thread is for, and you tell me about your daddy."

"You said you would show me pictures of my mom when she was my age."

"Yes, yes, that also."

"And the wedding sari with a thousand lotus flowers that you said you would give me when I grew up."

"Yes, child, yes," promised Nirmala.

The sari had been specially created for Nirmala's grandmother's wedding by a master weaver in Kanjeevaram. Somewhere among the fragile veins of gold and turquoise silk, among the two hundred cyan peacocks, three hundred magenta jasmine buds, the tangle of leaves, creepers and blossoms—somewhere in that grand outpouring of the weaver's imagination was hidden a gold elephant for luck and for strength.

When she was a girl, Nirmala had stretched the seven yards of silk across her grandmother's bedroom and searched for the elusive design. Her grandmother had never found it, and the sari had been passed on to her own mother and then to her. It lay there in her cupboard, wrapped carefully in tissue paper, with a slice of sandalwood in between. Every six months for years, she had shaken it out carefully—allowing the delicate smell of sandalwood to float out—folded it in a different way to prevent the gold thread from breaking and put it back in the cupboard.

"Yes," she said again. "And we will look for the elephant hidden in that sari."

Another cyclonic system followed on the heels of the one that had just passed and brought a heavier downpour. Now the people of Toturpuram, who had so longed for rain, cursed it with every breath. The water in the Big House compound, which had subsided a bit, began to lick again at the edges of the verandah. Brown and black worms, swept out of their holes in the earth, coiled and uncoiled like burning rubber on the damp tiles, and in the evening the house rustled with flying ants blindly hitting the light bulbs. By this time even the street urchins had stopped sailing their paper boats in the flooded streets. Instead they huddled under flapping plastic sheets, which were dubiously moored to the pavement with stones and bricks, wailing and fighting with each other. Hoardings crackled with the force of the gale. A small village nearby was swept away, all of its inhabitants killed except for an old woman in a mud hut. Miraculously alive, still surrounded by her chickens, a stray dog and a goat, she seemed blissfully unaware of the storm.

The schools had declared a holiday until further notice as the weather bureau had issued a severe storm warning. Some areas of the town were so heavily waterlogged that it was impossible to go anywhere at all. Fortunately for Nandana, there were the children in the apartment blocks to play with. Her escapades had made her a minor celebrity among them, and she was being constantly invited over. She was a heroine. She had ventured into the tunnel and survived. She had even been kidnapped by the crazy lady and come out of it unscathed. And she made the most of it, telling stories of the monsters that lurked in that dark tunnel, how they had threatened her and how she had thwarted them. However, she could not share with anyone the great empty feeling that had come to her in the lost girl's small, mournful room—the understanding that her parents were dead. Now she trotted alongside Nirmala, eagerly

chattering as if a dam had broken inside her. She was full of questions and comments: Why are there so many mosquitoes? Why
does it scratch when they bite? I don't like the taste of Indian milk.
I like chocolate cake, but my daddy's favourite was tiramisu. My
mommy said that there are lots of ghosts in the back garden, especially under the mango tree. Why do you walk so slowly, Ajji? I
want a kitten of my own, please. Only Ammayya was irritated by the
constant sound of that childish voice. "Pah, like a fly in a bottle she
is! I am getting a headache listening to her." But the rest of the
house was enchanted by her liveliness.

The morning when Sripathi's fever broke, Nirmala decided to
visit the Munnuswamys. She had made some fresh chakkuli to take
to their house—a token of her gratitude for their support the night
of Nandana's disappearance. Carefully balancing the tray of crisp,
golden rings, Nirmala put on her slippers and stepped gingerly off
of the verandah and into the front yard, which seemed to have dissolved into a brownish swill. The water was deeper than she had
expected and she almost lost her balance. She hitched up her sari
with one hand and waded cautiously towards the partially opened
gate through which water from the road gushed into the Big House
compound.

Nirmala had never been inside Munnuswamy's house. All her
conversations with Mrs. Munnuswamy had been conducted over
the wall or near the gates. It was a large and well-maintained abode.
Inside and out, the walls were painted a horribly bright shade of
copper-sulphate blue, but the dadoing was white and, mercifully,
relieved some of the pressure on the eyes. And at least there was no
sign of water damage. There were ornate ceiling fans in every room,
with small chandeliers dropping from their centres. Envy pinched
at Nirmala, and resentment too. So much money they must have
to keep such a big house so nice and clean, she supposed. She
thought about Big House, so rundown, its state of disrepair en-
hanced during the monsoons, when large patches of moss formed

on the walls and ceilings like maps of fertile countries. They hadn't even whitewashed it for ten or more years. She felt Mrs. Munnuswamy's eager eyes on her, but could not bring herself to say anything. Then suddenly she relented, guilty that she was repaying kindness with arrogance.

"Such a nice house you have built," she said. "Nice colour also, the walls and all." The lie didn't bother her much for the pleasure it gave the small, round woman before her.

"My husband got all that paint half-price from a friend. If you want, we can get for you also," said Mrs. Munnuswamy smiling bashfully. "My husband has lots of contacts. Any problem you have, he can take care." She paused. "If you want, only." She then begged Nirmala to sit down on one of the chubby, overstuffed chairs covered in a silky pink material.

"Please, you must take some refreshment," she pressed, and Nirmala yielded despite the initial prickling of guilt at going behind Ammayya's rigidly orthodox back. The feeling was followed almost immediately by annoyance—with herself. How could she, a grown woman, a grandmother herself, still be afraid of a senile old woman with backward ideas?

"Ishwara!" shouted Mrs. Munnuswamy, startling Nirmala with the strength of her vocal chords. She beamed happily at her guest and said, "Ishwara is a very holy boy. He gets dreams, you know. So clever, you can't imagine."

After tea, Mrs. Munnuswamy insisted on taking Nirmala on a tour around the house. Nirmala followed her from one bright blue room to another until she thought the sky had fallen into her eyes. But she said only the most flattering things, unwilling to hurt. In any case, who was she to comment? As if her own house was any better. The last stop on the tour was the terrace from where Nirmala had a good view of the surrounding area. Her own home dwarfed by all the apartment blocks, crouching sullen and nondescript in its pool of filthy water.

Mrs. Munnuswamy noticed it as well and, clapping a hand to her mouth, exclaimed, "Why drainage is so bad in your house only? Better do something. Call corporation people, maybe."

Nirmala nodded and peered uneasily at her home, old and forlorn, stranded in the middle of the rippling grey-green mess. She really ought to tell Sripathi—or Arun since her husband was still unwell—about this. Surely water wasn't supposed to stay for so long, even though it had been raining for days.

Just before Nirmala left, Mrs. Munnuswamy caught her arm, and said hesitantly, "There is something I wanted to talk to you about. Don't be offended, please. My son has been insisting, and I don't know what to do."

"Is it about my sister-in-law?" asked Nirmala, coming straight to the point.

"Yes. We will come and ask properly of course, but first I thought I should speak to you. It is hard to talk to your mother-in-law."

"Gopala wants to marry Putti?"

"Yes."

"Why don't you come over, with tambola and all, after Deepavali festival is through? I will take care of everything, don't worry. I know Putti will be happy also."

Nirmala was amazed at her own daring. To begin with, she would have to deal with Ammayya's hysterics. And Sripathi, how was he going to react? He had cut off their own daughter for marrying out of caste, religion, race. Would he support his sister now? Especially since it was this goonda fellow, the same man whose thugs had beaten up Arun twice.

"You are sure?" repeated Mrs. Munnuswamy, stunned by Nirmala's invitation. She had expected some resistance—shock, or perhaps anger, at the thought of an alliance between her son and the Brahmin girl. A sharp doubt entered her mind. Perhaps there was something wrong with Putti. That's why nobody had yet married her. She looked doubtfully at Nirmala now and got a warm smile in return.

"Yes, why would I simply say it?" said Nirmala.

"You should talk to your mother-in-law first, no?"

"Such matters ought to be settled fast. Neither Gopala nor Putti are young any more. How much longer do you want to wait? Till they lose all their hair and teeth, or what?" Nirmala laughed, in high good humour at her daring.

"What you say is right," agreed Mrs. Munnuswamy, bustling to an ornately carved sidetable with an assortment of silver boxes on a tray. She picked a small tin, opened it and offered it to Nirmala, who took a pinch of vermilion and smeared it in the parting of her hair. The familiarity of the ritual soothed her. If they could manage a half-foreign granddaughter, why not these people who at least had the same rituals?

Again she waded through the ankle-high water around Big House, wrinkling her nose at the stench of rotting vegetation that wafted up with every movement of her feet. God only knew what kinds of dirty diseases were breeding in the mess. She reached the verandah and, with an expression of disgust, squeezed the filthy water from the ends of her sari, bunching the cloth and twisting it vigorously. Then she held the fabric away from her legs and entered the house. Once again she was struck by the difference between the peeling walls of her own living room—the ancient furniture, the musty odour that muffled all other smells—and the brightness of her neighbour's. Again that sting of envy. And then Ammayya appeared, demanding to know whether she had been to the upstart's house, and Nirmala forgot about the water outside and the sad deterioration of their home.

"Yes," she said. "I took some chakkuli to thank them for their help."

"Why suddenly so friendly you have become with them?" asked Ammayya suspiciously.

Nirmala hesitated, wondering whether to break the news of the proposal that would be arriving for Putti. This was probably not the most propitious moment, she decided. She had to think of a strategy first. Tell Putti and Sripathi and Arun. Get them on her side before telling Ammayya. The old woman noticed her hesitation and pounced on it, shaking it like a rat.

"What?" she demanded. "What you are hiding from me?"

"Nothing, Ammayya. I was just thinking how kind they have been, and we . . ."

"Liar! Something else you are hiding. I know you too well, Nirmala."

Nirmala thought quickly. "Well, Munnuswamy's wife said she could get us some wall paint half-price, and I was wondering whether you could lend some money to buy. The house needs painting."

As she had expected, the idea of lending money put Ammayya off the scent immediately. "Money? My husband left me a pauper, and I have to live on my son's charity. Where do you think I will get money from?" she grumbled, retreating hastily into her room.

Nirmala made her way up the stairs, still holding her soggy sari away from her legs. First she would tell Sripathi about the proposal, then Putti, then Arun, and finally Ammayya. If her husband dared to do ooin-aayin about caste and creed, she would remind him of their Maya. Cruel tactic to get her way, but sometimes cruelty was necessary. Squelch-squelch-squelch, she climbed, her feet cold. But Nirmala barely noticed, so busy was she, plotting a marriage for her sister-in-law. A happy occasion was needed in this house. It could be a small wedding, no need to call the whole world. Maybe even an Arya Samaj wedding, which would be over in five-ten minutes and cost less than a traditional one. If everyone agreed, of course. It would be nice to have a full-scale celebration, but money was a consideration, naturally. In her stolid, practical way, Nirmala had decided that the best way to deal with her own loss was to put it behind her and forge on.

She went upstairs to tell Sripathi about the water around their house, hoping to find him awake. She found Arun sitting at the edge of the bed, conversing with his father.

"The boy has a job," Sripathi said, before she could open her mouth.

"What? When did this happen?" she asked, surprised.

"Why are you both so astonished?" Arun wanted to know. "Even Appu acted as if I had won the Bharat Ratna or something. It is a small job in Delhi."

"So far away?" Nirmala said.

"An environmental group—non-governmental, so the pay is not great—but it is what I want to do. I will be able to send some money home; I don't need much for myself."

Sripathi cleared his throat and said, "You might not have to. I am selling this house. I have decided." He didn't know when he had reached the decision, but now that the words had left his mouth it seemed perfectly right. "Yes, that is what I shall do."

"Why didn't you tell me all this? I always come to know last of all. Is this not my home too?" demanded Nirmala. "What will Ammayya say? You haven't talked to her about it, have you?"

"It is the best thing for all of us," said Sripathi. "This property is worth a lot of money. We will need money from the end of this year. I might not have a job for much longer."

"But what will you do sitting at home?" There was dismay in Nirmala's voice. "The whole day you will be here?"

"Don't sound so worried," Sripathi said ironically. "I will keep out of your way. Maybe I will start giving tutorials in English and mathematics." He leaned back against the pillows and stared out of the open balcony door at the apartment block. Soon, he thought, soon they would all be living in one of those boxes. He didn't mind after all. This house was like a grindstone around his neck. There were too many memories haunting it—some good, it was true—but it was time now to create new memories.

20

A
NEW DAY

THE DEEPAVALI FESTIVAL had come and gone. A number
of the apartments kept the strings of electric lights hanging
from their balconies, perhaps to make up for the heavy
darkness that had descended on Toturpuram since the rains arrived. Although they had decided not to celebrate the festival this
year, Sripathi had bought a box of sparklers, some fountains and
ground chakras for Nandana to play with. He had also bought her a
small packet of coloured pencils and a set of hair clips, dithering a
long time over the choosing of these gifts. It had been more than
twenty years since he last purchased something for a child. Nirmala, too, had got Nandana a new frock and some pretty, multicoloured plastic bangles, and had made a few delicacies to mark the
festival of lights.

"But should we be doing this?" Sripathi had asked on Deepavali morning, suddenly overcome with a bout of guilt at celebrating so soon after a tragedy.

"What is gone is gone," Nirmala had said as she rolled out thin
discs of puri dough in the kitchen, her bangles tinkling briskly.
"Wipe your hands and carry on, that is what I say. I will always miss
my Maya, but tomorrow's meal still has to be cooked, no? The
child's future is more important than past sorrows."

In the weeks that followed his breakdown and slow recovery, Sripathi watched his wife, admiring the sturdy resilience that allowed her to cut and cook every day, trudge up and down the stairs to oil, bathe, cajole and care for Nandana, or sing her to sleep after dinner. He had lived with her for thirty-five years, and still he had not learnt her optimism. He looked always over his shoulder at the night instead of waiting hopefully for the next day.

It was the middle of December now, and the cyclonic activity over the Bay of Bengal had again intensified after a brief hiatus. It was impossible to keep schools and offices closed indefinitely, although the streets were still drowned in water. People went about their daily lives with a shrug.

"What-what will happen, will happen-ay-happen," said Balaji, the bank manager, one morning, when Sripathi was squeezing through the gates of Big House. He had gone to Advisions, but only to work out the notice of resignation that he had handed in a month ago. Better that than to wait like a dog for Kashyap to throw him out. At least he had some dignity left.

Balaji continued to hold forth. "If my fate is to die of drowning, so be it." He adjusted the bright woollen balaclava cap, a size too small, over his large head and shrugged. There were many of those caps around Toturpuram this year. Beauteous Boutique was doing a roaring business in woollen caps and sweaters, not to mention mufflers, gloves and socks, as a result of the lingering cold. The cyclones had brought the temperatures in Toturpuram down several notches. Kumar Jain, the owner, had even managed to sell woollen jackets to the Palanoor family, who were convinced that the polar ice cap had finally made its move to Toturpuram. The shopkeeper had bought the consignment of woollens from a merchant in Kashmir, whom he had met on a family holiday in Delhi several years ago.

"Poor fellow," he had told the Raos when they had gone to buy Nandana's Deepavali dress. "It is my duty to help my Kashmiri brothers. He said that he did not even have money to feed his family

the next day. I was in tears, you know. Ask my wife. She will tell you
how I was nearly in tears."

His wife had nodded her head and looked worshipfully at her
husband. "He is a very sentimental person, too-too generous and
fond of doing charities of all sorts," she agreed.

"Rascally liar!" Ammayya had proclaimed on the way home. "He
must have got the woollens at a price too low to resist and hoarded
them till now. And made a 200 per cent profit. Have you noticed his
wife's new jewellery? Two diamond florets on her nose. And six
gold bangles that I have never seen before, latest pattern that too!"

The house smelled of damp clothes that had been strung up in
almost every room. Nothing dried, not even the thinnest of cotton
blouses. It was as if the rain had percolated into every pore of the
house.

This morning, Sripathi was busy filling water in the kitchen. He
heaved one pot out of the sink and replaced it with another. He
filled one last container and tiptoed into Ammayya's room, hoping
that she was asleep. In the dining room he passed Nandana, who
woke up absurdly early every morning. A few days ago, to her intense joy, Arun had brought her a bedraggled kitten. After much
debate, during which Ammayya protested loudly and ineffectually,
they decided to keep it in a closed basket in the dining room. The
child spent every available minute with the creature. She looked up
at Sripathi as he passed and gave him a small smile. She didn't
speak to him as freely as she did to the others, he knew. Sometimes,
while he was on the balcony, he would notice her peeping at him
around the bedroom door, disappearing as soon as he looked up.

Ammayya was wide awake in her favourite chair. She was in
a bad mood. "Oho, Sripathi," she started off when she saw him.
"There are too many mosquitoes in this house. Why can't you do
something? No sleep at all I had, and now I will fall sick."

"Please, no drama first thing in the morning. I have no time,"
he said briskly, peering into the bathroom. He knew that the

grumbling was a prelude to something else. Ammayya was not pleased about the sale of the house, although the thought of having an apartment of her own had mollified her. What she was actually upset about was the marriage proposal from the Munnuswamys' and Putti's obvious delight at the thought of being Gopala's wife.

"Tell me when the tank is full," he said and headed back to the kitchen. The child was still in the dining room, dragging a small toy on a string across the floor and giggling every time the kitten pounced on it.

"Don't you have school today?" Sripathi asked, watching her play.

"She does," replied Nirmala, who was also in the kitchen, measuring out cupfuls of ingredients for the snacks she was making for that evening. "The naughty one isn't getting into her uniform. That kitten is too much of a distraction."

"Why do I have to wear that stinky uniform?" Nandana whined. "Why can't I wear my jeans?"

"Sister Angie will get angry, my sugar," said Nirmala. "What is wrong with your uniform? You look so smart in it. Now go and wear it, or you will be late."

"But it scratches my neck and my arms," argued Nandana. "See, it gives me a rash, an itchy one. I am allergic to it."

"Nobody is allergic to uniforms. It is the starch that is making you scratch, that's all," said Nirmala firmly. "From tomorrow I will tell the dhobi not to starch your clothes. Now I am getting tired of all this fuss-muss. Go upstairs, otherwise I am going to ask Arun Maama to take that kitten back to wherever he found it."

"You are mean," grumbled Nandana, getting reluctantly to her feet. "I wish my mommy was here."

"Your mother was my daughter," said Nirmala. "She would have said exactly the same thing, my sweet chicken. I'll have a treat ready for you when you come back from school if you are a good girl. Okay?"

Just then the doorbell rang. "Three cups of sooji," she murmured. "Ree, will you remind me that I measured out three cups already? I'll see who it is." She hurried out of the kitchen, pausing to shoo Nandana up the stairs, and to the front door, which was wide open already. Over the sound of water running, Sripathi heard Raju's voice. He thought that he must be mistaken, that it was actually somebody who only sounded like his friend. A few minutes later, Nirmala came into the kitchen. "I'll take care of the water," she told him. "Raju is here. You better go. Something is wrong, I think. I will make some coffee and bring."

"What a surprise this is," exclaimed Sripathi as he entered the living room. "The sun is surely going to set in the east today! If we see it at all, that is. Come on, sit down. Why have you decided to visit on this stormy morning, my friend?"

"Oho! Finally you remembered us, Raju Mudaliar," remarked Ammayya from her chair. All around her were the week's supply of newspapers stolen from the Gujerati couple in the opposite block of flats. "To what do we owe this honour?"

"You know my situation, Ammayya," said Raju politely. Sripathi remembered that his mother had never liked this friend, a dislike largely fuelled by the fact that Raju always did better than Sripathi at school. He led Sripathi back onto the verandah to avoid any further interruption from Ammayya, who had abandoned her papers to listen to their conversation.

It was cool and wet on the verandah. Raju sat down on the solitary cane chair and Sripathi leaned against the door. "What a way to greet your old friend!" he said, smiling wanly. "Instead of giving me some hot coffee, you ask me why am I here?"

"Sorry, sorry. I was just so surprised. This early, too. And your coffee is already percolating, don't worry. Do you want some idlis also? Have you had breakfast?"

"No, but I am not hungry. I just came to tell you something." Raju paused and looked down at his hands. "Ragini died last night."

Sripathi stopped smiling. It seemed to him that the room had become very quiet, even though sounds came from everywhere else, magnified and unnaturally loud—Nandana's chuckles, the water running in Ammayya's room, even the thump of clothes being washed in the backyard.

Raju did not look up from his studied contemplation of his hands. "She seems to have stopped breathing for some reason," he added. "I called the doctor early today and he issued a death certificate. The cremation is at eleven o'clock. I came to ask if you will help me carry her to the burning grounds. You are like my brother. Can you take a day off from work?"

"She died in her sleep?" asked Sripathi sharply. He remembered the despair in Raju's eyes the last time they had spoken. And how he had said that he sometimes thought about ending the girl's life. Had his friend finally crossed the thin, ambiguous line separating thought from deed? And if he had, was he wrong to have done so? One by one, thought Sripathi, all his stiff certainties were sliding, leaning over, falling. A year ago, he would have cut all ties with Raju on the basis of that suspicion. He would have accused him of killing Ragini, instead of merely speculating. He would have been unshakably righteous, sure that in the same situation he would never have done something so drastic. But now he was a man filled with doubt.

"I don't think she was in pain," said Raju, still avoiding Sripathi's eyes. "I did all I could for her, you have to agree with me. I looked after her better than anyone ever could. Right? Right?"

"Yes, you are right," said Sripathi quietly. "Nobody could have done any better."

"And you will be one of the pall bearers? You can take leave?"

Sripathi realized that he hadn't seen Raju since Nandana's disappearance. "Don't worry, I will manage." He would have to phone Kashyap again. "I can take the time off," he assured Raju. "I will not be missed."

By the time Sripathi returned it was two o'clock in the afternoon. The ceremonies for Ragini had been done very quickly at Raju's request. The girl's body had looked so thin and flat, and her face so calm, that for a hallucinatory moment, Sripathi thought that Raju had made a mistake. Surely this was not that large, ungainly creature with the flailing arms, the wildly mobile face, who had occupied his friend's life for twenty-five years? The funeral van had taken them to the head of the small road leading to the burning grounds, where the bier was removed. Leaving their slippers in the van, they carried Ragini to the open field where a single smouldering pile of wood sent up a spire of smoke into the dull sky. Two of Raju's relatives had offered to help as well, in this last rite.

Back home, Sripathi waded through the slush to the rear door, shouting for Nirmala to bring a bucket of clean water. He had just returned from a place of death and needed to wash the sorrow away before he entered the house. He stripped off all his outer garments, shivering in the rain, and when the bucket was placed before him, washed himself down.

In the few hours since his absence, the house had been transformed. It was cleaner than Sripathi had ever seen it. All the doorways had fresh curtains, and Nirmala had hung a fresh garland of mango leaves over the front door, reminding him that the Munnuswamys were arriving on this auspicious evening. Another of his certainties eroded. He had never thought that he might one day end up as that thug Gopala's brother-in-law. Overlaying the odour of stagnant water were kitchen smells—of uppuma and bonda, vadai and laddoo—delicacies that Nirmala had made throughout the day.

"Our house might not be as good as Munnuswamy's," she told Sripathi proudly when he praised her efforts, "but our hospitality cannot be faulted."

The rotting sofa was draped in a bright new bedsheet, and the chairs in the living room had been drawn away from the wall, dusted and grouped around the rosewood and ivory coffee table. The air of excitement in the old house reminded Sripathi of the times when Maya had received her university admission letter, got engaged to Prakash, or when Arun had passed the college finals with a high first class. Even his son looked transformed somehow, and it took Sripathi a few minutes to notice his haircut and clean-shaven face.

In her room, Putti dithered before the Belgian mirror, anxiously draping one sari after another across her shoulder. Pink? Green? Navy blue? The last one, with its discreet pattern of magenta and green flowers, made her look older than the others. She liked it, though. She *was* old, why hide that fact?

"Ammayya, is it okay?" she asked her mother timidly, who sat in raging silence in her chair, her stick beating a sharp tattoo on the floor. Ever since Nirmala had broken the news, she had been like this. Putti hated that sound—tap-tap-tappa-tap—fracturing her happy thoughts, creating an unpleasant tension in her chest. She badly wanted her mother to give her blessings to this alliance. "Ammayya?"

Her mother pressed her lips together tight and glared at her daughter. "If you really cared about my opinions, you wouldn't allow that pariah dog from next door into this house," she snapped finally. "You are breaking my heart, I tell you. If I die tonight, it is on your head."

"But they are nice people, Ammayya," begged Putti.

"Yes, even our toilet cleaner is very nice, no doubt. Why you don't marry her son? Henh? Why not throw some more shit on our family name? Nice!" She coughed violently, a prolonged, choking bout calculated to fill Putti with guilt. When her daughter did not respond with her usual anxious queries, Ammayya said bitterly, "And don't think I will give you any jewellery to wear. From today you and I are strangers. You are a piece of dirt that my womb voided and that I kept by mistake, idiot that I am!"

"I don't want anything from you," replied Putti with equal bitterness. "You only said that if somebody really wants to marry me, he will not want any jewellery or dowry. Keep everything."

She swept out of the room and behind her Ammayya shouted, "Who do you think gave you that sari you are wearing? Or the blouse or petticoat? Who do you think gave you life in the first place? 'Don't want anything,' she says!" She hit the floor viciously with her stick. "And who else will marry an old spinster like you but a low-caste fool?"

An hour before the Munnuswamys were scheduled to arrive, the power failed, plunging the entire street into darkness. Ammayya was delighted, taking it as a sign that the gods were as furious as she at this unholy alliance.

"Inauspicious beginning, wretched ending," she chortled, swaying from one room into the other, getting in the way as Nirmala hurriedly lighted candles and kerosene lamps. In the kitchen, she found a tray full of laddoos and crushed a few of the perfect, golden, hand-rolled sweets. She found a tin full of fresh, crisp chakkuli that Nirmala had slaved over all morning and, under cover of darkness, stole the whole thing. She held it close to her stomach, draped her sari over it and hurried to her room, where she hid it under the bed. Nobody would look there tonight for sure. By the morning, she would have concealed it inside her cupboard. She settled down again in her chair to think of something nasty to do when the visitors arrived, so that they would be frightened off the match altogether. Or better still, to insult them thoroughly. Yes, that Munnuswamy milkman's son was too arrogant by far—offering for a Brahmin girl's hand indeed! As if there was a shortage of decent men for Putti. And as for Putti, Ammayya cringed to think how her daughter's shameless behaviour might have led to this. Too much television, no doubt, corrupting the poor innocent. Then all of a sudden, Ammayya felt sorry for being so harsh on Putti. She would have responded better to kindness, to good advice given away from the corrupting influence of Nirmala. Yes, she had been tainted by the denizens of this house, influenced by that Maya, by her shameless marriage to a foreigner. Couldn't Putti see where *that* had led her? Straight to Lord Yama's kingdom, that's where. Uh-*huh*!

In the living room, candles sent long, wavering spires of light all over, shadows swung out from behind shelves, cupboards, the television and chairs, even the ancient hat stand that was now used to hang umbrellas and raincoats. Outside a guttural chorus of frogs had started up, interrupted now and again by the thin wail of a nearby child. And the rain still poured out of the heavy sky.

The Munnuswamys arrived at six sharp, all of them with their clothes hitched up to avoid the brown water surrounding Big House. Koti had been posted in the verandah to offer the guests water to wash their dirty feet and towels to mop them dry. Putti, lurking in the shadowy living room, got her first glimpse of Gopala's large feet and went coy and shivery all over at the thought of those feet sliding over her own. She ran into the kitchen as they entered the house, overcome with shyness. Only after Sripathi had welcomed them, asked after their health and made sure that they were comfortably seated, did she emerge again.

"Ah, daughter-in-law!" exclaimed Munnuswamy with heavy good humour. "When can we carry you away with us?"

Ammayya snorted loudly from her room at the sound of that coarse voice. "Cheek!" she said. "Insolence! Low-class crooks. Taking our homes and our daughters and all."

There was an embarrassed silence.

"Beat up my grandson and steal my daughter. Think that will make you any better than you are? Only fit for collecting dung!"

Nirmala got up and shut the door on her mother-in-law, ignoring her indignant shouts.

She smiled at her visitors. "Please don't mind, she is old and doesn't know what she is saying. Such a problem it is, you know, but what to do? We will all grow old sometime or other, no?"

"I know what I am saying," bawled Ammayya from behind the closed door. "Putti, if you marry this loafer you will be dead for me for ever. My curses will be on your head. A mother's curse is the blackest of them all. Your children will be born deformed. They, too, will abandon you. And that evil fellow will beat you every single day!"

But Putti heard nothing. She was lost. Utterly. She and Gopala gazed at each other, transfixed. Her heart drummed rapturously in its curving cage of bones. She allowed her eyes to rest on his fierce, dark face, made fiercer and darker by the lack of light. And on his wide shoulders and muscled chest. She wanted to lick his nipples. Suck on his long, hanging earlobes that had been pierced as a child and still showed faint indentations. Miss Chintamani, with much giggling and nudging, had shown her a magazine article that enumerated erogenous zones in men and women. The article was particular about ears and nipples, remembered Putti. She wanted to squeeze his bunched, ropy muscles between her own tiny fingers. Once they were married, she would oil that wonderful manly body with mustard oil every morning, she vowed. Give him a head bath and then he could oil and bathe her. They would live in the steamy heat of the bath for the rest of their lives. Lost in her lascivious thoughts, Putti heard not one single word being shouted by her mother, and when Gopala's mother handed her a tray full of fruit to welcome her as her son's future wife, Putti could have swooned with joy.

21

THE
FLOOD

T HE RAIN FINALLY STOPPED the next morning. When Sripathi emerged from his room into the balcony, he was cheered by the sight of the sun, a yellow smear in the pale grey sky. He opened his box of pens and selected one at random, not sure what he wanted to write about today. The newspaper had yielded nothing worth comment.

The muted cacophony of the street swelled forth. The temple bell pealed continuously, and the long, wailing call of vegetable vendors, the clackety-clack of the knife sharpener on his ancient bicycle, the honk of buses, cars and scooters all seeped into the house.

"Ammai, flowers, ammai!" called a sing-song voice from the road. It was the young flower girl, Naga, with her basketful of fragrant jasmine and champa, roses and marigolds. Sripathi heard the front door being opened, and shortly after, his sister appeared near the gate. "Akka, do you want flowers today?" shouted the girl. "Nice and fresh they are." Her thin, bare arms raised to hold the basket on her head, gleamed in the morning light.

"Don't I buy from you every morning?" She had her sari bunched in one hand and hitched up to avoid the dank, squelching filth that covered the yard. "How much for a single mana?"

"Seventy paise, Akka."

"Rubbish! The temple woman sells for ten paise less, do you know that? Come on, you are charging too much."

"What Akka," protested the girl. "My flowers are so fresh you can smell the wind on them still. Picked at two o'clock this morning. That old hag at the temple plucks them the previous night."

She planted one foot on a large rock near the gate and lowered her basket onto her cocked knee. The jasmine, strung together with thin threads of banana fibre, alternated with coral flowers and fragrant herbs and lay neatly coiled in the leaf-lined basket. The roses, champa and marigolds were divided into separate heaps of pink and white, cream and gold.

"Well, how many lengths do you want today? One or two?" asked the girl. She drew out a string of jasmine for Putti to see how tight and full the buds were and how closely they were strung on the banana fibre.

"Two. And make sure you measure it all the way to your elbow. No cheating. I am watching with both eyes," Putti warned.

The girl held one end of the string between her index and middle fingers and allowed it to unravel until it reached the crook of her elbow before doubling it back. Then she carefully snipped it off with a small pair of scissors, folded it into a slice of banana leaf and handed it to Putti.

"You don't want champa or rose today? Very nice white roses, see. Smell and see," offered the girl, handing one to Putti.

"Silly girl, who smells flowers before offering them to God?" Putti dropped a few coins into the basket and turned away. There were rumours that the flower girls raided gardens before dawn for their baskets, but Sripathi could not imagine this delicate child thieving.

The Burmese Wife emerged on her balcony, her hair wound up in a thin cotton towel. "Girl, come up here also!" she shouted.

More women appeared on their balconies to summon the flower girl, and soon the world was awake. Sripathi put down his newspaper and writing material and made his way down the stairs. To his surprise, his mother was still lying in bed. Usually, she was up and ready for breakfast before he came down.

"Sripathi, will you go to Dr. Menon and get me some medicine?" she asked as soon as he came down. "I am feeling dizzy and sick."

"Just take a spoonful of the syrup he gave you the last time," he said. "I will be late for work again."

"Anyway, you are leaving that stupid job, so what does it matter when you go? I am really not well," whined Ammayya. She emerged from under the mosquito netting and shuffled slowly to the door of her room.

Sripathi looked at his mother, her shorn scalp silver with a dusting of new hair, her skin haggard and yellowish in the early light. She did look unwell. With something approaching sadness, he gazed at her, and saw beyond the craggy features the hope and beauty that had once been there. "I'll send Arun," he said gruffly. "You can tell him exactly what is wrong. But if you are really feeling bad, maybe we should take you to the hospital."

"No," said Ammayya flatly. "I want to die in my own home."

"Don't talk like that, Ammayya. You will be okay. It is probably all those laddoos you ate yesterday." Or because you cannot swallow the idea of Putti and that crook's son, Sripathi thought.

When he left to catch the bus to work he found a group of men clearing the debris in front of the house.

"Hello, brother," called Gopala from across the wall. "You won't have problems with my truck fellows any more." He smiled cheerfully. "You have any other problems you want fixed? Tell me, we are kin now."

"*Your* trucks? Those truckers work for you?"

Gopala smiled proudly. "My father owns six of them. Goddess Lakshmi has showered prosperity on us." He folded his palms and piously touched them to his forehead.

Sripathi did not know how to respond. He had never been crooked in his entire life so far, he had always followed the rules. He had plodded down the straight line of duty and honour, and here was this rogue clearing the mess with one wave of his violent hand. The mess that his own people had created, probably at his orders too. Come to think of it, the Munnuswamy house was the only one on the street that had a spotless stretch of road before it. Perhaps he and Arun were the fools in this world and Gopala was the wise man who used any means to survive. Did he ever feel a twinge of conscience? What if Sripathi asked him about the beating that Arun had received? Would he just smile his white, radiant smile and say, "We are kin now, and your son is like my nephew," and send his goondas out to fight Arun's hitherto unarmed battles with knives, broken bottles and sticks? And Putti, his foolish, loving sister, how would she live in that house, her own goodness compromised by the knowledge of her husband's villainy?

Gopala's rich bass tones interrupted his thoughts. "You want my car to drive you to work?" he asked.

"No, it is okay," said Sripathi hastily, unwilling to be the recipient of any more favours. "Thank you for clearing the gates for us. Very kind of you."

"You only have to ask, Sripathi-orey, that's all. I see that there is too much water collecting in your compound. If you want my Boys will fix that also. Simply have to break the wall at the back. What do you say?"

"I'll ask my mother, Gopala," said Sripathi, shuddering inwardly at the thought of how Ammayya would react to *this* offer of help. "She is very touchy about some things."

"Oh yes, oh yes, mother comes first." Gopala wagged his head and flashed another smile at Sripathi, who hurried away to the bus stop.

Clouds rolled in by three o'clock that afternoon and by evening it had started pouring again. Putti, unable to stand on the terrace that had become her refuge from Ammayya, was obliged to sit in the living room while her mother shot barbed comments at her from her veiled bed. To everybody's surprise, she refused to eat lunch, claiming that Putti had driven her appetite away by her shameless behaviour.

"Is she all right?" Nirmala asked uneasily. "She never refuses food."

"Ammayya has been feeding on anger," said Putti bitterly. "One day without food won't hurt her. Why can't she be happy for me? She never wanted me to get married, I know. Why should I care how she is feeling now?"

But at night, when Ammayya skipped her dinner as well, Putti's guilt overwhelmed her. "Why aren't you eating anything?" she asked her mother, peering through the dirty mosquito net. "Did you drink the medicine that Arun brought for you?"

"What do you care?" muttered Ammayya and then retreated into complete silence. She didn't respond when Putti offered to press her legs, as she did most nights before bed, or even to massage her head with warm oil. And when her daughter got into bed, she turned her back on her, refusing to gossip before drifting off to sleep as was her habit. Putti lay in the dark, miserably listening to the endless rain tapping on the window panes and against the verandah floor, and whooshing through the gutters. The fan creaked as it rotated. Light filtered in from outside through the stained-glass window panes and made the room glow eerily for a while. At about eleven o'clock, the power went off, plunging everything into a profound darkness. Putti heard Nirmala singing to the child, the kitten mewing in its closed basket in the dining room, and eventually the clock striking twelve upstairs. Finally, silence descended. The old house rocked gently on its heels and settled down to sleep.

At about three o'clock, a muffled thump woke Putti. She scrabbled around the bed sleepily, wondering what had made the sound.

Another thump, like an explosion. She peered through the mosquito netting, but it was too dark to see anything. If Ammayya did not close those wretched windows so tightly, she might have had some light from the street. But then she remembered, the power had failed. With a sigh, Putti reached in the gap between the two mattresses and fished out the torch. She shone it around the room and saw nothing. Now she could hear a gurgling sound, as if there was water bubbling somewhere. *Inside* the house, not outside where the patter of rain was loud and constant. Had someone left a tap on in the bathroom? With the torch in one hand, Putti pulled on the edge of the mosquito netting, releasing it from under the mattress where it had been tucked securely. She prepared to slide out quickly, so that no mosquitos could get in. Her bare feet landed with a splash in cold, oily water. Putti screamed and drew them back inside the netting. She turned the torch towards the floor, and the light shimmered and danced on the black water that was lapping quietly against the walls, reaching up the legs of the bed. Putti couldn't believe what she was seeing. For a few moments she wondered wildly whether the sea had somehow worked its way into Big House. She reached down cautiously and touched the surface of the water to assure herself that she was not dreaming. Something floating by brushed her hand, and when she shone the torch at it, she saw that it was a crescent of feces. Putti gagged in revulsion and wiped her hand frantically against the mosquito netting. She still couldn't fathom what had happened, but knew that she didn't want to drown in sewage. Soggy sheets of newspaper were slowly sinking into the water—all of Ammayya's stolen newspapers from under the bed, realized Putti. The thought of her mother brought her up short. If the sea was flooding through the house, they would be the first to drown. They had better go to the uppermost floor, and fast.

"Sripathi! Arun!" she shouted, hoping that somebody upstairs would hear and come down to help. There was no response. Putti yelled a few more times, intermittently shaking her mother and prodding her in the plump rolls of flesh that seeped out from the sides of the loose, faded blouse she wore to bed. Her mother merely swatted her hand away and continued to snore. Exasperated, Putti seized a pouch of skin close to her mother's belly and pinched it hard, feeling a definite pleasure in the violence of the action. All her anger against Ammayya and her strategies to keep Putti a spinster were expressed in that twisting, cruel pinch. She felt no guilt later on, assuring herself that she was only trying to get her mother out of bed and to safety. Ammayya responded with a squeal of pain and a flailing of her heavy arms.

"What?" she demanded blearily. "What?"

She screamed when she saw the dark shape hovering over her, the torchlight under her face turning her into a creature from nightmare. "Don't touch me! I'll give you everything," she whimpered, holding her arms over her face.

"Ammayya, it's me, Putti."

The old woman sat up quickly and glared at her child. "Why you are waking me up in the middle of the night? What is wrong?" It was the first time that evening that she had spoken to her daughter.

"Ammayya, the sea is inside our house. Big mess it is. We have to climb upstairs immediately," said Putti frantically.

"Henh?" said Ammayya baffled.

"Get out of bed. We have to go upstairs. Otherwise, we will drown," she repeated slowly. "Look at that."

She shone the torch at the floor, around the room, and a horrified Ammayya gazed at the water eddying around the legs of their bed and lapping at the rosewood dressing table. The lower edges of the Belgian mirror eerily reflected the net-shrouded bed like a white island marooned in the stinking, obsidian sea. For once she was bereft of words. She allowed Putti to rip the mosquito netting aside and push her off the bed. The stench assailed her as soon as they had begun to wade through the cold, disgusting mess.

"Why so bad it is smelling?" she whispered, clinging to Putti, who was gagging continuously now, the torch shaking in her hand.

"Ammayya, there's kakka in the water and all kinds of other dirty things," said Putti brutally, hating her mother for clinging to her, for having sucked her life away.

"I thought you said it was the sea," wailed Ammayya. "Now you are telling me that I am walking in shit water?" Her skin crawled at the sly touch of the liquid. "Ayyo deva! Ayyo swami! Ayyo-ayyo-ayyo!" she howled. She was polluted for all eternity. She was soiled for ever. Nothing could wash away this stink, this putrefaction, this muck that only the toilet cleaner ought to touch. She felt bile gurgling up her throat and retched drily. "Oh Sathyanarayana!" she called to her favourite god. "What treachery is this? What have I done to you to deserve this? Putti, are you sure?" she begged.

"Can't you smell it?" She shone her torch around and Ammayya moaned with disgust. She was *walking* in somebody's excrement?

"Whose is that?" she asked faintly.

"What do you mean *whose*, Ammayya?" demanded Putti. Now her anger had been replaced by contempt for her mother. How could she have been scared of this pathetic creature for forty-two years? she wondered. "All the drains on this road are connected. So it could be our neighbour's for all I know. Maybe Chocobar man's. Maybe Munnuswamy's. Does it have a name on it, you want me to check?"

"Why you are making fun of me, my beloved child?" asked her mother, trying to wade through the water without disturbing it. She shut her eyes tightly and allowed the tears to trickle out. Real tears. She imagined the foul liquid on the floor seeping up through her orifices into the sacred parts of her body, corrupting her from the inside out. She would never be able to clean herself. Never. She wailed once more and then fell silent, except for the violent retching sounds that burst out of her as they made their way to the staircase which, beyond the first three steps, was dry. Putti shook off her mother's clutching hand, forcing her to hold on to the bannister and climb up slowly. She yelled again for Sripathi and Arun and Nirmala, her voice bouncing off the moist walls, startling against the silence. She could hear shufflings and whispers of wakefulness as her shouts filtered through deep sleep and dreaming eyes.

"Was that Putti?" she heard her sister-in-law ask. "I heard someone shouting."

"Wake up, wake up!" screamed Putti. "We are all going to drown. The sea is here!"

"Sea? What sea?" That was Sripathi. "Is she dreaming or what?"

They all gathered sleepily on the first-floor landing. After a few minutes of what-ing and where-ing and why-ing, during which Arun ran down the stairs to make sure that his aunt was not hallucinating, Sripathi decided that the best thing to do was to call the Munnuswamys for help from the terrace. Ammayya wouldn't go anywhere until she had washed her legs with soap and water.

"Rama, Sita, Rama, Sita," she murmured, while she scrubbed her legs. She was trembling all over and had to be helped out of the bathroom by Nirmala, who wrapped her in a bedsheet. Nandana was roused, lifted out of bed by Arun, and the family climbed up to the terrace. She woke just as Sripathi finished his struggle with the bolts on the terrace door.

"Where are we going?" she wailed, rubbing her eyes.

"The sea has come inside the house," said Ammayya tearfully. "We will all drown, yo-yo-yo Rama, yo-yo-yo Sita!"

"We are all going to die? Like my Mommy and Daddy?"

"No, we are not," soothed Nirmala.

"Where is my kitten?"

They had all forgotten the little animal trapped in its basket. Nobody said anything and Nandana kicked her legs against Arun. "I *want* my kitten."

"Not now, my raja," said Nirmala, patting her legs. "Later on. He will be all right."

Nandana gave her a suspicious look but allowed herself to be pacified. They went outside and were soaked by the rain almost immediately. Ammayya moaned that her chest hurt, that she was dying, that this was God's way of showing his anger over Putti's betrothal.

Why, thought Sripathi, was his life in such chaos all of a sudden? Like King Harishchandra, was he too being tested by the gods? He glanced at Nandana cowering under a plastic sheet that Nirmala had found in her cupboard. The umbrellas were all stranded in the living room, so they had to make do with whatever they had been able to find in the small storage cupboard near the terrace door.

"Nobody will hear us if we shout!" he said despondently over the gush of rain in the gutters.

"I can climb down easily," suggested Arun. He had jumped from one compound to another often enough as a boy. "Best way. You all stay here till I come back."

He balanced for a moment on the wall of the terrace and leapt across to the adjacent balcony. He shinnied down the drainpipe and was lost to the darkness. A few moments later, however, they heard him banging on their neighbour's door, shouting for help. Doors opened, there were voices, and then a wide beam of light as Petromax lanterns flared whitely on Munnuswamy's terrace.

Only a moment later, it seemed, Arun leapt back onto their terrace. "Appu! The flood is only in our house. Must be a burst septic tank or something. We will have to go to the Munnuswamys' for the night."

"I am not climbing walls and all," declared Ammayya.

"No need," said Arun. "If you use the bathroom stairs on the first floor till you are level with the wall, we can lift you over."

"Bathroom stairs? Which the sweeper woman uses? Are you mad?" demanded Ammayya, her voice thick with rage. Wasn't it bad enough that her insides were swilling with filth? Now she was supposed to lower herself even further by using the untouchable stairs? "I am not going anywhere," she declared. "I will die in my own house, if necessary. My children will stay with me. Putti mari? Sripathi?"

They stared wordlessly at her. Again the pinch of pain in her chest that she had felt that morning. Everyone had let her down. All her life she had been betrayed and humiliated. By her whoring husband who stole her youth, her self-respect, even the fortune that should have sustained her in old age. By her son who had run away like a coward from medical school and robbed her of hope. By Putti, who was leaving her for a milkboy. And by God himself, who had sent this filthy flood into her room alone. Silently she followed the family to the bathroom. Silently she allowed them to hustle her down the curling wrought-iron staircase to the level of the wall, where Arun and Gopala waited to lift her over to the other side. Inside the blue Munnuswamy home, Ammayya lay on the divan, still unable to speak after the affronts suffered by her body and her heart that day. She could literally *hear* her stupid daughter simpering at that cowherd's son. Disgusting, disgusting, disgusting, she thought. Somewhere in the room, she could also hear Nandana asking querulously whether they were all going to die, and Nirmala exclaiming over the multicoloured marvels of the room revealed to her by the bright light of the Petromax lamps. She choked with fury when she realized how little she mattered to these people gathered here in this room. Simply an old woman with odd ways, that's how they thought of her. Even her beloved Putti, for whom she had saved and scrimped and stolen. And with that thought, Ammayya's ancient heart gave one more heave, dragging a fiery path of pain through her left side, and she cried out loud, surprised at the intensity of it.

Sripathi heard the cry first and, to his shame, ignored it, thinking that his mother was performing, as usual. Then it came again, fainter now, almost a gurgle followed by silence. This time he rushed over to the sofa and found Ammayya straining for breath, her eyes dilated horribly as if they would force their way out from her face, and her lips turned back from her teeth in a blue-tinged snarl.

"She is sick!" he said frantically. "My mother is sick. We need to take her to the hospital."

A hush fell over the room.

"Don't want hospital," whispered Ammayya, clutching at Sripathi's shirt as he bent over her. He was surprised at the strength of that grip. "Want Putti."

Putti hurried over to her mother and knelt on the floor, her protruding upper lip trembling with emotion. "Ammayya, I am sorry," she wept. "Don't be angry with me, please."

Ammayya released Sripathi's shirt and transferred her grip to Putti's wrist. She pinched it so hard that Putti's eyes began to tear. "I am dying," she hissed through her ragged blue lips. "And *you* are the cause. Remember that! Remember that when you crawl into his bed."

She panted and glared at Putti, who tried to wrench her arm out of her mother's terrible grip. When she finally broke free she found fingermarks etched into her skin, marks that would later dry and scab but would never entirely disappear. They began to resemble three staring, cartoonish eyes, causing Putti to wear dozens of bangles retrieved from her mother's trunk under the bed, all in an effort to hide the marks from her own guilt-ridden gaze. And after her wedding, when Gopala made love to her in their brand-new apartment—one of three that Sripathi had got in exchange for Big House—on a brand-new cot that had been purchased in Madras, Putti wrapped her wrist with a thick bandage to hide those ovals of jealous anger left on her by Ammayya.

"Get an ambulance," said Nirmala weakly, wishing that someone would take charge. Even the efficient, bustling Munnuswamy seemed at a loss. "Shouldn't we take her to the hospital? Call an ambulance?" she asked again.

"Phone isn't working," said Munnuswamy briefly, "but don't worry. We will take her in our milk van." He gestured to Gopala, who nodded and left the room. There was the sound of a vehicle being started up, reversing into the driveway and stopping.

Arun lifted Ammayya off the sofa and carried her to the van, which was also a bright shade of blue, with Ambika Milk Co-op stencilled in flowery letters on the side. He put her down on one of the long seats and Nirmala arranged a blanket over her.

"Putti," called Ammayya weakly. When her daughter's anxious face swam into view she whispered, "You also come with me. I want you to make sure those doctors don't take off my clothes and poke here and there with their instruments. If my own son were a doctor . . ."

Another wave of pain cut off all further speech, and then the van started up again. Putti clambered in beside Arun and Sripathi. Arun sat on the ridged floor of the van, which smelled of stale milk, and held Ammayya as they bumped and rattled through the pitted, flooded roads to Toturpuram's Vanitha Hospital, a new institution with a dubious reputation. But Munnuswamy said that he knew many people there, and so that was where he took them.

The emergency ward at the hospital was busy, even at that early hour of the morning. A bus had collided with an overloaded truck, bringing in three dozen wounded passengers. A harried nurse told them that they would have to wait in the corridor until someone was free to examine Ammayya. She lay on the ground against the bleached wall of the hospital corridor, her nose full of the odour of dead and dying bodies, her bulging heart full of the rage she had accumulated over sixty of her eighty years of existence.

After a brief conversation with Munnuswamy, which Sripathi could not hear, the nurse paged a doctor.

"Not to worry," said Munnuswamy with a satisfied air. "I told her who I was. You will get some good service. Now if you will excuse, I have to take my leave. The van will be back with my driver at seven o'clock. And I will get my Boys to clean up your house."

"I'm sorry," he said to Munnuswamy. "Very, very sorry for imposing on you like this."

"No problem, we are sambandhis now." He waved Sripathi's gratitude away with one hand and left.

Ammayya opened her eyes and called to Sripathi. "Unscrew my earrings," she commanded hoarsely. "And remove my mangalya and all the other chains. They will rob me otherwise. My earrings are blue jaguar diamonds. The best water. I want them all back when we go home. My vaaley, my mangalya, the rice-grain necklace, the mohan-maaley and my corals. I know what I am wearing. And under my bed—my *aurum* and my *argentum*—I know how much there is, so don't try to take anything."

She insisted that Sripathi do the job, and not Putti. "Nothing for you," she said when her daughter tried to help Sripathi with the unfamiliar task of removing a woman's earrings. "Not a single paisa of mine."

The doctor arrived shortly after Sripathi had wrapped his mother's jewellery in a handkerchief and placed it in his pocket. Two orderlies lifted Ammayya on to a gurney and started to wheel her away.

Ammayya clutched at Putti's sari. "Come with me," she whispered. "Tell them I don't want them to take off my clothes."

But one of the orderlies shook his head at Putti. "No madam, visitors not allowed inside operating area."

"Are you operating on her? But you don't even know what is wrong," said Sripathi surprised at this quick turn of events. The doctor hadn't even checked Ammayya's pulse or put a stethoscope to her chest. Wasn't that what they were supposed to do to begin with?

"Name of patient?" asked the doctor, ignoring his questions and scribbling rapidly on a form.

"Janaki Rao."

"Age?"

"Eighty-one. She was complaining of chest pains. Maybe a heart attack?" Sripathi suggested. "How can you operate without even checking her?"

"Please sign here, sir, and then I will answer all your questions," said the doctor, pointing his pen at a cross on the form. "Just to verify that you are releasing the hospital from all obligations in case of problems."

"What problems?" asked Arun. "Appu, don't sign till you read the form."

The doctor shrugged. "The longer you take, the longer it will be to help the old lady. This is simply a formality. Everybody has to sign it."

Sripathi took the pen and signed.

"Now, please pay at the desk."

"Pay?" asked Sripathi blankly.

"Yes sir, that is the rule here. You have to issue a cheque at the nurse's desk before we do anything for the patient."

"Is this a shop or a hospital?" demanded Arun. "First see if my grandmother is all right. We aren't going to run away without paying. We aren't thieves like you!"

"Your decision, sir," shrugged the doctor. He yelled to the orderlies who were wheeling Ammayya through a swinging door. "Bring the patient back. These people can't pay." He turned back to Arun. "Take her to the government hospital, it is free service there."

"No, no, it is okay," said Sripathi. "Please ignore my son, he is very emotional. I will pay. You take care of my mother."

For several hours, Sripathi and Arun and Putti waited in the corridor, which was now being swabbed by a peon in a khaki uniform. He worked his way backwards down the length of the waiting area, the wet rags that made up the mop slapping against the feet of those who waited in resigned silence for someone to attend to them. An odour of disinfectant permeated the air, mingling with the smell of cooking that emerged from the cafeteria. At eight o'clock, the doctor came looking for them with a grave expression on his face and facile words of condolence slipping out of his mouth. "We could do nothing for her," he said. "She was very old."

Ammayya was wheeled out, her body wrapped in a pale green hospital sheet, and for that Sripathi had to sign another cheque. Somebody had brushed her eyelids shut and she looked unusually gentle. It seemed to Sripathi that he had last seen such an expression on her face at his upanayana ceremony, when he was a boy of ten, just before his father's mistress had arrived. There were pieces of cotton wool sticking out of her nostrils, and her mouth was slightly open.

"She was angry with me, she didn't forgive me," whispered Putti, her face wet with tears. She clutched a bag of clothes that the orderly had handed to her.

Sripathi helped Arun carry Ammayya's stiffening body, which was lighter than he had imagined it would be, to the van that was waiting for them. He sat silently beside the body and wondered who he would lose next.

Back at Big House, one of the Boys stopped them on the verandah, which was slimy with mud, and said, "You will have to go from the back, sir. The water has gone, but it is very filthy."

He told Sripathi that the rear compound wall had been broken down to allow the water to drain. It would take several hours for them to clean and disinfect the house. "Oh, and we found something," he smiled, his teeth large and white against his dark skin. He went to a corner of the verandah and picked up a cardboard box. Inside it was the kitten. "We found this baby clinging to the curtains."

"Nandana will be happy," said Putti. She took the box and went to Munnuswamy's house to break the news of Ammayya's death to

Nirmala. Meanwhile, Sripathi and Arun went back to the van to re-move the corpse. This time they had to ascend the spiral toilet stairs to the terrace, holding Ammayya upright to negotiate the twisting metal path, through the bathroom and into the landing be-tween the two bedrooms. Arun spread out a fresh sheet on the floor and they placed the old woman on it.

It was Nirmala who finally washed Ammayya's corpse and dressed her in a length of unbleached cotton. And it was she who discovered the large vertical incision down her right side, ex-tending from one withered breast to her pelvic bone, a curving greyish-pink slash, the edges held together with black stitches like ants marching. She wondered why that cut had been made. True, Sripathi had said something about an operation, but even she knew that the heart was on the left side of the chest. Had they removed something from Ammayya's body? She remembered the old woman's dislike of hospitals, her fear that the doctors farmed out body parts, and thought about telling Sripathi of her suspi-cions. For a long while she looked at her mother-in-law lying on the sheet, the dry old body, the white shoots of hair emerging from her scalp, the peaceful face, the sweet smell of putrefaction beginning to waft up from her, and finally made up her mind.

"What is gone is gone," she whispered. "No point creating un-necessary problems."

22

THE HEART
OF THE SEA

T HE RITUALS HAD BEEN OBSERVED; dozens of friends and relatives had come to pay their last respects to Ammayya. They couldn't seem to believe that the feisty old woman was truly gone. Krishnamurthy Acharye had said the ancient prayers for the dead in his whispery old voice. Nirmala and Putti wept quietly in a corner of the room while Nandana looked on wide-eyed. Earlier she had asked Sripathi whether all dead people looked like Ammayya, and Sripathi had not known what to say. Was it right to let the child see all this so soon? He didn't know what was right any more.

"No," he whispered finally, over the solemn chanting of prayers. "No, everybody does not look like Ammayya. She was very old." And my daughter was young, he wanted to add. Too young to die.

Late that evening, after the cremation was over, Sripathi told Arun that he could go back home.

"Where are you going?"

"To the beach with Ammayya's ashes," Sripathi replied.

"I'll come with you," offered Arun, unexpectedly.

It was dusk by the time they got a bus to the beach. They made their way to the same secluded spot at which they had scattered Maya's ashes. The tide was coming in, curling waves lapped against their feet, and seagulls swooped and pecked at drying seaweed left on the sand. Further down, pariah dogs leapt at an upturned boat, trying to get at something dangling from the high side. Sripathi walked across the wet, squelching sand until he reached the water. With a sense of déjà-vu, he emptied the ashes and watched as they mingled with the waves. Poor Ammayya, what a long, unresolved life she had lived, he thought regretfully.

He went back to the cluster of mossy rocks where he had left Arun and sat down beside his son. They stayed there until the moon appeared, a silver semicircle ringed with concentric rainbow light. It would be sunny tomorrow. In the thick darkness the sea was luminous, a body of motion, living, mysterious, beautiful.

"You go home if you want to, Appu," said Arun, his arms locked around his raised knees on which he rested his chin. "I want to watch the turtles coming in."

"How do you know that they will be here today?"

"A few arrived yesterday and usually the rest follow soon after."

"I'll stay with you," said Sripathi after a moment's hesitation. He had lived all his life beside this same sea, and he had never spent an entire night watching it as it poured over the sand and sucked away, leaving a wavering lace of froth that it retrieved almost immediately.

The moon rose higher in the sky, the beach emptied slowly, and one by one the last of the vendors turned off their Petromax lanterns and left. Now all they could hear was the susurrating of the wind in the brief stand of palm trees behind them. Suddenly, out of the sea, a dark form detached itself and staggered slowly up the damp sand. And another and another. Dozens of them. No, scores. It seemed to Sripathi that the beach itself had risen up and was rippling away from the water.

"Can you see them?" whispered Arun. As if the turtles would be scared off by his voice when they carried the thunder of ancient waters in their small, swivelling heads.

They poured across the sand, wobbling and swaying, a hump-backed, crawling army drawn by some distant call to the shore on which they were born fifty, one hundred, two hundred years ago, to give birth to another generation. Across the water line they surged, each an olive-green dune in slow motion, until they were well out of reach of the waves. They stopped one by one and began to dig cradles for their eggs—their thick stubby hind legs powerful pistons spraying sand into the air—grunting and murmuring, moaning and sighing as they squatted over the holes and dropped their precious cargo.

Arun leaned over and whispered, "Each of them lays at least a hundred to two hundred eggs, Appu."

Sripathi nodded, too moved to comment. How many millennia had this been going on? he wondered, humbled by the sight of something that had started long before humans had been imagined into creation by Brahma, and had survived the voracious appetite of those same humans. In the long continuum of turtle life, humans were merely dots.

Soon the turtles were done and began to churn up the sand again, covering the holes, tamping them down tight, with slow, deliberate movements. And then the swaying trudge back to the gleaming sea. Sweeping their hind legs to erase every trace of their arrival, as meticulous as spies in foreign lands.

"See how cunning they are," whispered Arun again. "They are making sure predators don't find their nests by following their footprints."

The last of the turtles disappeared into the waters as silently as they had arrived. They would never see their babies hatch, would not return for one full year to lay another batch of eggs at the edge of the sea that had been there longer than even they had. Their young might live or die. The eggs they left with so much care might yield another generation of turtles—or not. Sripathi thought about the chanciness of existence, the beauty and the hope and the loss that always accompanied life, and felt a boulder roll slowly off his heart.

Perhaps in their long, unknown journey from one sea to another, across oceans and past shifting continents, a turtle might meet one of her offspring and glide by without knowing it. And half a century later, those baby turtles would return to this same shore, drawn by a desire that had been etched into their memories. Who understood the ways of those silent creatures who had claimed this planet aeons before we did? reflected Sripathi, stretching his stiff limbs. But he had caught a glimmer of the reason his son came to the beach at this time every year, when the clouds hung pregnant in the sky and the night was darker than a crow's wing. It had annoyed him, this annual ritual, when Arun disappeared at ten in the night and came home only after dawn—collecting the eggs, he had said elusively, so sure of Sripathi's disapproval that he had ventured no further explanation.

He looked down at his son, who was still seated, staring at the sea as if communing with the ancient creatures that it rocked in its depths. What a strange man he had fathered. Arun had slipped through twenty-eight years of existence gently, rewarded for it by Sripathi's irritation, his disappointment, even his contempt.

They sat until the tide started to recede and the fishing boats could be seen—dark, bobbing shapes against the lightening sky.

"Shall we go now?" he asked Arun in a gentler tone than he had ever used to his son.

Big House smelled of phenyl and bleach. The Boys had cleaned it as well as they could, but all along the wall, two feet off the ground, ran a brown line marking the height that the water had reached. The sofa in the living room had all but dissolved, and Nirmala had left it in the backyard for the Boys to take away. She seemed to harbour none of the reservations that Sripathi did about taking Munnuswamy's help. The windows in Ammayya's room had been forced open, and the stained glass washed clean except for pockets of black dirt that soap solution couldn't remove. All of the saris that Ammayya had stored in trunks were ruined. The jewellery was fine, if a bit odorous, although later, much later, when Nirmala and Putti took it all to the goldsmith on Krishnaiah Chetty Road to have it polished for the wedding, they would discover that it was fake—made of silver or brass dipped in gold water. Every single piece of it, the jeweller would tell them regretfully, except for the diamond earrings and the necklaces that she had given Sripathi in the hospital. All else that remained was a few gold coins and the bars of silver that she had hoarded in the years after Narasimha's death by selling newspapers and old saris.

"He cheated her," Putti would say on their way back. "My father gave her rubbish jewellery. My poor Ammayya. Good thing she didn't know."

"How do you know that she didn't?" Nirmala would ask. "Your mother was not a fool."

On the balcony, Sripathi sat in his old chair, surrounded by his writing paraphernalia. He had just finished the newspaper, which had a news item that he thought would have pleased Ammayya. The cyclone had struck Madras as well and flooded the chief minister out of her house. According to the report, she had been bailed out in a boat.

Now he opened the sandalwood box that he had removed from Nirmala's cupboard. He took out a stack of aerograms and envelopes thick with letters from Maya. He opened one of them carefully. She began, "*My dear Appu, Mamma, Arun . . .*" Always in descending order, according to age. He looked at the neat, slanting writing, and finally the tears spilled forth unchecked.

There was a small sound near the door of his room and he knew, without looking, that it was Nandana. "Are you crying because your mother died?" she asked.

"Yes, partly that," he replied. He wiped his face with one of the towels hanging on the railing.

"My mother also died."

"Yes, she was my daughter."

There was no response, but when Sripathi turned he saw that the little girl was still there, leaning against the door jamb, chewing on a strand of hair.

"What is in that big box on the table?" she asked pointing a finger at the unopened writing case.

"Come here, I'll show you. If you want," invited Sripathi.

She came slowly to him, sliding one foot after another, ever ready to turn and run. He opened the box and ran a hand over the pens arranged against the warm, reddish-brown wood.

"Pens!" she exclaimed. "So many! Are they all yours?"

"Yes, but you can choose one."

"To keep for ever?"

"Yes, for ever," Sripathi agreed. "How about this one?" He picked up the silver Hero, unscrewed the cap, and wrote *Nandana* with a flourish on a sheet of paper.

She frowned thoughtfully and leaned closer to see what else was in the box. He could smell her hair, the smell of sweetness and youth, he imagined.

"May I have *that* one instead?" she asked finally, pointing to a small red pen that he had bought for fifty paise from a roadside vendor when he was in college. It was the cheapest one in his collection.

"If you wish," he said, the beginning of a smile tugging at the corners of his mouth. Just like her mother, he thought. She liked to make her own choices. "What will you do with it?"

"I want to write a letter to Molly and Yee," she said importantly, settling down on the floor near him. "May I have a sheet of paper too?"

The temple bell that had been ringing ever since he had come home from the beach at dawn finally stopped. Sripathi waited for the lory bird to start singing, but instead the air was filled with an awful racket. It was Gopinath Nayak, the donkey, waking the world with his voice. Moments later, the sound was drowned out by a loud, sliding roar. From where he sat, Sripathi saw the lorry emptying its load of broken granite slabs in front of the gates of Jyoti Flats.

"Oy!" shouted the Gurkha, dancing out of the gates and waving his baton. "Is this your father-in-law's house, or what?"

And the lorry driver leaned out of his cab high above the ground and shouted back, "Is it your father-in-law's *road*?"

Sripathi drew his tablet of paper forward and selected a pen. He thought about his daughter and her husband, about Ammayya and his father, and about all that he had lost and found. How was he to put it all into words?

"*Dear Editor*," he wrote finally. "*Early this morning, at the Toturpuram beach, I saw the most amazing sight . . .*"

A NOTE ON THE AUTHOR

Anita Rau Badami was born in India and lives in Vancouver.
She is the author of internationally acclaimed novel *Tamarind Woman*,
now published by Bloomsbury.